"Are you asking for more company in there?"

Matt asked from around the doorway. "We usually keep this door shut when the room is being used," he drawled.

"Please pull it shut, would you?" Emmaline asked, the towel in readiness as she bent forward in the water, her knees pulled to her breasts.

"Sure you don't want company?" From just beyond the door, his voice reached her, tinged with taunting amusement.

"Please, Matt," she whispered, her words wispy with embarrassment.

He sighed mockingly as he reached one long arm within the room, his fingers grasping the knob and deliberately closing the door.

"Don't be late for breakfast," he called to her abruptly. "Maria only serves once. After that, you're on your own."

"And I hope you choke on yours," she grumbled as she stepped over the edge of the tub and enfolded herself with the towel she still clutched.

Dear Reader,

When a man and a woman with ties to the same orphaned girl marry for convenience, the results set the small town of Forbes Junction, Arizona, on its ear. Broken hearts, intrigue and loads of charm all play a part in this delightful Western from author Carolyn Davidson, who is making her Harlequin Historicals debut this month with *Gerrity's Bride*. We hope you enjoy the fireworks.

We are also pleased to bring you *The Welshman's Way*, award-winning author Margaret Moore's sequel to *A Warrior's Way*, which earned a 5★ rating from *Affaire de Coeur*. This tale of a Welsh rebel who rescues a Norman maiden from an unwanted marriage is an extraordinary story—don't miss it.

Bestselling author Theresa Michaels hits her stride this month with *Once an Outlaw*, the second book in her new Western series featuring the infamous Kincaid brothers. *Romantic Times* calls this delightful love story "an engrossing, not-to-be-missed read." And from Barbara Leigh, *For Love of Rory*, her new medieval story of a young woman who forces a wounded Celtic warrior to help her find her kidnapped son.

Whatever your taste in reading, we hope Harlequin Historicals will keep you coming back for more. Please keep a lookout for all four titles, available wherever books are sold.

Sincerely,

Tracy Farrell

Senior Editor

Please address questions and book requests to:
Harlequin Reader Service
U.S.: 3010 Walden Ave., P.O. Box 1325, Buffalo, NY 14269
Canadian: P.O. Box 609, Fort Erie, Ont. L2A 5X3

CAROLYN DAVIDSON

GERRITY'S BRIDE

Harlequin Books

TORONTO • NEW YORK • LONDON
AMSTERDAM • PARIS • SYDNEY • HAMBURG
STOCKHOLM • ATHENS • TOKYO • MILAN
MADRID • WARSAW • BUDAPEST • AUCKLAND

ISBN 0-373-28898-0

GERRITY'S BRIDE

Books by Carolyn Davidson

Harlequin Historicals

Gerrity's Bride #298

CAROLYN DAVIDSON

Moving from Michigan to South Carolina several years ago, Carolyn Davidson left behind a job in a large department store. Deciding she'd earned some leisure time, she began pursuing her dream of writing. More specifically, writing romance. So much for leisure! *Gerrity's Bride* is her third novel and now she finds herself caught up in a new career, busier than ever before. Combined with her roles as mother, grandmother and part-time clerk in a new/used bookstore, it makes for a fulfilling life. A life she shares with her husband, Ed, the source of her inspiration.

To Penny Bice, who has given of her talents with true generosity of spirit. My world became a better and brighter place the day we met.

And to Brenda Rollins, for allowing me the benefit of her skills and vivid imagination. I appreciate all you do. Thank you, my friend!

But most of all, to Mister Ed, who loves me!

Chapter One

Miss Emmaline Carruthers
Rawlings Farms
Lexington, Kentucky

It is my sad duty to advise you of
the death of your father, Samuel
Carruthers, who perished in a flash
flood, along with his wife, Arnetta,
on Tuesday last. We await your
instructions as to your interest
in their daughter, Theresa, five
years of age. Please advise as soon
as possible.
I remain your humble servant,

Oswald Hooper
Attorney

"Surely even Hades could not be as miserable as this godforsaken place." The whisper was spoken into the wind. The words were gone as quickly as they were uttered, and the disappointment inherent in those whispered syllables might never have been, except for the slender figure of the woman who still gazed with incredulous eyes at the barren landscape of Forbes Junction.

The train bearing her had stopped for a few moments to allow for her departure, then left her behind with a doleful blast of its whistle. Now it was but a dark stain against the horizon, its smoke trail dissolving into wispy tendrils in the still air.

The sun rode high in the sky, its rays reminding her of the unrelenting heat that had been her companion for the past hours. Since shortly after daybreak, she had alternately fanned herself with a folded newspaper and mopped her brow with a dainty handkerchief. Still, the dry, breathtaking heat had penetrated her traveling costume, leaving her with but a trace of her usual vitality.

"Arizona... Even the name sounds hot," she muttered as she lifted one foot to view the dust clinging to her fashionably booted foot. She stamped it against the wide wooden boards of the platform beneath her and surveyed the choices she faced.

A dusty road ran between a row of buildings, houses and business establishments, built along a fairly even line, for three hundred yards or so. Then it gave way to a sandy expanse that stretched to the horizon, broken only by scattered shrubs and a few stunted trees. The narrow road continued on, running in a straight line as far as she could see. It was less than inviting, she decided quickly.

Directly before her, an unpainted wooden door stood ajar. Beyond it lay a shadowed room, which appeared to be her most likely chance for shelter from the sun. The train station was small. Probably didn't get much use, she decided, bending to lift her carpetbag, leaving behind the trunk that held her clothing. The weight of the carpetbag dragged at her arm, reminding her of the books she had stubbornly packed within its voluminous depths.

"Why you want all those along with you is beyond me," Delilah had muttered. "You won't be there long enough to read them, anyway," she'd predicted.

"One can only hope!" As fervent as any prayer she'd ever uttered, the words fell from her lips and were wafted away on the hot wind that blew in unrelieved measure. With a sigh, Emmaline Carruthers squared her shoulders and lifted her feet, moving briskly through the open door.

The room was shady, and that was about all that was to be said for it. Small comfort, she thought as she stood in the center of the dingy station. An open window allowed a bit of cross-ventilation, and she took advantage of the moving air, such of it as there was. Her hand lingered over the top button of her suit, her fingers sorely tempted to loosen it. But better sense prevailed, and she approached the window with all her ladylike decorum intact.

"I beg your pardon." Such decorum, she had decided, was her only defense against the situation. It would sustain her now, as it had for the past hundreds of miles. Once she reached the boundaries of true civilization, she had recognized that only her status as a lady would protect her from the vulgarities that surrounded her.

"Yup...just a minute." The drawling reply came from beneath the counter, and she stifled the impulse to bend over the narrow ledge to seek out its source.

Two thin lines of perspiration ran down each side of her neck and settled against the white fabric of her collar, dampening it before it soaked through, cooling her flesh. She resisted the urge to brush at the drop that was even now making its way to her eyebrow, and stiffened her spine resolutely.

"What can I do fer ye?" The stationmaster rose to his full height, his stiff collar tight about his skinny neck. He peered at her through spectacles, which slid down his nose, then lifted one bony finger to settle them back into place.

"I'm expected," she announced with brittle dignity. "There was to be a vehicle here to meet me from the Carrutherses' ranch, but I don't see anyone about. Have you any message for me?"

"Well, I might and I might not," he quibbled. "Tell me who the message would be fer."

"I'm Emmaline Carruthers."

His eyes widened behind the thick lenses, and he pursed his lips as he took a renewed interest in her. Hesitating only briefly on her bonnet, his look roamed with admiration over her flushed features and paused with a trace of wonder as he viewed the curves that filled her dark dress.

"Yep, you surely are," he allowed. "Got the look of yer pa about ye, through the eyes—not to mention the hair."

"Indeed?" Her mouth pursed as she considered his assessment.

"Yep. Yer brother's comin' to pick you up." He turned from the window, his duty accomplished with the delivery of the message.

Emmaline bit with vexation at the inside of her lower lip. "Who is coming?"

"Yer brother," the stationmaster said again, and returned to his position beneath the ledge.

She glowered at his back, lifting on tiptoe to lean over the counter. "I don't have a brother." The words were clipped, her exasperation apparent. Surely he had mixed the messages. "I'm here to meet my sister, Theresa. I have no other relatives here," she said emphatically.

But I have a sister, she thought with joy. Theresa. She whispered the name, savoring the syllables. Theresa. Five years old . . . daughter of Samuel. That definitely made the child her sister.

"Sorry to hear about yer pa," The stationmaster said with a frown. "Don't pay to get caught in a dry creek bed."

She nodded her thanks. As much a surprise as the news had been, she'd wasted little time in sending her reply. It was difficult to scrape up much sorrow for the man who had fathered her. He was but a distant memory that had never been encouraged to flourish.

Perished in a flash flood. The telegram's wording had been most specific. Her father had died, along with his wife. Samuel and Arnetta Carruthers . . . strangers who had borne the same last name she did.

"Did you know him well?" she asked on a sudden impulse.

"Eh? What's that? Do I know yer brother? 'Course I know him," the man stated with dour confidence. "Ever'-body in Forbes Junction knows Matt Gerrity."

"No, I meant . . ." Her voice trailed off as she backed away from the window. Tiny lines of consternation furrowed her brow as she considered the situation. Any more questioning on her part seemed a futile exercise, she decided with a sigh of frustration. Surely someone would arrive soon. She nurtured the thought. Soon . . . she thought. Soon, she'd meet the child. With anticipation, she straightened her skirts and adjusted the tilt of her bonnet.

"He'll be here afore long, lessen he gets tangled up talkin' with some female or another on his way through town. He draws them women like flies," the man said, before he lowered the shade over the narrow window and effectively cut off the conversation.

"Like flies..." Emmaline repeated dryly. "That sounds—"

"Time fer lunch," the now disembodied voice announced from beyond the barrier.

Emmaline sighed as her stomach notified her that breakfast had been too many hours ago. And not much to brag about, at that. The leftover bread from last evening's repast had been a bit beyond stale, and the peach more than ripe. Train travel left a lot to be desired, she'd discovered long before she reached Kansas City.

A wavy mirror on the wall faced her, and she stepped up to it, glancing into its depths, in hopes her appearance would bolster her sagging spirits. It was useless, she decided mournfully. Violet shadows rimmed her blue eyes, and a smudge marred her left cheekbone. Not to mention the stubborn curls vying for attention beneath the brim of her bonnet. She pushed at them with one finger, subduing them only until they were released, to escape in a flyaway fashion.

She peered at herself, and her sigh was deep as she pronounced, "I'm a wreck!"

"Now, I wouldn't say that."

She spun toward the door, her mouth open in dismay, her eyes wide and indignant, and faced the man who loomed in the doorway.

"I beg your pardon?" She couldn't manage haughtiness, not with sweat streaking her neck and forehead, and errant curls poking out every which way. She settled for arrogance.

He grinned while his forefinger poked back the wide brim of his hat, leaving a crease across the expanse of his forehead. The hand that lowered to his waist was brown, the fingers long and tapered. It rested against his belt, and then the fingers slid into his pocket, until only the thumb looped over the wide leather circling his waist.

Her eyes moved back to his face, and she glowered at him. That he'd caught her surveying herself in the mirror was bad enough. He didn't have to be enjoying her discomfort.

"I wouldn't say that." He repeated his words in a raspy voice that held a trace of amusement. "I'd say that you're the best-lookin' wreck I've ever laid eyes on."

She inhaled sharply, irritated at his impudence. Then, with swishing skirts and tapping of booted feet, she turned from him to face the shaded window.

"You don't want to be rude to the man who holds the reins, ma'am," he said softly into her ear.

He was right behind her. She felt the warmth of his body against her back, and she stiffened, her spine straightening imperceptibly. Ahead of her, the shade twitched to one side, and the stationmaster peered around the edge.

"Howdy, Matt. Yer sister's been waitin'."

She closed her eyes against his words, then opened them slowly. "I don't have a brother." Each word was spoken with the emphasis due such a denial. Her aggravation was plainly apparent to both men.

The man behind her had the advantage, and he took it. His hands lifted to rest on her shoulders, and he bent to speak once more, his breath warm against the side of her neck.

"Turn around, Miss Emmaline. I'm here to represent your family."

Emmaline's mouth narrowed, and she shrugged as if she would loosen herself from the fingers that even now were forcing her to face him, tightening her shoulders as he silently brought her about. Her eyes were dark with suppressed anger as he accomplished his aim, and she tipped her head back to meet his sardonic gaze.

"I don't know who you are," she snapped. "I've come from Lexington to meet my little sister, Theresa Carruthers, and I'm waiting for a ride to the Carrutherses' ranch." She took a deep breath, availing herself of a double lungful of hot desert air. "I am no relation of yours."

"Ah, but that's where you're wrong, ma'am," he drawled, his brow lifting in an arrogant gesture. "I'm just a shirttail relation, so to speak. But genuine kin of yours. My mama was Arnetta Carruthers, and when she married your daddy, I became the most interesting part of the bargain.''

He released her and stepped back, then bowed in a parody of elegance. His next words were underlaid with an emotion she could not have put words to.

''Welcome home, Miss Emmaline Carruthers.'' His eyes glittered with the intensity of his appraisal. ''We've been expecting you.''

The buckboard wasn't much of an improvement over the train, Emmaline decided before they'd traveled a mile.

''Do you ride in this thing often?'' she asked, clinging to the edge of the seat.

His eyes swept her with a hooded appraisal. ''Havin' a hard time keepin' your seat?'' The corner of his mouth twitched as he slapped the reins against the broad backs of the two huge animals trotting in tandem. Accordingly, they increased their pace, and Emmaline gripped more firmly to the wooden board beneath her.

''Surely you have a buggy of sorts that would have been more suitable,'' she suggested, her voice vibrating with the rhythm of the springless wagon.

''Buggy don't hold much in the line of supplies,'' he told her, casting a glance at her pursed lips and furrowed brow. It was really more of an initiation than he had planned. Piling discomfort on top of distress wasn't exactly playing fair, he admitted to himself as he noted the paleness of her cheeks, flushed from too much sun.

Pulling back on the reins and bringing the team of horses to a halt, he sighed. ''Look, little sister...''

Between gritted teeth, she spit the words, barely moving her lips. ''I'm...not...your...sister!''

His grin was quickly covered by a swipe of one large brown hand, and he turned to her with a suggestion of his amusement still vivid in his narrowed eyes. ''Whatever you want to call it, we're related, lady. Now, since that's been established, let's get you a bit more comfortable. You can't sit in the sun with all those clothes on, stranglin' you and holdin' all the heat in. You'll have heatstroke before I get you home, and then what good will you be to that little sister of ours?''

She sat in a huddled lump of bedraggled dark linen and considered his words. Then, as he reached toward her, obviously intent on loosening the buttons that marched up the front of her suit, she moved quickly. Her hands were there before his, her fingers moving stiffly as she set free the plain black buttons and turned back the lapels to reveal her throat.

Her eyes closed in pure pleasure as an errant breeze cooled the heated flesh she had exposed, and she breathed deeply of the scent of desert blossoms that the southerly wind carried to her nostrils. Scarcely had she inhaled, barely had she stretched her slender neck from within its folds of fabric, when she felt his hard hands on her wrist.

She opened her eyes, blinking against the glare of the afternoon sun, to see him undoing the buttons that closed her sleeve. She watched in stunned silence as he rolled up the cuff as far as it would go, almost to her elbow, then reached across her to grasp the other hand and repeated the motion.

Emmaline watched, aware of the total lack of respect he was displaying, aware of the proximity of their bodies as he bent to his task, and more aware than she wanted to be of the rough texture of his fingers against her pale skin. She swallowed back the flood of saliva that rushed to fill her mouth.

For just a moment, a swirling sensation in her stomach prompted her to consider anew her refusal of his offer of lunch. That is, until she decided that it wasn't simply pangs of hunger she was feeling, but rather an unusual awareness of the man who handled her so casually. And then, with a grunt that might have signified approval, he straightened and retrieved the reins.

"Feel better?" he asked as he once more set the team in motion.

"Ummm," she managed to reply.

"Once we get to the ranch, you'd do well to get out of those stockings and whatever you're wearin' under all those layers of clothes," he suggested in an offhand manner.

Emmaline straightened on the seat, oddly refreshed by the loosening of her jacket, but hovering on the edge of anger at his casual mention of her underclothes. "I beg your pardon," she said stiffly. "What I am wearing is no more or less than any lady would wear."

"You won't find any of those harnesses and piles of pet-ticoats on a ranch, Miss Emmaline," he said with dry precision. "The ladies wear light colors, and not too many layers."

"I'm in mourning," she announced primly, even as her honest heart prodded her. It was difficult to mourn a father she had little memory of, but she had dutifully donned the required black garb and yards of veiling on her hat. That the veiling had gone by the way after she discovered how hot it was behind the layers of gauze was not to be admitted, she thought warily. Now she'd allowed this...man, this ranch hand, to handle her clothing, and...

The memory of his work-roughened fingers against her skin was the final straw. He was bossy, she decided, not to mention arrogant, and she was still too hot. Her eyes blinked and narrowed against the unrelenting sunshine. Not only that, she was too tired, and sick of being jolted about on this sad excuse for a wagon, she thought as she fought the weary tears that burned behind her eyelids.

His voice saved her from the disgrace of tears. "We've arrived," he announced as they passed beneath a sign proclaiming that they were on Carruthers land. But it was not to be a quick arrival, she noticed, watching the group of buildings in the distance. Indeed, it was another twenty minutes before the wagon halted.

As if it had sprouted from the desert, the house sprawled in several directions, its sand-colored walls dotted with windows and doors. A wide roof provided overhanging shelter, forming a shaded spot on the eastern side of the building. Appearing from the shadowed doorway, a woman stepped forward. Wiping her hands on the front of the white apron she wore, she smiled her welcome. Behind her, the open door revealed a dim interior, and Emmaline yearned suddenly to step within that shady area, out of the sun that beat upon her with unrelenting brilliance.

She shifted upon the seat, and, as if spurred by her movement, the man sitting next to her leaped to the ground and then turned, hands reaching to lift her from the seat. She moved nearer and then, fingers clutching his shoulders, felt him take her weight as he circled her waist with hands that held her firmly. He swept her to the ground, providing support while she gingerly tested her weight on limbs that were unaccountably shaky.

"Got the ground under you, ma'am?" he asked, his eyes mocking as he watched her closely. She was a slim little mite, he decided, flexing his fingers against the boning of the undergarment she wore. 'Course, once she took off the corsets, or whatever it was they called those idiotic things women wore, she might spread out a little.

She stirred against his hands and he released her, his eyes hooded as he watched the sway of her skirt, the graceful steps of her slender booted feet and the tilt of her head under the bonnet she wore.

"Thank you, Mr...." She groped for a name as she stepped away from him.

"Just Matt," he said bluntly. "We don't deal in formalities around here, sis."

She stiffened. "All right. Thank you, Matt," she said, declining the argument he'd resurrected with his reference to their relationship.

"Come in, come in," the woman on the doorstep said, stepping back to allow Emmaline room.

"Maria, this is Miss Emmaline," Matt said. "Maria is our housekeeper, Emmaline."

The woman nodded quickly. "I've been watching for you. You must be hot and tired. Hungry, too, unless this man fed you in town. From the looks of things, you need something cool to drink and a place to sit and rest a bit." Maria bustled ahead, Emmaline trailing behind as she looked about the large room, drawn by the simple beauty of its furnishings.

Blinking against the dimness, she basked in the cooler temperature within the house. On the outside wall, the windows were covered with white curtains, sheer and filmy with deep ruffles that were held back at the sides. Large pieces of leather furniture sat about the room, deep chairs with reading lamps close at hand, and a pair of sofas that faced each other before an enormous fireplace on the far wall. A game table, surrounded by heavy wooden chairs, filled another corner. Whitewashed walls, dotted with paintings and an assortment of hanging rugs and tapestries, caught her eye. The floor beneath her feet was wooden, scattered with woven rugs across its wide planking.

A quiet, cool welcome enveloped her as she stood in silence . . . a welcome she had not thought to discover in this place.

Behind her, she heard the murmur of voices and then the bustle of men carrying in the contents of the wagon.

"Take Miss Emmaline's bags to the guest room," Maria instructed the men from the doorway.

"I only have my carpetbag and a small trunk," Emmaline said quickly. She'd trusted her trunk to fate when the train conductor deposited it on the platform earlier. There it had remained until Matt shouldered it easily and dumped it without ceremony in the back of the wagon.

"I didn't bring much with me," she added. Her smile was distracted as she watched Maria. The woman waved her hands at the men hustling to do her bidding, alternately scolding them and shaking her head at them.

"Will your other things be coming later?" Matt asked from the doorway.

"No." Turning to face him, she slid the bonnet from her head and brushed at the curls that sprang to life, vibrant against the darkness of her mourning dress. "I didn't plan on staying long enough to need many things."

His brow rose, and he braced his feet apart, one hand resting negligently against his hip, the other holding the belt and holster he had just slipped off.

"Oh?" The questioning syllable hung in the air.

Her chin lifted a bit as she silently defied him, determined to set the pattern for their short future together. "I only plan on staying long enough to hear the will read and make arrangements to take my sister back to Lexington with me."

Only the sharp intake of breath warned her of another presence, and that only for a second. Then a wail of anguish filled the air and set her in motion.

"*Noooo...*" cried a child from the far side of one of the sofas, where she peered over the high back. "I'm not going away! I'm not going to Lexing with her, am I, Maffew?" she wailed piteously.

"'Course not, Tessie," he assured her, reaching her in several long strides, his gun belt flung onto a peg on the wall as he moved.

Emmaline was right behind him as he gathered the child into his arms. The little girl wrapped herself about him, burying her face against his broad chest.

The look he slanted at Emmaline clearly told her she had made her first blunder in this place.

"This is your little sister. Too bad you couldn't have made a better first impression," he said bluntly.

Emmaline drew in a deep breath and considered the situation. Taking another step closer to where the child huddled in her brother's arms, she watched the narrow shoulders shudder, her heart aching in quick sympathy.

"Theresa, won't you look at me? I've come a long way just to see you," she said coaxingly. She reached out to touch the fingers that lay against Matt's collar, and the little girl shivered.

"No, I don't want to see you! Make her go away, Maffew!" she demanded loudly.

"Miss Emmaline, why don't I show you where your room is," Maria suggested softly from behind her, and Emmaline turned quickly, thankful for the suggestion.

"That would be fine," she whispered with a nod. With only one short look over her shoulder, she left the room, only to hear the words repeated in a firm, carrying voice from the child she had alienated so quickly.

"Make her go away, Maffew."

His answer was delivered in a husky murmur. "She won't be here long, short stuff. Everything will be all right. She's just a citified woman come to look us over. She won't be here long," he repeated firmly.

Emmaline's lips tightened and her eyes narrowed at his words of reassurance to the child, and she spun on her heel toward the hallway where Maria was leading the way.

"A lot he knows about it," she muttered beneath her breath. "Citified woman, am I? The man doesn't know a lady when he sees one! And I didn't come all the way to this blot on the desert for nothing. We'll just see about that!"

Chapter Two

Warily eyeing the tortilla on her plate, Emmaline poked at it with her fork. As breakfasts went, it was definitely different from the usual ham and biscuits she was accustomed to at home.

"Eat, eat!" Maria urged her from her post at the doorway. "I put in plenty of eggs and meat for you. It gives lots of energy for the whole morning."

Emmaline returned her admonition with a smile. Then, with determination, she cut into the strange offering that was called breakfast in this foreign place and ate the first bite.

"I just made fresh coffee," Maria said from around the corner. Bearing the coffeepot, she bustled through the doorway. Emmaline nodded, her mouth full.

"Mr. Matthew finished up early this morning," the rotund woman said as she filled Emmaline's cup. "He's gone out to check on the new foals."

"Where is Theresa?" Emmaline asked, and cut with more enthusiasm into the breakfast she had almost scorned. Whatever it was called, the combination of ingredients was surprisingly good.

"With her teacher, doing schoolwork," Maria answered, moving about the table as she cleared and straightened. For a moment, she hesitated, and her eyes were warm as they rested on the young woman before her.

Emmaline's hair was brilliant, a golden red that haloed about her in a cascade of curls. Her eyes were blue, wide-set, and bright with unveiled interest as she took in her surroundings. Her features were strong and symmetrical, calling to mind the handsome man who had fathered her. And it was that thought that brought a sense of nostalgia to the Mexican woman who had managed this household for over a quarter of a century.

"Miss Emmaline, you make me think of your papa, you know," she said with gentle yearning. "He had the same curls, so golden in the sunshine, so full of fire in the shadows." Her sigh was deep. "I remember the day your mama took you away, how your papa held you in his arms. Your heads were pressed so tightly together, I couldn't tell one curl from another, so alike they were."

Emmaline looked up unbelievingly. "You remember me? From twenty years ago? I didn't know you were here then, Maria."

"Ah, yes. Your mama was so full of sadness, so unhappy with our sunshine and the dry spells and the spring rains. She said so many times how much she wanted to go where there was green grass and cool breezes." Her ample breasts rose and fell as she breathed deeply, as if she would express sympathy with the long-departed woman.

"Mama always shuddered when she spoke of this place," Emmaline remembered as she propped her elbow on the table and leaned her chin on her hand. Mama shuddered a lot, she thought with resignation. She picked up her cup and sipped at the hot brew within.

"And what do you think of our sunshine?" Maria asked. "Perhaps you have some of your papa in you that craves the heat and the open spaces."

Emmaline shrugged diffidently. "I haven't given it much chance yet. Yesterday was a real experience, what with riding on that wagon and traveling in the hottest part of the day." She slid a glance at the woman who was still considering her intently. "I suspect Matthew was trying to put me through a trial, perhaps seeking to discourage me from staying."

Maria grinned. Her smile widened to express her agreement, revealing brilliant white teeth. "*Sí*... he may have set out on the wrong foot. Then, too, he did have to get supplies from town, and the buggy doesn't hold as much."

"Well, at any rate, I may not be here for long," Emmaline said quickly. "I'll make arrangements to see Mr. Hooper and find out what I need to do about the will, and then—"

"And then you'll fold up your tent and steal away, I suspect, city lady," said a husky voice from behind her.

Emmaline stifled the urge to toss her coffee at the tall man who stood in the archway, instead looking over her shoulder at him with disdain.

"I don't steal away, Matt. When the time comes, I'll leave the same way I came, only with my sister in tow."

His snort of disbelief only served to bring her to her feet in a rush of movement. She spun to face him, and her skirts swished about her.

Matt's gaze moved slowly from the tips of her neatly shod feet to the wide skirt of her dress, then across the fitted bodice to where the buttons marched up to fasten beneath her chin. Tilted at an angle, her head was like a bright blossom above the dark mourning colors she affected. The sight of such radiance, shimmering in the early sunshine, which poured through the unshaded dining room window, set his teeth on edge.

She was too good-looking for his peace of mind, he had decided last night. What with the sassy mouth pouting when she got aggravated and those eyes sparking fire at his teasing, she was more than he had bargained for.

"Thought you heard what Tessie had to say last night," he growled at her. "She's not about to go clear across the country with you. This is her home."

"She's my sister, just as much as she's yours," Emmaline reminded him firmly. "I didn't come all the way out here to see her for a few days and then forsake her."

Matt stepped closer, the smell of dust and horses and leather making her aware of where he had been this morning. "Don't sniff your elegant nose at me, lady," he said roughly. "What you smell is good honest sweat, and Arizona dirt. Not that you'd recognize it."

"On the contrary." Emmaline's voice slid like silk over his irritation. "You have the distinct odor of a horseman, and that doesn't change much between Kentucky and Arizona. I'm well accustomed to the smell of a barn.''

"Do you know how to ride a horse?" he asked bluntly, his narrowed eyes taking in her smug stance.

She smiled, and her expression was benevolent. "I've probably sat on richer horseflesh than you've ever dreamed of."

"Too bad you won't be here long enough to prove it," he ventured.

"I'm being tolerant of you this morning, given that you know nothing about me or my intentions, save that of gaining guardianship of my sister. But don't push me, Mr. Gerrity." She clenched her hands and thrust them into the pockets of her gown, unwilling that he should know the extent of her aggravation.

He knew. His brow lifted, and a grin teased at the corner of his mouth. "Somehow I suspect you don't have a tolerant bone in your body," he drawled. "Especially when it comes to me."

Her shrug denied him the satisfaction of a verbal reply, and she turned away. *Suit yourself,* she thought, then left the room, aware that she was too easily drawn into a war of words with him.

"Miss Emmaline!" he called after her, bringing her to a halt midway along the wide passageway that led to the living room. He'd followed her through the archway. She took a deep breath before she turned once more to face him.

"Yes."

The word was terse—not much of an invitation, he decided. "Oswald Hooper will be here shortly. Would you care to join us in the library?"

Her nod was abrupt. Better that she knew right away just where she stood in the scheme of things here. The situation was far from what she had expected; certainly, the presence of Matt Gerrity had not figured into her plans. But surely her father's will would effectively place Theresa in her care.

"Just let me know when he arrives," she requested, striving for a gracious tone. Already her hands were damp with the sweat of anxiety, and her breath caught as she contemplated the issues at hand.

For too long she had yearned for the closeness of family ties. Her mother had been sickly, tending to stay close to her bed or couch, finally succumbing to pneumonia without a struggle. Her grandparents had been kind, in an aloof sort of way, providing her with all she required in order to become a lady and prepare for life as a wife and mother.

It had not been enough. The message from Mr. Hooper had opened her eyes to the solitary existence she had lived for so long. That she was bonded by blood to a five-year-old child, that the closeness she yearned for might be within reach, was the impetus that had brought her here. Even the rude welcome she'd received from the girl was not enough to discourage her. She would woo her and win her, Emmaline had determined during the night hours. She would make Theresa love her.

"Will you be in your room?" Matt's eyes narrowed as he watched her. She'd been deep in thought. His words had shattered that privacy, and now she straightened her shoulders and lifted her head. With a tightening of her mouth, she nodded at him in silent acceptance.

"I'll send Maria to fetch you."

Once more she nodded and turned away, and he watched her walk down the hallway. He grinned unwillingly as he noted each twitch of her skirt, and the way the heavy fabric clung to the curves beneath.

"I don't believe it." Spoken in a whisper, Emmaline's words hung in the silence of the library. Her hands clenched at her sides, she spun and walked to the window. Only the rigid strength she had willed to her spine held her upright, and she stared unseeingly out onto the small patch of grass that comprised the front yard.

The man at the desk watched her with concern. Emmaline was the daughter of his friend, and Oswald Hooper had predicted this very reaction. His smile was wry. Anyone with a grain of sense could have predicted her reaction. Samuel was probably well out of it, he decided shrewdly. If her father were here, Emmaline Carruthers would no doubt be more than indignant. As it was, she looked fit to be tied.

Her voice was jerky, and her words were abrupt when she spoke. "Was this your idea?" she asked.

There was no doubt in his mind. Matt knew she was speaking to him. Leaning negligently against the wall, he ran one thumb across his bottom lip while he considered her. Her silhouette was dark against the brilliant sunlight that filtered so easily through the white curtains. The slender length of her was garbed in black, the fabric heavy against her layers of petticoats. Only the glimpse of small, fisted hands and the pale line of her cheek and forehead brought relief to the somber costume covering her.

Shaking his head and silently cursing the man who had brought about this situation, Matt straightened and approached the silent figure. "Your daddy didn't need any help from me, Emmaline. He dreamed this up all on his own."

Her lips barely moved, and Matt tilted his head to hear the words. "I can't do it."

His shrug was eloquent. "Then don't. Just get yourself on that wagon and I'll cart you right back to Forbes Junction, and you can catch the next train headed east." His drawl had become more pronounced when she turned to face him.

He said with innocence, "Why, I'll bet you could be in Lexington before the sun rises on Sunday."

"Wouldn't you just love that!" she said through clenched teeth. "Wouldn't you just!"

"Why, no, ma'am." He slowly rolled the words, as if he were jesting with her. Truth to tell, he'd been enjoying the faint accent she placed on each syllable as she spoke. The contrast of her soft, cultured voice and the anger flashing from her blue eyes pleased him.

"I suppose you'd prefer the alternative," she suggested scornfully.

For just a second, his eyes glistened with unholy glee, and she inhaled sharply.

"Well, ma'am," he drawled, "I'd say that I'm not in a position to decide that, one way or the other. I'm willing to go along with your wishes."

It was so tempting, Emmaline thought. He was so close she could see the tiny squint lines beside his eyes. She could stamp her foot or swing a closed fist at him or spout the swear words she'd heard the trainers use back in Lexington.

She swallowed the words, and kept her hands tightly clenched. Her feet were another matter. Her toes were twitching inside the slender boots she wore, so badly did they want to deliver a punishing blow to the instep of the arrogant man who taunted her.

She moved quickly, fearful of revealing the anger bubbling in her depths. He lifted his brow in surprise as she spun to face him fully, and hid a smile as her feet sounded firmly against the carpet.

"My wishes are not the issue here, Mr. Gerrity," she said with biting sarcasm. "My late father has shown no regard whatsoever for my needs or desires in this matter."

"Miss Carruthers," the man at the desk said mildly, anxious to turn this conversation back to the matter at hand. "We need to hear the rest of the will before you make a hasty decision."

As if she had forgotten his existence, Emmaline's eyes widened in recognition. "There's more?"

Since the terms of the will had been read, just minutes ago, she'd been thrown into a state of shock, she realized. That her father could have tied up this ranch, the money in the bank and the fate of her sister with such horrendous terms was unbelievable.

As legal documents went, it was quite simple, really, she thought glumly, remembering each word.

It is my decision that my daughter, Emmaline Carruthers, join with Matthew Gerrity, my stepson, in a marriage that will ensure the heritage of my father being passed on to coming generations. Therefore, I grant joint custody to Emmaline and Matthew, in the case of my beloved daughter Theresa, so that she may be raised with the influence of both her brother and sister. So long as Emmaline and Matthew live on this property, they will be joint owners and joint caretakers of my daughter, Theresa. Should they decide not to enter into such a marriage, neither of them will inherit from me anything other than personal items which shall be listed below.

The lawyer cleared his throat and adjusted his spectacles. "Yes, there is more." His face became suffused in a rosy hue, and Emmaline's eyes sharpened as she sensed his discomfort. As though he were sending her a silent apology for what was to come, he glanced at her somberly.

"Allow me to continue," he said.

However, if they decide to abide by the above terms, and should there not be issue from the above described marriage within two years, I declare that neither Emmaline Carruthers or Matthew Gerrity shall remain as owners, but said ownership will revert at that time to my daughter Theresa. Matthew Gerrity will remain in his present position for as long as he desires. A suitable guardian shall be appointed for Theresa and the property held in trust for her until the age of twenty-one.

"He can't do that!" Emmaline's words were anguished.

Oswald Hooper looked at her sympathetically, as if he could not bear to deny her claim.

Matt had no such compunction.

"Looks to me like he did do exactly that," he said with a humorless smile.

"There's not much more," said the lawyer. "Just some bequests to the people here, and some legal processes to take place, ensuring the rights of the child. Other than that, you've heard the gist of it. Once you two are married, the deed will be changed to include both of your names."

"Matt Gerrity has no right," she blurted. "He's no blood relation."

"Your father chose the terms, Miss Carruthers," the lawyer reminded her gently.

"I won't do it," she vowed with whispered determination.

"Don't be so quick to decide, Emmaline." Matt's voice was deep, demanding her attention. She looked up quickly to meet his gaze. "If you turn down the terms of the will, I'll have no choice but to send you on your way. You'll lose contact with Tessie."

"And what about you? What will happen to you?"

His shoulders lifted once more, negligently. "Well, I suppose I'll just stay on here as ranch foreman. The will gives me that option, if I'm not mistaken."

"It could be interpreted that way," Mr. Hooper said, prompted by Matt's questioning look.

"And you'll have Theresa," Emmaline said bitterly.

He nodded as he repeated her words. "And I'll have Theresa."

"I won't allow that to happen," she declared, her chin lifting another notch. Her nostrils flared delicately, and her eyes shone with barely repressed fury. "I'll do anything I have to."

She was a fighter, Matt decided, watching the lines of her face firm up before his eyes. Her jaw was clenched, and her lips tightened as she awaited his reply.

With an edge of anger, he accepted her challenge. "So be it."

Old Samuel had had the last laugh, he thought grimly. He had always told him he'd like to see the day Matt met his match. And this daughter of his damn sure looked like it.

Chapter Three

"*Si*, Mr. Matt has been in charge here for two years. And every unmarried woman in the territory has been making eyes at him," Maria added for good measure.

Emmaline's mouth pursed as she considered the statement. "I'll bet he eats it up," she said finally.

Maria shrugged and smiled. "What young man wouldn't? The ladies have always taken to Mr. Matt, and now..." Her shoulders lifted once more.

"And now?"

"Everyone will be thinking he has been left the ranch. A man with property will not go unmarried for long."

"Does he have..." Emmaline paused delicately, unwilling to ask such a question.

Maria frowned at her. "If you had come to breakfast earlier, you might have been able to ask him yourself," she said firmly, as if that would settle the matter.

Emmaline smoothed her fingers over the hem of her napkin once more. True, she'd appeared for breakfast just as Matt and Miss Olivia were leaving the table. At home, meals had been served at more civilized hours. Surely no one had an appetite at dawn.

Then, too, in her experience, servants were not as outspoken as Maria. But things were done differently here, she reminded herself. Lexington was a long way from Forbes

Junction. Informality was a way of life. Why, Theresa and Matt didn't even wear mourning, she realized, not for the first time, as she looked down upon her own black silk gown. She shivered, mutely deciding Arizona was a long way from civilization.

Annoyance was riding the edge of her voice when she finally managed a reply. "It isn't a question a lady can ask a man. Besides, I asked you, Maria. All else aside, Mr. Gerrity is not the easiest man in the world to talk to, you know."

The housekeeper shook her head. "Since he is to be your husband, you have the right to ask him anything you wish." Her sparkling eyes belied the prim pursing of her mouth as she tossed a quick look at Emmaline. "I owe as much allegiance to Mr. Matthew as to yourself."

Emmaline cast her an unbelieving look. "I doubt if I will ever be given as much," she muttered beneath her breath.

The husky voice from the doorway cut with precision into her thoughts.

"Just ask away, Emmaline. My life is an open book," Matt said with deceptive softness. "Don't make Maria feel uncomfortable. She's loyal to the family, and that splits her between us."

Emmaline's brow raised as she turned to face him. "You consider me family?"

He hesitated only a moment. "Maria does," he said flatly. "That's all that matters."

"*Sí,*" the older woman said quickly. "You are your father's daughter, Miss Emmaline. You are family, as if you had never left."

The words touched Emmaline more deeply than she wanted to admit, and she smiled with trembling lips as she rose from the table. "Thank you, Maria," she murmured quietly, one hand lifting to rest for a moment upon the housekeeper's shoulder as she paused by her side.

Her head bowed for a moment as she considered her position here. When the only truly friendly face she'd come across in the past two days was that of the housekeeper, it was difficult to feel at home. Matt's words of welcome had been flippant, and his manner had run the gamut from mocking to moody, especially during the session in the library. Since then, he'd retreated into a shell that bespoke his feelings eloquently.

His eyes had been upon her more than once, but the message they conveyed was guarded. He'd be happiest if she hightailed it out of here, she thought.

"Emmaline." His voice brought her back from her meanderings.

He stood in the doorway, his hands tucked into the slits of his pant pockets. "What do you want to know about me?" he asked, with a taunting grin that made her clench her jaw.

She shook her head mutely, unwilling to allow her irritation free rein. Where he'd been and what he'd been doing for all his life was none of her business, she decided swiftly. Better that she tend to today's business and forget his yesterdays. She might find out more than she wanted to know. And besides, she probably would soon be learning more about him than she had ever planned on.

With long fingers, he set his wide-brimmed hat upon his head, covering his dark, glossy hair and tilting the brim to shade his eyes, hiding their expression from her view.

"You missed your best chance," he said evenly. "See you at supper time." With a nod toward both women, he left the room, and Emmaline was left to wish she'd asked him just one question.

How did Matt Gerrity feel about entering a forced marriage?

Her heart pounded in an accelerated rhythm as she considered the thought. Somehow, Matthew Gerrity didn't appear to be the sort of man who would take kindly to being forced into anything, she decided. Especially something as final as a marriage. A marriage that would, by necessity, involve the birth of a child.

Bathing every day was a habit deeply ingrained in Emmaline. She had responded to Matthew's suggestion that she take a dip in the shallow creek several miles to the north with utter silence. His mocking grin had infuriated her.

The alternative was a procedure involving pails of hot and cold water, and the aid of others. There was no help for it, she'd decided by the third day. Sponge baths in her room were inadequate, and she yearned for the luxury of being wet all over.

The tub was large, sloped at the back, and longer than the one Emmaline was accustomed to. "I can almost lie full length in that," she said to Maria as the housekeeper supervised its filling. The bathing room was just off the kitchen—a rather primitive way of doing business, Emmaline thought privately. Two of the hired hands carried brimming pails of hot water and dumped them quickly into the tub. Then Maria pumped cold water in the kitchen and sent two buckets along to lower the temperature to Emmaline's liking. Another pail of steaming water was left next to the tub, should the bath cool before she finished.

"Your papa needed a big tub," Maria told her with good humor. "He was a large man, and didn't like to have his knees poking out of the water."

"I remember him a little, you know," Emmaline said wistfully. "He seemed a giant of a man to me—all legs, in fact, until he picked me up. I remember him holding me, and then sometimes I wonder if it might be just wishful thinking on my part. Maybe my memories and dreams get all tangled up in my mind."

Maria moved behind her to plait the abundance of hair flowing to the middle of her back. "I'll pin this up to keep it out of the water," she offered, her fingers quick as they formed the loose braid and attached it to Emmaline's crown with a bone hairpin. Her hands dropped to the younger woman's shoulders, and she sighed, shaking her head at the memories Emmaline's words had brought to life.

"I think we have many pictures in our minds, Miss Emmaline. If you remember your papa at all, it is because his love for you was so strong. Don't think badly of him. He only wished that you had received his letters and could have answered. But he never held it against you."

"He wrote me?"

"*Sí,* every month he sent a letter. For years he hoped... but your mama or your grandparents... Well, it's done now," she finished briskly. Her face brightened. "When Arnetta Gerrity came here, his life changed. He decided you were lost to him, I think." She bent to test the bathwater, dismissing the subject.

"I have left towels, here on the stool," she said briskly. Quickly she patted once more at Emmaline's hair, testing the security of the upswept braid, and her eyes were moist with tender feeling. "So like your papa," she whispered, shaking her head as she left the small bathing room, pulling the door shut behind herself.

Emmaline's movements were slow, her fingers deliberately undoing the row of buttons on her dress. That her mother had kept so much from her was almost unbelievable. If her father had truly written letters to her all that time, what had happened to them? Carefully she stripped her petticoats from her body, silently condemning them to perdition.

"You're right, Matthew Gerrity," she muttered through clenched teeth. "It's too dratted hot here for civilized clothing." The black dress, with its yards of skirt, received a baleful glance, and she stepped carefully into the tub of water. And then she sighed with contentment as the scent of lilacs wafted about her.

Bringing her own soap along had seemed a luxury while she packed for the journey, but now it was a dire necessity, she decided. The sudsy fragrance she used washed away her tension, even as it removed the dusty residue and perspiration from her body.

"Are you still here?" asked a small voice from the doorway, even as the knob squeaked at being turned by the child's hand.

Automatically Emmaline slid beneath the surface of the water and turned her head to peer at the intruder.

Theresa watched her with wide, hostile eyes. "I thought you'd be gone," she said, her chin jutting forward as she eyed the unwanted woman who'd taken up residence in the bathtub.

Emmaline chose her words carefully. "I came to see you, Theresa. I can't leave till we get to know each other. We're sisters, you know."

The child sniffed and sidled into the room. She propped one hand on her waist and assumed a belligerent stance. "I don't need a sister," she declared firmly. "I have Maffew, and he's my brother."

"I know," Emmaline answered softly, aware of how gingerly she must tread. "But all girls need a sister, you know. I've always wanted one of my very own. And now that I've found you, I really want to get to know you."

"Why?" Theresa frowned, pushing her lips into a pout.

Emmaline hid her amusement at the look. "Because I'm sure you're a nice girl and we'll get on well together. I can show you how to play some games I know," she added gently, coaxingly.

"Games?" Theresa's eyes lit with interest for a moment, then the frown settled back in place and an uncaring gesture lifted the small shoulders in a shrug.

"I brought along some things I thought you'd like to see," Emmaline said as she began once more to wash. She lifted one leg and used the cloth with long strokes, enjoying the sensation of the rough fabric against her flesh.

There was a long moment of silence. Then the child spoke, in a small voice that struggled to be offhand. "What kind of things?"

Emmaline cocked her head and looked over her shoulder, her mouth pursed as if in thought. "Oh ... I have a set of jackstraws, and a skipping rope." She slanted a glance at Theresa once more. "Can you skip rope?"

Theresa's head shook as she took another step closer.

"Oh, I almost forgot," Emmaline said, as if in surprise. "There's a package from France that I found in my room back home in Lexington that I thought you might like."

"From France?" Her eyes widened as Theresa sank onto the bath stool, oblivious of the towels beneath her bottom. "My Miss Olivia says that's a place across the ocean."

Emmaline nodded agreeably and resumed her washing, donning a façade of nonchalance. "Of course, you might not like playing jackstraws. But...we could skip rope." She dared another look at the child, who had leaned even closer. "But then, I'm really a very good rope skipper, and you might have a hard time learning."

"Oh, no," Theresa said quickly. "I can learn real fast. My Maffew says I'm smart as a whip." Her mouth drew down suddenly as a new thought struck her. "You won't be here very long, anyway. Maffew says you'll be leaving soon."

"Well..." Emmaline turned quickly to the child, but it was too late. She had jumped from the stool and, with only one backward look, was gone, slipping through the doorway and running through the kitchen.

"Where've you been, pigeon?" The deep voice sounded beyond the half-open door, and Emmaline slipped once more beneath the surface of the water, sloshing it precariously close to the brim of the tub.

"Talkin' to that lady," Theresa said. "She's takin' a baff."

"With the door open?" Tinged with a trace of amusement, the voice came closer, and Emmaline reached for the towels Maria had left.

"Are you wantin' more company in there?" Matt asked from around the doorway. "We usually keep this door shut when the room is being used," he drawled.

"Please pull it shut, would you?" Emmaline held the towel in readiness as she bent forward in the water, her knees pulled to her breasts.

"Sure you don't want company?" From just beyond the door, his voice reached her, tinged with taunting amusement.

"Please, Matt," she whispered, her words wispy with embarrassment.

He reached one long arm within the room, his fingers grasping the knob, and deliberately closed the door.

"Don't be late for breakfast," he called to her abruptly. "Maria usually only serves once. After that, you're on your own."

"And I hope you choke on yours," she muttered as she stepped over the edge of the tub and enfolded herself in the towel she still clutched.

The last rays of the sun set the sky aglow in shades of pink and orange contrasting with the darker bands of purple that chased the daylight below the horizon. The porch

faced west, and Emmaline sat on the top step, her arms
wrapped about herself as she watched in awe, her eyes wide.

"Never seen a sunset before?" he asked in a faintly teasing fashion.

She shrugged, the movement lifting her shoulders, then
allowed her glance to meet his. "Lots of them," she answered, her arms dropping from her waist, her hands
clasping easily in her lap.

"Looked like you were all wrapped up in this one." He
nodded toward the sky in the west, where the scudding
clouds were still gleaming at the edges. The pink had darkened to cerise, rimming the gray, ominous cloud bank as
though a paintbrush had been swept across the upper edge.

"It's different," she admitted quietly. "Stronger, somehow. Maybe just because there's so much more of it." She
turned back to the vision that was even now fading rapidly
beneath the horizon, and her sigh was audible.

"There'll be another one tomorrow night." He made his
way to where she sat, his stride long and his boots loud
against the wooden porch. In an easy motion, he sat down
beside her and stretched his long legs before him.

She eyed him from beneath lowered lids, her glance
making a guarded survey. His pants were snug, wrapped
about his thighs and calves as if custom-made to fit the
muscular shape they covered. Dusty and worn at the seams,
they were standard-quality denim, but on Matthew Gerrity they became something else.

She thought of the men she'd known who wouldn't be
caught wearing common pants from a store shelf, men who
had their riding clothes made by tailors who measured and
sewed each seam with precision. None of them could hold
a candle to this man, she decided.

There was about him a sureness, a quality of masculine
perfection that defied description. He wore a cotton shirt
that tucked neatly into his pants, a bandanna tied casually

about his throat, his belt snug about his waist—below his waist, really, she amended with a silent chuckle. The pants rode the top of his hips as he walked, she remembered, and her face flushed as she recalled that walk.

That slim-hipped, flat-bottomed stroll that had caught her openmouthed as she watched. The masculine body that began with broad shoulders and long arms, arms that were thick beneath the shirtsleeves he rolled to within inches of his elbows. Hands that were wide, and fingers that were long and tapered and strong.

"Emmaline?" The voice was close to her ear, and she jerked as it brought her from her thoughts.

"Have you made up your mind? Are you planning the wedding?"

She shook her head. "Not yet."

His look was cynical. "Begging off already?"

"I told you I'd do anything I had to, didn't I?"

"Is it so bad? Marrying the ranch foreman?" His tone was clipped and cold.

"You won't be the foreman if I marry you. You'll own the place."

"Half of it. Your name will be on the title, too. That ought to make your folks happy, you bein' a landowner."

She shrugged and eyed the darkened horizon, loath to look in his direction. "It's still not what my grandparents planned for me. Certainly not what my mother had in mind for her only child."

"In other words, you could do better back in Lexington," he said tonelessly.

"Could you? Could you do better?" she asked, and then dared the question she'd been mulling over. "Was there someone else in the picture before I arrived?"

He was silent, and she ventured to cast a quick look at him. His jaw was taut, and his eyes were narrowed. Certainly not an approachable man, she thought. He gave no indication of his thoughts, and she'd begun to regret her question when he shifted toward her.

"No one that should matter to you," he answered shortly.

"Will you break her heart? Or is there more than one?"

He shook his head in a slow movement, his eyes on her. "Hardly. I don't have time to chase after women."

"Maria seems to think you don't have to do much chasing."

"Maria talks too much." His grin was cocky.

"You didn't answer my question. Are you going to break some woman's heart if we marry?" She tilted her chin and waited for his answer.

It was enigmatic, as was the look he sent from beneath lowered brows. "Most women don't have hearts that are broken so easily."

She sighed, wondering how long it would take to get a straight answer. "Will you give her up?"

His smile tilted one corner of his mouth disdainfully. "Does it matter?"

Her cheeks were pink as she considered him. "There isn't any hurry, is there?" she asked finally. "We don't have to be married right away. Because if you're having second thoughts, or if you're planning on—"

"You didn't answer me, Emmaline." His lips twisted into another half smile that taunted her, even as it eased the harsh lines of his face, and her eyes were drawn to the movement.

Was his mouth hard, she wondered, or would it soften when it touched the flesh of a woman's lips? Would he be gentle with his caresses, or would those hard hands be rough against tender skin? Thoughts of those forbidden secrets, things that happened between men and women, flooded her mind, and she blinked in confusion.

"Yes . . . yes, it matters," she whispered.

"Even cowhands have honor," he said roughly. "I won't be lollygaggin' around in town after we tie the knot, Emmaline."

"But you don't really want to, do you?" she asked.

"I told you, lady, the offer's still open. I'll cart you to Forbes Junction to visit the preacher whenever you say. But, to tell the truth, I'd be just as well off putting you on the train. I can make it without you. I make a good living at my job, and I keep a close eye on my sister. I'm satisfied with what I've got right now. Theresa's all that matters to me."

Her heart thumped against the wall of her chest, and she knew a moment of dreadful sorrow. What she had dreamed of in her childhood years was never to be. Matt Gerrity had no warmth to spend on her, only derision and a calm acceptance of his fate. Could she be satisfied with that? Did she have a choice?

"Can you marry me, without feeling anything for me?" she asked boldly.

His grin was quick. "Oh, don't worry, honey. I'll feel something, all right."

With a graceless movement, she stood, color riding her cheeks as she smoothed the wrinkles from her skirt. "This is a big game for you, isn't it?"

His eyes were guarded as he rose to tower over her. "I don't play games, Emmaline. I play for keeps. But let me tell you one thing. If you marry me, you'll have nothing to complain about. I'll give you all the attention you want."

So quickly she was barely able to catch her breath, Matt loomed over her, his big hands grasping her shoulders. He lifted her against his hard body. With a smothered growl, he drew her to him. And then their lips met, hers opening to protest, his open to consume the lush softness of her mouth. With measured restraint, he covered her, taking no notice of the murmurs she uttered within the depths of his mouth.

Emmaline's hands were helpless against his broad chest, and her toes barely touched the wide boards of the porch. She hung in his grasp and closed her eyes, her face and throat flushed and warm, her mouth tamed to his liking.

A tingle of warmth simmered low in her stomach, but she fought the urge to soften against him. He'd taken hold of her as if she were a hussy in a saloon, and he'd brutally invaded the virgin territory of her mouth as if it were his due. A flush of anger at his treatment covered her cheeks, and Emmaline was overwhelmed suddenly by a sense of despair at the treacherous response of her own body. A sob rose to vibrate within her chest, bringing tears to her eyes. And even her tightly closed lids could not stop them from sliding down her cheeks.

Perhaps it was the dampness against his face that cooled the force of Matt's ardor. Perhaps he'd begun to regret his irate, impetuous behavior. Whatever the cause, he loosened his grip on her, lowering her feet to the floor, lifting his head to rub his cheek against hers. Her face was rosy, her eyes were tightly closed, yet still the tears flowed, and he felt a pang of regret.

It had been an impulse, and he was too old to be impulsive. Silently he cursed the urges she managed to arouse in him. Emmaline wasn't used to such rough handling, he reminded himself. He'd have done better to keep his hands off. Here she was, a lady from tip to toe, and he'd just treated her like a woman upstairs at Katy Klein's Golden Garter.

Putting put her away from his aroused body, he held her in place, waiting until she caught another shuddering breath. Her tongue came out slowly, moving across her lips, testing the tender surfaces and tasting the residue of his mouth. She shivered once more, then shrugged out of his hold, her eyes opening slowly, focusing on the front of his shirt.

"Is this what I have to look forward to?" she asked stiffly.

"Are you gonna cry every time I kiss you?" Matt countered in a harsh growl.

She gritted her teeth and watched as his chest rose and fell with each breath he took. "Was that the way you kiss all your women?"

"Only the ones I plan on taking to bed," he answered roughly.

She stiffened, and her head lifted until her eyes met the darkness of his. "You are not a gentleman, Matthew Gerrity," she managed to whisper.

"I never said I was, Emmaline Carruthers." His index finger touched her mouth before she could move away. "Hold still," he said quickly, his other hand gripping her shoulder. That single finger slipped easily, slowly, over the fullness of her mouth, and was eased by the moisture he had left there. He watched intently as he traced the path her tongue had taken only seconds ago.

His words were raspy, contrasting with the gentle touch of his callused finger as he completed his inspection and cupped her chin easily in his palm. "Maybe I'll be nicer next time, honey," he said roughly.

"Maybe there won't be a next time," she snapped, pulling from his touch and hurrying to the door that led into the house.

He watched her go, and his mouth set into a grim line. "Don't bet the ranch on that one, lady," he said deliberately, then considered the final twitch of her skirts and the arrogant tilt of her head.

Chapter Four

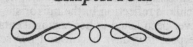

The box was glossy, with an allover design of flowers, blue forget-me-nots and pale pink roses entwined in heart-shaped bouquets. It lay in solitary splendor on the bed, a splash of delicate color against the white coverlet.

Theresa appeared in the doorway and imitated her brother's stance, her hands stuffed into her pinafore pockets, her feet apart and her head tilted to one side. Carefully she kept her eyes averted from the temptation that lured her. The package had been in the same place every day for three days, the same three days the door to Emmaline's room had been left ajar, allowing for easy inspection of the interior.

The box, beguiling her with its mystery, had brought the child this far, the faraway land of its origin provoking her curiosity.

Miss Olivia had shown her a map of Europe and pointed out the orange area that represented France. Theresa had been disappointed. Certainly that blob of color was not what she had expected, and the map had not satisfied her yearning to know more about the source of the enticing box that lay just beyond her reach.

Prodded by the child's questioning, Miss Olivia had dug deep in her satchel of books to find a slender volume that contained reproduced pictures of the French countryside. Grainy photographs of elegantly dressed Parisian ladies strolling down shop-lined boulevards had awed the child. She'd gazed with wonder at the Arc de Triomphe—Napoleon's concept brought to life, offering welcome to the city.

Certainly such a marvelous place could only offer inde-
scribable treasures.

And such a treasure resided in the box that lay on Emmaline's bed. Only Theresa's inherent dignity kept her from
it. Only her reluctance to accept the presence of Emmaline
denied the eager curiosity that glistened in her dark eyes.

From the dressing table near the window, Emmaline
watched the child's reflection in the mirror she faced. Patience had never been listed in her personal catalog of vir-
tues, but the past few days had found her seeking that
quality with a persistence that would have given her grandmother immense gratification, had she known. Now she
watched as the child in the doorway struggled with temptation.

"Would you like to come in?" Feigning ignorance of
Theresa's dilemma, Emmaline turned on the padded seat
and smiled a careful welcome.

A lifted shoulder was her answer, together with a shuttered glance that denied interest.

"I've been hoping you'd come to see me." This time the
child met her gaze fully.

"Miss Olivia said I could leave off writing my letters till
later if I wanted to," she offered diffidently. One hand crept
from her pocket and rubbed against the muslin of her skirt.
"I just thought I'd see what your jackstraws looked like."

Emmaline released her breath, relief and delight min-
gling to create a gentle smile. "I'd love to show you all the
things I brought with me," she said, rising slowly, as if she
feared to startle a small wild creature.

Another step brought Theresa within the room, and she
halted there, her eyes moving over the small evidence of
Emmaline's presence. A silver-handled brush and mirror
lay on the dressing table, next to a crystal bottle of toilet
water and a delicately painted china hair receiver. The open
wardrobe displayed the meager contents of her luggage,
and a paisley reticule hung from the wooden knob of the
open door.

But the treasures she had planned to lure the child with
lay within the depths of her carpetbag, and she turned to lift
it from the floor behind the bed. Carefully she ignored the

beribboned package that lay precisely in the center of the feather bed she had slept in for three nights. As if it were a worm on a hook, she had displayed it there with casual unconcern, hoping for just such a visit as Theresa had finally chosen to make this morning.

Reaching into the bag, Emmaline drew forth a jump rope with finely carved handles. "Have you ever tried to skip rope?" she asked.

Theresa's head shook from side to side as she took another step forward, lessening the distance between them. "No, ma'am," she said quietly, remembering her manners. "I've never played jackstraws, either. Miss Olivia said she played them when she was a little girl, though."

Emmaline allowed a small grin of triumph to escape. Apparently Theresa had discussed this venture with her tutor. Certainly she'd been impressed enough to make her way here without further coaxing.

"Would you like to see my books?"

The child cast one yearning glance at the bed and then harnessed her curiosity with obvious effort. Her sigh was deep. "I do like books, ma'am."

"Maybe you could call me Emmaline," her sister suggested quietly. "What would you like me to call you?"

"I'm Theresa. Only Maffew says I'm his Tessie." She stepped closer, her soft slippers silent against the wide planks of the bedroom floor. One small hand lifted to brush against the quilted coverlet, its fingers careful to stray no farther than inches from the edge of the bed. For a moment, her eyes darted once more to the flowered box, and then she tamed the errant glance.

"Oh!" Emmaline feigned dismay with a soft cry and a pursing of her lips. "I almost forgot about the present I brought you from France."

"You did? You almost forgot?" Theresa's eyes widened in wonder at such a lapse.

With shameless satisfaction, Emmaline reeled in the prize she had won. "There, on the bed," she said with a lazy movement of her hand. "I left the box out in case you came by."

Theresa's mouth formed a soft circle of wonder as her small hand edged across the coverlet to allow slender fingers to trace the fragile flowers that graced the shiny prize she coveted.

"This is for me?" she whispered hopefully.

Emmaline nodded, her smile guardedly triumphant as she watched. "Open it, why don't you?" she urged softly.

With an eagerness that brought a startled burst of laughter from her elder sister, Theresa clambered onto the bed and then, with anxious eyes, glanced back for approval.

"Go ahead, open it," Emmaline said encouragingly as she approached the foot of the bed. She was heady with success, and her cheeks were rosy with excitement.

Pretty as a picture. The words that described the scene flew into being as Matthew Gerrity watched from the doorway. Unseen, unnoticed by the two, who were deeply engrossed in their own involvement, he hesitated outside the room.

A strange emotion tore at his heart, a painful surge he recognized as jealousy tightening his jaw, and his eyes narrowed as he surveyed the woman who had begun to usurp his place. With feminine skill, she had brought about this happening, knowing intuitively what would whet a small girl's curiosity, what would draw the child into her orbit.

"Sneaky," he said in a casual accusation as he left his watching post to shatter the fragile picture burning in his mind. Unwilling to admit the beguiling of his senses, he chose to break the tenuous moment of vulnerability that had seized his control. He thrust away the moment of envy, the sense of standing outside the magic circle, his mouth tightening with the effort.

Emmaline glanced at him quickly, her smile smothered by the shuttered look he cast in her direction.

"Not sneaky, just devious," she told him softly. "I need every foothold I can manage."

Oblivious of the adults who spoke civilities over her head, Theresa was involved in the process of lifting the cover from the box, her fingers already foraging beneath the tissue, which had kept the contents from damage during the long journey.

With a gasp of delight and a whisper of wonder, she drew forth the beautiful bisque doll Emmaline had brought for her. With bonnet and gown barely wrinkled, with delicately hand-painted features smiling demurely in her direction, the loose-limbed creation enthralled Theresa completely. The doll's hands were lifted carefully and examined, the slippered feet treated with tender regard.

Then the child's small head lifted, and for the first time, Emmaline saw the sister she had traveled so far to meet and claim as her own.

"Oh, thank you, Emmie," she said with joyous haste, her small tongue shortening the ponderous length of her sister's name.

Emmaline cast a glance that reeked of triumph in Matthew's direction and then allowed her features to soften as she sat down beside the girl, who held the doll with careful hands.

"Emmie?" she asked carefully, her heart rejoicing at the implied intimacy.

Theresa looked up and shrugged. "Emmaline is too long to say." Her eyes darted to the tall form of her brother, who watched silently. "Do you like my present, Maffew?" she asked with obvious restraint as she awaited his opinion.

To his credit, Matt Gerrity smiled and nodded his approval. Unwilling to dampen the pleasure of his small sister, he faced the knowledge that his solitary relationship with her was at an end.

"Your sister knew just what you would like, didn't she?" he asked, his question directed at both females.

Emmaline's chin lifted defiantly as she allowed her smile to widen in response. "You had a head start, Matthew," she said carefully.

Theresa looked from one to the other, as if she sensed the undercurrents that lay beneath their words.

He relented, unwilling to cloud the small face looking at him with a trace of uncertainty. "It's a beautiful doll, Tessie," he assured her. "I'm glad your sister brought it to you."

The gathering cloud vanished. Theresa embraced the doll, her arms holding the stuffed body with care and her head bent as she crooned softly against the delicately rouged cheek.

Matt's glance brushed with tenderness over the small form as she rocked the doll within her arms, and Emmaline's breath caught in her throat as she glimpsed the warmth of his regard.

Just for a moment, an errant thought pierced Emmaline's satisfaction as she hugged her small victory. Just for a fleeting second, she wondered how it would feel to have that same tender look bestowed upon her own being. And for the space of that moment, she felt alone, bereft of human touch, once more the lonely girl who had been searching for a lifetime and until now had never caught a glimpse of what she sought.

"You're getting married?" The words were shrill and carried easily to the hallway, where Emmaline had paused. Voices from the library had alerted her to the presence of a visitor, and she had hesitated, unwilling to intrude upon a private conversation. With one hand, she leaned against the wall beside her, vacillating between advancement and retreat.

The murmur of Matthew's voice was blurred by the rapid speech of a woman who appeared intent on overriding his explanation.

"I don't understand! I just cannot believe you've dragged a bride out of the woodwork!" she exclaimed with the same shrill vehemence.

"Now, Deborah," Matt said firmly.

A silence settled against her ears, and Emmaline leaned forward a bit, listening for the reply she was sure must be forthcoming. No longer was she tempted to retreat to her bedroom. Gone was the ladylike urge to ignore the passionate exchange in the library. The woman was talking about her, and Emmaline's eyes were wide with annoyance.

"I was hardly dragged out of the woodwork," she muttered beneath her breath.

A muffled sob reached Emmaline's hearing, and then a whispered flow of words caused her to change her position. She took her hand from the whitewashed wall, jammed it in her pocket and moved carefully down the hallway, bent on catching sight of the unseen female who had managed to put a blight on this morning.

Hesitating before the open door of the library, she stiffened, her mouth tightening in disapproval. Matthew's hands were busy, one distractedly patting a slender back, the other in the process of wiping away tears with a large white handkerchief. The woman who was allowing such familiarity with her person was sighing and sobbing with dainty purpose, the sounds at variance with the shrill comments she had been making only minutes ago.

"Am I intruding?" Emmaline asked from her vantage point. She schooled her features into a concerned mask and stepped forward.

Matt looked up and glared at her over the head of the woman he was attempting to comfort. "I'm not sure this is the time for a formal introduction, Emmaline," he said bluntly.

The woman in his grasp shuddered once more, then straightened her shoulders and took charge of the handkerchief he held. Walking to the window, she pulled aside the white curtain and looked out upon the view from the front of the house.

Emmaline lifted one eyebrow in an unspoken question and, with a delicate movement of her hands, signified her willingness to retreat, backing away from Matthew's apparent frustration.

"Never mind leaving." He changed his mind and reached for her hand, clasping her fingers in a grasp she knew would be easier to accept than to wiggle out of. "This probably is as good a time as any," he muttered, contradicting his first reaction to her appearance.

"Deborah," he said briskly, and then waited while the woman at the window slowly turned to face them.

"This is Emmaline Carruthers, the woman who will be my wife."

Not "my bride" or "the woman I've asked to marry me," but, bluntly, "my wife." Emmaline struggled to look pleasant. She knew she couldn't manage friendly, and welcoming was far beyond her capacity for the moment. Pleasant would have to suffice.

With but a passing glance, the woman turned her attention to the tall man who had delivered her a telling blow. His jaw was set and rigid, but his eyes held a trace of pity Emmaline could not help but notice. Perhaps it was the unwanted suggestion of such an emotion that tightened the woman's own features into a civil expression marred only by the flaring of her nostrils as she spoke.

"Congratulations to both of you. I'll admit I was a bit surprised at the news, Matt, but then, you always were full of surprises," she said, dropping her gaze, to brush with one hand at the unwrinkled expanse of her skirt.

"This is Deborah Hopkins, the daughter of our nearest neighbor," Matthew explained as he drew Emmaline closer, his fingers tightening on her own as she reluctantly stepped next to him.

"I really must leave. I only dropped by to invite you to Sunday dinner, Matt," the blond creature said, her breasts lifting as she stifled a sigh. Her eyelashes fluttered in a sad little gesture Emmaline noted grimly, and then, fastening her gaze on the man who stood across the room, Deborah smiled. Pathetically, her mouth trembled in a way designed to tug at a man's heartstrings.

Only as she made her way past them to the doorway did she deign to look directly at Emmaline. Her eyes swept from the top of her unruly curls, down past the black mourning dress that hung in heavy folds to the floor. In a gesture that dismissed Emmaline as insignificant, Deborah moved past her, and it was only when she reached the front door that Matthew moved.

"Let me walk you to your buggy," he offered, releasing Emmaline's hand and reaching Deborah's side with long, easy strides.

She looked up at him with a brave little smile and nodded, stepping back so he could open the door.

Emmaline shook her head in disgust and walked back to watch from the window as the couple approached the buggy standing in front of the house. A small, dark mare stood patiently within the harness, tied to the hitching rail that was just beyond the patch of grass.

How odd, she thought. The woman would make a wonderful actress, changing from feigned sorrow to acceptance to disdain in a matter of moments. And for the life of her, Emmaline couldn't put a finger on which emotions were genuine. That the girl truly cared for Matthew was probable. This likely was the one he had referred to. The one he said would not be heartbroken by his marriage.

She tended to agree with his judgment. "I don't think anyone could break her heart," she said beneath her breath as she watched them. Matthew assisted Deborah onto the high seat of the buggy and then untied the mare, turning the buggy with one hand on the harness. Lifting a hand in a farewell, he watched as the horse broke into a rapid trot at the urging of her mistress.

He turned back to the house, his eyes fixed on the window where Emmaline waited, narrowing as he caught sight of her there. With long, measured strides, he went back to the porch and up the steps to cross to the wide front door. In moments, as long as it took her to turn aside from the window and move halfway across the room, he was back, framed in the doorway, his face a dark cloud of anger.

"All that was far from necessary," he said with rough impatience. You should have kept your nose outa here, Emmaline. This whole thing was none of your business."

A twinge of guilt stabbed her, and she hastily threw up a barricade of irritation to thwart its interference. "My name was mentioned. That made it my business," she said pertly. "After all, I'm the bride you dragged out of the woodwork," she added with soft emphasis.

"If you hadn't been eavesdropping, you wouldn't have heard that remark," he growled defensively. His jaw firmed and his eyes glittered as she glowered at him.

"I was coming from my bedroom down the hallway. I couldn't help but hear," she explained with lofty hauteur.

"Well, you should have trotted right back down that hallway. You could tell that Deborah was upset," he said with measured anger. "I had only just told her that we were to be married, and she spoke too quickly."

"Are you defending her, Matthew?" Clasping her hands behind her back, Emmaline surveyed him cooly.

"Deborah doesn't need defending. She's more than able to take care of herself," he answered bluntly.

"Perhaps just the sort of wife you need." Emmaline's suggestion was coated with subtle sarcasm.

"Perhaps." The word dropped between them, and Matthew wished immediately that he could retrieve it, unsaid. This had gone on long enough, and he sensed Emmaline becoming more agitated by the moment.

"Look, it's beside the point, Emmaline. I'm not marrying Deborah. I've never even discussed the subject with her. She's a neighbor and a friend. Let's just forget the whole thing."

"Maybe you never discussed marriage with her, but your friend certainly had it in mind, Matthew. And what was I supposed to think when I came and found you...*together?*" she asked emphatically.

He glared at her impotently, unable to deny her statement. "She was crying. What should I have done? Shoved her away?"

Emmaline shrugged. "I'm sure a gentleman like you would never do that."

She could really get his dander up, Matt acknowledged glumly. And in a way, she was right. Certainly Deborah had been considering him as a husband. He'd have been a fool not to recognize it. And he probably should have been more considerate when he broke the news to her. But a few kisses and stolen caresses didn't add up to marriage, in his book. Deborah had probably set her cap in his direction, and his innate honesty forced him to admit silently that it likely would have come about...had not this fiery little baggage come into his life.

But she had, making an impact he was still attempting to absorb. His aggravation at her interference and the rush of emotion she managed to let loose within him combined as he approached her with measured tread.

Too late, she attempted to sidestep his grasp. He was upon her before she could maneuver past him, and his hands were reaching for her. His eyes flared with a hot purpose that had her retreating, struggling against his hold, turning her head from the warmth of his appraisal.

"Let go of me," she demanded, her hands rising between them and fisting, to pound against the width of his chest.

"Not on your life," he growled. "You sauntered in here and claimed your rightful place. Don't deny it, Emmaline. You knew exactly what you were doing when you came through that doorway."

She met his eyes with a wary look, and her hands unclenched, her fingers spreading against his shirt and pressing against him, as if to retain some small space in which to defend herself.

"No, I..." she began carefully, attempting to explain her actions, then stopped, knowing he was right. She probably should have retreated to her room and left Matt to his explanations. Better yet, if she'd stayed in her room just a while longer... No matter. It was done. She'd known he'd be angry with her interference, and, too late, she wished she could undo the events of the past several minutes.

He held her shoulders firmly, his eyes focused on the myriad expressions that flooded her features. Then his gaze lowered, sweeping over the same dark dress Deborah had surveyed with such scorn. His mouth quirked at one corner, and his fingers shifted their grip, sliding a few inches down her arms. One eyebrow lifted a bit as he watched her, unwillingly admiring her defiant stance.

Emmaline felt heat radiate within her as he surveyed her, from the uptilted thrust of her chin to the soft curves of her breasts. She faced him proudly, fighting the urge to cross her arms over the cushion of her bosom, her senses vibrantly alive beneath the dark intensity of his gaze.

With heavy-lidded precision, his eyes lazily surveyed her slender form, and his movements were careful as he allowed his hands to slide to her waist. Then, moving them upward, he clasped her ribs, just beneath the swell of her bosom, and with a steady urgency his thumbs moved, resting against the lower curve of her breasts.

She flushed, feeling the pressure there, where no man had ever dared to trespass before. Where no gentleman had even cast a lingering glance in passing. She was taken aback by his forward behavior, and yet within her she felt a spark of excitement that would not be denied. A flaring need brought tingling life to the part of her that he touched . . . a warmth that begged to be brushed against, a heat that cried for the movement of his hands. But good sense, and her rigid upbringing by Delilah, prevailed.

"Don't." The single word whispered from her lips, was a plea he could not deny. He lifted his gaze reluctantly from the vision that tempted him and looked instead into her eyes.

As quickly as it had filled him, Matt's flaring anger was gone, washed away on a tide of regret. As much as Emmaline had deserved his harsh disapproval, she was not deserving of his crudeness.

His hands dropped from her, and his nostrils flared as he inhaled abruptly. "I'm sorry, Emmaline. I shouldn't have touched you in anger."

"No . . ." She shook her head.

For a moment, she swayed, her own breathing irregular, her heart fluttering within her breast like a captured bird that strained to escape. Once more his hands framed her shoulders, and he steadied her, his jaw firm, his gaze sober, only the strange light in his eyes giving her a glimpse of the emotion he held in check.

Her laugh was uneven and forced as she tilted her head to one side. "You've really done it now, you know," she said, her voice trembling.

"Have I?" He muttered the words through lips that barely moved.

"Yes, you've let the cat out of the bag. You told Miss Hopkins that you're going to marry me. The whole town will know it by nightfall, if the Arizona Territory is anything like the state of Kentucky. And I suspect people are alike the world over."

"Maybe," he conceded roughly.

She tilted her head back, her eyes meeting his. "Are you going to marry me?" she whispered, and he nodded without hesitation.

"When?" she asked in the same whisper, as if she could not raise her voice beyond the soft questioning that was but a breath of sound.

"As soon as I can make the arrangements."

Her mouth formed a soft O and he yielded to the temptation of her lips, his mouth descending to cover them with his own.

She shivered in surprise, bracing herself for the same sort of assault he had launched on the porch only days ago. Instead, Emmaline found that the mouth he pressed to hers was all warmth and tenderness. His hands slid up to either side of her head, holding her with gentle purpose as he explored the textures of her face. Her eyes closed and she caught her breath as his caress brushed against her cheek and then to her temple, his nose burrowing in the curls that lay in abandon against her brow.

She was caught up in the pleasure he offered. With only a moment's hesitation, she leaned into his embrace and relaxed against the broad firmness of his chest. Tentatively her fingers crept to his shoulders, and she grasped handfuls of his shirt.

He gentled his touch, only his mouth paying homage to the softness of her skin, the curve of her throat, and again to the lips that inhaled his scent.

This time he growled a wordless sound of triumph as he parted her lips and edged his tongue against the tender skin. "Open your mouth for me," he said with dark purpose, his lips brushing carefully with coaxing movements.

She shook her head, moving against his grasp. Her eyes opened in dismay as his demand penetrated her lassitude.

His sigh was deep and his regret enormous as he drew back. A trace of humor lit the depths of his eyes and his mouth twisted in wry acceptance as he viewed the flushed face of the woman he intended to marry.

She wore his brand—the glow of latent passion that lay just beneath the surface of her bewilderment. He tamped down the surge of desire that billowed once more within him.

"You'll open for me next time," he promised her in a lazy drawl that told her of his satisfaction at this turn of events.

She dropped her hands from him, confusion darkening her eyes as she considered what he had demanded of her. Then, the determination within caused her to her stiffen against his grasp. She shook away his hands, stepping back from the nearness of his big body.

"Don't count on it," she said softly. "Don't count on it, Gerrity."

Her skirts swished about her, her head lifted in defiance, and he let her go as she brushed past him, turning to watch as she left the room.

It wasn't until she closed the door of her room behind her that Emmaline crumpled. Leaning against the heavy planks, she slid down to sit on the floor, burying her face in her hands. Her fingertips traced the path his lips had taken, barely touching the surface of her flesh where the heated kisses had burned against her.

"Oh, Delilah," she whispered against her palms. "You didn't tell me about this. You didn't tell me!"

Chapter Five

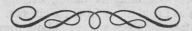

Olivia Champion could be an attractive woman, Emmaline decided. If only she weren't so grimly determined to look like a typical teacher. Her primly clad body and her smoothly scraped-back hair advertised her calling, as did the subservient air she wore like a garment.

Like a chameleon against the sand, she blended into the atmosphere of the house, and only here at the breakfast table had Emmaline heard more than one-syllable replies from the woman. Apparently this was a daily routine. Matthew questioned and Olivia answered, reciting Theresa's schedule for his approval.

Her dark eyes focused on Matt's face as Olivia placed her napkin carefully across her lap. Emmaline watched as a faint softening of the other woman's features was quickly concealed by the lowering of her head.

So that's how the land lies, Emmaline thought with awakening interest. The words spoken described lessons and books, but the subdued glances and carefully orchestrated movements told a different story.

"Today we'll be working mostly on letters and numbers," Olivia said quietly, her eyes limpid as she lifted her lashes in Matt's direction. "I've planned a geography lesson for this afternoon, but that will depend on Theresa." She glanced at Emmaline, her expression tolerant, as she elaborated. "Sometimes she gets a bit cranky after noontime and needs a short rest."

Emmaline nodded, striving to hide the smile that begged to curl her mouth. "I seem to suffer from the same problem some days," she agreed. Glancing at Matt as if she were seeking his reinforcement, she continued. "She's only five years old, Miss Champion. You're not pushing her too rapidly, are you?"

Olivia shook her head. "Certainly not. Mr. Gerrity wants his sister to be more than literate. His plan is to send her back east, to a university, when the time comes. But for now she is only beginning the basics, learning her letters and numbers as I read to her from the classics. We look at pictures of other countries and read about them, learning history and geography at a primary level." Her gaze swept across the table to rest with tender concern on Theresa, whose own eyes had moved from one adult to another.

Well said, Emmaline thought with a trickle of humor. The woman was a teacher to the bone, with hardly a shred of impetuosity within that dignified frame. Except for the sidelong glances that Matt seemed so oblivious of.

"I'm sure you have the situation well in hand," Emmaline murmured, her attention on the butter knife she was using with a lavish hand.

Across the table, Matt's dark eyes focused on the two women. Even as he listened to the words they spoke, he measured them in his mind. It was unfair, he decided. The contrast between them put Olivia at a distinct disadvantage. Next to the bright curls that surrounded Emmaline's head and cascaded down her back in an early-morning frenzy, the tutor's dark hair was commonplace, slicked back into a tightly wound knob at the nape of her neck. Only the somber clothing each wore placed them on common ground; Olivia's dark gray morning dress just shades lighter than the black silk that adorned Emmaline's curves.

He frowned as he considered the covered buttons that divided Emmaline's fitted bodice, ending at the small stand-up collar circling her throat. Covering all the soft flesh there, except for an inch or so in front, where he caught sight of the vulnerable hollow his lips had touched only yesterday.

"I want you to put away the mourning, Emmaline," he announced as he cut the beefsteak that lay on his plate.

"Really." She managed to put subtle emphasis on each syllable as she softly defied his edict.

His fork waved in her direction. "Yes, really. You're not likely to meet any members of high society out here, and the rules of behavior you followed in Kentucky don't apply."

She glanced at him with barely concealed disdain. "Rules of behavior never vary when it comes to civilized people," she said politely.

Olivia Champion swallowed the last bite of her breakfast with almost indecent haste and snatched the white napkin from her lap to cover her mouth. "May I be excused?" she asked softly, and her eyes were shuttered as she rose from her chair. "I must prepare for Theresa's lessons."

Matt's nod was curt, but Emmaline found her tongue. "Certainly, Miss Champion. We'll look forward to dinner."

His gaze was morose as Matt watched the young woman leave the room. "You've had a week to look her over. Is she any good?" he asked in an undertone. "I mean, do you think she'll do for Tessie?"

Emmaline's left eyebrow lifted as she considered him. "Why on earth are you asking me? Didn't you check into her credentials before you hired her? How long has she been here?"

He shrugged diffidently. "For three months, just since Tessie's birthday. My mother hired the woman, sight unseen, from a newspaper ad, when she decided that it was time for Tessie to begin schooling."

"Well, I suppose she's doing well. She seems to like Tessie, and she certainly admires you."

"Me?" Matt shook his head as he swallowed the last bite on his fork. "What do I have to do with anything? You're just trying to ignore the issue."

Blankly Emmaline looked at him. "What issue?"

His hand waved in her direction, encompassing the darkness of her attire. "That black thing you insist on wearing," he muttered with disgust.

Emmaline's chin lifted, and her eyes glittered. The man was totally blind to the attachment Tessie's teacher was forming for him, and yet managed to notice every detail of her own appearance. How dare he criticize her dress?

Matt chewed calmly, surveying the arrogant picture she presented, his own eyes lowering to his plate as he fought to hide the gleam of amusement he could not suppress.

"This black thing," she announced with genteel anger, "is made of the finest silk, imported from France and sewn by Lexington's most accomplished dressmaker." Her head nodded once when she'd completed her announcement.

His drawl became more pronounced as he inspected her carefully. "Well, it sure won't do for summertime in the Arizona Territory."

"I beg to differ with you," she said smartly. "We've had this conversation once before, if I remember correctly, and my position has not changed. I intend to remain in mourning for at least six months. Given the circumstances of our marriage, I consider that sufficient."

His chair pushed back, silent against the thick rug that covered the dining room floor, and Matt rose to his feet. He spread his palms flat on the heavy pine table and leaned to confront her, parroting her words precisely.

"Given the circumstances of our marriage, I insist you send for some more appropriate clothing from Kentucky. Either that, or I'll take you into Forbes Junction to sort through the ladies' things at the dry goods."

A flush rose from her throat to cover her cheeks, and Emmaline swallowed the angry words that formed in her mind. Just who did he think he was? This misbegotten . . .

"Well?" He leaned closer, and she fought the urge to scoot her chair back, fought the inclination to put more than a few inches between his hard-bitten features and her own.

Her fingers clenched into fists as she pounded them on the table, her elegant manners flying to the four winds. She met his arrogance in equal measure.

"Well, what?" she said between gritted teeth. "Who gave you the right to judge my wardrobe, Mr. Gerrity? Until I stand before a preacher and say all the right words, you have no right to dictate to me! About anything!"

His eyes flashed with smothered amusement as he assessed the haughty demeanor of the woman who faced him. He'd ruffled her feathers, that was for sure. He decided he might as well finish the job, as long as he was at it.

One hand lifted from the table and snaked out to cradle the curls that covered the back of her head. Fingers gripping securely, he pulled her forward, balancing himself with the other hand that pressed firmly against the table between them. Tiny flecks of amber glowed within her blue eyes as she tilted her head against the pressure of his wide palm. Not fear, he noted with satisfaction, but defiance, lit those gently slanted eyes. Her lips were firmly closed, her jaw clenched, and her nostrils flared with the force of her indrawn breath as he lowered his mouth to stake his claim.

As kisses went, it wasn't much, he thought ruefully. She had clamped down hard, her teeth held tightly together, like a bulldog with a bone. He molded her lips with his own, amused by the pursing and pushing at him, and then, with a growl, he bit at the lower lip that protruded, nipping it gently until she protested.

"Um... bffft..." The words were captive within her mouth, and he quickly followed his attack with a gentle bathing of his tongue against the fullness of the flesh he had grasped between his teeth.

Then, as quickly as he had leaned forward to take hold of her, he released her and stood erect, his damp mouth slanted into a grin that bespoke his victory.

"I have the right, Emmaline," he told her quietly. "I'm in charge here, over everything and everyone on this ranch. Most especially, my dear bride-to-be, I'm in charge of you. That gives me the right to be concerned for your welfare."

He waited for the explosion that was sure to follow, but she only watched him warily, her tongue exploring the cushion of her bottom lip.

The worrying of her mouth had not hurt, she realized, only caught her attention, which was no doubt what he'd had in mind. He'd caught her attention, all right. Twice before, he'd kissed her, first with a harshness that branded her as his prey. The second time had been an awakening, a tender, careful perusal of her lips that had beguiled and tempted her into hazy desire.

Now, in a demanding fashion, he had arrogantly taken her mouth, riding roughshod over her muffled protest. As hard as his hand had been, holding her in place, as determined as his mouth had been, tasting of her own, she could not be afraid of his dominance. Only of the strange emotions his touch had forced into being within her.

"And what if I decline your generous offer, Mr. Gerrity? What if I choose not to shop at the dry goods?" She rose from her chair and waited, her eyes speaking her defiance.

His grin became a smile of anticipation as he allowed his own gaze to slide downward over the bodice of her dress, admiring the slender curves beneath the black silk.

"Why then, Miss Carruthers, I'll have to find something appropriate of Maria's for you to wear," he said with mocking assurance.

"Maria's?" Her glance was skeptical, questioning his intelligence without words.

Arrogantly he ignored her insinuation, viewing her dark garb measuringly. "You'll need a different outfit, if you expect to go riding with me. We'll just have to make Maria's fit."

"I hardly think so," she said, denying his suggestion. "We just aren't built the same."

His grin caught her unawares, and she bit at her lip. His threat to stuff her into Maria's clothing had been mere foolishness. No two women could be more different. Once more he'd managed to rile her with his teasing.

And then he relented, his smile shamefaced now. "Peace? A truce of sorts?" He lifted his hand in a placating gesture, waiting for her nod of agreement. "I have just the thing for you to wear," he said softly.

Matt Gerrity in the role of a supplicant was not to be believed, and Emmaline privately gloated at the sight. She could afford to be generous, she decided, then smiled and shrugged eloquently.

"You're going to have a chance to make good on your claims," he told her, reaching for her hand as he reminded her of her boast. "I'll get you outfitted, and then we'll see just how well you can ride some good Arizona horse-flesh."

"Whose is it?" she asked as she smoothed the soft leather garment with the palm of her hand. Dark against the pristine white of the coverlet on her bed, the riding skirt was spread for her approval. Made of tanned leather, sewn with careful stitches, it was certainly not Maria's. Slim at the waistline and flaring into a full, separated skirt, it was obviously some woman's prized possession. Her hand brushed once more at the creamy texture of the leather as Emmaline admired the garment.

Matthew Gerrity's jaw clenched, tightening for a moment as he watched her slender fingers. "It belonged to my mother," he said finally, his voice clipped, as if he found the words difficult to speak.

Emmaline's eyes widened as she stood erect, clutching the skirt to her breast. "Oh...well, maybe I shouldn't..."

He shrugged, lifting one shoulder, as if it were but a minor detail, this protest on her part. "It's too fine a garment to go to waste," he said soberly. "I don't think she'd care if you wore it."

As if a veil had lifted, his mouth twisted into a smile when Emmaline nodded, accepting the gift he offered.

"Thank you," she said gently. "I'll be very careful with it."

His smile widened into a grin, quick and unexpected, taking her by surprise. Another side of this man, she realized, one she hadn't expected. A warmer, softer element that had caught her unprepared.

Then, as quickly as it had appeared, the grin vanished and the taciturn rancher once more stood before her. "Get ready," he said gruffly. "I'll get someone to saddle up a couple of horses."

She nodded, lifting the soft leather to brush it against the curve of her cheek, watching Matt as he turned away to leave her room. Deep within her body, a coiling heat radiated, bringing about a tingling awareness of him. Of high cheekbones and dark hair, a strong jaw with deep slashes defining his cheeks, wide shoulders and hard, heavy muscles beneath the cotton shirt he wore.

The door shut behind him quietly, and she closed her eyes, intent on recapturing the purely masculine look of him to ponder for a moment. The width of his shoulders, the strength of those wide-palmed hands that had lifted her so casually, taking her weight as if it were nothing. Her heart pounded more rapidly while she remembered the moments on the porch, when he'd held her and kissed her with harsh intent. Yet his kiss had not repulsed her or caused her to fight his embrace.

It was a puzzle, she decided, her eyes blinking open. And nothing in her sheltered past had prepared her to interpret the feelings that ran rampant within her. To give her his mother's riding skirt... She shook her head unbelievingly, inhaling the fine scent of the leather.

And this was the same man who was intent on riding roughshod over any objections she might have to offer against his manipulating her life. Biting her lip against the thought, she shook her head. "I don't begin to understand you, Matthew Gerrity," she murmured.

Even as she uttered his name, she heard the telltale sound of his boots in the corridor outside her door.

"Ten minutes, Emmaline," he called impatiently through the closed panel.

"Bossy," she grumbled as the footsteps moved on, and then she sighed as she crossed to the heavy wardrobe to find a shirtwaist that would be suitable for her ride.

The mount he placed her on was small, a compact cow pony with muscular haunches and leashed power that surged between her knees. The saddle was strange, high in back and equipped with a knob in front, cradling her in its depths. She held the reins as Matt directed, both across her palm, guiding the horse with the pressure of the narrow leather strips across his neck.

"Not exactly what you're used to, is it?" Matt's wide palms were lodged against his hips, and his eyes glittered with unconcealed glee. Watching her and assisting her in mounting the gelding had been an experience he'd thoroughly enjoyed. Holding her left foot in his palm, he'd hoisted her easily, one hand at the waistband of the skirt she wore. Regrettably, he hadn't been able to fit her as neatly with boots. The ones he'd found in his mother's room were a size too large, but he'd stuffed the toes with batting that secured her feet for safety.

"I've ridden astride before," she told him. "But we box our reins and hold them with both hands." Her palms rested on the horn of the saddle, and she scooted about in the cradle, seeking a spot where she would feel comfortable and yet in control of her mount. Her legs clung to the pony's sides, and she spent a moment sending a prayer heavenward that she'd not disgrace herself on this first day. A vision of falling headlong in front of Matt or losing control of the horse she rode caused her to tighten her grip on the reins. Her horse pranced sideways, sensing her unease.

"Let up on the reins!" Matt said sharply.

"I am!" she retorted, attempting to soothe the animal. Ears back, the gelding was skittering toward the corral fence, and Emmaline realized she was facing her first test.

With soft words and a gentle, even pressure on the reins, she turned the horse and then allowed him to move out at a quicker pace. Automatically, she rose to meet his quick trot, and behind her Matt howled his dismay.

"No... not like that! You can't post on a western pony. Just ride the trot...keep your rear end in the saddle and get used to the motion." He shook his head in scorn at her eastern ways. "You'll be laid up with liniment on your bottom at this rate," he said, catching up with her as she rode beyond the confines of the corral.

She glanced at him with as much dignity as she could muster, given the bouncing ride she was coping with. "I'd like to see you on a saddle with one of our big hunters between your legs and watch how you handle it!" she snapped.

"You'll never find me perched on one of those pancakes you call a saddle. We don't ride for pure fun, lady. Out here, our horses are just equipment that allow us to do our work."

"Well, I certainly don't call this ride pure fun." But, gradually, she caught the rhythm of the animal she rode and settled deeper into the saddle, rolling more easily with his gait. One hand slid from the leather of the saddle to smooth the mane, which flowed against the dark neck of her mount.

"Does this animal have a name?" she asked.

He shrugged at her question. "I think Claude calls him Brownie."

Her hand ceased its motion.

"Brownie?" The word dripped with derision. "You actually call a horse Brownie?"

He swept her a mocking bow from his saddle, and his eyes sparkled. "Actually, I don't call him anything. What would you call him back in Kentucky?"

"Our horses all have names they've been registered with, and we usually call them by some part of that name. Mine is Rawlings Sweet Fancy. I call her Fancy."

"Well, today you're riding a cow pony named Brownie, bred for cutting cattle," he drawled, urging his horse into a slow lope. Hers followed suit, and she settled with relief against the saddle.

Emmaline scanned the horizon, where low hills melted into each other, covered with a dark underbrush and dotted with taller scrub. Before them lay a sparse pasture where mares and foals were kept. Surrounded by a double strand of barbed wire, the mares appeared to have docilely accepted their confinement. But the foals were frolicking, kicking up their heels and racing to and fro, carefree in the hot sunshine with their mothers close by.

"We'll be working with these foals later today, if you want to watch," Matt said, his gaze ever alert to her. She'd changed, thawing before his eyes as she watched the young ones leap and play in the pasture. A faint smile hovered over her lips, and the rigid control she'd donned at the beginning of this ride had slipped, to reveal the softening of the woman within.

"I'd like that. I've helped with the young ones back home," she told him casually, and then, as her smile broke into a wide grin, she lifted her hand to point at one particularly adventuresome colt.

"Look at that little fellow," she said with a chuckle. The long-legged dove gray creature had overestimated a leap and gone spraddle-legged in the grass, shaking his head and looking about in surprise.

Their horses had slowed as they spoke, and now they walked abreast of one another. The air between them was free of the abrasiveness they had set out with.

"Thank you for the loan of the skirt," she said finally, after a few long minutes of quiet.

"No problem," he answered curtly. "My mother was generous. She'd approve."

"Tell me about her," Emmaline asked, aware that her request might well be denied. Matthew Gerrity didn't strike her as the kind to confide in anyone.

He surprised her, tipping his hat back and resting one hand on his thigh. "She was raised here in the territory—a real native, you might say. Her daddy was a brave from a tribe who took a shine to her white mother. That made her a half-breed, and not good marriage material. But she was pretty," he said, his words tender as he thought of the young girl who had been an outcast.

"Anyway, when Jack Gerrity breezed by, he snatched her up and took her along with him. She was young when I was born, just sixteen, and too innocent to see through the black-hearted Irishman who fathered me," he said with a twisted grin. "He was foreman on a good size ranch fifty miles or so west of here, and she made do as best she could. We lived in the foreman's shack there on the ranch, and my mother took home the laundry from the big house." His mouth tightened as he remembered those early days. "You sure you want to hear this?" he asked abruptly.

She nodded, almost afraid to speak, lest she break the thread of his story.

He shrugged and settled back into his saddle. "Jack Gerrity wasn't a kind man." His eyes flickered once in her direction, and the look in them was bleak. "Anyway, one day when I was about five or so, he hightailed it to town on payday, along with the rest of the ranch hands." He lifted his reins, and the horse beneath him quickened his pace.

Emmaline looked at him with impatience, jostled in the saddle as her own mount followed suit. "And then what happened?" she asked after a moment of silence.

"We never saw him alive again," he said. "He headed for town to drink and gamble away his monthly pay, and died when he slipped an ace up his sleeve."

Her brow puckered and she shook her head. "What caused him to die?" she asked innocently.

"The gun of the fella across the table who caught him cheatin' at poker," Matt replied sardonically.

Her heart thumped wildly in her throat as Emmaline envisioned the bloody scene. "Whatever did your mother do?" Her voice trembled as she thought of a young woman left alone with a child to care for.

His shrug was eloquent. "We had to move to make room for the new ranch foreman. She managed to get another job, cooking for another rancher. Took me along and raised me in the kitchen."

"How old were you then?"

His hand fisted against the solid flesh of his thigh, and his voice tightened into a deep growl. "Old enough to stay out of the way when the old man who owned the place got drunk." He went on deliberately, as if he wanted to have the words spoken and done with.

"One day, my mother loaded me and all our belongings on a wagon and headed out. Your pa found us on the road and took us home with him. When the old man caught up with us, your pa sent him on his way. Paid him for the horse and wagon and told him to clear out."

"Did they get married then?" she asked quietly, almost unwilling to interrupt, but wanting to know the rest of the story.

"No…she cooked and kept house for him until he heard that your mother had died, just ten years ago." He scanned her with eyes gone hard and cold. "He thought you'd come back home then."

"I was only twelve years old," Emmaline said, defending herself. "My grandparents were heartbroken, and I was all they had left of her. I couldn't leave them." Her chin lifted defiantly. "To tell you the truth, I didn't want to. My father had never shown any interest in me, anyway."

His look was scornful. "We both know that isn't true. I remember all the letters he sent, till he finally gave up on you."

Those letters again. Maria had told the same story, and she'd spoken with such ringing sincerity, the words had begun to raise doubts in her mind. She shrugged them away, her heart unwilling to release the anger she had clung to for so long.

"Seems to me he had a family right here," she said haughtily. "You and Arnetta filled the bill for him. He didn't need a daughter." As she spoke the words, a twinge of pain needled its way into her heart, and she recognized the envy that blossomed within her. "He didn't need me," she repeated stoically.

"You're wrong." Matt's voice was firm, adamant, as he denied her claim. "He felt bad every time one of his letters came back unopened. Then he finally stopped sendin' 'em."

She was silent, digesting the news he'd just delivered, tempted to admit her ignorance of the facts she'd just been faced with. But not for the world would she betray her grandparents, though dismay gripped her as she repeated his words to herself.

His letters came back unopened.

It was too late for mourning, she decided as her back stiffened. But unwanted tears burned against her eyelids, and she struggled to contain them. If he really wanted her, he'd have come after her, she reasoned painfully. She allowed herself one sniff, breathing deeply as she pacified herself with the thought, her eyes on the ground.

"What did you want to show me?" she asked abruptly. "Surely there must have been a reason for this jaunt."

He glanced at the set expression she wore and scowled. One day he'd make her listen, he vowed. She was due for an eye-opener where her daddy was concerned.

"Just thought you'd like to take a look at the near pasture, and then ride to the top of that highest rise ahead of us,'' he answered. ''You can see the stream over east of here, and from the high spot we can see all the way to the summer ranges, where the horses go for pasturing.''

''You send them away?'' she asked, relieved that he'd allowed her retreat.

''Yep. We round up a good share of the stock and herd them north from here into the high country to graze. Leave a couple of men there for the summer to tend them. They stay in a line shack and watch for mountain lions and keep an eye on things.''

''What about the young ones? Do you send them, too?''

He nodded. ''Except for the nursing foals and the ones we keep here to train for saddle. The rest we'll sell off as we need to.''

''To whom?''

''Whoever,'' he said. ''Some go north, some to the army. We make most of our money from the ones we break and sell to ranchers or send east.''

''Break?'' she asked.

''Well, eastern lady, what do you call it when you get a horse to let you on its back and give you a ride?'' His tone was amused as he teased her.

''I can't imagine breaking an animal,'' she said briskly. ''Back in Kentucky, we train them, starting with a foal, just days old. By the time we're ready to mount them, they're used to being handled and are ready to be ridden.''

''And I suppose you know all the tricks of the trade,'' he suggested mockingly as he watched her roll with the easy gait of her horse. Once she got past the rough trot, she managed well, he thought with silent admiration.

''I watched the trainers work, from the time I was a child,'' she said, and her mouth tilted in a smile of remembrance. ''I used to sneak out to the barns whenever I could. And when I was older, our head trainer, Doc Whitman, let me help.''

''I'll bet your mother didn't know,'' he surmised with a lifted eyebrow.

''No.'' Her smile faded as she straightened in the saddle. ''How much farther?'' she asked briskly.

''A ways yet,'' he returned, acknowledging her retreat.

The level land began rising in a gradual ascent, and her pony chose his way without her guidance, moving at a steady pace that ate the ground beneath them. She followed just a few feet to Matt's rear, aware now of the value of the high-backed saddle as she settled into the rolling gait. Her eyes scanned the land about her, yet returned like a compass pointing north to the man who rode before her, his back straight, his shoulders held proudly as he traveled the land he'd been entrusted with.

The highest of the sprawling hills was ahead, and Emmaline felt the hot rays of the midmorning sun penetrate her white shirtwaist even as the breeze kept her reasonably cool while they rode. Matt had handed her a wide-brimmed hat to wear when they began this trek, but she'd left it hanging down her back. Now she tugged it into place.

"You're 'bout guaranteed to have a sunburned nose tomorrow," he told her, casting an assessing glance over his shoulder. "That's a case of too late, you know."

"I've never been very concerned with a lily-white skin." Her nose wrinkled, and she laid fingers against it. "I suspect you're right this time. I can feel the heat there already."

"I'll warrant you were a trial to your folks, growin' up," he suggested mildly, taking in the sight of her rosy complexion.

"You'd be right. But I cleaned up really well, once I grew up," she added with wry humor.

His mouth pursed at her words, and he grunted in agreement. "Yeah, I'd say so."

The horses traveled a narrow path as they neared the crest of the hill, moving along ridges that had not been apparent from far off, but had obviously been used for trails regularly. Single file, they moved along at a quick pace, Emmaline a few yards to the rear, until they broke onto level ground. Their pace picked up and the horses settled into an easy lope.

Then, with a scattering of small pebbles and dust, Matt drew his reins and held out a hand to halt her next to him. "Look, out there," he instructed her as his other hand swept the horizon.

Before them was a valley that led into a canyon between two roughly hewn hills. A stream trickled down the center of the valley, coming from the side of the rocky heights above.

"Is that the beginning of the mountains?" she asked as she tried to trace the canyon out of sight.

"Just foothills," he said. "The mountains are farther north, where the stream begins. It dries up down here during the hot spells, but up north a ways, it flows year-round. That's where we send the horses."

"It's desolate, isn't it?" Her eyes swept the horizon, where not a moving shadow or creature caught her gaze.

"Some folks would say so."

She looked at him quickly. "But not you?"

He shook his head and swung his horse about with a quick movement of his reins across the cow pony's neck. "Time to get back. Maria will have dinner gettin' cold before we show up."

It was gone. The sense of closeness she'd felt with him had vanished.

His glance was quick as he nudged his horse into a trot. "Can you keep up?"

She bristled and urged her own horse along. "Try me," she called challengingly.

"One of these days, city lady," he drawled. "One of these days, I'll take you up on that."

Chapter Six

The rounded flank of the horse shone in the sunshine like warm mahogany, and with each stroke of the currycomb, Emmaline sent dust and loose horsehair flying. It was satisfying work, she decided, this grooming of horses. The sound of soft nickering from the mares and colts in the corral, the scent of hay and leather, and even the more earthy smells associated with the barn, brought back memories she cherished.

An affinity with the majestic animals had been her salvation through her childhood, when her mother had almost abandoned her, languishing in her dark, silent rooms. In the home where her grandparents observed all the rules of proper behavior and struggled to instill them in their reluctant grandchild.

She'd felt an outsider, there in that pillared mansion where guests were greeted beneath a welcoming portico. She'd greeted them herself, more than once, and smiled and talked obligingly with the finest citizens of the county. All in the cause of family. And since the death of her mother, she'd spent ten long years struggling to come up to the standards of the society her grandparents enjoyed.

Her hands slowed as she considered the past, reflecting on the proper behavior, the elegant posturing, the strict rules of etiquette she had adhered to, suffering in the doing. Only her hours spent in the barns had given her escape from the rigid way of life that had ruled her days.

She lifted her head and looked about her, at the wide span of the corral, the open doors of the barn and the flat pasture that was still green from the spring rainfall. Her gaze halted as she inspected the adobe house, which hugged the earth and seemed almost part of it. With thick walls and high ceilings, it held the cool night air long into the daytime hours, and offered a welcome for her that she had felt with increasing depth.

Even the people within those walls had begun to treat her as a part of the household. Emmaline smiled as she considered the sister she had come here to claim.

Theresa had spent half an hour before breakfast practicing her rope skipping, with Emmaline's willing encouragement. The session had ended with a tentative embrace on the child's part, and Emmaline had tried to be satisfied with the half hug she received before Theresa scampered off to the breakfast table.

"Out exercising so early?" Matt had come upon her unexpectedly, and she'd wondered for a moment if he'd watched as she took turns with her sister, showing her the fast-paced stepping to the rhythm of the rope as it spun about her body.

She had turned to face him, flushed and still breathless when she met his teasing glance. Irritated at being caught off guard, she'd muttered a hurried excuse and slipped away, aware of her disheveled appearance.

She spent a few moments before her mirror to prepare herself for the morning table. She'd washed her face with warm water and a cloth, and then quickly brushed her hair before she tied it up with a ribbon to match her dress.

At the table, Matt once more had become the man in charge, questioning Olivia, prodding Tessie to eat her breakfast, his earlier lapse into teasing forgotten, it seemed. But the slanting look he cast in Emmaline's direction as he left the table had been filled with a veiled warmth she hugged to herself.

Now she took it out and examined it, that glance of his. Her eyes slitted against the brilliant sunshine, she brushed contentedly at the side of the horse she tended and wondered at the softening of Matthew's hard features. His eyes had glowed with some indecipherable emotion that dwelled there, just behind his shuttered gaze.

Her arm kept up the steady movement as the horse edged closer, his own eyes closed as he welcomed her attention.

"I swan. You're spoilin' that critter, Miss Emmaline," said Claude from the barn door, where he watched. "Ol' Brownie's never had it so good in his life, since you started ridin' him."

Emmaline grinned. The lazy teasing of the man behind her, combined with the prospect of a long ride in the morning sunshine, pleased her immensely.

"I like grooming him," she answered, finishing her task with a final flurry about the neck of the gleaming animal, bending to step to the other side as she brushed. One hand rubbed at his velvet muzzle with affection.

"Well, he's never had so much attention in his young life, and he's just eatin' it up." Claude tipped his wide-brimmed hat back as he surveyed the scene before him.

He watched as Emmaline flicked the blanket onto the pony's back, then lifted the saddle to swing it into place. She hesitated and lowered it, taking a breath as she once more prepared to hoist it. It was heavier by far than the small riding saddle she had used in Kentucky. And when she rode sidesaddle with the larger horned version, her mount had always been prepared for her.

"Here, let me do that," Claude said, quickly dropping the halter he'd been holding and hustling over to where she stood. His hands reached out to grasp the heavy saddle and take it from her hands.

She relinquished it readily and brushed her palms against the leather of the riding skirt she wore. Once more the soft texture of the garment caught her attention, and she looked down at it, appreciating the gesture of the gift. The thought brought a flush of color that ridged her cheeks as she recalled the hours she had spent with Matt that day.

She would ride alone this morning, always within sight of the house and barns, she had promised at the breakfast table. Matt would be working with horses in the corral, unable to join her. She watched as Claude tightened the cinch and dropped the stirrup into place, ready for her to mount.

Leading the horse, one hand on his bridle, she walked with him until she lined him up with a mounting block Claude had placed for her use next to the barn. She could manage without it, but the gesture had pleased her, and she knew he watched as she stepped up onto it, smiling in his direction in silent thanks.

The horse edged away as she put her weight in the stirrup, and she spoke quietly to him, swinging her other leg over the saddle and gathering the reins into her left hand.

Like a demented animal, the cow pony flung his head back and snorted, then bowed his back and kicked out with his hind legs. His loud whinny rang out, and then, in a surprise movement that had her clutching at the saddle horn and dropping the reins at the same time, he leaped with all four legs off the ground, slamming once more against the hard sand, jarring her teeth together.

"Whoa...whoa there, Brownie!" Claude's hoarse voice rang out in near panic as he watched the young woman clinging for dear life to the animal she rode.

From the corral, three men came running to the scene, Matt Gerrity at the front, his booted feet eating up the ground in long strides, his eyes focused intently on the drama before him.

She was holding her own, he'd give her that. But the reins trailing and whipping through the air seemed to spur the horse on to even greater effort as he sought to dislodge the slight weight on his back. He leaped once more into the air, and this time skewed sideways as he returned to earth.

It was too much. Her body flew off at an angle and Matt was there, between bucking horse and fallen woman. Moving quickly, he scooped her from the ground, even as the two other men captured the horse. Brownie stood, spraddle-legged, blowing and wheezing while he shivered and shuddered beneath the empty saddle.

"What the hell happened?" Matt's voice boomed out in anger. He stood just out of reach of the animal, holding Emmaline's inert form against his chest.

Claude shook his head, his wizened features perplexed. "Don't know, boss. He was fine just a minute ago. Miss Emmaline was pamperin' him, and he was havin' a good time, just eatin' it up. Then I swung his saddle on and cinched it up good, and she clumb up on her block and got on. Just like yesterday and the day before.''

"Well, something happened," Matt growled, "and you'd better figure it out, old man."

Matt turned with his burden and stalked toward the house, leaving the three men staring in his wake.

"Do ya 'spose she's okay?" asked the man who held Brownie firmly.

Claude shrugged and shook his head, perplexed. "Who knows, Tucker? She shore did bang herself a good one... 'Peared to me she was out like a light.

The third man, Earl, was busy with the cinch, working at removing the saddle Claude had just moments before put in place. "Let's get ol' Brownie dried off," he said. "We'll get a good look at him."

Tucker picked up the halter from the ground. "This one Brownie's?" And without waiting for a reply, he slid it over the horse's ears and into place, removing the bridle in a reverse motion.

Claude watched silently as Earl disappeared into the barn with the saddle, and his sigh of disbelief was deep.

"I shore can't understand that'n," he muttered, his gaze following Matt's tall figure through the double doors into the house. "Nope, I shore can't figure that out at all." His gnarled hands ran over the animal who stood before him, quiet now, a far cry from the bucking cow pony of moments ago.

"She'll be fine, Mr. Matthew." The words were confident and softly spoken, and Emmaline heard them through a painful haze.

Maria, she thought, recognizing the woman's voice. And then she spoke the name.

"Maria." It was loud in her mind, but the sound that passed between her lips was but a whisper. Two heads bent low, but Matt's fingers reached to grasp her hand, and it was to him that her head turned, her eyelids fluttering open for just a moment.

"Emmaline?" He sat gingerly on the edge of the bed, still carefully holding her hand, his index finger slipping up to the inside of her wrist. His other hand lifted to brush her hair away from her face, and the fiery tendrils caught and curled about his fingers.

Drops of blood were smeared on her forehead, and already a lump had risen. A quickening of emotion thickened his throat as he recognized the vulnerability of this woman. So easily she could have been taken from him, even before he'd come to fully know her, before he'd had a chance to claim her as his own.

The thought startled him. It was a stranger to his solitary existence, this yearning to claim another human as part of himself. Not as he'd taken other women in casual encounters during the past several years. They'd been like falling leaves, held for a few moments and then released. And with the thought, he dismissed the memory of them from his mind, as if they were whisked away by the winds of chance. For chance encounters were all he'd ever known...until now. Until this mercurial creature had come into his life and wiggled her sassy little self into his plans for the future.

The fact that old man Carruthers had dictated that same future no longer seemed nearly as important to Matt Gerrity as he sat by the side of the woman he was determined to marry. What was important now was that she be guarded against any further mishap, that he keep her safe and secure.

He bent lower and whispered her name again. It was a low, breathy sound that called to her from the dim edges of awareness.

"Yes..." She spoke the single word and once more attempted to lift heavy eyelids, but the effort was too much, with the pain that sliced through her head and the bright light that shone from the window.

"Head hurts." She blinked, her free hand lifting to rub at the offending spot.

"I've sent for the doctor from town." Matt's large palm spread over her forehead and temple, his eyes inspecting the swelling and bruising beneath the dust and smeared blood that clung to her skin.

"I'm all right," she managed to say, silently trying to assess her own injuries as she shifted against the mattress. Her feet and legs seemed fine, and although she sensed she would be lame and a bit stiff and sore, the only thing that concerned her was the pain radiating from her head.

"Lie still, Emmaline." Though spoken softly, it was a command nonetheless, halting her movement as she turned her head on the pillow.

"Can't...it hurts," she murmured, closing her eyes once more, shielding them from the bright sunshine flooding her room.

Immediately his hand released hers, unclasping it from the firm hold he had taken. Her limp fingers twitched once, as if they searched for his touch, and then stilled against the coverlet. His palm enclosed the base of her skull for a moment, and his long fingers carefully and tenderly worked their way through her curls, searching out the contours of her head.

She grunted when he touched a swollen area just above her ear. "Ummm...right there."

"Yeah, that's quite a knot you've got there, honey." Bending closer, he brushed the hair aside. "The skin's scraped up a little, but that lump's not bleeding."

"I'm fine... Need to rest." Her words were slurred, barely audible to the two watching her.

Maria shook her head, her worry evident as she bent low over the bed. "We need to wash her up and put on her nightgown, so the doctor can look her over."

"No..." Emmaline whispered, her forehead wrinkled against the ache and stinging pain. "Lemme rest...call me for dinner."

"Fat chance," Matt grumbled beneath his breath. He bent lower, until his lips were at her ear, and he blew in it gently. "I don't want any arguments. Let Maria help you, like a good girl, or else I'll have to stick around and do it myself."

Emmaline glared at him for a moment through slitted eyes, then, with a sigh of resignation, relaxed against his big body. For just a few minutes, it was easier to let him take charge, she decided. For now, she'd surrender gracefully.

"Just need a nap," she breathed in a final sally, aware for a fleeting moment that his chuckle followed her into the dreamless sleep that claimed her.

Maria stood by the bed, hands clasped at her waist. "What happened, Mr. Matt?"

He shook his head. "I'm not sure. Brownie threw her. Bucked like a new bronc out there for a minute. Doesn't make sense to me." He eased to his feet and stood watching the even breathing of the woman on the bed.

"You can bet your boots I'm sure going to find out what happened. You'd better believe that, Maria."

The sharp piece of iron had been wedged into the leather of the saddle, underneath, where it would not be seen, and toward the center, where no one would touch it during the normal movements it would take to lift it onto a horse's back.

"Who found it?" Matt's voice was harsh as he tugged at the almost hidden object. "It's a good thing she's not heavy," he said as he managed to loosen it and pull it from its place. "A man's weight would have jammed this thing in good."

Claude nodded in agreement. "As it was, ol' Brownie just got a good scratch out of it. 'Nough to set him off, though."

"I found it, boss." Tucker stood in the doorway of the tack room. "I was wipin' down ol' Brownie and saw blood on the rag. Took a look at the underside of his saddle and thought you'd better take a look."

"Anybody been around?" Matt asked as he thumbed the sharp object he held.

"Dunno," Claude answered. "Not that I saw. But then, I been out with the colts this mornin'."

"Can't imagine who'd do such a thing," Tucker said mildly. "Could have really..." His voice trailed off as Matt shot him a glance.

"Well...someone did it. And when I find him..." Matt's jaw tightened, and his eyes darkened with anger.

* * *

"She is a very stubborn lady."

"You don't mean Emmaline, by chance, do you, Maria?" Matt's worry lines were soothed by the doctor's pronouncement that Emmaline would be fine, and was in a mood to be agreeable.

But the woman standing just outside the closed bedroom door, holding a supper tray, did not appear nearly so pleased with the state of affairs.

"Mr. Matt, she says she will get up for supper tonight. And when I told her the doctor wants her to stay in bed for the rest of the day, she just said, 'Pooh on him!' And that's no way to talk about our doctor." Her indignation was simmering, but Maria had backed off from the battle, aware that Matthew Gerrity was much more capable of waging this war of words.

His grin bespoke confidence, and Maria gladly surrendered the tray to her employer. She hurried down the passage toward the front of the house, her head bobbing in time to the words she muttered.

"More like her papa every day. Just as redheaded and just as bullheaded."

Balancing the tray on one hand, Matt turned the door knob and eased his way into Emmaline's room. One knuckle rapped on the opening door as he called out a greeting.

"Emmaline, I found Maria in the hallway with this tray of food. How about sharing it with me?"

"You could have knocked before you opened the door," she stated haughtily from her perch on the side of the bed. Slender white feet hung below the bedding, several inches from the floor, and the cotton gown she wore covered the rest of her admirably. Only her hands and face were left to his view. One hand had scabs already forming across the knuckles, the other wore a bruise that covered its palm and ran up beneath the ruffle that cuffed her sleeve. She was pale, and her mouth was pinched against the headache still plaguing her, but her face was unmarred. Her hair, haloing her head, was the sole spot of brightness against the white bedding and gown she wore.

"Do I look that bad?" she asked. "You're frowning." Her mouth formed a pout as she glowered at him from eyes that wore faint violet shadows beneath their lower lids.

"Yep, you sure do look like the very dickens, lady. And you sure as hell don't look to me like you ought to be threatenin' to climb out of there and trot right down to the dining room for supper." He examined her for a moment. "In fact, I'd say your best bet is to lay back down on that bed and behave yourself."

"Well, I would have been dressed and ready for supper in just a few minutes," she said defensively, only too aware of the pillow behind her that beckoned her to return to its comfort.

"Not a chance, honey." His smile was cheerful, but his stance belied his good humor.

She opened her mouth and closed it. Suddenly the thought of moving from the bed had lost its appeal, even though her pride was making demands.

"I've never been thrown from a horse before," she admitted, brushing at the scratches on her fingers, unwilling to meet Matt's eyes while she made her confession.

He relaxed. She was giving in, almost without a murmur. Lowering the tray to the table next to the bed, he paused for a moment to absorb her words. A smile twisted the corner of his mouth as he turned to her, one long finger lifting her chin, the better to see her face.

"Wish I had a nickel for every time I've eaten dust in the corral," he admitted.

Her eyes swept open and widened as she gauged his words. "Really? You've been bucked off?"

Matt's chuckle was rich with humor. "Honey, when you break horses for a living, you might as well figure on hitting the ground once in a while."

"I didn't mean to cause all this fuss." One hand waved at the supper tray, even as the other tugged the sheet up higher to cover the front of her nightgown. "I'm sure the doctor told you I'm just fine."

"Not quite. The doctor said you probably have a mild concussion and need to stay in bed for a full day. If your head still hurts by the day after tomorrow, he wants to know about it.''

"He said that?" Her eyes blinked against the prickly tears forming, and she pulled away from the finger he'd propped beneath her chin. She'd turned down the tray Maria offered because she didn't want to be a burden to anyone, but Matt certainly didn't act as if she was a problem at all, if the concerned look he wore was any indication.

"Emmaline?" He squatted at the side of the bed, his face on a level with her own. "You're not crying, are you? Do you hurt anywhere? Does your head pain you?" He eased her feet back up beneath the covers, his big hands warm against her ankles. And then he rose to lower her to the pillow, relieved when she offered no protest.

"No, I'm not crying. I never cry," she said stiffly, blinking furiously at the evidence of her lie.

He settled at her side, within easy reach of the tray of food, and considered the problem. Then, with careful hands, he lifted her in his arms, her face buried against his chest and propped two more pillows behind her head, until she was elevated to his satisfaction.

She inhaled once more, catching a last whiff of his shirt, which held the faintly musky, male scent of him. "Do you know that men smell different than women?" she whispered whimsically, relaxing against the pillows.

His hands, ready to lift the tray, stilled suddenly as he glanced at her, his eyebrows raised in surprise. "Well, I reckon I knew that, honey. But I wasn't sure that you did."

Suddenly weary, she nodded solemnly. "I do now. Your shirt smells sort of like leather and horses and lye soap, but I could smell your skin, too."

"Well..." He lifted the tray and held it on his lap, the grin he'd worn earlier returning to twitch his lip. The thought of that straight little nose sniffing at his chest brought to life another problem, and he gritted his teeth against the fullness he felt in his groin.

"I like having you take care of me, Matthew." Emmaline blinked again, and then her eyes closed for a moment.

"I can't believe I'm saying such things to you. My head feels all muzzy inside again."

"Probably the medicine Doc gave you," he murmured. His hands were busy with the food, uncovering the soup Maria had prepared, unwrapping the napkin that held the thin slices of bread she had buttered and cut into narrow wedges. "You can chatter all you want, sweetheart," he told her with a wry grin. "But I suspect you won't be happy with yourself tomorrow, if you talk too sweet to me tonight."

"I'm not talking sweet. I gave Maria a hard time, didn't I?" she asked wearily. "Tell her I'm sorry."

He grinned agreeably. "Yeah, you were a real pain in the patoot, honey. Now open wide." Bringing the soup spoon toward her lips, he waited for her to obey, one hand holding a napkin beneath it.

She obeyed and savored the chicken broth for a moment before she swallowed it, murmuring her approval.

"Here, let me fix this." With one hand, Matt spread the napkin across her chest, easing one edge beneath her chin and lightly smoothing the cloth into place. Beneath his palm he felt the rise of her breasts and her sudden intake of breath.

"Shhh . . . it's all right," he said quickly when she cast a startled look at him. "Just making sure your gown doesn't get splattered with soup."

"I think you're taking advantage of me." Choosing her words carefully, she peered at him from beneath heavy eyelids. "I'm not sure you should even be in my bedroom, you know."

"Here." He quieted her with another spoonful of broth. "We're going to be married, Emmaline. I'll be sleeping in your bedroom before long."

She swallowed quickly. "My grandparents each have their own room. I think that would be a good idea for us, too. I'm not used to sharing a room with anyone, and I'm certain you would sleep better without me taking up half your bed."

He held the spoon before her lips. "Quit arguing with me, Emmaline. We'll settle it another day. Right now, I just want you to eat your supper. How about a little of Maria's fresh bread now?''

She nodded slowly and accepted the narrow slice he gave her, biting and chewing with precision. ''Hmmm...don't you think it's about time for me to win an argument?'' she asked, waving her hand at him imperiously as she savored the fresh bread.

He shook his head. ''Not this one, honey.'' Reaching out, he claimed her hand and examined it for a moment. The scratches and bruises would heal quickly, he thought, but the memory might take longer. She was feeling the effects of the medicine Doc had given her this morning and Maria had dosed her with later in the afternoon. Tomorrow might be a different matter, when the recollection of her fall was not clouded by medication.

Lifting her other hand in his, he pressed his lips to the scraped flesh and touched the tip of his tongue to the injured skin. Then with gentle care, he placed it in her lap, only to pick up the other hand and give it equal treatment. The bruise would remain for a while, he decided. Already it had turned dark, and he pulled up the ruffle at her wrist to view the extent of it. Once more he lifted her hand to his mouth and kissed it with soft, silent brushes of his lips.

''Matt?'' She lay back, her hair tangled and curled against the pillow.

''Hmm?'' He tucked the second hand beneath the sheet and bent to press a kiss against the pale skin of her forehead, where the bruises cast a purple shadow.

''I remember when I was very small, my father used to kiss my bumps and scrapes for me. He said a kiss would make anything better.'' Her voice was wispy and unsure, as if the memory was faded and blurred in her mind. ''I shouldn't be able to remember that, should I? I was so young when my mother took me away.''

''We always remember the important things, Emmaline,'' he said soothingly, his breath stirring the curls at her temple.

''I'm glad you kissed me.''

''Which time?'' His lips moved against her forehead.

She was quiet, and he lifted from her to look into her face. Eyes half-closed against the lamplight, she peered at him, her skin pale and translucent. "Tonight," she decided. "And the other time, when you acted like you really liked me."

"Oh, I really like you, honey," he assured her, with the same cocky grin she had elicited from him earlier.

"Will you kiss me a lot after we get married?" Smothering a yawn, she watched him closely.

He could no longer contain the laugh. It bubbled up within him, a relief from the tension of the long day and the worry of her injury. "I'll be doing a lot of kissing, Emmaline. And so will you."

Her eyes were closed. "I don't know how," she whispered.

"I'll teach you," he promised.

"You look mighty fetching in the moonlight."

"I haven't given you leave to speak to me with such familiarity."

His laugh was low and raspy, and the jingle of his spurs told her he had moved closer. "You owe me more than the right to make a pretty remark, lady," he growled.

She stepped back, measuring her length against the back wall of the barn. "I don't owe you anything...yet," she said in a voice that fought to be calm.

"You didn't say you wanted her dead," he reminded her with chill emphasis. "You just wanted her scared enough to go back east."

Her words were whispered, but no less cold than his own. "If it comes to that, can you do what has to be done?"

He laughed again—it was a sound of anticipation. "I reckon I can do anything I have to, if the reward is rich enough."

Her smile sparkled in a ray of moonlight that broke through a cloud. She stepped closer to his still figure.

"I told you how much it's worth to me to have her out of the way. Didn't you think it was enough?"

His eyes swept her form, and his smile took on a feral quality. "Not unless the rest of my payment comes up to snuff," he whispered roughly.

Her eyes flashed a promise. "I think you'll be pleased by what I can give you," she purred.

His hand reached for her, and she sidled out of his grasp. "Not yet," she whispered softly. "Be patient."

Chapter Seven

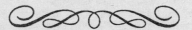

"Samuel's will is cut-and-dried," Oswald Hooper stated emphatically. "I made sure of that when I wrote it for him."

"Didn't mean to get you in an uproar," Matt said from across the desk in the lawyer's office. "I just wanted to be sure her grandparents couldn't give me any trouble."

Oswald's eyes raised in a silent question. He cleared his throat and waited, dignity denying him the privilege of asking it aloud.

Matt did not disappoint him. His big shoulders lifted in a shrug, and he smiled with wolfish pleasure.

"I wired for her things from Lexington first thing this morning." His teeth gleamed as his smile widened, and he leaned forward in his chair. "I told them we were getting married," he confided. Glancing at the clock on the wall of the small office, he rubbed the fingers of his right hand against the hard muscle of his thigh. "Should be getting an answer back pretty soon."

Matt stood and reached for his hat from the peg by the door. "Guess I'll take a walk over to see Harley Summers at the train station and see if they've had enough time to wire me back."

"When is the wedding?" Oswald asked, rising from his chair.

"I'm going to see the preacher after I talk to Harley. Might be as soon as tomorrow, if I can find a dress at the dry goods for her to wear," Matt said. "And I'm plannin' on lookin' real hard."

* * *

Matt's mouth drew down with irritation when he heard the news from Harley Summers. No answer from Lexington. Probably shocked them right out of their socks, he thought as he headed for the small parsonage next to the white church.

He'd tied his buggy to the hitching rail in front of Abraham Guismann's Mercantile Establishment, and he wished for a moment that he'd ridden into town. Only the fact that he wasn't sure how much he'd be buying at Abraham's place had prompted him to use the single-seated buggy this morning.

All this walking is good for only one thing, he thought, stomping his way down the wooden walkway that fronted the line of buildings. Managing to get rid of his aggravation halfway to the parsonage, he had to chuckle at his own impatience. He hadn't been this eager for time to pass since he'd been a kid waiting for Christmas, back in his early days, before things got bad.

The visit at the parsonage was successful, and Matt's mood improved as he headed for his next stop. Reverend Tanner would be happy to officiate at his wedding at a moment's notice. Josiah Tanner had not been surprised by his visit, and Matt had grunted his thanks, fully aware that the whole town was privy to his plans.

Thanks to Deborah, everyone in the county knew he was getting a bride along with the Carruthers ranch. Emmaline had pegged her right.

Ruth Guismann greeted him as he made his way across the wide-planked floor of her husband's store.

"Good morning, Mr. Gerrity," she said, with the formality he had come to expect from her.

He nodded and tilted his hat back as he approached. "Good morning, ma'am." Feeling the eyes of several of the womenfolk of the town upon him, he was suddenly reluctant to complete his mission. Might as well bluff it out, he decided after a moment.

Sliding his hands into his pockets, he looked at the bolts of fabric that stood at attention on a shelf behind the polished walnut counter. Next to them, a wall of drawers climbed to the ceiling, each containing bits and pieces of women's fripperies and men's underwear and stockings. To his right a series of shelves held folded garments, and it was to these that he directed his attention.

"I need to see a ready-made dress." His tone was low, designed to carry just across the counter and no farther.

"What size would you need?" Mrs. Guismann asked, her eyes gleaming with mischief at his discomfort.

"She's not very big." His big hands formed a circle and his head tilted as he estimated the size of Emmaline's waist. "Well, a lot smaller than Maria," he added helpfully.

Ruth Guismann's mouth tightened to hide the smile that threatened and she turned her back on him to sort through a stack of dark-colored clothing.

Matt cleared his throat again. "Ma'am?"

She turned, a navy blue shirtwaist dress in her hands. "Yes, Mr. Gerrity?"

He pointed briefly at a section farther along where bright colors vied for attention. "I don't want anything quite that somber." He nodded toward the dress she held.

"Is it for a special occasion?" she asked brightly.

He looked about him, and the women whose eyes had been focused on him immediately turned away, their whispers silenced as they enjoyed his quandary.

Enough was enough, he decided. He refused to be the center of this gaggle of women's amusement. Standing erect, he pulled his money from the front pocket of his denim pants and flourished the small roll of bills.

"I need a wedding dress for my bride," he announced loudly, a dark frown in place. "I want something bright, maybe green or blue, with some ruffles or bows or something to dress it up. It needs to be about this big around the middle." Once more his fingertips touched, his thumbs spread wide, to show her the size of Emmaline's waist, as best he could remember.

The navy blue dress was folded quickly, and Mrs. Guismann stepped briskly along the shelving to sort efficiently through several items. Her search bore fruit, and she turned about with a flowered garment that, even folded, gave evidence of ruffles that peeked from its depths. Unfurling it, she held it before her for his inspection and waited for his approval.

Matt's eyes narrowed as he imagined the shapely form of Emmaline Carruthers within the hourglass lines of the blue flowered dress. It surely had enough ruffles to please any woman, he thought judiciously. They lay in layers from midway down the skirt to the hem, and the dress even boasted one about the neckline, in place of a collar.

"This has elastic at the waistline," Mrs. Guismann pointed out as she stretched it across her ample front. "It will fit nicely, if you have gauged her right." She laid the sleeve on the counter before him and fingered the mother-of-pearl buttons that fastened the wide cuff. "These are the latest fashion in New York," she said with pride.

"Kinda hot with those long sleeves, isn't it?"

"A lady never exposes her arms in public," she answered primly, tugging at her own sleeve, which came exactly to the bone at her wrist.

He nodded, deferring to her better judgment, and took the dress from her hands. He held it before him. The length was about right, he decided as he brushed the hem close to the floor, estimating the level of her head against his chest.

"This will do fine," he said gruffly, aware of the audience of women who had stopped their own shopping and were openly watching him. "Do I need anything else to go with it?"

Mrs. Guismann was coming into her own, and she beamed benignly at him. "Why don't I just see what I can find?" Not awaiting his permission, she turned to a wall of drawers he feared would contain enough female froufrou to relieve him of all the money he'd brought along this morning.

"Yeah, whatever you say." He rested his weight on one foot, then the other, eager to be on his way—at any cost.

The pile before him grew, and he watched in stoic silence, finally turning away when he caught sight of a fragile fabric that looked suspiciously like silk. Or at least what he imagined silk to resemble. Resigned to it now, he shrugged and grinned at the nearest woman, Hilda

Schmidt, who approached at this first sign of encouragement.

"We heard there was going to be a wedding," she said cheerfully. "I told Mr. Schmidt just yesterday the sewing circle was going to make a quilt for your bride."

Matt's eyes darkened. "How long have you known?"

"Oh, several days now. Ever since Sunday church service."

The day after Deborah's visit to the ranch, he recalled grimly. She hadn't wasted any time. He'd have to be sure to congratulate Emmaline—she'd pegged Deborah as a blabbermouth right off the bat.

"We're not havin' a real wedding," he said firmly. "Just a private ceremony at the parsonage."

"That's all right," she allowed, though her mouth curved down in obvious disappointment. "We'll come calling after the honeymoon." Her head nodded firmly, speaking for the listening ladies who had drawn closer to the morning's entertainment.

They nodded in return, almost in unison, and Matt suppressed a groan. Like hens in a chickenyard, they gathered about him, and he turned to the counter once more.

"Have you got it all gathered up, Mrs. Guismann?" he asked, a note of desperation apparent in his voice. He was determined that, no matter what her answer, he would be on his way.

She tipped her head to one side and bit at her lower lip, her eyes scanning the pile of merchandise. With a nod she indicated that her work was finished, and then reached for the roll of paper that stood upright just to her left. Estimating the length needed, she pulled the cut edge toward her and reached for the pair of scissors that hung from a ribbon at her waist. She cut the paper, laid it on the counter and, with swift calculations, jotted down the prices of the items she had chosen for him.

His eyebrows lifted a bit as he glanced at the total, but without hesitation he peeled off the bills required and handed them to her. Slipping the money into her pocket with a polite murmur of thanks, she lifted the pile of clothing to smooth the length of paper beneath it. With deft movements, Mrs. Guismann wrapped his purchases and, reaching above her head, pulled several yards of string from a holder suspended from the ceiling. Securing the bundle quickly, she tied it with a double knot and clipped the ends with her scissors.

"There you go, Mr. Gerrity." Her smile gave away her satisfaction as her fingers slid into the pocket that held the money he had given her. "I'm sure your bride will be lovely," she added, turning to make her way to the big cash register, which gleamed darkly on the shelf at the back of the store.

As he opened the door to leave, Matt turned back for a moment and tipped his hat once more to the other women, who had murmured their own farewells in his wake. The cheerful ringing of a bell signified the deposit of his money into the register, and it blended with the closing of the door as he made his escape.

It was late afternoon when the buggy stopped before the barn. Earl stepped from the darkness beyond the wide doorway and reached up to hold the head of the chestnut mare, who had every intention of hauling the buggy into her stall.

"Whoa, girl," he muttered in a husky voice. "Your supper's a-waitin'. Let's just get you out of this harness first." He watched Matt climb down over the high wheel of the vehicle.

"Need any help, boss?" he asked, wondering at the parcel that filled the right side of the seat.

"Nope, I can get this." Matt grasped the large package firmly, carrying it by the string that was wrapped about it several times. After all the discomfort he'd gone through to buy the blasted things, he planned on carrying them in the house and right to Emmaline's bedroom himself.

"The rest of that stuff has to go in the tack room," he told Earl, indicating his purchases from the blacksmith's shop.

He made his way to the house, the reply from Lexington resting in his shirt pocket. Fighting to suppress a smile of triumph, he thought of its contents. Harley Summers had scratched out the words on lined paper and handed it to him over the counter at the train station.

They hadn't even argued, they'd just agreed to send her belongings. In a week or so, she'd have the contents of her wardrobe all lined up in his bedroom.

He'd move them both into the big room at the far corner of the house, he decided as he climbed the two steps to the porch at the back of the house and entered the kitchen door. Maybe he'd have Maria do it while he took Emmaline into town for the wedding. The vision of her black kid boots and slippers lined up at the foot of the bed next to his own boots tickled his sense of humor, and his mouth widened in a smile of pure pleasure.

The screen door banged behind him and he made his way across the empty kitchen to the dining room doorway.

Emmaline sat in her usual place, with Olivia across from her and Theresa on her left. Maria was just about to place a platter of meat and vegetables before his own seat at the head of the long mahogany table when she turned to look over her shoulder at him as he entered.

"We waited for you until the meat was getting cold," Maria said with a shrug. "Come and sit down."

His eyes sought those of Emmaline, but she was busily placing her napkin across her lap, and he grew impatient at her dithering.

"Emmaline," he said quietly, standing just inches from her chair.

She looked up reluctantly, and her eyes were defiant. "Yes?" The single word was sharp and crisp.

His mouth thinned with the force of his irritation. The package fell from his hand, and the soft thud as it hit the carpet by her chair brought not a sliver of response from her.

From the other side of the chair came the hopeful voice of his sister. "Did you bring me something, Maffew?" she asked as she looked up at him over Emmaline's head.

"Matthew." The correction came in Olivia's firm voice. She ignored Tessie's glare. "We've discussed this, Theresa. You are old enough to speak your brother's name properly."

Matt looked exasperated. "Do we need lessons at the supper table, Olivia?"

Her look was startled. "I'm only trying to—"

"Not now." His voice boomed in the silence and Olivia cast her gaze into her lap, where her fingers knotted tightly.

"Maff... Matthew..." Tessie mumbled the name, unwilling to give up her chosen version of his title.

"Yes, Tessie." Matt bit off the words, barely moving his lips.

She repeated her question bravely. "Did you bring me something?"

He shook his head firmly. "Not this time, Tessie."

"That whole parcel is for Emmaline?" she asked with wonder, leaning almost into her sister's lap to view the paper-wrapped package.

"Every bit of it," he said, stepping back to take his seat at the head of the table. The confounded woman was in a snit over something, and he'd probably not find out the reason until after they ate.

He was right, he discovered as the meal progressed. Emmaline spoke with Miss Olivia about Theresa's schooling, suggesting the use of a book she'd brought from Kentucky with her and agreeing to show it to them both at breakfast. She was gracious to Maria, complimenting her on the meal and the bread pudding that was served for dessert. She told Theresa a story about a dog she'd had as a child and agreed to show her a picture she had in her carpetbag that included that very animal.

But for the man who sat at her right, she had only silence and guarded glances. By the time he'd finished eating, Matt was on the verge of dragging her from the room and shaking some of that arrogance from her.

He settled for gripping her by the right wrist as she rose to leave the table when everyone finished their meal. With a nod, he excused Miss Olivia and Tessie, and then, picking up his parcel with his other hand, he led his reluctant bride to the big bedroom at the end of the hallway in the north wing of the house.

He opened the door and ushered her into the room. With a well-placed heel, he closed the heavy door behind them.

Emmaline glared at him scathingly. "It is not considered proper to be alone in a bedroom with a woman who is not your wife," she announced primly.

"I was alone in your bedroom with you just a few days ago, when you got bucked off that horse you're so crazy about," he growled as he bent over her. His face was just inches from her own, and he saw the apprehension that darkened her eyes just before she lowered her lids and looked down at the floor.

"That was different. I was not myself."

"No, you sure weren't. You were almost nice to me." He turned away and then spun back to her, hands on his hips and eyes blazing with more anger than he'd felt in a month of Sundays.

"Just what has your bustle in an uproar?" he shouted.

Her head lifted quickly and her eyes were wide with astonishment. "What a horrendous thing to say to me!" she snapped, her hands pushing at his chest as she sought to make room between their bodies.

It was somewhat like pushing at the side of a mountain, she decided. He didn't budge, and wasn't about to, if she was any judge of it. She might as well speak her piece and have done with it.

"Maria told me you went into town to make plans for our wedding."

He straightened and looked down at her with astonishment. "Is that why you're mad?"

Her mouth opened and closed and then opened again. "Yes, that's why I'm mad." She spouted the words with a volume that almost matched his own.

"I did it for you!" His answer was a muted roar. He ran his hands through his hair to keep them from gripping her shoulders, and mumbled beneath his breath.

"Well, thank you very much!" she snapped. "I might have wanted to have some say in my wedding plans, don't you think?"

"Why?" He was astounded. "What is there to plan? We're gonna go to town and see the preacher and he's gonna marry us. I wanted to get the details out of the way. I was tryin' to do you a favor." He was blustering now, aware finally that he had stepped on her toes in the worst way possible.

Her look was unbelieving. "Marrying me is just a detail in your life?"

He sighed and closed his eyes. "Awww...come on, Emmaline. Don't be mad. I didn't mean that the way it sounded. I guess I just didn't think about you wantin' to go along."

"You were afraid I'd want a real wedding, weren't you?"

He was silent.

The color left her cheeks as she endured the few moments of silence, and her voice quavered as she asked the question that had been born in her mind during that time. "Are you ashamed of me?"

"Hell, no!" The words burst from his lips, and Emmaline had no doubt as to the truth of his vehement reply. She was quietly relieved, but not entirely so. She pressed her lips together and stepped back from the towering man who stood before her. His hands were clenched into fists against his hips, and he leaned forward a little, his jaw jutting angrily, his eyes narrowed and flashing darkly.

"Please do not curse in my presence," she said with precise enunciation.

"You sure manage to pull my cork, Miss Priss," he growled. "And if you think that was cursing, you oughta hear me when I really get fired up."

She flared her nostrils delicately and retreated another half step. Matt Gerrity in a royal snit was a sight to behold, she decided. Even his scent was threatening—masculine and musky, overriding the dusty outdoor aroma he wore like a second skin.

"Don't do that again!" he roared. "You sniff at me like I'm fresh from the barn and stick that little nose of yours up in the air like I'm not good enough for you!"

She shook her head, her eyes widening at his words. "That's not true," she cried, aghast at his accusation. "I've never thought that. I'm not a snob, Gerrity! Not like you, certainly!"

"And just what does that mean?" he asked, his voice toned down to an acceptable growl.

"Just because I'm from back east, you seem to think I'm not fit to be a ranch wife. You're planning to marry me in a hurry-up wedding, so your friends won't have a chance to make fun of your bride."

"Ah...hell!" With fierce intent, he reached for her. His hands were like iron bands that clamped her shoulders, dragging her forward the few inches it took to bring her against his chest. His grip loosened as his hands slid around her back, meeting at her waist and tugging her closer, until her slender body was plastered with indecent familiarity against his hard length.

She felt the heat of him through her clothing, felt the bone-melting, pulsating fever of his frustration burning between them. Her breasts were flattened, straining with a strange urgency against the ungiving breadth of his chest. Her belly was snug against his groin, soft cushioning for the hard evidence of his arousal, and she held her breath as she recognized what it portended.

His head was tilted, and his eyes blazed with frustrated anger. Yet the lips that touched hers were almost gentle in their taking, brushing against her softness, asking her compliance. She felt his intake of breath as he lifted from her, and heard the harsh, guttural words he spoke before he lowered to her once more.

"You drive me crazy, woman," he muttered against her tender flesh, his mouth once more taking possession of her lips. Not so gently this time, he kissed her, branding her with the touch of his tongue at the corner of her mouth, edging it carefully along the crease of her resilient flesh until he found the opening he sought.

She took a shuddering breath, and his tongue slid to capture the ground she had unknowingly surrendered. Searing a path across the soft inner flesh of her lower lip, he measured the width of her mouth in a heated fashion that coaxed a small moan of surrender from her throat.

His grunt of satisfaction was galling, she decided with mute frustration. So easily he had forced her into his embrace. So readily he had subdued her body and brought about her acquiescence. Even the invasion of her mouth, the indignity of his tongue between her lips, had only served to meld her closer with his male form.

And she couldn't even complain with dignity, she realized. It was hard to be ladylike when her whole body was in such close proximity to a man, when all her mind could concentrate on was the searing pleasure of his mouth.

His hands were gentle and his aggravation was spent as he set her away from him. His smile, however, hovered on the edge of victorious as he swept his gaze over the length of her trembling figure.

"Now, Miss Emmaline, do you have any doubts about my wanting to marry you? Do you really think you're being judged on whether or not you'll make a good ranch wife, whatever that's supposed to be?"

She shook her head, not sure he expected a reply to his sardonic query. Her hands lifted to her face, her fingers flat against the warmth that had invaded her cheeks, cooling the heated flesh and then moving to pat into place the tendrils of hair framing her face.

His hands covered hers and squeezed them carefully, forming them into small fists, which he enclosed within his own.

"Leave those pretty curls alone," he ordered her softly, his eyes moving with tender regard over the rebellious locks that would not remain subdued by pins and combs.

She met his eyes, intent on knowing the truth of his purpose. "If you want to marry me, you'll wait until we can plan a decent wedding," she announced stiffly, her chin jutting forward in defiance.

"If I want to marry you?" he ask unbelievingly. "I thought I'd made that clear."

"Well, either I go into town and talk to the parson and make some arrangements, or—" She stopped, unsure what threat would hold water with this man, who stood and gazed at her with such apparent irritation.

"I'll go with you."

"We'll see." Her eyes lowered in a gesture of feminine capitulation…quickly, so that he could not take note of the determination those long lashes hid from his view.

Chapter Eight

The sky was turning pink outside her bedroom window, and Emmaline watched as the dawn chased the night from the sky. She'd felt beleaguered and bedazzled by turns through the long hours of darkness. Matthew Gerrity was a scamp, she'd decided. He held the reins and was tugging them with a vengeance, beguiling her with the power of his kisses and planning her future without a thought for her own wants and wishes.

Truth to tell, she'd about decided to postpone things until her head was back in control, instead of that treacherous heart of hers. Maybe she'd be better off—no, for sure she'd be better off—if all she had to think about was Tessie and her welfare. At least for now. The wedding could surely be put off for a while...or could it? Maybe there was a way out of the conundrum. Maybe the lawyer could find a loophole, even though he'd said she had no real choice in the matter.

It might be worth a try, anyway.

Sneaking out of the house had been the easy part. Saddling Brownie, riding from the barn toward town and convincing Tucker of the validity of her trip had taxed her ingenuity to its fullest.

Pangs of hunger were a silent companion as she rode, thinking of the breakfast Maria would serve. Then she thought of the man who would undoubtedly be fast on her trail, once her absence was noted. Her heels dug into the sides of the brown horse as she considered the consequences of Matt's anger this time.

But she had to try. It was worth a try, and Oswald Hooper would know the answer...if there was one to be had.

The bullet had whizzed in front of Emmaline almost before she heard the sound of the gun firing. She flinched at the whine of its passing and heard the impact as it hit one of the small stand of scrubby trees she was riding past.

"Dratted hunter," she snapped, glancing off to her right, hoping to catch a glimpse of the careless gunman.

The horse beneath her snorted and pulled at the bit in his mouth, dancing sideways as he responded to her hands on the reins. She relaxed her hold and reached to pat him, speaking soothingly as she looked behind her once more.

A flash of color caught her eye, and she squinted against the morning sun. Just past her field of vision, the figure of a horseman disappeared into a gully, and the blurred image struck her mind with force.

"Next time I see a man wearing a red shirt, I'll be ready to tear into him," she muttered, urging her mount into a lope. "The fool could have hit me instead of that tree." She craned her neck to scan the horizon, her hand shading her eyes.

"I sure don't see any game. Wonder what he was shooting at?" she puzzled. And then she shrugged as she settled into the saddle and rode quickly toward town.

Her chair was empty. Matt's frown deepened as he considered the cushioned seat and delicately wrought wooden frame of the piece of furniture that should have been covered by the person of Emmaline.

"Where is she?" he asked abruptly as Maria placed his plate before him. Steam rose from the generous pile of scrambled eggs she'd prepared for him, and the steak that flanked them was still sizzling from the griddle.

Yet it was not enough to take his mind from the absence of the woman he'd expected to see next to him this morning.

Maria stepped back and wiped her hands against the white apron that covered her dress. "I'm sure she'll be here in a few moments, Mr. Matt."

"Have you seen her this morning?" he asked as he ground the pepper mill across the expanse of his plate.

She shook her head. "Not since I took a cup of coffee to her room an hour ago."

"You have enough to do without carrying coffee to us in the mornings, Maria." He grumbled the words, knowing they would fall on deaf ears. They'd had this discussion several times over the years.

She shrugged and allowed a benevolent smile to spread over her face. "Don't growl, Mr. Matt. You know you enjoy your coffee before you shave."

He gave in, allowing her to win this small battle once more. Maria was set in her ways, determined to care for her family as she pleased.

The eggs and beefsteak were hearty fare, and Matt tucked into them with zest. The day promised to be a long one, spent herding the cattle from the far western range back toward the barns to be culled and branded. He'd carried on with the Carrutherses' tradition of growing their own beef and selling off the excess each year, holding the size of the herd to a manageable level. Cattle were a small part of the picture. Horses were the mainstay of the ranch.

Olivia and Theresa had joined him at the table and eaten their own meals before he sensed an uneasiness tugging at him.

"She should have been in here by now," he muttered abruptly, shoving his chair from the table and rising.

"Emmie's not comin' to breakfast, Maff—Matthew," his small sister announced with barely a stumble.

He glowered at her. "What do you mean, Tessie?"

She waved her hand in a nonchalant motion, and her voice matched the insouciant gesture. "She's gone to town already. Real early."

"To town?" he repeated. "To *town?*" The second time he said them, the words were a roar.

"We'll see," Emmaline had said, oh-so-compliantly, he remembered. And then she'd left him standing there. And he'd let her go, sure of his victory.

"Drat you, Emmaline Carruthers," he growled, shoving his hat angrily atop his head.

"Confounded woman, you need a good trouncing," he snarled, throwing the saddle on his horse's back and tugging at the cinch with quick, hard movements.

"Did she go alone?" he asked Tucker, the hand who had been watching him from wary eyes.

"Yessir, boss, she sure did. I offered to saddle up and go along, but she said she'd be fine, so I didn't argue with her."

"Don't let that woman leave this ranch alone again, do you hear me?" Matt said, in a deceptively quiet manner.

"Yessir, I hear you fine." Tucker's eyes were wide with trepidation, aware that Matt Gerrity in a temper was not a man to be messed with. "I'm sure sorry I didn't tell you she was goin' ridin', Matt, but I didn't know she was headin' for town till she took off thataway."

Matt's reply was unintelligible as he swung into the saddle and turned his horse quickly, applying pressure with his heels in the animal's ribs. He'd catch her, but not till she was already in Forbes Junction, he figured. She'd had too much of a head start.

Oswald Hooper was unlocking the door of his office when Emmaline slid from the brown gelding in front of the building housing the law office. He shielded his eyes against the bright sunshine as she approached.

"Well, good morning, Miss Carruthers. Sure didn't expect to see you today." He greeted her with a smile. "And I have to say you're lookin' a bit ruffled."

Her own smile was forced, and she brushed distractedly at her hair, smoothing it back from her face.

"Well, someone took a shot at a rabbit or something a ways out of town, and the bullet went wild. Missed me by a bit, but I'll have to admit—"

"Whoa! Back up there!" he exclaimed, reaching out to grasp her arm. "Someone shot at you?" He looked her over quickly, as if he might spy evidence of the bullet. "Missed you, you say?"

She patted at his hand, where it clutched her wrist, and shook her head. "No, no, I don't think he was aiming at me," she assured him quickly. "It was probably someone after game, and he missed his shot."

Oswald Hooper swallowed and blinked twice. Then his fingers squeezed once more, reassuringly, against her flesh before he let go his hold.

"Well, I'm sorry you got such a fright," he told her warmly. "And on such a beautiful day, too." He beamed at her with sudden humor. "Sure didn't expect to see you here this morning. Thought for sure you'd be home getting ready for your wedding."

"Did you now?" she said with as much aplomb as she could muster. "It sounds like Mr. Gerrity has notified you of his intentions, then?"

"Well, he made the arrangements, I understand." Oswald Hooper spoke slowly, aware suddenly that he was treading on dangerous ground. Emmaline's toe was tapping a quick tattoo on the boardwalk before his office door, and he cast an apprehensive eye at that sure sign of feminine aggravation.

"Tell me this," she began, one hand against her hip, the other clenched at her side. "Is there any legal way possible I can gain custody of my sister and not have to marry Matthew Gerrity?"

Oswald Hooper's eyes widened and his mouth opened in disbelief as he considered the young woman who faced him. Then he shook his head solemnly.

"I'd thought you were set on getting married, ma'am. Is there a problem I can help with?"

She took a deep breath and shook her head. "I've just been thinking it might be wise to wait a bit and not rush into this." Rushing her was not half of what Matt Gerrity was doing, she thought with a quick flush of anger. He'd made his plans and then expected her to just follow along like a well-trained pet, and she wasn't feeling like anyone's lapdog this morning.

"I'm surely surprised to hear that," he said slowly. "But I can't think of any way offhand that you can squeeze out of a wedding, Miss Emmaline."

"No loopholes?" she asked hopefully, as if she must pursue any chance of success.

"Well, let me tell you this," he said brightly as a thought occurred to him. "The circuit judge came into town last evening. He knew your pa and he knew about the will. Old Samuel talked it over with him a year or so back. It may be that he'd know something that I don't about the law in a case like this." He gestured toward the hotel across the dusty expanse of the road that ran through the middle of town. "He may still be over there, in the dining room."

Emmaline took a deep breath, snatching at this final straw. "Thank you, Mr. Hooper. I'll just take a chance on catching him."

She looped the reins of her horse over the rail provided in front of the office building and hurried across the road, waiting impatiently for several riders to pass midway across.

In a moment she was stepping up onto the wooden porch of the hotel, where early-morning loafers were assembled. Nodding, she passed them as she made her way inside. The open doorway of the dining room beckoned across the lobby, and she moved quickly in that direction.

"Do you want a table for breakfast?" a young woman asked her from just beyond the archway. Garbed in a prim uniform of black, with a heavily starched white apron pinned to her bosom, the girl watched her with sharp interest.

"No, thank you." Emmaline glanced about the almost empty room quickly, wondering as she did just what a circuit judge would look like. Surely not that rotund gentleman with a bowler hat plopped next to his plate. Or either of the two dusty, denim-clad men who were shoveling biscuits and gravy down their throats with indecent haste.

She turned from the distasteful sight and centered her attention on the young hostess. "Has the judge had his breakfast yet?"

"Oh, yes, ma'am. He's long gone over to Katy Klein's place." The girl flushed. "I mean to say, the Golden Garter, ma'am. There's gonna be court this morning. Those two over there—" she nodded her head in the direction of the busily eating cowhands "—they're witnesses to a shoot-out. Probably be a big crowd there for the hearing."

Only two words had stuck in Emmaline's mind. "Golden Garter?"

"Yes, ma'am. That's the biggest building in town. Till the courthouse gets built, that's where they hold circuit hearings." She nodded for emphasis, her curls bobbing about her face.

"Yes... well, thank you," Emmaline said distractedly, turning about to cross the wide lobby once more. "Holding court in a saloon," she muttered beneath her breath. "I've never heard such a thing!"

Once more on the porch, she looked up and down the street, her eyes drawn to the brightly painted signs that designated the two favorite haunts of the local menfolk. The Silver Bullet was at one end of the main street, the Golden Garter at the other. Over each establishment hung a colorful depiction of those more-than-colorful titles.

It was to the latter building that she headed, her eyes drawn by the glittering golden garter painted in minute detail on a wooden sign over the doors. Her booted feet kicked up small puffs of dust as she hurried to her destination, and her hair caught fire in the bright sunshine.

The doors were painted a bright red and hung just high enough that she could not see over them into the dim recesses of the saloon. If she bent just about double, she could look beneath them, but the indignity of that position erased the thought almost immediately from her mind.

Instead, she pushed with one palm against the center of the two doors, and they obligingly swung back as she shouldered her way between them. It was rather dark, she realized, only the shuttered light from the door and the two windows in front of the building spreading dim rays of sunshine across the cluttered room.

Tables and chairs were scattered about, the legs of the chairs poking into the air from atop the tables, while a young man energetically swept the floor. Motes of dust flew in profusion in the wake of his endeavors, and Emmaline squinted as she sought to locate the man who would make this barroom into a courtroom sometime today.

"Miss?" From behind the long, polished bar at one side of the room, a white-shirted man caught her attention. "Can I do something for you?" he asked gruffly as she turned to face him.

Emmaline approached slowly, uncertain now as to whether or not she should have ventured into this establishment. Grandmother would have a hissy fit if she could see me, she thought with trepidation. Although surely it was safe enough at this hour of the day, she decided stoutly. Later, the menfolk who patronized this place would make it hazardous for a decent woman to enter the door, she was certain.

The thought of the judge who might be able to answer her questions firmed her steps, and she stood before the bar with resolution in her gaze.

"Is the circuit judge here?" she asked quietly.

The barkeep nodded to a corner table just beyond the path of light that was shed through the doorway. "Over there, ma'am," he directed her. "Judge Whitley's his name." His smile brightened suddenly. "Say, aren't you old Sam Carruthers's girl, from back east?" He leaned forward, his broad face easing into a friendly smile.

She nodded in answer, her eyes intent on the shadowy corner, where a lone man sat at a square table.

"Heard tell you were in town. 'Course, I could tell by the red curls anyway, ma'am. You sure have the look of yer pa about you," he continued as she turned her back and made her way across the room.

"They're not red, just bright auburn," she whispered, and her hands clenched, her nails biting into her palms as she skirted the table in her path.

The man was dressed in black, with a glistening white shirt that buttoned up to the collar, and was bedecked with a black string tie. His hat was wide and cocked low over his brow, so that his eyes were shadowed beneath the brim. He was big, she could see that much. Even sitting down, he was a giant of a man, and she stopped before the table where he sat, unsure now, as his gimlet eyes took her measure.

"Judge Whitley?" She was proud of the firm tone she was able to produce.

He nodded once.

"I need to talk to you," she said, unsure of her welcome, but determined to accomplish her task.

"Talk away, young lady," he growled from the other side of the table, where one hand clutched a full glass of some sort of liquid.

Surely he wasn't partaking of hard liquor so early in the day, she thought distractedly. Yet, even as she considered him, that big, fleshy hand lifted the glass to his mouth and he tipped his head back as he drained it of its contents.

"Be quick about it, girl," he said harshly. "I'm holding court in a few minutes."

"I'm Emmaline Carruthers," she said carefully, wondering how to begin her quest.

"I figured that already, what with that headful of red hair, and that Carruthers look you're wearing," he said gruffly. He leaned forward a bit, and his gaze was searching.

Emmaline stiffened. "I beg your pardon? What is the 'Carruthers look' if I may ask?"

"You're a lot better-lookin' than your daddy, but you've got that same determined chin he had." The judge's eyes narrowed and his lips pursed as he surveyed her. "I suppose you're wondering about the will he wrote, aren't you?"

Emmaline nodded vigorously. "Yes, I am. I want to know if there's any way it can be broken. I want my sister, but I don't know if I want to get married right now. I'd like to maybe wait awhile."

This is all Gerrity's fault, she decided with an irritated toss of her head. If he weren't so pushy, so bossy, so... She couldn't come up with a word that described him best. That masculine, hard-edged attitude that irritated her so. The aggravating way he'd maneuvered her last night that had spurred her into this morning's mission.

And yet there was the softer side of the man. The side that appealed to her, that had caused her to be acquiescent to his bid for marriage. Not to mention the power he held over her when he touched her and held her and—

She shook her head distractedly. Her mind was made up. If this wedding could be postponed without her losing the chance to have her sister with her, she'd surely be better off.

The night spent with the memory of him had convinced her. He would capture her heart if she let him. He'd hold her in the palm of his big, callused hand, like so much booty acquired from the reading of the will, if she allowed it. Already she was halfway in his thrall, and he'd accomplished it with a few kisses and a little sweet talk.

"Not any way to circumvent that will, Miss Carruthers. Your daddy sewed it up tight as an old maid's pucker." Judge Whitley made the pronouncement and leaned forward, his hands folded on the table before him.

Behind her, the doors flapped open again, and she realized that it was not for the first time. Gradually the room had been infiltrated by several men, who stood about as if fascinated by her presence here. Now heavy-booted footsteps approached, and the flesh on the back of her neck shivered as a chill of foreboding passed over her body.

Before she heard his voice, she knew who it was at her back. Before she felt his hands on her waist, she knew whose touch would burn through the layers of cotton and leather to sear the flesh of her body.

"You've met my bride, Judge," Matt said gently as he gripped her and held her immobile. He spoke over her head to the magistrate, and was met with a look of devilish delight.

"This young lady is less than eager to marry you, young man," Judge Whitley intoned.

Matt's mouth twisted in a wry grin. "She's hard to persuade," he allowed as his hands tightened imperceptibly against her.

"Let go of me," she whispered through unmoving lips.

"Not a chance." His voice was a murmur in her ear, his mouth brushing against her vibrant hair.

"Now, let's just settle this thing, once and for all, and then I'll get on with my business," the judge announced, rising to his feet and towering over the table.

Emmaline swallowed. He was even bigger, taller and wider, than she'd thought. More than formidable, he filled her vision, and she found herself sheltering against the firm body of the man who stood behind her.

"Matthew Gerrity, do you understand that you must marry this woman in order to gain custody of your sister and ownership of the Carrutherses' holdings? Are you agreeable to that?"

His words carried over the whole room, vibrating in Emmaline's ears even as she heard the answer that came firmly from Matt.

"Yes, I do."

Emmaline heard his voice resound in her ear. It was a confirmation of the desires of her father, and Matt was more than agreeable. She was fully aware of that.

"And you, Emmaline Carruthers," the judge continued. "Are you aware that in order to inherit from your father and hold custody of your sister, you must marry this man and live with him and bear his child? Do you understand that?"

Emmaline was silent. Of course she understood the terms of the will, and so did half the population of this town, thanks to the judge's booming voice. She sighed. So much for privacy. And if this man was certain there was no way out of it, she'd have to abide by those terms. A sense of relief swam through her as she realized the whole thing was out of her hands. The choice was made.

"Miss Emmaline?" The judge was prodding her for an answer.

What had he asked her? Did she understand the terms of the will? Would she marry Matthew?

"Yes, of course," she said succinctly, aware of the firm grip of strong hands about her waist, the heated length of Matt's body against her back. Then she felt the *whoosh* of air that escaped his lungs, even as the judge thumped once on the table with his fist.

"Well then, according to the laws of the territory of Arizona, and by your own agreement, I pronounce you man and wife. Kiss your bride, Matt."

A buzzing not unlike that of a hundred bumblebees clouded her hearing and a haze surrounded her, threatening her vision. Her feet stumbled against the wooden floor as she was turned within his grasp. Then Matt's hand was beneath her chin, tipping her head up. As if from afar, she saw his mouth widen in a grin and his eyes narrow with tiny creases at the corners. But it wasn't until his head bent, his lips lowering to rest against hers, that she allowed the darkness to overtake her, and she collapsed in his arms with a tiny muffled moan of protest.

He'd lifted her and carried her out of the saloon, whistles and whoops of laughter following in their wake. Faintly she remembered the shouts of encouragement from the onlookers who'd witnessed her defeat at the hands of this man, and she squeezed her eyes shut at the memory.

She felt one strong arm about her back, the other beneath her knees, and she sensed the security of his embrace as he held her tightly to his chest. The sunlight burned against her closed eyelids, and she caught the scent of horses and dust and the man who held her.

"Might's well open those eyes, Emmaline. I know you're awake," he said teasingly as he strode with her toward the hotel.

She opened them just enough to peer at him through her lashes, and her teeth gritted at the look of triumph lighting his features.

"I was just faking," she announced with brittle precision. "I've never fainted in my life."

"Well then, you did a pretty good imitation of it back there," he said, laughing at her pouting belligerence.

Reaching the porch of the hotel, he allowed her to slide to her feet and held her with careful hands until she caught her balance.

"Are you all right now?" He kept his grip firm, plainly unwilling to let her go until he was sure she was steady.

She twitched away from him, lifting her head and biting at her lip as she looked about her. Across the street and down a ways, in front of the saloon they'd just left, was a scattering of men, all intent on watching the entertainment of the morning. Several ladies were in front of the dry goods store, next door to the hotel, busily taking note of Emmaline's dishevelment. She smoothed her shirtwaist and brushed with little success at her hair. More than one admiring glance was aimed at the man beside her, and she glared her disapproval at the boldness of the daring females. Foolish women were all over him every time he showed his face. No wonder he was so confounded cocky.

And to top it all, they were giving her the once-over, too, as if she were on display for everyone's amusement—and all of it was Matthew's fault.

"I hope you're satisfied, Gerrity," she spouted with fervent anger. "You've managed to make me the laughing-stock of the whole town."

He looked about with interest, and tipped his hat to the ladies who watched. "Not quite the whole town, Emmie," he said with good humor.

"Maybe not, but it'll be all over town before the day's through."

He grasped her elbow and guided her toward the doorway of the hotel and ushered her within.

"You didn't have breakfast, my dear wife," he said briskly. "That's probably why you passed out back there."

"I just lost my breath for a minute," she argued, unwilling to concede him the battle.

"Well, before we go any farther, you're going to eat something." He grasped her elbow, aiming for the doorway of the dining room, where the same white-aproned girl stood guard.

The growl that rumbled beneath her pleated shirtwaist was in full agreement with him, and Emmaline nodded. "I could use a piece of bread and butter, I suppose," she said grudgingly.

"You'll eat breakfast, and then we'll decide where to go from there," he told her as they were shown to a table near the front window. He held her chair for her to be seated, then bent low to whisper in her ear.

"I'll be back in just a minute. You can order, if you like. Just coffee for me, though." He turned and made his way quickly through the tables to the doorway, and Emmaline watched him go, caught up in the sheer bewilderment of the day.

The hotel room was large, the best in the house, the desk clerk had assured them.

The bed was large, at least, Emmaline decided as she finally allowed her gaze to fasten on that enormous piece of furniture. She'd ignored it studiously since Matt had guided her into this room, still sputtering from her outrage at his insistence that they spend their wedding day and night here.

Rather than make a fuss in the lobby, in full view of the clerk and the assorted guests who had been amused by the sotto voce arguing, she had clamped her lips together until they should achieve some degree of privacy.

Unwilling to look at him, sure his face would reflect the triumph of his victory, she glanced instead about the room. It was heavy with crimson velvet and gold braid, lavishly draping every window and hanging in rich folds from the canopy over the bed. The walls were covered with a flocked wallpaper of flowers of some sort and, as if that were not enough, had been garnished with ornately framed pictures. She pretended interest in the landscapes and walked about from one to the other, aware all the time of the man who watched her from near the door.

"You might as well look at me and have your say, Emmaline," he said finally. "We're going to stay right here in this room till we make peace of some sort between us."

"I didn't know I was allowed to say anything. Seems to me you've had it all your own way up to this point."

"It was your choice to go to the saloon," he reminded her. "I was intending to speak my vows in front of the preacher."

She spun to face him. "That judge tricked me, and you know it."

His face softened and his smile faded. "I know it, Emmaline. Believe me, that wasn't what I had planned. But you never can count on old Judge Whitley to do what you expect. I reckon he just thought to get the deed done and send us on our way. He was a good friend of your pa's, you know. Maybe he just wanted to perform the ceremony himself, sorta for old times' sake."

"Ceremony?" she asked unbelievingly. "You call that a ceremony? It was a farce."

"It was legal. You're my wife, Emmaline Gerrity," he told her stubbornly.

"I don't feel legal," she admitted glumly.

"Would you feel better if the preacher said the words?" He took three steps toward her and raised one hand, palm up, as if he were begging for alms.

Her eyes fastened on that callused hand, and she recognized the significance of his gesture. He was asking her compliance. He was willing to find the preacher and make it easier for her to accept.

Once more he'd surprised her with a degree of understanding she'd not credited him with. Lifting her hand, she offered it to him, allowing him to draw her to his side.

"Let's go do it again, Mrs. Gerrity," he said in a whispering, rasping invitation that brought a wistful smile to her lips.

"I don't have a wedding dress," she said ruefully.

"No, but you're getting married in something borrowed and old, and you've got a blue ribbon tied in your hair back here." His fingers circled the nape of her neck and rubbed with gentle comfort. Then, turning, his hand brushed in a lingering caress over the hair hanging down her back, and his fingers tangled in the curls that clung tenaciously to his rough skin.

"But nothing new." Her lips trembled as she looked up at him.

"Maybe that can be arranged," he told her, allowing the bright ringlets to slide free from his touch. His gaze held hers for a moment, and then he bent to drop warm kisses across her forehead, closing his eyes to better savor the silken texture of her skin. It would be so easy to claim her now, he thought. To melt the last shreds of resistance she was clutching so fiercely.

"Arranged how?" she asked, her voice slurred with the warmth of passion that had begun to stir within her. The old restraints drilled into her by a vigilant Delilah over the past years had begun to fall away during the past days. Until the mere touch of his hands against her laid siege to her barriers, and she was vulnerable in strange new ways to this man who held her future in his keeping.

"Secrets," he murmured against her temple. "Let's just call it a surprise. We'll hold things up here for another hour or so, all right?" Hopefully his earlier trip from the dining room would bring about the desired results. "Are you sure you won't mind the wait?"

Mind? With his arms about her and his lips warm against her face, she was tempted to agree to almost anything. Just being here was surprise aplenty, she thought with dark humor. Certainly nothing more could shock her on this day of strange happenings. She shook her head slowly.

"No...I don't mind waiting," she answered, wondering at his grin as he stepped back from her, releasing her reluctantly.

"I'm expecting a package to be delivered pretty soon now. Why don't I order you a nice bath brought up and give you a chance to fix your hair, and when the package comes, I'll bring it up to you?"

The bath had been warm, comforting, and of necessity cramped, given the short length of the tub he'd had delivered to their door. She stood in front of the oval mirror that hung over the washstand and inspected herself in the wavy glass. Her skin gleamed, shining from the scented soap he'd managed to find for her. Her mouth curved as she remembered.

"Thought you'd like this," he'd said diffidently, holding out the wrapped bar as the hot water was carried past them, behind the tall screen, where the tub awaited.

"Thank you," she'd said simply, accepting his offering, aware that it was somehow a turning point, this giving and receiving of a simple bar of soap. He'd done it for her pleasure and comfort, and she acknowledged it with a tremulous smile.

Still wrapped in the length of white toweling, she brushed at her hair, twisting it and looping it in various ways, aware that her final choice must be simple. She had only a few hairpins in her possession, and a short length of blue ribbon.

A quick rapping at the door caught her attention, and the turning of the key scraping in the lock assured her of the identity of her visitor.

"Matt?" she called hopefully from her hiding place behind the screen.

"Yeah, it's me." He closed the door behind himself and looked about the empty room. "Where are you, Emmaline? Still in the tub?"

"No, I'm trying to fix my hair," she answered, watching the expanse of wall visible from where she stood.

"I brought you something," he said from across the room. "Want to see it?"

"I'm not dressed," she answered primly, blushing as she spoke the words.

"Wrap up in something and come on out," he told her. "I want to show you this. I just had it brought in from the ranch."

She peeked around the corner at him and caught him unawares. One hand was running through his dark hair, the other was weighted down by the large package he carried. The same package he'd brought home last night.

Her eyes were curious as they fastened on the bundle. "What is it?" she asked cautiously.

"Come take a look." He coaxed her softly, his eyes lured by a bare shoulder that edged beyond the screen.

She clutched the towel well above her breasts and, with the other hand, held it in place at her waist. From there it draped her slender form to well below her knees. Still, she hesitated, looking down at herself doubtfully. She was quite presentable, she decided, bearing in mind that she was legally married to the man who waited across the room.

But by the time she'd taken three steps, she no longer felt the least bit presentable. His burning gaze had glittered over every inch of bare skin exposed. Over rounded shoulders and naked, slender arms. Past discreetly covered inches of her body, to where her curved calves and slim feet were uncovered and open to his scrutiny.

He'd seen her bare feet before, had admired the high arches and straight toes that were even now curled into the carpet covering the floor. But the satin-smoothness of her shoulders held him enthralled, and his fingers itched to touch the skin glowing from her bath. Aware of her innocence, he forbade his lustful fingers the delights they yearned to sample. Certain of her unworldliness, he sought to temper his own needs in order to gently persuade her closer.

"Come see what I have for you," he said with casual ease, turning to place the bundle on the bed. Bending, he pulled his knife from his boot and, with a quick motion, cut the string holding the paper wrapped about his gift. With deft movements, he unwrapped the things he had purchased the day before. Was it only yesterday that he'd chosen the dress?

He held it up and watched her intently. She stepped closer, forgetting her unease for a moment as she reached to touch the fine cotton fabric he held for her inspection. The flowers were blue against a field of white, with green leaves and stems traced delicately between them.

"It's lovely," she said finally, her eyes misting with tears. She drew in a shuddering breath and relaxed her grip on the towel at her waist, allowing it to hang loosely about her. Matt draped the dress over her arm and she received his gift with a murmur of thanks.

"You chose it?"

Matt nodded and cleared his throat as he stepped back, away from her, tempted almost beyond the edge of his endurance. She was a vision, wrapped in a simple length of toweling, her hair in total disarray about her face and spilling across her shoulders. Her eyes were shiny, her mouth was soft and smiling, and she was the most alluring female he'd ever laid eyes on.

On top of that, she was his wife, and unless he turned and walked out of the room right this minute, he would be likely to mess up his whole wedding day. His hands trembled with the urge to touch her, and he shoved them into his pockets before he gave in to the temptation that beguiled him. Before he carried her to the wide bed that beckoned, and took her like a stallion in the breeding barn.

Before he took her without giving the preacher a chance to speak the words that would satisfy her woman's heart.

Chapter Nine

The knot was well tied. And try as she might, Emmaline could not fathom how such a day had come to be.

We've managed to get ourselves married, well and good, she thought mournfully. Not only that, but we're about to spend our wedding night right here in Forbes Junction.

She shot a furtive glance at the man who sat across the table from her, calmly cutting an enormous beefsteak into pieces. He looked up unexpectedly, grinned with humor and proceeded to lustfully make short work of the meal on his plate.

"You're enjoying this, aren't you?" she asked accusingly.

"Ummm . . . you bet." He swallowed, wiping his mouth with a gleaming white napkin.

"I don't mean the meal, I mean the whole day. I mean staying here—" she gestured toward the lobby, visible through the wide archway "—where everyone in town knows that we just got married."

He looked up at her, chewing another bite of steak, and his eyes lit with delight. "Twice," he said succinctly, and reached for a thick slice of bread. "I'd bet my bottom dollar that we're about as well married as any two ever were." His fork speared another piece of meat and delivered it to his mouth. "Twice," he repeated with unrepentant glee.

"The preacher was expecting us," she reminded him primly. "It was only right to be married by a man of the cloth."

"Whatever you say, Emmaline."

She squirmed in her chair, lifted a bite of baked potato on her fork, then dropped it back on her plate. "Anyway, you know what I mean. They all know that when we go upstairs, it will be our wedding night." Her cheeks were flushed with a pink stain that had hardly left her all day, and now it deepened, until her throat, too, was painted a delightful shade of color.

Matt watched her blush, saw the shimmer of tears glistening from her wide-set eyes, and wanted nothing more than to hustle her up those stairs and begin the wedding night she was referring to.

"Emmaline, my dear," he said in a low voice, leaning over the table, "there isn't a married couple in this town who haven't shared a wedding night."

At the look of dismay on her face, he decided his words were small comfort.

"That's what I mean," she whispered, wiping at her hands with the napkin she held. "They'll all know!"

Matt picked up his cup and sipped at the coffee that had grown cool while he enjoyed his steak. He pointed one long finger at her plate, and she looked automatically to where he directed her attention.

"What? What's wrong?" she asked, peering at the perfect specimen of beef she'd been served and managed only to cut up into small pieces. It lay next to the baked potato she'd cut in half and carefully forked about in distraction. The carrots were barely disturbed, and her slice of bread, though torn asunder, waited patiently for her to take the first bite.

"You need to eat, Emmaline," he said quietly. "You haven't touched your supper and, to my knowledge, you didn't eat any noon meal. The only thing that's passed your lips today, besides a lot of argument, was the bread and butter you managed to call breakfast."

"That was well past breakfasttime," she said politely. "And besides, I'm not hungry." Placing her fork down, she folded her hands in her lap.

"Well, don't come crying to me at midnight, complaining your stomach's growling," he admonished her, scraping the last of his potato onto his fork.

"I don't plan on complaining to you about anything," she vowed in a tight little voice, casting another glance about the dining room.

"No one is looking at you, Emmaline." He struggled to be patient. "No one is going to pay any attention to us at all."

"Oh, no? Deborah Hopkins just came in the door with a man. And she's headed this way."

"Try to look happy," he ordered her quickly, as he reached across the table to filch a piece of her steak.

Obediently she managed a cool, polite smile and lifted her fork once more, spearing a bit of carrot.

"Well, so this is the bride," Clyde Hopkins announced heartily, stopping just inches from the table.

"Hullo, Clyde," Matt said jovially, rising in deference to Deborah. "You're right. This is Emmaline, my wife. My brand-new bride."

His voice registered the proper degree of pride, Emmaline decided as she added her own discreet greeting. Her smile widened until she was sure every tooth in her mouth was on display, then she managed to blush even deeper at Clyde's all-encompassing survey of her.

"Yessir, she's quite a little charmer, I'd say. Wouldn't you, Deborah? Managed to haul you off to the altar, did he, Mrs. Gerrity?"

Emmaline looked about distractedly, aware they were now definitely the center of attention. Almost every eye in the dining room was directed at them, and she wondered desperately if she could just rise and leave with some semblance of dignity.

"The altar?" she asked, fumbling for a reply.

Clyde grinned deviously. "Well, I understand you had to settle for a tabletop in the saloon, but then, a wedding's a wedding, I always say."

"I've always said that Matt was full of surprises," Deborah put in mildly. "I'm sure his decision to marry his bride in the Golden Garter was just one of the many he has in store for her."

She smiled benignly at Emmaline, then smoothed down her already perfectly coiffed hair. Just in case everyone in the room hadn't already tuned in on the conversation, she leaned closer to Emmaline. Guaranteed to carry to the farthest corner, her words warbled sweetly: "Maybe he'll take you to the Silver Bullet for a honeymoon."

"That's enough, Deborah," Matt growled. His teeth were clenched, his eyes were narrowed and dark, and he clamped his hand over her fingers, which waved dangerously close to Emmaline's face. "You've just insulted my bride, and if you were a man, I'd drag you out in the street and shoot you down."

Deborah's face whitened at his words—not to mention the pain his clenched fist was delivering to her fingers. As if the touch of her flesh were repugnant to him, he dropped her hand and sat down once more, his eyes fastened on Clyde Hopkins this time.

"Take your daughter and get out of here," Matt said quietly. Determinedly, he reached across to where Emmaline sat and scooped up her plate in one hand. Holding it inches above the table, he nodded to the door.

"Leave now, or Deborah will be setting a new style when this food decorates the front of her frock."

Eyes gleaming with pure hatred seared Emmaline as Clyde glanced once in her direction. Then, with as much dignity as he had available, he led his daughter from the quiet dining room.

"Please, let's leave," Emmaline pleaded beneath her breath.

"We'll go in a minute," Matt assured her. "Just drink some water, Emmie. Take a bite of your bread or something. I'm not letting them chase you out of here."

"They won't be chasing me. I was ready to run for it before they ever got here," she admitted with grudging humor.

His eyes were tender as he assimilated her confession. "You don't have to run from me, sweetheart," he said softly. Leaning closer, his elbows rested against the pristine tablecloth. "And if you do, I'll be right behind you."

It's going to take some doing to get her in a wedding-night mood, he thought, aware of the skittish condition of her emotions. It had been bad enough before Clyde got here, and now he had to start all over again.

"Please?" The whispered plea announced her intention to depart, and Matt nodded agreeably.

"Sure, let's go."

With his hand pressed firmly against her waist, he guided her from the dining room, relieved that the others present tended to their own business. Once they were in the lobby, he steered her to the wide stairway that led to the upper story, where their room awaited them.

Her feet dragged against the carpeted stairs, her palm was damp with moisture against the curved walnut banister, and her heart thumped unmercifully against her breastbone. Emmaline was in the midst of being seized by pure, unadulterated panic by the time Matt unlocked the door of room 209 and ushered her within.

"I don't have a nightgown," she blurted out as the bed loomed into view. Turning on her heel, she faced him, her eyes wide with hope. "We'll have to go home, out to the ranch, Matt. I can't go to bed without a gown."

The temptation to smile was almost more than he could resist. But resist it he did. That he make Emmaline any more upset than she was at this moment was not to be considered.

"That's all right, honey. You can sleep in your petticoat or something. Maybe that silky thing that was in the stuff I bought for you."

"My chemise? You want me to sleep in that? It's almost transparent!" she said distractedly, squeezing her hands together at her waist.

"Yeah, I know," he muttered, remembering the scrap of soft fabric he'd seen for just seconds at Abraham Guismann's dry goods store. A vision of Emmaline garbed in the sheer garment filled his fertile mind, and he sensed a heaviness in his groin that threatened to expose his manliness before the time was right.

"We can't just go back to the ranch, can we?" she asked hopefully, already knowing the answer, but willing to try once more for clemency. Surely she would die tomorrow morning if she had to walk back into that dining room and face those people, who would know she had just survived a wedding night.

"Emmaline, just what are you so dang scared of?" It wasn't what he'd intended asking her. The words had been blurted out before he could halt their progress. Oh, well, better to know than to wonder, he decided, lifting his hands to rest them on her slender shoulders. "Surely you know I won't do anything to hurt you, don't you?"

"I don't know what I'm afraid of, Matt. That's the whole thing. I just don't know... anything," she admitted. "Oh, I know the general idea. You know, I'm aware of using a stallion to breed a mare, and I know how puppies are born, and I've seen the birds in the springtime flutter around, and I think they were—you know..." She stopped, suddenly aware she was discussing this forbidden subject with her husband.

"Oh, Emmie," he said, his voice as tender as the smile he wore. "Men and women aren't quite the same as the horses or dogs or the birds—though I'm not sure just what you saw, watching those birds in the spring. Now, if you want to watch the chickens and the rooster, they may provide you with a little education," he added teasingly.

She bristled and jerked away from his touch. "I know they're not the same, Gerrity. I know that!"

"Do you, honey?" he asked gently, reaching for her once more and turning her about to face him. His hands fit beautifully about her narrow waist, he noted. In fact, he had the notion they'd fit together well in more ways than one as his gaze traveled over her lithe form.

Remembering the satin warmth of her bare shoulders above the towel earlier, he knew an urgent need to have her out of the dress she had on. The thought of stripping the stockings she wore down the length of her shapely calves almost made his hands tremble, and his mouth was dry as he considered the rounded firmness of her bosom.

"Don't look at me like that," she warned him, her senses alert to his wandering gaze. She was warm, a tingling, traveling sensation of heat blooming where his hands and eyes touched her.

"Turn around," he said, his words more order than invitation. And, as suited his purpose, he turned her, his hands moving about the circumference of her waist.

She obeyed, fascinated by the rough texture of his voice, the warm pressure of his hands.

Then those same hands moved with ease down the length of her dress, releasing the row of fine mother-of-pearl buttons from the buttonholes that had contained them all afternoon. The buttons ended just below the widest part of her hips, and as soon as the last one was undone, she felt those same hands reach about her to unfasten the identical ones that closed her sleeves.

His arms, of necessity, were about her shoulders, his hands holding her own directly in front of her breasts, and his fingers worked carefully at each button. That the inside of his wrist brushed against the side of her breast as he completed his task surely was an accident, she thought, her heart fluttering once more in an uneven fashion.

When he pulled the sleeves down her arms, the bodice of the dress followed suit, until she felt the first brush of lace across her chest. Her hands pressed against the collar, holding it at half-mast, and her eyes widened in dismay.

"What are you doing, Matthew Gerrity?" she squeaked, tugging at her dress to no avail. She looked over her shoulder at him, and he smiled disarmingly.

"Just helpin' you honey."

"I got into it without your help. I can get out of it the same way," she breathed, aware that she was not in total control of the situation.

"Come on, Emmaline, let me help you," he said reasonably, his hands rising to cover hers with gentle strength.

She took a deep, shuddering breath and released her hold, then closed her eyes as the yards of fabric slid to the floor. Bending her head, she opened her lashes just a bit and stared down to where it lay, in a circle of blue flowers, about her feet.

"Step out of it, Emmaline," Matt said softly. "You don't want your new dress to be wrinkled, do you?"

"No," she said, looking down at her chest, where the gentle rise of her breasts lay exposed to him.

"I thought it fit you well," he said in a conversational tone, bending to pick up the garment. He stretched the elastic that had been inserted into the waistline to ensure its fit. "This is quite a novel idea, isn't it?"

"Yes," she muttered, watching his hands in fascination.

He hung the dress on the wall, a handy hook being provided for the occasion. Then, turning to her, he focused deliberately on her face, aware that her full petticoat left a good share of her upper chest exposed to his view.

"Do you need help with the rest of your clothes?" he asked helpfully, his eyes never straying from her pink cheeks.

She shook her head. "No."

His smile was rueful. "Can't you say anything but yes or no, Emmie?"

Once more she shook her head. "I don't know what else to say," she admitted forlornly. "And I don't need any help. You didn't get me a corset."

His brow lifted. "I don't think the women hereabouts wear them much. Doubt if anyone on the ranch owns one. Too blamed hot to bind yourself up like a trussed steer," he said dismissively.

"Well, when I send for my things from Lexington, I'll have mine if I need it," she said, searching wildly for conversation that would put off the disrobing process.

He almost told her. But his better sense prevailed. No point in opening that can of beans tonight, he decided firmly. When the stuff arrived was soon enough to let her know he'd already told her grandparents of his intentions.

Outside the windows, the sun had reached the horizon, the sky providing a magnificent display of color in the west. Soon it would be dark, for when the sun went down, twilight lasted only a matter of minutes here, she'd found. It was the dark she craved. Not in her wildest imaginings could she fathom climbing into that bed with just a thin chemise covering her while it was still light in the room.

"Can I have some privacy to wash up?" she asked with sudden inspiration.

Matt eyed her with speculation, then shrugged in capitulation. She was clean as a whistle already, but if she wanted to splash around in the basin a bit, so be it.

"Sure," he said agreeably. "I'll just sit over here by the window and keep an eye on the street, and you can go behind the screen and do whatever you have to do."

She squirmed as she considered her next request. "Well, part of what I have to do requires more privacy than that," she blurted out finally.

"Uh-huh..." He should have known, he thought in hindsight. "I won't be long, Emmaline," he told her, heading for the door. "I'll just take a walk out back for a few minutes."

He couldn't have made it any plainer than that, he decided as he made his way down the back stairway and past the lingering cowhands who were gathered in the alleyway behind the hotel. He'd give her ten minutes. No more.

She took up barely a third of the bed. The portion she'd claimed was farthest from the door, he noted as he closed it behind himself.

Covered to the chin with the sheet and coverlet, she lay flat on her back, a slender form that he hoped fervently was clad in no more than the lawn chemise he'd bought her. His eyes intent on her, his hand slid up from the knob to shoot the bolt that would ensure them privacy.

Emmaline heard the sound of metal against metal and swallowed. *I'm locked in this room with him,* she thought. *We're really married, and I don't know what to do.* She bit fervently at the inside of her cheek, worrying the small bit of flesh as she watched him. *How I wish Delilah had told me what to expect!* She breathed unevenly against the crisp white sheet that almost covered her chin.

"Sleeping, Emmaline?" he asked softly as he approached the bed, one hand busy undoing the buttons on his shirt.

"No," she whispered into the sheet. Thank goodness, it was almost full dark, only the last shred of twilight remaining to blend with the light of the moon, chasing the shadows from the room. He stood in the moonbeams that

cast a ray of muted light in the direction of the bed and released the belt holding his denim pants in place. They
sagged against his hips as he pulled his shirt free and slid it
from his body.

Turning his back, he walked to the wall to hang the shirt
on a hook next to her dress, and she was struck by the intimacy attached to the act. Forevermore, their clothing
would share the same wardrobe space, their bodies would
share the same bed. Such closeness could hardly be imagined.

He sat on the straight wooden chair next to the bed and
bent to remove his boots. With a grunt, he tugged the right
one free, then tackled the other. Placing them upright beside the chair, he took off his stockings, reminded that he'd
not been able to act out his fantasy of peeling Emmaline's
from her slender legs.

The thought jolted him, and he felt the urgency he'd been
struggling to hold in abeyance once more run rampant
within him. Rising, he dropped the denims to the floor and
stepped out of them, wearing only his short underwear.

Picking up the sheet, Matt slid beneath it, relishing the
coolness of the starched linen. With casual ease, he slipped
his hands beneath his head, his arms stretched wide on the
pillow, and made a great show of settling into the mattress.

After a moment, he lifted his head a bit and looked in her
direction. "Got enough room over there?" he asked
cheerfully.

"Umm..." she said, not sure how to answer the question.

"Well, that beats yes or no, I guess," he said, chuckling
despite himself.

"When are you going to do it?" she asked abruptly, torn
between the anticipation of the event and the endless waiting. Surely he would put his hands on her soon, or maybe
he would just... just what?

"Do it?"

She sat upright and was silhouetted in the pale glow from
the window, her filmy chemise a small covering against the
moonlight. Within it, her breasts were round, proud be-

neath the fine fabric, the agitation of her breathing causing them to rise and fall with each intake of air.

It was almost more than his meager amount of self-
control could handle.

He tugged at her hand, and she turned toward him, her
face pale, filled with the unknowing of this act of intimacy. His second tug caught her off-balance, and she
leaned in his direction. Carefully his wide palm circled her
shoulder and he drew her down to him, easing her into
place against his chest. Tenderly he brushed back the
abundance of hair she'd released from the ribbon, his fingers tangling once more in the curls.

"I like your hair, Mrs. Gerrity," he murmured against
her temple.

"Thank you." She shifted against him, her face cushioned by the black hair that curled across his chest.

"So polite," he said softly. "What would you say if I
told you I like your pretty shoulders and your smooth
skin?"

She inhaled deeply, a shuddering breath, and nudged his
chest with her chin as she shook her head. "I don't know."
The pause was long, and then she whispered with longing,
"Do you? Like my shoulders?"

"Oh, yes," he assured her, his palm shaping her arm, his
fingers aware of the pulse beat at her narrow wrist. He
clasped her fingers between his, tracing the length of each
and rubbing with gentle care at each knuckle, as though he
considered this the safest place to begin his investigation.

"You have nice hands," she volunteered as he lulled her
into a semblance of comfort.

"They're full of calluses," he murmured against the top
of her head, his nose buried in the scented glory of her
gleaming curls. They were almost golden in the moonlight, he decided, inhaling the fragrance of her.

Cautiously he moved his other hand, easing it up her
back, until it cradled her head. She was acquiescent as he
turned it, tilting it back until his mouth could reach hers.
Her lips were warm, and he covered their satin-smoothness
carefully, aware of the shiver that vibrated with gentle
tremors through her body.

"You said you liked me to kiss you," he reminded her, their lips brushing together with each word he spoke.

"Yesss...." The word was a hiss against his mouth, and he felt the small shiver of her response as he claimed the prize she had given into his keeping.

The fingers that had run the length of her arm and clasped her hand traveled on. She felt them moving in a gentle quest across the narrow width of her shoulders, the heat of his touch warming her through the fragile covering she wore. Then his palm was flat against her back, each finger imprinting itself against her skin, exploring the length of her spine, imparting a tingling awareness that seeped into her body and settled there.

He surrounded her, from the hand that clasped her head and held her in place for the gentle invasion of his kiss to the wide palm that was pressing her against the heated length of his solid frame. Flattened between their bodies, her hands were teased by the texture of the curls that sprang from his chest. Covering the width of him with a lush carpet, they coaxed her fingers to bury themselves in their curling depths.

He closed his eyes at her touch, the grasping of her fingers, the rasp of her nails against his skin, the tugging of the short curls as she explored with unconcealed eagerness. The arousal he had been aware of this whole livelong day was more than noticeable, he was sure, even to her untutored body. It was sure as hell driving him crazy, he thought with grim determination, and her hands were only multiplying the problem.

His mouth lifted from hers, his lips tugging at her soft flesh with gentle suction, as though he were reluctant to break the contact he had established between them.

"Hey, Mrs. Gerrity," he whispered hoarsely against her cheek, his breath warm and fragrant with a blend of mint and coffee.

"Mrs. Gerrity?" She repeated the title slowly and inhaled deeply, bemused by his nearness, by the calling of her name. It was going to be all right, she decided dreamily. He was being so careful to treat her like a lady. This being married might be just the thing, she thought, and she snuggled closer.

"Just wanted to know if you'd answer to it," he murmured in her ear.

"Of course," she whispered. "Now that I'm your wife, that's my name."

He grinned in the darkness and eased back, tugging her with him until she was in the center of the bed and he was leaning over her, his chest pressing firmly against the softness of her breasts.

"But you're not... not really," he informed her gently.

"Yes, I am." Her tone was indignant as she denied his claim. "I'm as much your wife as a circuit judge and a preacher could make me!"

His chuckle was ripe with amusement. "Ah, but that's where you're wrong, Mrs. Gerrity. All those words couldn't do the trick. I'm the only man in the world who can make you my wife."

She was quiet, her eyes blinking in confusion. He watched her, waiting until she should take in the meaning of his words.

"We're in bed together," she blurted out.

He nodded.

"You've been kissing me and touching me and everything."

"There's more," he told her quietly, even as his rebellious body surged against the warmth of her thigh.

She moved restlessly within his arms, away from that nudging hardness, and he slid his hand down to pull her back against himself.

"Don't you know what that is, Emmaline?" he asked gently, wondering how long he could hold out against the throbbing tension that was fast taking hold of his aching groin.

"Is this the part... is this when I have to be submissive to you?"

"Is that what you think is going to happen? That I'm going to hurt you?" he asked, lifting his leg to nudge hers apart.

"I don't know much about this, and I'm not very good at being submissive," she warned him in a harsh whisper, aware suddenly that he was lifting himself to lie above her and had somehow insinuated himself between her knees.

"I'll show you how, Emmie," he murmured, lowering himself against her as he wondered how he would manage to ease the chemise from her. It was tangled about her thighs and stretched taut over her belly. He slid one hand down to tug at it, lifting it from her and pulling it free.

"You're uncovering me," she said, her voice wispy, as she considered the movement of his hands against her limbs and beneath her bottom. There was a hardness about him, a strange tension in him, his muscles firm and tight. She thought to protest, closing her eyes as he pushed himself to his knees between her legs. But he took her breath away as he lifted her, stripping off the chemise in one easy motion.

And then her own eyes betrayed her, opening, sweeping down over the naked length of her own body, widening in disbelief as she realized that there was not a single shred of clothing between them.

"This is what happens when people make love, Emma-line," he said quietly. "This is the part that makes us husband and wife."

He was so dark. From his head of black hair to the shadowed width of his chest. He was like a creature of the night, upright against the softness of her thighs. Her eyes lowered to where their bodies touched, and she watched as his fingers stretched wide across the lowest part of her belly.

"You'll carry our baby here, Emmie," he said in a curiously hushed voice. "You don't know how that happens, do you?" he asked, resigning himself to his task as teacher. Why hadn't someone taken it upon herself to tell her? he thought. Surely her grandmother, or someone . . .

Her head rolled back and forth against the white pillow in silent negation. "I've seen women who were in the family way," she supplied helpfully.

"Yeah . . ." He dropped his head, breathing deeply, his eyes closed. Then, leaning forward, he captured her chin in one hand and slid his long body the length of hers, announcing his presence against the softness of her belly as he bent to kiss the mouth she offered so willingly.

She wiggled beneath him. "Matt?" She mumbled against his lips. "I feel so warm."

"It's okay, honey," he whispered, coaxing her mouth to open, laving the softness of her with his tongue as he moved his hips in a circular motion. "You feel so good, sweetheart," he groaned, reaching down to raise her knees on either side of his taut body.

He bent lower, his mouth finding the firm flesh of her breast, and he molded his lips to the rising slope, careful to ease his way gradually as he shaped the lush fullness with his hand. He suckled her, gently and tenderly, aware that this was virgin territory, as much so as the woman part of her that was pressed against his groin.

Emmaline writhed against him, her breathing hampered by the harsh pounding of her heart. He was touching the forbidden places that she had never thought to submit to him, to anyone. His mouth was hot against her, tugging with rhythmic movements and causing waves of heated pleasure to pulse throughout her body until the pleasure was centered in the very pit of her belly. There, where his hard presence pushed against her with a steady pressure.

She moaned his name, and her voice was high and wispy as her hands slipped through his dark hair, holding him in place, lest he leave her, robbing her of the strange spiraling pleasure he brought her.

Carefully his other hand slid between them, his fingers gentle as he discovered the warmth of her woman's flesh, relieved at the discovery of her readiness. He could wait no longer.

"Hold still, honey," he whispered against the softness of her breast, moving against her carefully, cautiously positioning himself and praying fervently that he would not bring her pain.

It was a futile hope. She was wonderfully snug, gloriously tight about him, and he pressed forward with all the tenderness he could manage. Breathing deeply, eyes closed against the passion that surged within him, he heard her gasp of pain, felt her buck against him, and then recognized the barrier of her innocence as it blocked his way.

His hands slid to grip her hips, holding her in place, and his mouth tightened against gritted teeth as he took her with one thrusting movement.

She cried out, shuddering against the invasion of her body. But then, with a trembling acceptance, she enclosed him within the cradle of her embrace, her arms tight about his back.

"Is that all?" she asked in a tight little voice against his shoulder.

He shook his head, concentrating on holding back the flood tide that begged to be released from his aching loins. "No, honey, there's more," he groaned, holding himself still, waiting for her tender flesh to accept him.

"I feel so full," she ventured, shifting her hips to ease the aching pressure.

"Lay still," he cautioned her quickly, unwilling to spill his seed without bringing her pleasure from their joining. Easing back, he allowed room for his fingers to reach her soft woman's flesh once more, and she shivered.

"I'm not hurting you?" he asked, ceasing his gentle movements.

Her answer was a moan and a subtle lifting of herself against his hand. He felt the muscles of her bottom tighten as he held her firmly in place, and he soothed her, squeezing gently against the soft flesh. Her knees lifted higher, and her breathing quickened, her moan becoming a soft cadence of whispered words.

"Oh, please, Matt...please... I can't...." Her voice was a pleading cry, and her head tossed on the pillow as she surrendered to the fierce pulsing pleasure of his caress.

He slid his arms beneath her, up her back, until his hands clasped her shoulders, holding her against him as he lifted himself and slid deeper within the narrow channel he'd claimed. Again, and then again, he sought the depths of her woman's warmth, his breath shuddering against her throat. Until, with a final groan, he surged within her.

"Emmie?" He lay against her, aware of her silence as his weight pressed her slender body into the mattress beneath him. The word sounded harsh to his ears. His lungs were expanding more slowly now as his breathing became normal. "Emmie?" he repeated, lifting his head to gaze at her with hooded eyes.

Wordlessly, he watched her, watched the slow tears that slipped from beneath her lids, leaning to brush them with his own cheek. "Don't cry, baby," he whispered. "It won't hurt the next time."

She looked up at him, blinking against the tears that fell, smiling as she lifted her fingers to touch his face, tracing the wide lines of his forehead and down the hard angle of his jaw. She shook her head in an almost imperceptible movement, and her words were soft as she eased his worry.

"I'm not crying because it hurt."

"Then why?" he asked roughly, bending to steal another tear, this time with the tip of his tongue.

"Because of...all of it," she breathed. "You...me...the touching, the closeness of our bodies. I feel like I'm part of you," she said in wonderment.

His grin was teasing as he moved, shifting with a subtle motion that reminded her of his position. "Are you now?" he asked as he brushed back the hair that curled against her forehead and temples, his fingers tempted once more by the silky texture. And then he bent to string a line of damp kisses across the flesh that he'd exposed, unwilling to meet her gaze as he felt the tendrils of caring tighten about his heart.

Chapter Ten

The face peering back from the mirror was a bit flushed, a bit anxious, but not what Emmaline had thought to see. Most certainly, it was her own, but somehow she had expected . . . what?

She frowned, one finger tucking at a stray curl that refused to be contained within her bonnet. Surely she should look different. Certainly the events of a wedding night should have made her look older, or more mature, or . . . something.

"Emmaline, are you ready to leave?"

She whirled to face the man who had entered the room while she was gazing at herself so intently.

"Don't creep up on me," she blustered. "You startled me."

His gaze encompassed her, from the top of her bonnet to the tips of her shoes, which peeped from beneath the hem of her dress. He took his time about it, grinning as she clutched at her skirt with nervous fingers. Her cheeks were rosy with the same embarrassed confusion she'd struggled with since early morning. And, even as he watched, it intensified until she blinked and lifted her hands to lay cooling palms against her flaming skin.

"Reckon I know now what the phrase 'blushing bride' means, Emmaline," he drawled with humor.

"Don't look at me like that," she blurted. "I hate it that I always blush."

He was before her in two quick strides and his hands were spanning her waist, drawing her against his long, lean frame. She stiffened for a moment and opened her mouth to protest, but he shook his head.

"Hush, Emmie," he whispered, in a raspy, deep admonition that widened her eyes as she obeyed. "I like your blushes," he said, in that same whisper, and she felt the tension once more grip her, aware with sharpened senses of the strength in his hands as he held her firmly, yet with a gentle touch. With narrowed eyes he focused on her mouth, and he smiled as he bent to bestow a brushing caress against the lips tempting him.

Her lashes drifted closed, and she drew a breath, caught up in the emotion that clutched at her. With a teasing pressure of his mouth against hers, he once more called into being a strange, mind-boggling awareness of him that pervaded her body at his touch. It filled her, this combination of scent and texture, as she inhaled his essence and moved her lips against his in a cautious exploration.

She reveled in the sense of triumph flowing through her like warm molasses, savoring the joyous knowledge that he wanted her. Hadn't he said so? In the hours of the night past, hadn't he whispered those very words into her ear?

"I want you, Emmie," he'd muttered, just before he—

Her gasp of dismay as she recalled those heretofore forbidden and unknown intimacies was smothered by his mouth. But he lifted his head as she moved abruptly within his grasp.

Her eyes opened, fastening on the grin he wore. "What is it, Emmaline? Afraid I'll cart you off to bed again?" He rocked her within his embrace, his arms tightening and his hands moving to fit themselves against her back. "I won't, you know," he said, a touch of regret lacing his words. "We need to head out to the ranch this morning. Tessie will be wondering what happened to us."

She shook her head. "No, I wasn't thinking that at all."

His low chuckle mocked her. "I'll bet you've spent more than a few minutes this morning worrying about being a bride." His keen eyes rested on the telltale movement of her mouth as she bit against the corner of her lower lip. "Was it so bad, Emmie?"

Her eyes met his, and she shook her head again, more slowly this time. "No, it wasn't bad at all," she answered with inherent honesty. "Just..." Words failed her. It had been a revelation, an awakening. Nothing had prepared her for Matthew's loving during those night hours. The unexpected pleasure she'd found in his touch, the joy she'd discovered within his embrace and the tenderness he'd brought to their lovemaking, were memories she would cherish. But she certainly couldn't talk about them!

It was enough that she couldn't escape the memories this morning. *I've become a carnal woman,* she thought mournfully. *Just like those unmentionable creatures who make themselves available to men. The ones that Grandmother talked about when she warned me about impure thoughts.*

"I never knew before what happens between men and women," she said, her words a whisper as she admitted her ignorance.

"I kinda figured that," he said gruffly, his hands still against her slender back. "Didn't anyone ever talk to you about it?" His brow furrowed as he wondered at the lack in her upbringing.

She shook her head, her eyes fixed on the second button of his shirt. "Delilah just told me that when I married, I must be a good wife and submit to my husband."

His snort of disbelief tightened her lips, and she lifted her chin defensively. "Grandmother warned me against impure thoughts and told me to always be a lady," she said, with precise emphasis on the words. "You made that very difficult for me to do, Matthew."

"To tell the truth, honey, I'm amazed we made it through as well as we did, what with all the wonderful ideas that must have been floating through that curly head of yours." He clasped her shoulders with gentle strength. "Look me right in the eye, Emmaline, and listen to this bit of advice to a new bride. You don't have to submit to your husband. I just want you to enjoy what we do together." His grin was knowing as he watched her eyes widen with comprehension.

"I'm not sure we should be talking about it like this," she said primly, and she pushed with futile pressure against his broad chest.

He laughed, a full, robust chuckle that caught her unawares, and his eyes lit with delight. "I doubt I need to worry about you being too submissive to me, anyway, Emmaline. You're about the least pliable woman I've come across in my time."

"Really. And have there been a lot of women 'in your time' to compare me with?" she asked tartly.

"Probably not as many as there could have been," he said bluntly. "I'm twenty-eight years old, Emmaline, and I've met up with a few females along the way. But I'll tell you one thing right now. You don't need to worry that there will be anyone besides you in my life from now on."

The welcoming committee was out in full force as their horses neared the house. "Someone must have seen us coming," Matt mused. "Sure looks like all the females in the place are ready to pounce, doesn't it?"

Emmaline nodded, her thoughts in a quandary. Already she was aware of the telltale warmth of her cheeks as they drew rein near the back door of the low, sprawling building. The thought of facing Maria, Olivia and the hired men as a new bride was daunting, but the anticipation of scooping Theresa into her arms for a welcoming embrace was heartwarming.

And there her little sister was, balancing on one foot as she gave them her best scowl. "You didn't come home last night," she said darkly. "I didn't have a good-night story." Her eyes were focused on Matthew, but they slid quickly to Emmaline as she thrust her lower lip out and frowned her displeasure.

"I'm sorry, Tessie," Matt began as he swung from his mount. "We got held up in town longer than we thought and just couldn't make it back before dark. So we spent the night at the hotel." He dropped his reins to the ground, moving with long strides to where she stood. His smile was warm as he reached down to pick her up, and she clung to him, her smile matching his own.

With Tessie held high in his arms, he stepped back to where Emmaline waited, still astride her horse. "Did you know that Emmaline is going to live here from now on?" he asked the child, his mouth next to her ear.

She shook her head. "Nobody told me anything, Maff—Matthew," she complained dourly, and she poked out her lower lip as she considered her sister.

"We wanted to tell you ourselves, Theresa." She smiled at the swift brightening of the little girl's doleful countenance, and cupped the small chin as she bestowed a warm caress on her brow.

"You're never gonna go back to Lexing—that place where you came from?" Tessie asked hopefully. "You're gonna stay here with Maffew...I mean Matthew...and me for always?" Her eyes darted to Olivia, and then she whispered, for Emmaline's ears only, "I keep forgetting."

Emmaline nodded and bent once more to kiss the child. "It's all right. We all forget things, sometimes."

"Not Miss Olivia," Tessie confided. "She reminds me of things all the time."

Emmaline's glance met that of the dark-haired woman watching the tender scene and caught a look of cold derision aimed in her direction. Olivia's lashes fell quickly, covering the evidence of chilling animosity she'd made no attempt to conceal. Emmaline felt a shiver snake its way up her back, and she blinked disbelievingly.

I must have been mistaken. Surely the woman could not feel so hateful. Why would she?

She chanced another look. Olivia's hands were smoothing her skirt, her eyes were still downcast, her face was placid and unreadable. *I was wrong,* Emmaline decided, relief flooding her.

"Emmie, are you gettin' down off that horse pretty soon?" It was a plaintive query, and Emmaline responded with a laugh.

"I certainly am, sweetheart. We have something to tell you." Lifting her right leg, she rose in the saddle, ready to slide to the ground, but Matt was quick to lay a hand on her knee.

"Here, Tessie. Get down for a minute," he said, lowering the child to the ground. Then, with a possessive gesture that caught Emmaline unawares, he held her by the waist and lifted her from her mount, hesitating while she kicked free of the stirrup, and then lowered her to the ground to stand facing him. With one arm possessively about her waist, he turned her to where Maria and Olivia waited.

"Emmaline and I got married in town yesterday," he announced briefly. Theresa tilted her head back and gazed at them with wide eyes. Maria's smile was brilliant, and she nodded as she stepped off the low porch.

"*Sí*, I figured that out when you sent for the bundle of things you bought for her. Tucker said you were at the hotel and looking very pleased with yourself."

Emmaline glared at Matt as he shrugged diffidently. "Things went well, I thought," he allowed, tightening his grip on Emmaline's ribs.

"My congratulations to you, Mr. Gerrity," Olivia said smoothly, smiling politely as she waited near the porch. "And good wishes to you, Mrs. Gerrity," she added, her eyes veiled, once more calm and self-assured.

"Thank you," Emmaline replied, intent on escaping from the confining grip Matt had placed upon her. She bent to embrace Theresa, and Matt's hand slipped from her waist, freeing her reluctantly.

"I've got things to tend to," he said, his eyes already seeking the figures that moved about the barns. Claude lifted a hand in greeting and Matt stepped to take the hanging reins of both horses, his mind already focused on the chores that awaited him.

"I'll try to be in for dinner, Maria," he said over his shoulder as he led the animals behind him, his strides long and purposeful, heading for the men who awaited him.

"I killed chickens this morning," she answered. "We'll have dumplings."

Emmaline's nose wrinkled. "You killed the chickens?" she asked unbelievingly.

"*Sí*." Maria nodded firmly. "Who else would do it? I don't let those men in my hen yard. They are all big hands and loud yells, and they scare my laying hens." She glanced slyly at Emmaline. "Maybe that would be a good job for you. You could feed them and gather up the eggs."

Emmaline shook her head. "I don't think so. I don't know anything about chickens, except that they somehow get from the coop to the table."

"You can't cook?" Maria was disbelieving.

Emmaline shook her head again. "I've never been in the kitchen much," she admitted. "Our cook didn't like anyone in her way, and I didn't expect I'd ever need to know how to, anyway."

Maria inspected her with measuring eyes. "I think you will find it a little different here," she said, gathering her skirts and turning to step up onto the porch. "Everyone has to be able to take care of themselves on a ranch. And that means knowing how to cook."

Emmaline shuddered at the thought of what must surely be involved in the process of killing chickens for dinner. "I think I could get vegetables from the garden and fix them," she offered, willing to be obliging. "But I've always been more interested in working in the barn with the horses than wondering what goes on in the kitchen."

Maria shook her head in wonder. "Ladies don't work in the barns where the men are. Hired hands come and go, and ladies have enough good sense to stay away from them. Mr. Matt would not want you out there."

Emmaline followed her into the house, intent on explaining her position. "I've been out with the men. Well, with Claude, anyway."

Maria turned to her and shook her finger admonishingly. "You are safe with Claude. Perhaps with the others, too, but it is not a good idea. You let Mr. Matthew decide that. You are a pretty woman, and now the lady of the house. You must do what your husband says, you know."

"Oh, you sound like Delilah and my grandmother," Emmaline said scornfully. "I may have married Matt, but that doesn't mean he can tell me what to do," she announced with a trace of scorn.

"Matthew tells us all what to do," Theresa said primly from behind her. "He runs the place, doesn't he, Miss Olivia?"

"Your brother owns the ranch, Theresa. And we don't argue with those in authority." Olivia spoke her piece as though it were well rehearsed.

"Oh, pooh!" Emmaline snorted. "Any woman worth her salt could learn how to take care of the horses."

"Emmaline!" His voice was strident behind her, and when she spun to face the door, Matt towered before her.

His eyes were dark and his face was set in harsh lines as he scowled at her upturned face. "The least of your worries right now is taking care of horses!"

"Whatever are you fussing about?" Her eyes were wide with disbelief as she faced him.

"Fussing? I'm mad as hell, Emmaline!" he snarled. "You didn't have enough sense not to ride alone, did you? And not even enough sense to tell your husband when someone takes potshots at you?"

She inhaled sharply as she remembered. Was it only a day ago? She shook her head disdainfully. "It was just someone out hunting, or maybe target shooting. And how did you find out, anyway?" she asked quickly. "I only told Mr. Hooper in town."

"What happened?" Maria wanted to know. "Who would shoot at Miss Emmaline?"

"Well, apparently our Miss Emmaline didn't think it was worth talking about," Matt said scornfully. "But after she set off for town by herself yesterday, somebody came close to killing her."

"That's not true," Emmaline protested. "And I didn't mean not to tell you. I just had other things on my mind," she mumbled as he leaned closer.

"Well, if Tucker hadn't run into Oswald Hooper in town yesterday afternoon, I still wouldn't know about it, would I?" he asked harshly.

Emmaline's hands clenched at her waist, and her chin tilted defensively. "I don't think he meant to fire at me. He probably didn't even see me."

Matthew Gerrity looked down at his bride in disbelief. "You are the most confounded aggravatin' woman I've seen in a month of Sundays. Don't you ever go out riding alone again. Do you hear me, Emmaline?"

"I could hardly help but hear you, Mr. Gerrity," she answered with flaring fury. One slender finger emerged from the fists she had formed, and poked at his chest. "You are shouting at me, and you have no call to tell me what I can do. I've been riding all my life, and I'm not about to need a nursemaid along at this stage."

His hand swooped down and grasped the prodding finger, enclosing her whole fist in his and holding it immobile. "Don't poke at me, Emmaline," he ordered her firmly. "I'm your husband now, and you'll do well to remember it. I give the orders hereabouts, and I expect them to be obeyed. Can you get that straight?"

Small hands pushed against her skirt, and Emmaline looked down distractedly. Teary eyes met hers, and Theresa shook her head as she spoke.

"Don't fight, Emmie." Tessie's lashes blinked at the evidence of her distress as the child held firmly to the soft leather of Emmaline's riding skirt.

Understanding filled Emmaline's countenance as she took in the child's distress. Then, bending, she pulled her hand from Matt's grasp and lowered it to Theresa's shoulder. She shook her head, forcing a smile to curve her lips for the little girl's benefit.

"We're not fighting," she said quietly, denying the child's words. "Your brother and I are just discussing a situation."

From above her, Matt growled several words beneath his breath, then stooped to hold his small sister within the circle of his arm.

"You shouldn't say those bad words," Theresa said primly, gazing into his eyes with reproof. "Mama used to scold Papa when he said bad things."

His grin was forced but his tone was cajoling as he agreed with her. "I apologize, Tessie. You're right." He glanced to Emmaline, and his mouth tightened. "Your sister and I will discuss this later," he said, his look filled with a promise that needed no words of explanation.

Rising, he smoothed the dark hair from the child's forehead and patted her reassuringly. But his eyes were on Emmaline, and the look of anger he cast in her direction was barely suppressed.

"We'll talk tonight," he promised her, his words quiet, his mouth thinned into a line of disapproval.

They watched in silence as he stalked from the house back to the barn, and then Emmaline heaved a deep sigh and turned to face Maria.

"I suppose you'll tell me again about obeying my husband," she said with resignation.

"No, I think you know yourself what you have to do, Miss Emmaline. I'm just surprised that you said nothing to him about someone shooting at you."

Emmaline's hands waved distractedly, as if she were pooh-poohing the importance of the whole thing. "I wondered for a moment about it, but certainly it was just an accident, Maria. No one would have any reason to shoot at me." Her look scorned the idea as she brushed aside the issue. "Now, what was it Matt said that I didn't catch? It sounded like another language."

"Oh, he always says stuff in Spanish when he gets mad," Theresa said hastily. "I can understand it sometimes, but I don't know what the words mean."

"And you don't need to, either," Olivia put in firmly.

A grin teased at the corners of Emmaline's mouth. "I agree with you, Olivia," she said. "In fact, I'll have a little talk with him about it."

The door closed firmly behind Matt, and he leaned against it, his eyes intent on the woman who sat before the mirrored dressing table across the room.

"Don't start yelling at me again," she warned him, eyeing him warily in the reflecting glass. "I would have told you about what happened if I'd thought it was important. Besides, I didn't even think about it again till today."

He was silent, unmoving but for his eyes. Dark and assessing, they traveled over her seated form, taking note of the robe she wore cinched at the waist, flowing to the floor, where bare toes peeked from beneath the hem. His gaze bored into her, as if he saw beneath the cotton fabric to her flesh, and she felt a pink flush rising to her cheeks as she watched his intent appraisal in the mirror.

Swinging about on the seat, she faced him, her breath taken by the piercing scrutiny he offered her.

"Matt?" It was a whisper of sound, but it brought his eyes to her face, and he read aright the look of uncertainty she wore.

"Are you done with speaking your mind, Emmaline?" His tone was quiet, almost frightening in its intensity. Unmoving, he watched her, and she felt a flutter of apprehension.

"I don't think I know what you mean," she said, her voice a tentative murmur as she placed her hairbrush on the dressing table. Her curls were alive with color in the lamplight, glowing against the white robe she wore, and she brushed distractedly at the locks that fell forward over her shoulder. They curled about her fingers with a life of their own.

His eyes followed the movement of her hand. "You know what I mean," he said, still with the same quiet nuance underlining his words. "If you're finished telling me how unimportant the shooting incident was, I'd like you to listen to me for a minute."

She folded her hands in her lap, her lips pressed together, her eyes rebellious.

He stepped toward her, and his hands lifted for a moment and then fisted and settled on his hips. His feet were spread, and his stance was so like that of a gunfighter ready for a showdown that she felt a chill lift the hair on her arms.

"We have a problem, Emmaline. It was no accident when you got thrown from your horse the other day. Someone stuck a piece of sharp metal under your saddle."

Her face was pale in the glow of the lamplight and her expression was stunned as she absorbed his words. "Are you sure?" she asked in a hushed voice, disbelief obvious on her expressive face.

He nodded and slid his fingers into the pockets of his denim pants. "Yeah, I'm sure," he admitted reluctantly. "Just about as sure as I am that you almost got yourself killed yesterday morning."

She swallowed hard against the lump that formed in her throat. "I was sure it was just someone out hunting...or something," she finished weakly as she considered his words. "Why would anyone want to..." She couldn't bring herself to say the word. *Kill.* "I didn't think..." Her mind rejected the thought, and she shook her head against the idea.

"Did you see him, Emmaline?"

She shook her head again. "No...not really." She closed her eyes, envisioning the moment when she'd heard the sound of gunfire. That single shot, startling her, striking a tree off to her left. Her eyes opened and she studied Matt for a moment.

"Matt, surely if whoever it was wanted to hurt me, he wouldn't have..." She hesitated, thinking again.

"Wouldn't have what, Emmaline?"

"Wouldn't have missed me by so far," she said firmly. "The bullet hit a tree. It didn't come anywhere near me, you know. It had to have been an accident."

"Did you see him?" he asked again.

"No, just a glimpse of a red shirt."

"Was he on a horse?" At her quick nod, he stepped closer. "What color was it?"

"Dark...I think." She shook her head. "I don't know, Matt. I told you, I just caught a glimpse of him. It happened so fast." Her fingers trembled as she brushed at the fine fabric of her robe. She clenched her fist as she recognized the betraying tremor.

His eyes narrowed as he watched the gesture, and the anger he had fought to set aside surged within him once more as he considered how fragile she was. That anyone had lain in wait for her, that anyone could even now be planning to hurt the woman who watched him with such innocent eyes, was beyond comprehension. Why? Who would want to cause her harm? The thought gnawed at him, tightening the muscles of his arms, filling his mind with a helpless fury.

Jerking his hands free from the confines of his pockets, he busied himself with the task of unbuttoning his shirt, his gaze never leaving her face. Impatiently he watched, forcing a slow, precise cadence into his movements.

She stiffened, catching a quick breath as she turned her head away. His mouth twisted wryly. "What's wrong?" he asked, sliding the shirt down his arms and then tossing it to land on a chair beside the bed.

"You're undressing. The lamp is still lit, Matt," she reminded him needlessly.

"I'm getting ready for bed, Emmaline." Loosening his belt, he moved to sit on the edge of the bed. He bent to tug at his boots, pulling them off with a muffled grunt and making short work of his stockings before he rose to his feet again.

"Wait, I'll turn out the lamp," she said quickly, hurrying to the square table that stood next to the bed. Carefully she kept her head averted from him, reaching for the small metal handle to turn down the wick. She concentrated on the flame, narrowing her eyes against its brilliance as she lowered the oil-soaked cotton wick, breathing a sigh as the light flared briefly and then died.

She heard the rustle of his clothing on the other side of the bed, then the whisper of the bedclothes as he lowered himself to the soft comfort of the feather tick. Her hands loosened the tie of her robe, and she slid it from her shoulders, allowing it to fall to the floor, where it lay in a pale half circle about her feet.

"Get in bed, Emmaline." His voice was low and harsh against her ears, and she shivered.

"Are you angry with me?"

He sat up abruptly. "Hell, no, I'm not mad."

She backed away, just a step, until the reflection of the moonlight, falling in a path from the open window, illuminated his face. It was drawn into harsh lines, his eyes hidden in the darkness beneath lowered brows, his mouth unsmiling and grim. But the hand reaching toward her was open and inviting.

"Come to bed, Emmie. Now."

"Yes." It was a drawn-out syllable—a breath of relief—and she accepted his hand, clasping his fingers with her own. She took the short step to where he waited. He lifted the sheet and she slid beneath the white muslin, her head cushioned in the depths of the goosedown pillow.

"It's all right, Emmaline," he said carefully. "I'm not angry with you. I was upset for a while, but I'm over it."

He raised on one elbow to rise over her, and she turned her head to seek his gaze...that penetrating, narrowed gaze that shattered her composure so easily. Trembling at the fierce tension that flared to life between them, she breathed through parted lips, her senses filled to overflowing with the power of his presence...the musky, male scent that teased her nostrils, the familiar appraisal of his eyes as he watched her with barely concealed hunger.

She breathed deeply once more, freeing herself from the captivity of his gaze. Her eyes scanned the harsh planes of his countenance. Dark hair fell across his wide forehead, coaxing her fingers to explore, and she clenched them tightly, lest she yield to yet another temptation. His jaw was rigid, his mouth tight and unsmiling, as he allowed her this surveillance of his features. Intently she measured him, as if she sought reassurance from the familiarity of his face.

Her sigh whispered between them as she yielded to the temptation he offered, and her hand lifted in an involuntary movement to press gentle fingers against his furrowed brow.

"Are you going to kiss me good-night?"

He shook his head slowly and carefully. "No, not yet, Emmaline."

Her eyes widened as he lowered his head, and then her lashes fell to blot from her vision the hunger that painted his harsh features.

"I'll kiss you good-night later," he promised, in a rasping whisper, which brushed against her ear.

But, untamed as his ragged breathing was, his mouth was gentle, his need restrained, and the touch of his hands careful against her flesh. He drew her tenderly into the realm of pleasure they had explored in the hours at the hotel. Now, with desire that had been fed throughout the day while he waited impatiently for the sun to set, he coaxed her with gentle, tender caresses.

She followed where he led, her body supple beneath him, her movements untutored and so even more of a delight than she could know as he drew her into new depths of passion. He whispered dark, delicious promises against her flesh, and she shuddered as he fulfilled each vow, bringing her to a shattering awareness of his power over her slender body.

Yet still she clung to him, even after the tremors had subsided to faint shivers that caused him to press damp kisses against her throat and across the narrow width of her shoulders. His face was shadowed, hidden against her breasts, and she threaded her fingers through his hair, thankful for the darkness that cloaked her.

For surely he would know...if he was to see her face, he would recognize the emotion she struggled with. The sure and certain knowledge that the man who had claimed her body had taken possession of more than the flesh and bone that was Emmaline Carruthers. For she had given more than her body in this act of marriage. As surely as he had received her virginity the night before, tonight he had been gifted with her love.

In the darkness, the soft, triumphant sound of his laughter vibrated with sensual pleasure against her throat.

"Now I'll kiss you good-night, Emmie." The words were whispered against her skin. He shifted against her until she felt the heat of his breathing against the rise of her breast.

"There?" she managed to gasp as his tongue feathered across the tender flesh.

"Well..." he drawled in a husky, muffled whisper, "I'll start here." His mouth suckled for a moment, drawing a startled cry from her. He laughed again, pleased by her response. "Of course, it may take a while, Emmie," he said, his lips teasing her once more. "I'm sure I'll get to your mouth in just a little while."

She moved beneath him, her legs twining about his as she closed her eyes, the better to savor the tingling sensations he brought to life deep within her. His limbs were heavy against hers, but she welcomed the weight of his body as it pressed her into the mattress. Then she lifted her hands to hold him, yielding to his strength.

It was dark beneath the tree, where heavy branches shielded her from the moonlight. Watching as the stealthy figure approached, she pressed against the rough bark behind her, and her hands clenched into tight, angry fists. Her mouth twisted as she considered him, and the words that greeted him told of her frustration.

"You missed." Her accusation was a taunting whisper in the night air.

He reached for her and then, thinking better of it, leaned one hand against the tree whose shelter they shared. "I didn't miss," he said, denying her claim. "I aimed ahead of her horse. I meant to scare her out."

Her laughter was scornful, a bitter sound in the darkness. "She thought you were a hunter."

"How do you know what she thought?" he mumbled, aware that this night would gain him no prize from the woman who stood before him.

"She told the lawyer in town, and everyone on the Carruthers ranch knows that she brushed off the whole thing. Some gunman you turned out to be!" The woman huffed in disgust, turning her back on him. "I may have to find someone else to handle this."

"No." It was a harsh denial of her threat. "I said no. Did you hear me?"

"I heard." A tinge of boredom touched her reply.

"I'll take care of it," he vowed. "I told you I'd get rid of her. I was just gonna do it the easy way, scare her back east where she belongs."

"She's still here," she said, walking away.

"Wait." His call was hushed in the still air of the night, but she sauntered on, her slim figure dark against the paler shadows of moonlight.

His mouth drew down, and beneath his breath, his words of frustration promised a quick end to the issue.

Chapter Eleven

Matt was at the breakfast table. With his arrogance firmly in place, he watched Emmaline enter, and she refused the demand of his gaze. Her eyes lowered, she slipped into the chair awaiting her and unfolded the napkin that lay close at hand. Deliberately she edged her fingers against the silverware set precisely on either side of the flower-bedecked china. With great care, she moved the knife a fraction of an inch, the fork even less. And then, with defiant daring, she raised her head and lifted her eyes to the man at the head of the table.

And damned her daring. He was laughing at her! Beneath the cool exterior of his calm facade, he was enjoying her discomposure. Within the depths of his dark eyes, lingering traces of passion glimmered and unholy amusement glittered as he watched her attempt to gain back her hard-won semblance of dignity.

"We'd about given up on you, Emmaline," he drawled. He lifted one eyebrow, his gaze moving over her person in a caressing fashion. "Tessie was wondering if you were going to sleep all day, but I assured her that you'd be up before noon, at least." He smiled at his young sister and then, with a nod of his head, continued. "I told Tessie that you'd be spending some time with her today, if that's all right."

Emmaline looked at him, her mouth pursed, her hands clutching the edge of the table. "Will you be planning all my days, Matthew, or is this an exception?"

He bowed his head for just a second, then lifted it to meet the aggravation flaring in her eyes. "Until we decide just where the threat is coming from, I want you to stay in or close to the house. Today seemed like a good time for you and Tessie to set up a regular routine. Now that you're in charge of the running of this household, you'll probably have changes to make."

She shook her head, then looked up at Maria, who hovered in the doorway. "I think the house has been in good hands. I'm willing to go along with things as they are for a while."

Serving platter in hand, Maria approached the table. With deft touches, she filled the plates, spooning out heaping mounds of fluffy eggs, then garnishing each serving with thinly sliced ham. Beside Emmaline's chair, she paused, her hesitation a tribute to the young woman.

"You are the new mistress of this house," she said firmly. "We will spend many years here together, Miss Emmaline, and today will be the beginning." She emptied her platter and stepped back, her ever-observant eyes checking every detail. "I think you all need some more coffee. And some milk for Theresa."

Emmaline shifted in her chair and picked up her fork. She sought the smiling face of her sister. "May I sit in on your lessons this morning?"

"That sounds like a good idea," said Olivia, slipping with decorum into the dining room and finding her seat at the table. "Please pardon my lateness," she added apologetically. "I lingered later than I had planned at my early-morning reading."

"Then plan on me joining you," Emmaline said, with a tender smile for her little sister.

At Tessie's delighted and exuberant nod, she relaxed. She tasted the steaming eggs, eyes half-closed, savoring the faintly spiced flavor. Then, reluctantly but with determination, she looked at Matt, her face serene, her uncertainty subdued.

Beneath the amusement that still lit his eyes was a renewed glimpse of the passion he had bestowed on her in such lavish detail throughout the night. She shivered with a barely discernible tremor. The daring of the man, she thought, lowering her eyes once more to her plate, her tongue tracing the edge of her lip. He looks like a barn cat stalking a poor little field mouse, she decided, unaware of the rosy hue that tinted her cheekbones.

At the end of the table, the object of her thoughts was more than aware of the flux of emotions his scrutiny had set flowing within his bride. *She looks like a paragon of housewifely virtue,* he thought with delight. And of all the occupants of this room, he was the only one who knew that her slight tremor had signified her awareness of him. The flush painting her cheeks with delicate color gave away the memories running rampant in her mind, even as she solemnly chewed on the bite of ham she had delivered to those pink, full lips with total equanimity.

He bent to his plate and made quick progress, his gaze never far from the figure of Emmaline, speaking only in short replies to the questions that Theresa aimed in his direction. Could she go riding this afternoon? Would he like to see her drawings from yesterday? Did he think the new puppies were ready to sell yet? To all her queries he gave succinct answers, and Tessie smiled and pouted in quick sequence.

"Why can't I go riding, Matthew?" she asked, with only barely subdued arrogance. "Tucker says I'm pret' near as good a rider as Miss Olivia."

His chin lifted as he considered her rebellious stance. Quietly he turned her words about and delivered them with deliberation. "Tucker says you are almost as good in the saddle as your teacher, but you need a lot of practice in handling the reins, Tessie. You're just a little girl, and bragging about your accomplishments isn't polite."

"Then maybe I really need some more practice," she said quickly, brushing aside the intended chastisement of his words and smiling brightly in his direction.

"I could work with her this afternoon," Emmaline volunteered, her mouth quirking with amusement as she watched Tessie wheedle her way past the refusal her brother had issued.

"I won't be around this afternoon. I have to go out with a couple of the men to check the herd of cattle we're sending to the stockyard in Yuma. Maybe tomorrow," he said, his look slanting toward Emmaline in warning.

Her chin lifted, and her eyes defied the unspoken refusal he'd issued. "We'll see," she said demurely, her words sweetly spoken and her smile turned with sisterly approval on Theresa.

"Emmaline, walk me out to the porch!" It was a direct command, and he issued it with barely concealed anger.

"Certainly," she said, folding her napkin carefully and placing it beside her plate before she rose and left the table.

He strode ahead of her into the hallway and then turned abruptly to face her. She faltered at his sudden movement and was caught off guard when he reached for her. Dragging her by one hand, he headed for the door at the end of the short corridor and spun her to wedge her against the hard wooden surface. She was breathless, wide-eyed and aghast at his behavior. Her mouth opened to protest his high-handedness and her eyes glittered with disapproval, but he gave her no room in which to vent her displeasure.

With practiced aim, he covered her mouth with his own. His hands were hard and ungentle as he grasped her shoulders and, with a strength she marveled at, lifted her against his rigid body. Not until he had her quiet, subdued and malleable against his hard form did he relent. And then only in the degree of pressure he had used against her soft curves and within the depths of her mouth.

She was plastered against his length, breathless and totally at his mercy, and she searched her heart for the anger she was certain was her just due. To her dismay, the urge to press herself even closer to his hard body was overcoming the need to protest his actions. Her eyes were closed, but beneath her lids she saw a display of color, splintering across her vision and magnified with each touch of his mouth against hers, each brush of his tongue and each movement of his lips.

Her hands were clenched against his chest, and she felt each bone as a separate entity as she splayed them against the firm width of him, edging toward the handhold of his shoulders. But it was only his slight unbending that allowed that process to be complete and, with a sigh that quivered in her breast, she reached her goal, her hands gripping him with a strength that pleased him, her fingers clutching for purchase against the rough cotton of his shirt.

He lifted his head, and his eyes were dark, penetrating and perceptive. He saw the quivering of her mouth, the flaring of her nostrils as she breathed in his scent and the flutter of her lashes as she lifted them reluctantly. That this woman, this bundle of feminine wiles and softly rounded curves, was his to possess was almost more than he could accept as his due. But the fact was, she was well on her way to hauling him in and putting the bit in his mouth, he realized darkly, and the thought tightened his grip as he flexed his hands at the back of her waist. She had beguiled him throughout the night hours and aggravated him almost beyond the boundaries his temper would bear this morning. Now she lay against him in surrender, and he was seized by the urge to carry her to the bedroom he had left just an hour ago and spend his frustration upon her fragile form.

She blinked once more and looked at him in confusion. His hands were hard against her back, his long length was ungiving against her breasts and belly, and he glared at her with eyes that sparked fire.

"Look, Emmaline," he said, in an undertone that did not lack force. "I can't be doin' my work if I'm worrying about you. I need you to promise that you'll stay inside or with Claude all day. Don't be meandering about, gettin' into trouble, you hear?"

Her chin tilted even more, and she felt the strain in the back of her neck as she fought to meet his gaze with equal force. "I don't intend to 'get into trouble' today," she said emphatically, albeit softly, aware that their voices would carry to the dining room. "I intend to spend the day with Theresa and Maria and perhaps work in the corral with Claude and my sister this afternoon. If that meets with your approval," she added with proud finality.

He stepped back from her, and his grin was cocky once more. Deliberately he lifted his hat from the rack on one side of the hall and placed it squarely on his head, crushing the dark hair beneath its brim. His nod was polite, but his eyes were alight with the same amused glow that had met her earlier, as he lifted her to one side before he opened the door.

"That's exactly what I wanted to hear you say," he told her cheerfully as he strode past. And then, as he bypassed the steps and jumped to the ground, he laughed. It was a full, hearty sound that brushed her ears and drew her lips into a thin line.

Not for the world would she reveal her chagrin. Not for a moment would she allow him this victory. And so she forced the light note into her voice that would get his attention and stepped out onto the porch as she sang out the words that would halt him in his tracks.

"But I'll be spending most of the day planning our party, Matthew," she warbled.

His back stiffened and he skidded to a stop, midway across the small grassy expanse that made up the backyard. He turned, and his expression stunned her.

"Good," he said, his smile triumphant. "That oughta keep you busy for a couple of days."

"Oooh!" She drew out the sound, hiding her dismay. Where was the anger she had anticipated, the irritation she had been certain he would not be able to contain?

"Yep...best idea you've had all day, Emmaline," he said cheerfully, tipping his hat to her and setting off once more to the barn.

She stamped her foot and looked about quickly, lest she be caught in such a childish display. Her eyes narrowed as she glared at his retreating back, and she thrust her hands into the deep pockets of her dress. And yet she could not erase the faint warmth lingering within her as she turned to the door and entered the house.

It seemed a party would include the whole of the countryside, Emmaline finally realized. Maria had taken up the banner with little urging and was busily planning a menu that sounded more appropriate for a jamboree than for a wedding reception.

There would have to be a compromise of sorts, Emmaline decided firmly. Something between a barbecue and a dinner party, with the barbecue being the choice of Matthew, of course. Glumly she realized that her thoughts of a rather formal introduction to the neighboring ranchers and the townspeople would be going by the boards. More likely was Maria's suggestion, complete with a whole steer turning on a spit over an open pit. Somehow the thought was gaining a bit more of her approval as she dwelled on the idea of having the party outside, keeping the community outdoors, beneath the scattering of trees that bounded the area between the house and the barns.

Maria sighed with satisfaction. "I think we've listed everything we'll need from town," she said. Passing her list across the table for Emmaline's approval, she narrowed her eyes as she concentrated. "We'll need to decide on tables and benches, too."

Emmaline glanced up from the paper she'd scanned, still wondering at the enormous amounts of food Maria deemed necessary. "We need tables? Can't they all sit under the trees and eat?" she asked, considering the task of locating seats for so many guests.

Maria chuckled and shook her head. "The young ones will be happy to sit on the ground, but the men will sit about the tables and argue and tell stories for hours."

"What about the women?" Emmaline wanted to know.

Maria shrugged. "They will serve their men and have their own place to sit and eat."

"How will we locate so many tables and benches?" Emmaline looked at the list she held. The planning was assuming immense proportions.

"Our men will make them, out in the barn. They have a stack of wood, ready to use for new stalls or putting up partitions. They just use it for tables this time, and then for something else later."

Such temporary measures were foreign to Emmaline. Used to fine china and formal dining, she was finding it difficult to form a picture in her mind of the party to come.

Serving the menfolk was not her pleasure, but she supposed that for Matt's sake she could be a docile wife for one day. She laughed as she thought of herself acting that part, but then sobered as she realized that already she was fitting into the mold he expected her to fill.

"I'll leave it up to you, Maria." She rose and gripped her list firmly. "I'll have to write out the invitations and have them delivered."

"One of the men can take them to town, next time we send someone in for supplies," Maria said. "The rest can be given to the neighbors as we see them. Someone is always stopping by."

Such a haphazard way of doing things was beyond her, Emmaline decided forlornly as she went down the hallway to Matthew's office. There she pulled his large armchair from behind the desk and plopped into it, feeling small against the high-backed piece of furniture. Made to fit her father's big frame, it dwarfed her, and she snuggled into its soft leather depths as she sensed another facet in the circle of her life here.

He'd sat here, the man who had fathered her and loved her for two short years. Dimly she remembered being in this room as a child, a baby, really, not old enough to climb into this chair by herself. She recalled looking over the wide expanse of the desk, held firmly in the arms of the man who cuddled her here. There, in the doorway, she remembered her mother, slim, fair and unsmiling. Always unhappy, always speaking in a fretful voice, which, even now, was imprinted on her memory.

She closed her eyes against the vision, but it returned still more clearly. Amazed, she recalled the deep, harsh sounds of her father's words. Not the meaning, just the tones that had sent her flying to her mother's arms for comfort as he argued against the peevish words that beat against her ears.

It had been the day they left, she realized. He'd been holding her and hugging her to himself, and then her mother had come for her, had commanded her to leave his arms, and she'd done so, ever the obedient child. Only with her father had she been laughing and mischievous. Early on, she had learned that in her mother's presence she must behave, must be quiet and subdued.

She frowned and her eyes opened at the memory. Even in her growing-up years, she'd learned to withhold her laughter, relaxing only in the barns, where she was accepted by the men who dealt with the horses and who welcomed her with gentle courtesy.

And now, here with Matthew, she'd once more felt able to break the mold, that tightly restricted life that had labeled her a lady, had kept her dignity inviolate and preserved her to this point. She'd been a girl on the verge of womanhood, needing only the impetus of Matthew's touch to propel her into his arms and the knowledge that she was where she belonged, finally.

It's come full circle, she thought. My earliest memories are here, in this room. And now I've returned. To the man my father chose for me. The rebellion she'd harbored over that choice—or the lack of it—had somehow become subdued, almost forgotten, in the days past. Unconsciously she'd begun to accept her father's will as just that...his will for her life, his inheritance to her.

"He really cared about me," she whispered in the quiet of the room. "He wanted me to be here, and this was the only way he could be sure I'd be able to stay." The thought warmed her, and she hugged herself as she relaxed into the chair, pulling her feet up to curl beneath her bottom.

It was there that Matt found her, her head tipped against the leather upholstery, her hands lying loosely folded in her lap, her eyes shut and her mouth soft as she breathed slowly, relaxed in sleep.

He stood in the doorway and gazed his fill, aware of the rare treat he was offered. Bristly more often than not, well armed against his every suggestion, she pitted her soft feminine strength against him with fierce splendor. He reveled in every battle, every word spoken, every thrust of her barbed tongue. He had let her have her way while it pleased him, and then reeled her in for his pleasure, delighting in her sputtering and feasting on her sparkling wit and flashing temper.

Now she was quiet, asleep in the shadowed room, unaware she had taken the prescribed siesta that she had opposed as unnecessary. Other days since her arrival, she had retreated to her room during these silent afternoon hours when the whole house shut down for a peaceful repose, but he was sure she had written letters or read one of her innumerable books while everyone else settled back for an hour of quiet rest.

His smile widened as he approached her and, bending, he lifted her into his arms, soothing her murmured protests as he gathered her close and retreated to the deep cushions of the leather couch beneath the window. There he laid her gently on her side, snug against the high back. Quickly he pulled off his boots and lay down beside her, molding her slender form close to his own muscular body.

She smiled, as if she were caught up in a particularly pleasant dream, and snuggled against him, seeking the warmth that radiated through the layers of clothing that separated them. Her murmurs were soft against his throat as she tilted her head up to nuzzle his flesh, and he shivered at the sensations she evoked.

It was enough, this tenderness she gave him. Although his body readied itself for more, he suppressed the reflexes that urged him to press her against the evidence of his need. For now, he would hold her, bask in the gentle movement of her mouth against the weathered flesh of his neck, enjoy the pressure of her breasts against his chest and sate himself with her fragrance. His eyes flickered shut as he held her with a possessive yearning, his arms about her, his hands curved to hold her close, one about her rounded bottom, the other across her back. Gently he slid one leg between hers and felt the clasp of her thighs as she tightened them about his knee. A low growl passed his lips before he could stop it, and he shuddered again as he restrained the urges that prodded him.

If she heard the sounds of the household about them as the afternoon passed, Emmaline gave no sign. She lay asleep in his arms for over an hour. All the while he held her, his own thoughts were too rampant to allow him to sleep.

When she awoke, her eyelids fluttered, once, twice, and then in a rapid succession against his throat that brought a deep chuckle from within his chest.

"Matt?" It was a bewildered little sound, and he chuckled again, unable to resist.

"Matthew Gerrity! What are you doing?" she sputtered against his shirt, shifting and wiggling against him. "This is broad daylight, and you're lying down with me right here where anyone can see us!"

"I closed the door, Em," he drawled softly, unwilling to release her from his hold, yet aware that this time of quiet had come to an end.

"I don't care," she said vehemently, lifting herself from his embrace and smoothing her dress with one hand as she struggled to escape. "Get off me," she said through gritted teeth, and she pushed at him.

He raised his brow and grinned up at her. She was clamped between his big body and the back of the sofa. "Now, Emmaline, if I was on top of you, you'd have somethin' to holler about. I'm just layin' here, takin' a siesta with you."

She pushed at him again and gained a few inches of space. Gathering herself together, she reached for him. Then, catching a handhold on his leather belt, she pulled herself over and atop him and slid to the floor. Before he could turn over, she had scrambled to her feet and was running her fingers through her hair, attempting to comb it into some semblance of order. She tugged at her dress, pulling it about her waist and brushing distractedly at the wrinkled skirt.

"Just look at me," she muttered. "I'm a mess!"

"I am looking." He stretched to his full length on the leather sofa, his hands folded against the breadth of his chest as he watched her flustered movements. "I think you look just fine, Emmaline. A little wrinkled around the edges, but then, if I'd taken your dress off before I laid you down, you probably would have woke up."

"Taken my dress off! Not likely!" she said tartly. Her frown deepened. "My other dresses are both in the wash, Matt. I'll have to go to dinner looking like this."

"You can make do for today, honey," he said soothingly. "You'll be all decked out before long. You'll be getting some baggage from Lexington before you know it."

She stilled her motions and looked at him askance.
"What on earth do you mean?" she asked slowly, narrowing her eyes on him.

He lifted his hands and then replaced them against his
chest before he answered, chagrined at his disclosure. "I
mean that I sent a telegram to your grandparents and asked
them to send your things here."

"I don't believe you," she whispered.

"Better believe it, Em," he said cheerfully. "I sent the
wire when I went into town and got your dress and things
and talked to the preacher. The stuff should be here in a
couple of days or so, depending on how fast they get it
packed up."

"What did you tell them? What did you say in the wire?"
she asked quietly, her face pale in the subdued light.

"Told them we were going to get married and you would
be needing your things since you weren't goin' back east.

"I don't believe you!" She was vehement in her doubt.
"You wouldn't just tell them that way."

"Oh, but I did," he said, disagreeing with her judgment
of him. "Didn't know any other way to say it, so I just said,
'We're getting married. Send her things.' Or something like
that," he amended.

"Didn't you think I'd want to tell them myself?" she
asked with deceptive calmness.

He grinned at her, pleased with her. Doggone, she wasn't
even angry, he thought. Here he'd taken the whole thing
out of her hands, planning the wedding and announcing it
to her family. And then the honeymoon, such as it was.
She'd been a good sport about it, he decided. *She even
spent the night in my bed without squawkin'*, he mused, his
grin widening.

He should have been warned. He should have recognized the fury that smoldered within the depths of her eyes.
She'd agreed to most everything he said...till now. Too
late, he realized he'd pushed her beyond her limits.

"Damn you, Matthew Gerrity!" The words exploded from her lips with the fury of a keg of dynamite being set off. "Who do you think you are, pushing me around this way? You must think I'm some sort of a ninny, that you can run me around in circles!"

He lifted himself from the couch, soon realizing the full extent of his folly. But it was too late. She had turned to the desk, desperate for a weapon, and had hurled the first thing her hands fell upon.

The heavy crystal inkwell hit him midchest, and the ink spewed forth with a vengeance, splattering his shirt generously, missing his eyes by the barest fraction of an inch and freckling his face with tiny spatters that stood out against his tan, like spots on a blue tick hound. With a thud, the heavy missile hit the floor, where it lay draining its last against the flowered carpet.

Emmaline gasped, pale with dismay, as she viewed the results of her temper. Then, as if unable to face his wrath, she turned and fled the room, tugging for a moment at the doorknob before she managed to turn it and open the heavy door. Her steps were hurried, just short of a run, as she traveled the corridor to the big room at the corner of the house. Once within its shelter, she leaned against the door, panting, her chest heaving as she filled her lungs over and over again.

It was several long minutes before she heard him coming and she stepped aside, aware that her strength would be futile against his when he opened the door.

Strangely, he knocked, and she suppressed a gasp as she leaned closer to speak through the barrier.

"What do you want?" she asked, her voice trembling, much to her distress.

"I want to come in, Emmaline," he answered with infinite patience.

She caught her breath, her head swimming at the relief she felt. He didn't sound angry. He didn't even sound upset. Her hand rose to grasp the doorknob, and she opened it slowly, stepping back as his tall form stepped over the threshold.

He was naked from the waist up, his chest bare but for the wide thatch of dark hair that curled there. And splashed over that whole area was the evidence of her fit of temper, the dark stain of ink that had penetrated the thick mat of curls and coated his skin. Below and above the hair, he wore small droplets of ink, which were scattered in profusion—even on the muscles that flexed in his arms. But it was the pinpoint specks on his face that drew her eyes, and she found herself backing away as he approached, one hand lifting to cover her mouth as she viewed the full extent of her deed.

He was silent, one foot prodding the door closed. He watched her as he moved closer, intent on the stunned expression she wore.

She'd gone as far as she could go—her legs were pressed against the bed—and still he watched. "Matt..." The single word was not much more than a whisper, muffled in her hand.

"Yes, Emmaline."

"Would you believe me if I told you that I'm sorry?"

He shook his head. "I don't think so."

"Why not?" she asked, with as much dignity as she could muster.

"Probably because I can tell you're having a hard time not laughing right now," he said matter-of-factly.

She shook her head vigorously. "No, I'm not," she vowed, finally daring to take her hand away from the mouth that yearned to widen in a grin. "Well, I might laugh, if I weren't afraid that you'd really be mad," she admitted after a moment. She leaned forward, looking at him searchingly. "You don't look angry, Matt," she said finally, relief apparent on her expressive face.

His shrug was an answer in itself. He approached her slowly. "I'm not sure I can be mad at you, Emmaline. You had a right to pitch a fit. I've run roughshod over you for a couple of days now, and I guess I shouldn't be surprised that you finally got your back up."

"You're really not angry?" she repeated hopefully.

He shook his head. "Nope." The trace of a grin tilted the corners of his mouth. "It was almost worth it just to see the look on Maria's face when she saw my shirt. She had it snatched off me quick as a wink, and I left her scrubbin' away at it in the kitchen. Hated to tell her she might as well throw the dang shirt out and work on the carpet instead.''

"You don't think it'll wash out?" she asked anxiously, peering at his face.

He shook his head. "You owe me, Emmaline."

"I do?" she squeaked, then cleared her throat.

He nodded solemnly. "Yeah. I reckon this is about the worst thing you've done to me."

"It is?" Dolefully she considered his face once more. Her eyes narrowed. "What else have I done to you?" she asked suddenly, aware of his accusation.

"I don't think you want me to name everything, Em." He reached for her with a quick movement she was too slow to evade. "Let's just say you're about to make payment."

"Oh…" The word was a surprised whisper as he drew her into the circle of his arms and bent to nuzzle at her throat.

"Will this pay the debt?" she asked, gripping his shoulders and leaning into his long frame.

"Nope," he stated firmly. "It'll take a long time to pay me off, Em. Years and years and years…"

Chapter Twelve

"What do you think, Emmaline?" Matt whispered the words in her ear just as she felt the warmth of his arms enclose her, and she was thankful for the shadowed corner shielding them. His hands slid about her waist and met, clasping her close against the hard length of his body.

"I think I've never seen such a big cow in my life," she said as she watched the enormous spit revolve over the open firepit. She leaned back against him, nestling her head beneath his chin.

"It's not a cow, Emmaline. It's a steer," he explained patiently, suppressing the chuckle he knew would rile her.

She waved her hand in an imperious gesture. "They're all cows, as far as I can see, Matt. I just hope there's enough there to feed all these people."

He bent his head to drop a kiss against the nape of her neck, nudging her head forward to give himself access. She'd done her hair up in a twisty sort of sunburst on top, and he'd watched as she poked the final pin in place. Now, appreciating the vulnerable curve of her neck and tasting the sweet scent of her skin, he decided that being married had some definite benefits.

"Can I take out these pins after a while, Emmie?" His breath was warm against her ear.

She shivered at the intimacy and released a low, unsteady laugh. "Stop, Matt," she whispered, tugging at his hands where they pressed firmly against her midriff. "Everyone will be watching us."

He glanced about, his mind still intent on the woman whose warmth was nestled against his own needy flesh. *Needy*... the one word that summed up his condition these days.

"It's a good thing our company can't get a good look at me right now, Em," he murmured beneath his breath. "It's probably a good thing they're more interested in givin' my bride the once-over."

She breathed deeply and pried away his fingers. He chuckled at her attempt and tightened his hold, his hands clasping her waist. "Matthew Gerrity! Just quit that!" she said tightly, attempting at the same time to nod a greeting to the Reverend Josiah Tanner, who was approaching with his wife.

"That's all right, they know we're newlyweds," he answered in a teasing undertone, unwilling to give up his advantage. "This is our party, Emmaline. These people expect us to cuddle a little bit."

Her groan was almost inaudible, swallowed as it was by the greeting she spoke to the parson.

"We're so pleased you could come," she said politely, too aware of the long, lean form of Matt Gerrity plastered against her back.

"It's a fine party, ma'am. Accept our best wishes, won't you?" He leaned a bit closer and lowered his voice. "I'm just pleased to have been in on the beginning of this marriage. I'll admit I had my doubts, what with all the to-do in town that day, but I'm certain that your daddy would be most pleased to see you back home, Miss Emmaline."

"This is where she belongs, all right," Matt put in firmly. "Why don't you folks grab yourselves a plate and try some of that beef we've been cookin' all day?" He nodded at the open pit that yawned near the barn. Glowing embers sent heat radiating in visible waves to the turning spit above, the barbecued beef emitting a savory scent that enticed the hungry crowd.

"Don't mind if we do," Josiah Tanner answered, ushering his wife to join the group.

"Are you hungry, too, Emmaline?" Matt's whisper was soft against her ear. "We could get a couple of plates and park under that big tree over there and watch the folks havin' a good time."

"Later," she said, relaxing for just a moment against him. "Listen, the violins and piano are tuning up."

"Fiddles, Emmaline. They're fiddles." He squeezed her a bit, shaking his head as he corrected her. "They're gettin' ready to play for dancin'. Before you know it, that floor will be full of foot-stompin' ranch hands."

"Matt, I want you to—" Emmaline's good intentions flew to the four winds as she narrowed her eyes in dismay.

"I didn't know you'd invited your old sweetheart," she snapped coldly, nodding at the man and woman who were walking across the wide expanse of the yard.

Matt's arms were firm about her, and she tried in vain to ease away from him unobtrusively, but to no avail.

"Let go of me." She gritted the words out between her teeth, determined to dislodge the embrace she thought smacked too much of ownership.

Stepping to her side, his long arm still around her, he tugged her into place against his hip. "Don't fuss, Emmaline. Just look like a happy bride and greet your guests."

The wooden smile she forced into place masked the whispered words she hissed in his direction as she looked up at him with a semblance of coyness. "Did you have to invite her?"

"She's a neighbor." His eyes met hers in a narrowed warning. "Now be polite."

"Is this my polite look?" she asked, her jaw clenched, her eyelashes fluttering in his direction.

"Behave, Emmaline, or I'm gonna get downright aggravated!"

"Threats, Matthew Gerrity?" she asked sweetly, her voice a mere whisper against his cheek as she stood on tiptoe to deliver her query.

He closed his eyes for a moment, and his hand clenched tighter against her waist. "Just you wait till I get you alone."

"Why, look who's here! The bride and groom, all cuddled up in the corner." Clyde Hopkins stepped before them, hat in hand, Deborah on his arm. Jovial and red-faced, he swept them a bow and then placed his broad-brimmed hat back in place, his chill gaze belying the warmth of his greeting.

"Afraid he'll get away?" Deborah asked brightly, tossing her head in Emmaline's direction. With a practiced flicker of her lashes and a pouting gesture of pleading, she lifted one hand to Matt's cheek, running her fingertips down the hard line of his jaw.

"Surely you can let him loose long enough to have a dance with an old friend," she said sweetly, her eyes flashing a sidelong glance toward Emmaline's frozen countenance.

"I'm sure Matthew isn't glued to me, are you, dear?" Somehow the words emerged with just a touch of mockery, and somehow Emmaline managed to widen her smile as she met his eyes. They were crinkled at the corners, and his amusement was apparent.

"The music hasn't started yet, Deborah. They're just gettin' tuned up," Matt pointed out dryly, his hand snaking up to clasp her wrist and drag the offending fingers away from his face, even as his attention clung unwaveringly to his bride.

"Well, you shouldn't be hiding your bride here in the corner." Deborah was clearly irate about the attention he denied her. "Let her go meet her neighbors, Matthew. We can get the dancing started."

Reluctantly his eyes left Emmaline's face, and the warmth that had kindled his gaze disappeared, leaving a dispassionate chill in its place. "Doggone if I haven't promised the first dance to my bride," Matt drawled with deliberation. "Sorry I can't accommodate you, Deb. I'm sure you'll have plenty of ranch hands flockin' around when the music starts."

Emmaline watched silently from within the circle of Matt's arm as Deborah gave him a last glance. Then, as if conceding a temporary defeat, the young woman tossed her head and walked away to join a group just within the barn.

"You could have danced with her, you know," Emmaline said softly. Matt looked down at her with a trace of skepticism. "Could I, now?" he asked. At her nod, he laughed aloud. "I' tell the truth, Em, I'd rather do the askin'." He bent his head in a gentlemanly gesture and released his hold on her waist, stepping before her to offer his hand.

"Is this a waltz?" she asked in an undertone. "It seems awfully fast, but the tempo is right."

Matt grinned, swinging her about, his hands at her waist as he kept time with his toe to the beat of the music. "I don't know what you call it, honey. We just dance to it," he said, sweeping her out onto the wooden floor. "You'll do fine, Em," he murmured against her ear, bending to plant a damp kiss on the tender skin at her temple. Sawdust, scattered across the wide boards, made the floor slippery beneath them, and he held her close as he caught the rhythm.

His feet moved rapidly, and she sensed the timing of his steps, joining him in the quick rotation as he danced the traditional box step of the waltz. Within seconds her skirts flew about her legs as they set a fast pace about the floor, their dancing accompanied by the clapping cadence of the watching neighbors and townsfolk, more of whom swarmed into the barn, encouraging the newlyweds as they made their way the length of the barn.

Down to the end of the long aisle, past the empty, whitewashed box stalls, to where the musicians played in double time, they danced, Emmaline's cheeks flushed and her eyes sparkling as she kept up with his twisting and twirling steps. About them, couples joined in and the barn rang with laughter and the sound of hard boots and sliding slippers across the slippery floor.

He swept her closer, and her hands crept from their position on his shoulders to twine about his neck as she melded her slender form against his firmness. And for the space of several magical moments, they were caught up in the music, the intimacy of the dance, the careless, carefree pleasure afforded them.

"I feel like a real bride," she managed to say, her voice little more than a whisper. She was breathless, her eyes sparkling, as they swung once more past the doors.

"Dancing does that?" One eyebrow lifted as he grinned into her rosy countenance. "Here I thought I'd been making you feel like a bride for a couple of weeks already."

She scowled at him, but the pretense was too difficult to maintain. Her pleasure in the music, the friendly faces that watched them and the man who held her would not allow the sham of indignation.

"I'm out of breath," she declared as the music finished with a final flourish of sound. The fiddlers' bows extended skyward as they bowed, accepting the applause of the dancers. The piano player spun on his stool to wave at the crowd that gathered close at hand to call out requests for favorite tunes.

Matt drew her toward the doorway, and they stepped out onto the hard-packed dirt. Another buggy pulled under the trees across the way, and a stout man climbed down, only to reach up and lift down his equally sturdy companion.

"That's Otto Schmidt and his missus. He runs the livery stable in town," Matt told her, in a low voice that carried only as far as Emmaline's ear.

Hand extended, the older man approached, wife in tow. "We're in time for dinner, I see, Matthew. I told Hilda you'd be barbecuing a steer for the occasion." His head nodded with emphasis as he spoke, his wide smile exposing the gleam of a gold tooth near the front of his mouth. Beside him, Hilda Schmidt beamed her best wishes silently, nodding almost in unison with her husband.

Emmaline smiled, unable to restrain her pleasure at their open enjoyment of the occasion. "We're so glad you came. I'm Emmaline."

Hilda Schmidt nodded vigorously. "I figured as much. I was in the emporium the day Matthew bought you that dress. Did he tell you that the ladies' sewing circle is making you a quilt?"

"No..." Emmaline answered distractedly, looking back over her shoulder at Matt, who was being hauled in the other direction by Mr. Schmidt, to where a circle of ranchers was gathering about the tailgate of a wagon.

"Just leave them be," Hilda said, clucking her tongue at Emmaline's look of bewilderment. "The men have to have their snort from old Tyler Mason's jug before the party gets to going good, you know. Matthew'll be lookin' you up in no time.''

"My, doesn't that look good!" Hilda clutched at Emmaline's hand, drawing her to where white-aproned men were doling out generous servings of barbecued beef. "Have you tried any yet, Emmaline?"

"Here's an empty plate for you, Mrs. Gerrity," a nearby woman called out.

"That's Ruth Guismann," Hilda said in an undertone. "Her husband owns the store in town, and she's the one who picked out all the fancy things Matthew got for your wedding."

Emmaline blushed, imagining the scene. "Who else was there?"

"Oh, my, half the ladies in town were in the store that morning. We just had the best time, watching him get all flustered while he tried to choose things for you."

Emmaline groaned, imagining Matt surrounded by these women while he did his shopping. They'd all seen the lacy underthings she wore even now.

"Here you go, here's your plate. Now you just step right up there and try some of your husband's prime beef," said the woman at her elbow, ushering her forward to be served.

"Thank you…Mrs. Guismann, wasn't it?" Emmaline asked as she accepted the plate and held it in readiness. Within seconds, two slices of steaming meat centered it and she was pressed in the direction of the serving table.

"Land sakes, girl, you just call me Ruth, like everyone else does." Her face beaming with humor, the shopkeeper's wife ushered a bemused Emmaline before her, spooning generous servings to surround the beef.

"Havin' a good time, Miss Emmaline?" Across the table, Claude, drafted for the day by Maria and resplendent in his own white apron, beamed at her. Carrying a platter of fried chicken, he searched for a bare spot to place it.

"It's wonderful, Claude," she complimented, glancing about at the women who gathered about her as if they would take her to their collective bosoms.

And wonderful it was, she decided a short while later, when she had somehow escaped and found herself beneath a tree, plate laden high with salads and meat and topped with an irregularly shaped slab of bread, generously slathered with butter by some helpful soul. Beside her, Tessie bounced on her heels as she squatted for a moment, a chicken leg clutched in her fingers and eyes glistening with excitement.

"Oh, Emmie, isn't it the most fun ever? Did you see the man playing the piano? His fingers just fly so fast, you can hardly see them," Tessie breathed, eyes wide with wonder.

"Don't you need a plate for your chicken, Theresa?" Her tone faintly admonishing, a plate of her own in hand, Olivia approached.

"Won't you join us, Olivia?" Emmaline asked, patting the quilt beside her.

Tessie's eyes lost a bit of their sparkle. "I didn't think I had to use all my manners today, Miss Olivia," she said carefully. "This is a picnic."

"Manners are never to be discarded, no matter where we are," Olivia reminded the child firmly.

Emmaline bit at her lip for a moment, but the words would not be withheld. "I think we might understand if Tessie is excused her table manners, just for this once. It's a special occasion, after all."

Olivia bowed her head in acquiescence. "I'm sure you know best, Mrs. Gerrity."

"I gotta go," Tessie said quickly, shooting a quick grin at her sister before she scampered away, chicken leg in hand.

Olivia was silent for a moment, contemplating Tessie as she skipped through the yard. "That child would have done well with a mother," she said quietly.

Emmaline's mouth dropped open, her face a study in stunned surprise. "She has me," she said finally.

Olivia waved her hand dismissively. "A real family would have been ideal. Theresa requires a firm hand."

"Did you have anyone in mind?" Emmaline's query was quiet.

Again Olivia's hand dismissed the other woman's words. "It's too late now, anyway," she said. "And, after all, I'm only the teacher."

Emmaline was stunned, her eyes round with surprise, as she watched Olivia walk away. And then her gaze fell with relief upon the tall figure of Matt sauntering through the groups of people. As though he sensed her watching him, he turned his head in her direction and his mouth tilted in a secret smile that brushed her heart with a silent message. Halted by one person and then another, he nevertheless made his way to where she sat, his eyes focused upon her, homing in on the bright beauty that drew him like a candle flame in the night.

"Where'd Olivia get to?" he asked as he stooped beside her.

Emmaline shrugged and shook her head, her hands clasped loosely in her lap. "I don't know."

He sank to the ground with limber ease. "How'd you manage to get abandoned over here all by yourself?" he asked, settling next to her and reaching for the bread she'd shoved to one side of her plate. Picking up a slice of the beef she'd been given, he held it between two fingers, then placed it squarely atop the bread. He folded the whole thing in half, then took a bite.

"Umm...good," he pronounced, relishing it with appetite.

"I'll share with you," she offered, motioning at her plate and handing him her fork.

He looked at her askance. "Aren't you hungry, honey?"

She nodded quickly. "Of course! It's just that I'm excited, and I've already eaten some...." She gestured at the plate.

"Hmm...not much, Emmie," he noted. His eyes were keen as they swept over her face. "You all right?"

She looked up at his solemn face. "Olivia says Tessie needs a mother." Her mouth tightened suddenly. "I don't think she approves of me."

"I'll talk to her," he said abruptly. "Guess I haven't paid much attention to her lately. Maybe she's gettin' too big for her britches, sayin' something like that to you."

"No, don't do that." Emmaline shook her head. "I don't think she meant anything. Except maybe she thought Deborah would have done better as your wife than me."

Matt grunted disparagingly. "Not likely. Olivia hasn't got the time of day for Deborah."

"Maybe she had herself in mind," Emmaline suggested quietly.

"Not on your life." Matt's words were loud and clear, and Emmaline shushed him quickly, vowing silently to put Olivia's words out of her mind.

"How about another dance, Mrs. Gerrity?" Matt suggested, tugging her to her feet before she could protest. Hands clasped, they made their way to where the fiddles were playing a fast-moving tune, caught up in the music.

The sun had gone down in splendor and the shadows of evening had fallen when Emmaline sought the quiet of the house. Bending over the basin in the kitchen, she rinsed her face in cool water, drying her hands on the towel as she looked from the window. The night was dark, the sky scattered with clouds, with only a few stars peeking through to lend their light.

About the yard, shadowed figures moved in a silent dance of their own, silhouetted against the glow from the embers in the barbecue pit. The spit was gone, but several platters full of beef were left on the table, where muslin cloths draped the food to keep it clean.

Emmaline sighed deeply, aware of the quiet of the house about her, the music that the breeze carried to her ears and the occasional sounds of laughter from neighbors who walked about beneath the trees or sat on bales of hay within the barn.

"Where's Emmaline?" she heard Matt ask from a distance, and then watched as he left the brightly lit barn to walk across the yard. Her face was wreathed in a smile at the sight of his long-legged, slim-hipped stroll, her eyes fixed on the lean strength of his body, shadowed in the light of the fire.

"Emmaline!" he called, facing the line of trees that bordered the long lane.

She went swiftly to the door and pushed it open, stepping onto the porch. He was walking away, and she moved quickly, wanting to catch him. Her mouth opened, the words that would call him to her on the tip of her tongue.

And then a silent figure hiding in the darkness next to the kitchen door moved.

One step brought the man close behind her. One rapid movement of his hand effectively halted her words. About her waist, his arm swept her from her feet, and she was carried around to the side of the house, gasping beneath the fingers that clutched with cruel strength against her mouth.

She kicked her feet wildly and squirmed against his side, hanging like a sheaf of new-mown hay, his arm solid about her middle. Wordlessly he made his way to the narrow line of brush beyond the house. His steps were long and swift, covering the ground quickly, and she dangled helplessly in his grasp.

Against the night, a horse waited, dimly visible as they approached. Its reins were looped over a branch on a scrubby short tree, and as they neared, the animal lifted his head and nickered softly.

"Listen, you stand up right in front of me and don't make any trouble...hear?" The rough voice was close to her ear, and the words were hard and succinct.

Emmaline shuddered, the taste of salty, grimy flesh on her lips, the chill of fear slicing at her spine, and her legs trembled beneath her weight. She almost fell, but he caught her once more, handicapped by the need to keep her mouth covered.

"Damn, I said stand up," he growled, and his hand on her shoulder tightened bruisingly. His other hand snaked to the saddle horn, where a rope hung. His fingers snagged it neatly.

Emmaline's eyes widened above the hand that held her in a harsh grip, watching as he formed a loop in the rope and then passed it over her, binding her arms to her sides.

For just a moment, his hand moved, so that the rope could slip into place about her waist. And that moment was all she needed. Her lungs filled with air, precious, clean air. She screamed. Screamed while the anger of her captor washed over her in audible waves of vile curses. Screamed while he scrambled into his saddle and tugged at the rope that cinched her waist tightly. She was still screaming when he reached down to lift her into the saddle with him.

His arm was in front of her face, and she leaned into it, her mouth already open. Through the dark cotton of the shirt he wore, she chomped down, her teeth the only weapon she had.

It was all she needed. His howl of pain must have carried almost as far as her shrill cries had traveled. Her teeth held fast like a bulldog's in a pit, and she squeezed her eyes shut as she hung on grimly. The horse was moving in short hops, snorting and tossing its head. She was hard-pressed to stay on her feet, dangling at the end of the rope her captor held.

"Damn fool woman," he snarled finally as he heard the shouts from the back of the house. Letting loose of the rope, he swung his arm about, catching Emmaline with a solid fist against the side of her head.

"Emmaline... where the hell are you?"

It was Matt, Matt's voice, coming from a distance.

"Here... I'm here, Matt..." The words were whispered as she fell. Then, against her face, the ground was cool and she felt the vibrations of the horse's hooves.

"I bit him." The words were a slurred whisper. "I bit him." Her lips moved against the dirt, just as she felt warm hands lift her.

Chapter Thirteen

"Got any ideas, Claude?"

"No, sir, can't say that I do." The old man's dark eyes surveyed the shadowed corners of the barn, and he shook his head. "It's pretty bad when you start lookin' for trouble on your own place, ain't it?" Sitting abruptly on a bale of hay, he motioned with a curt gesture to indicate another just a few feet away. "Might's well rest your bones awhile, boss. Chompin' at the bit, the way you been doin' for the last couple a days, is like to wear you out."

Matt shrugged and lowered himself to the fragrant bale, drawing a deep breath as he rested his elbows on his knees. He clasped his hands loosely and focused on the callused skin that ridged his palm just beneath his thumb.

"I figure it has to be a maverick. Maybe some cowpoke who's out for a buck. But then, who'd be hiring him...and why?" He shook his head and his eyes squinted against the sunlight from the wide doorway. His mouth drew down at the corners in a frown. "Then again, maybe somebody's carryin' a grudge or something. I don't get it, and that's a fact." His words vibrated with anger and frustration.

"Well, somebody sure ain't took a shine to Miss Emmaline, I'd say," Claude drawled. "Can't get it through my head why anybody'd want to cart her off thataway, though."

"Bet he hadn't reckoned on ropin' a hellion." Matt ground the words out, thankful as he thought of Emmaline's brief battle.

"Yeah, she is that," Claude agreed. "All that spunk and red hair came true from her daddy, you know. You imagine that low-down skunk'll think twice before he lays hands on her again?"

A frown furrowed Matt's brow and tightened his jaw. "Sure hope to hell he never gets another chance to touch her. And he won't, if I can help it."

"You can't tie her to that bed forever, boss," Claude told him shortly. "She's gonna want to be out and around, and you know you can't keep her off'n her horse. She's taken to ridin' with the little miss purt' near every day."

"Well, she won't be riding without me from now on," Matt answered abruptly. "And in the meantime, she's not gettin' out of my bed till tomorrow at least. Doc says he wants to be sure her head's okay." He lowered his voice and leaned forward. "'Course, he's draggin' it out just a little. I told him I needed a few days to sort things out before I was ready to cope with her runnin' free."

A grin creased the old man's face, his eyes crinkling with laughter. "I heard from Maria that Miss Emmaline is accusin' you of puttin' bars on the windows next. Sure didn't think you'd go that far, boss."

Matt glared at him, then rose in a lithe movement, hitching his low-slung pants a bit higher on his hips as he stood. He faced the open doorway and tucked his fingertips into the flat pockets that rode his hipbones. "Doubt if bars would stop her," he admitted glumly. "She's one determined woman, Claude. But I sure as hell don't want anything to happen to her. I was only raggin' her, anyway...about the bars," he muttered. "I don't know how she'll take the news, but I'm afraid Miss Emmaline is gonna have to curtail her runnin' free for a while."

"We'll all keep a good eye on her, boss." Claude navigated his body to an upright position, a low grunt signifying his effort. "My old joints sure feel like they could use some wagon grease," he muttered, following the taller man from the barn.

On the porch, Maria raised her hand to ring the big bell for dinner. It was enough to prod Matt into motion. His hand lifted to tilt the brim of his hat as he set off for the house.

"Pret' near too hot to eat," Claude grumbled, quickening his gait to keep up with Matt's long-legged stride.

"That'll be the day" came the drawling reply. "You know, Maria killed a couple of old hens this morning. My guess is that we're havin' chicken and dumplings."

Claude's bushy brows lifted, and one corner of his mouth twitched as he considered the thought. "Well, I reckon I could manage to take a little nourishment, since Maria's gone to so much trouble."

"Yeah, I reckon you could," Matt agreed. Ignoring the shallow steps, he stepped onto the porch and halted. His eyes squinted as he caught sight of the slim figure standing behind the screening on the door. "Damn it, Emmaline, what are you doin' out of bed?"

"Good afternoon to you, too, Mr. Gerrity," she said with haughty precision. "In case you're interested, I'm tired of eating from a tray and counting the flowers in the wallpaper. I decided to get up and get back to normal." Her fingers were clasped behind her and her chin was lifted in a posture he knew only too well.

Coming to a halt just inches from the door, he glared at her through the screen. "You got a lump on your head the size of a man's fist, Emmaline, and your hands are all scraped up. I watched the doctor clean dirt out of your cheek—" He took a deep breath, his jaw clamped shut, and he scanned her with concern in his eyes.

It was the soft reply that threw him. He'd expected an explosion, at the very least a snapping rejoinder. What he hadn't expected was the smile that lit her face, turning it into a glowing welcome as she pushed the door open and offered her hand.

"I'm sorry... I know you've been worried, Matt. I truly appreciate it. But I need this—I need to be out of bed, I really do. Please don't be angry with me." She moved back as he reached for the door, and then he was over the sill and reaching for her.

Hard and callused, more suited to holding a recalcitrant calf or the reins of a bucking horse, long fingers and hard palms closed about her waist with a tenderness that betrayed him. He drew her against him, ignoring the hiss of her indrawn breath when she caught sight of Claude, close at hand.

His dark head was tilted, and his mouth and nose were buried in the fragrance of her hair. Inhaling deeply, Matt savored the freshly washed scent and closed his eyes. What is it about this woman, he wondered with a surge of fierce passion that tightened his thighs and brought him to needy arousal with astonishing speed?

He held her with barely concealed frustration, bending his head low to speak to her with hushed intensity against her curls. His voice was a low growl, the sound muted and rasping.

"You can eat dinner with us, and then you'll go back to bed, Emmaline. Or I'll carry you. Afterward, I'll just stay there with you for an hour or so," he promised with seductive intent. His mouth lowered to brush against her ear, and his whisper was warm and beguiling. "What do you think, darlin'?"

Her gasp was indignant, and she pushed with all her might against him, forcing her arms between their bodies to press against his chest.

"You can't budge me, sweetheart," he said, that same deep growl once more smothered in her curls.

Her head tilted quickly, and then he was face-to-face with snapping eyes and scarlet cheeks. Her nostrils were flared and her teeth were clenched, but not too tightly for words to escape from rigid lips.

"I tried to be nice, Gerrity. I even said please! And all I get from you is a nasty ultimatum."

"Yeah, *please* is a word that seldom gets spit out of that sassy mouth of yours, I'll admit that," he drawled, struggling to control the amusement that begged for release.

She glared up at him as he compressed his lips and shook his head. "I reckon I know what a chore it was for you to use that word, Em," he acknowledged, with as much sobriety as he could muster. "I'll even reconsider my—"

"It won't do any good. I'm not going back to bed today, and that's the end of it." Her mouth pouted, the bottom lip pursed and plump, and it was more than he could resist. Claude or no Claude, he had to taste it.

His head dipped quickly the few inches it took to cover her mouth with his own, and he gathered her even closer to himself, her arms and hands imprisoned against his chest. His lips were warm, firm and demanding, begging and gaining entrance to the secrets of her mouth. She resisted for only a moment, then gave him what he asked for.

She'd lost the battle. Relaxing against his hard body and tilting her head to one side, she savored the flavor of him. That clean man taste she'd learned to relish over the past weeks. His embrace was hard and ungiving, his possession of her mouth a masculine force that held her in thrall, and she basked in the heated desire emanating from his touch.

He retreated slowly, his mouth softening and becoming tender against her flesh. Then, with a final sound of satisfaction, he lifted his lips from hers and watched the hot flush of anger she'd worn fade into a rosy blush that pinked her cheeks. Her eyes opened, languid and heavy as her lashes blinked twice.

"You haven't kissed me like that since..." she began.

"Shh..." he said, lowering his head once more.

"Reckon I'd better head around to the other door, so's I can get some dinner," Claude grumbled from the porch. "Seems like some folks aren't as fond of Maria's dumplings as the rest of us."

"Oh, my..." Emmaline squeezed her eyes shut in dismay.

"No point in gettin' all flustered, Em," Matt said, turning her about and heading her toward the dining room. "Claude's pretty closemouthed, you know. He won't tell anybody that we hug and kiss like married folks."

He looked back at the man in the doorway and nodded toward the kitchen. "Go on and wash up, Claude. I'll be right behind you." One big hand on her shoulder halted Emmaline's progress, and she waited. Then, turning about, she peered past him.

"It was bad enough at our party that you kept putting your arms around me, Matthew. I'm mortified you kissed me right in front of Claude." She wore the look of a woman who was struggling between passion and pride, and her eyes met his accusingly.

"Well, you weren't mortified a few seconds ago," he reminded her. "And besides, old Claude knows all about kissin' and huggin', Emmaline. Anyway, I wouldn't have kissed you if you hadn't looked so tempting in that pretty dress, with your curls all ruffled and your eyes all shiny."

Her mouth pursed and she shook her head. "Don't think you can sweet-talk me, Gerrity. I'm on to your tricks."

"Yeah?" His grin was back, and she slapped at the hand that reached for her.

"Go wash up." Her finger stabbed at his chest. "Maria won't let you eat at her table with half the barn on your hands."

He reached for her, his big fist enclosing her finger as he bit gently at the tip of it. His eyes swept her face, and his husky voice spoke her name with soft emphasis. "Emmaline."

She blinked at the sober tone. "What is it, Matt?"

"I don't want you to leave the house alone. You can stay up today, but stay indoors, you hear?"

He left her no room to maneuver, and she acknowledged it with a nod. "All right, for today," she conceded. "We'll talk about it tonight."

He planted a soft kiss in the center of her palm before he released her.

He'd gained a small victory, he decided. One more day... But soon she'd balk at his ties on her. His frown was back in place, the tension of not knowing radiating to every nerve, and he readied himself for dinner in silence.

"This is the best part of being married," Emmaline whispered into the quiet night. Curled against his long, firm length, she felt the warmth of that solid body against her back. Her feet pressed snugly against the hard length of his shins and his arms surrounded her, wrapping her with tender strength against him. Gently, so gently against her flesh, his hands formed themselves to fit with exquisite care, one nestled just beneath the soft swell of her breasts and the other pressed against the curve of her belly.

The soft batiste of her nightgown clung to her, providing a fragile shield against his touch. Carefully, tenderly, his fingers moved, skimming the curves and hollows of her form. His hard, muscled frame cradled her, exuding a warmth that penetrated to her very bones.

"Sleepy?" he asked against the top of her head.

"Umm..." Her mouth curved in a smile she was sure he could not detect.

"And what is that mumble supposed to mean?" His words were a rumble above her head, and amusement was rampant in his tone.

"I'm almost asleep." Her eyes shone with anticipation as she felt his fingers move with lazy purpose, gathering the fabric of her gown into his grasp, easing it up the length of her legs.

"The hell you are," he growled, sliding one hand across her belly and then scooping his palm beneath the firm, plump breast that had been tempting him ever since he'd nestled behind her. His big hand cradled and gently squeezed, lifting the firm flesh he'd captured with such ease.

Carefully, with practiced movements, he turned her onto her back, regretfully abandoning his prize for a moment, tugging her hands into place about his neck.

She felt the chill as he moved his warmth from her breast, suppressing the need to draw him back, marveling at the yearning of her very flesh for the friction of his fingertips, the touch of his callused hands. With renewed senses, she recognized the teasing mood his lips were creating. Now, brushing phantom kisses across her forehead, then down the short length of her nose, murmuring nonsense as he went.

"Don't curse at me, Gerrity," she muttered, nudging him with her knee as she lifted it to one side of his long leg.

"When?" he groused, and then recalled his words. "I didn't curse. I just doubted your claim. You don't act sleepy to me."

"You don't think I should be tired?" she asked with a yawn that lacked substance. "After all, I spent the whole afternoon and evening mending your shirts and putting the hems down on Tessie's dresses. And I was almost asleep when you crawled in here with me."

"Liar," he murmured as he lifted his hands to the buttons that closed her gown. He slid one from its buttonhole and sought her eyes in the faint light from the window. "I planned this all day, Mrs. Gerrity, and if you were almost asleep when I snuggled up to you, I'll be a monkey's uncle." His fingers concentrated on the row of buttons as he spoke, and they submitted to his handiwork quickly, until a narrow strip of pale skin lay exposed, almost to her waist.

"I'll be chilly. I've been under the weather, remember?" Her words teased him as she moved her fingers through the heavy, dark strands of hair that fell against his neck.

"I'll keep you warm," he promised gruffly, tugging the gown to her waist, freeing her arms in the process and lifting her against his bare chest as he pulled the gown down her back. She lifted her arms once more to curl about his neck, raising herself until her breasts were flattened against him, and his hands worked to shove the gown down her legs, to be lost in the sheets. She relaxed and lay back against the pillow.

"I could have gotten up and taken it off." She smiled, peering up at him, her mouth tilting in a smile that promised much.

"I don't mind doin' it myself," he said, settling himself against her softness, leaning on his elbows with both hands surrounding her head, his fingers spread wide and moving gently against and through her hair.

He caught the faint scent of her, a blend of the soap she used and the sweetness of her woman's flesh. Inhaling it gently, he tasted the creamy skin that covered her cheek, just the tip of his tongue flicking against her flesh.

"Umm…" With a satisfied murmur, she turned her head away so that his mouth would brush instead along the curve of her ear.

"Like that?" he asked, his breath warm against her. His head dipped, and he kissed the tender skin that lay just under the curve of her jaw. Then his nose nestled into the sensitive hollow behind her ear, and she shivered.

"You give me chill-bumps."

"Yeah?" His mouth pressed damp kisses against her throat, and he shifted against her, moving lower, his hands following the line of her shoulders and arms, until he enclosed her fingers within his own and brought them to his chest.

"Touch me here, Em," he said roughly, guiding her to the dark hair that covered him almost to his waist.

"Where?" Her hands moved slowly, fingers tangling in the softness of his curls.

"I'll let you know when you get to the right place," he said thickly, his voice muffled as he bent to drop another kiss on her brow.

He lifted again, rising once more on his elbows, and watched her with anticipation as she moved beneath him, her hands brushing and caressing, her eyes wide in the dim light, intent on his every change of expression. His lashes lowered suddenly and his jaw clenched as he swallowed a moan that begged to be heard.

"Matt?"

"Yeah, honey," he breathed. "You're doin' just fine."

"Do I give you chill-bumps, too?" It was a quavering whisper.

"Oh, yeah, you sure do, honey," he agreed with a sharply indrawn breath. Her fingers moved against him, more knowledgeable now, teasing the small buttons she'd located, and her breath caught in wonder as she recognized the force of his arousal.

"I don't think I can take many more of your chill-bumps tonight, Emmaline." Shifting from her touch, he moved with relentless purpose against the soft contours of her body. Grasping the slender fingers she had spread against the expanse of his chest, Matt lifted them once more to rest against his shoulders.

He bent low over her, his breath a hot brand against her flesh. His mouth was hungry, seeking her with a needy passion he had controlled for too long. She felt his lips open wide, and then his teeth were against the plush cushion of her breast. He suckled her flesh, leaving his mark, knowing with a savage delight that a small bruise would remind her of his touch when she looked into her mirror in the morning.

Against her softness, his murmur was low, but the words reached her through the haze of desire he had woven with his touch. "I didn't hurt you?" he asked gruffly, his tongue already soothing the surface he had claimed, the desire to brand her warring with his need to treasure the gift of her body.

She shook her head, aware only of the fluid heat that filled her, of his openmouthed kisses and caresses, which even now were seeking another goal.

Capturing the crest that promised greater purchase for his lips, he drew on her gently, then with stronger purpose, felt the shiver that swept through her body and heard the low groan of surrender she smothered against his brow. Her head tipped forward and her hands grabbed him tightly, holding him firmly to where he lavished her with the pressures of his mouth and teeth.

"Matt...Matt..." She could speak only his name, in a small whisper that gripped his heart with an emotion beyond his ability to describe. Emmaline clutched at him, her hands tight against his head, her legs moving in an urgent dance, coaxing him to settle in the cradle of her body.

"Em, let me..." He slid down her body, kneeling as he lifted her knees to make room for himself, careful as he moved her about, aware of the relative innocence of his bride, his touch gentle against the fragile flesh he was arranging for his pleasure.

"Matt?" Her whisper was wondering, but her fingers were eager against him as her hands moved to touch where she could, running her fingers with frantic brushes against his skin, reaching as far as she could over his shoulders and then back to the muscular width of his chest once more. As if eager to trace every inch of flesh, she explored, trembling with anticipation, even as her breath quivered within her chest.

"Emmaline," he growled, the name a plea against her softness. Again he called her name, this time with a tender voice he'd used with no other woman. "Emmaline?" It was smothered against her flesh, but she heard it, heard the questioning sound of her name on his tongue, heard it and knew it for the plea that it was.

She drew in her breath, her heart pounding in a thundering cadence within her. "I'm here, Matt." Her whisper was soft, trembling in the quiet of the room, and her hands clutched against the dampness of his head.

Within her, the churning, swirling pressure he had created curled like a living presence, and her hips shifted beneath him, sensing that only his possession would free her from its grip.

"Please," she gasped, tugging at him, drawing him up to fit against her body, her hands clutching wildly against the slick surface of his skin. He obeyed the unspoken command, and sought the embrace she offered. Her arms enclosed him with eagerness, her legs twining with his as she twisted beneath him. And then she was lifting to surrender herself to his seeking manhood.

He needed no further urging. With a groan of delight he came to her, with muffled words of encouragement he coaxed her to his will, and with a soaring sense of fulfillment he took her with him to that place called pleasure.

"I knew you weren't overly intelligent, but I didn't think you were stupid." The words were spit from the woman's lips with impetuous fury, and she spun on her heel, her anger visible as she stalked the length of the barn.

Deep within the shadows, his voice followed her, sniveling and contrite. "It looked like a good chance to grab her. She was all alone in the kitchen, and I was just gonna scare her a little when she came out on the porch. An' then I thought I'd just tie her up and leave her someplace for a few hours. Thought I'd just scare her some."

His voice trailed off and the woman glared her frustration. "I don't want her scared," she said, malice coating her words. "I want her...out of the picture."

His eyes lit with greed at the thought of this new demand and his shoulders lifted in a shrug. "I'm thinkin' the stakes ain't high enough, lady. If you want her dead, you shoulda said so."

"I want her gone! One way or another—out of here!" The woman tilted her head, her gaze challenging, her mouth twisted in a parody of mirth. "Now I'm wondering if you've got the guts to do—"

His snarl was her only warning. Her shoulders were seized with brutal strength, his hands harsh, his fingers grasping with vicious force.

"I've got more guts than brains right now," he told her, his words a guttural threat, reinforced by the bruising grip he maintained.

She squirmed against him, her words pouring forth in a vile litany of disgust. And above the scalding diatribe, he laughed, his lips pulled back in a grimace that was almost frightening to the woman he held.

Almost. Sensing his delight in her helplessness, she stilled her struggle. "You forget who is in charge of this whole thing," she reminded him. Beneath his hands, her flesh cringed, but the eyes that met his flashed a warning he could not ignore.

He released her and watched her walk away. "You gonna go back on your word? You told me we'd spend time together." He watched her, squinting his eyes as he counted the paces she walked, reaching the far wall, then turning back, nearing his corner with deliberation. "You promised me—" he began, but her derisive laugh choked the words in his throat.

"You haven't given me what I asked for," she reminded him, halting just feet away, her smile mocking.

He stood straight, forsaking the dimness and stepping closer. "Next time, I won't give in so easy, lady. You're gonna be nice to me, one way or another. And I'm gonna up the price."

She relented, recognizing his anger, reluctant to push him beyond the limited control she maintained. "Whatever it takes, I told you."

His nod accepted her capitulation. "I've got a plan. You'll get what you want." *And so will I,* he thought, his eyes sweeping over the woman who tempted him. *So will I.*

Chapter Fourteen

The arrival of four horses on the afternoon train was the highlight of the stationmaster's day. That they were accompanied by an elderly couple dressed to the nines only served to add to the excitement. Within a few minutes, word reached the mercantile, where Abraham Guismann was deeply involved in a discussion with the preacher. Over at the livery stable, Otto Schmidt had already harnessed up a mare to his light buggy. So, by the time Abraham arrived on pretense of business, the easterners were headed out of town. Behind the buggy trailed the four horses, on a lead rope.

Abraham watched the dust settle in the road and scratched his head. "Who do you think they are?" he wondered, sorry that he hadn't gotten a better look at their finery. Eastern fashions were the coming thing, and the black-and-white drawings in the catalog he'd sent for from St. Louis left a lot to be desired. He sighed as he rued the lost opportunity to view the fashion plates, who had probably worn the very latest styles.

"Couldn't say for sure, but I'm thinkin' they were Emmaline Gerrity's grandparents," Otto replied. "That's where they're headin', and they're takin' those horses to her for a weddin' present, they said."

"Fine-looking animals," Abraham decreed, although his judgment was based solely to his view of four twitching tails and the hindquarters to which they were attached.

"Well, I'm thinkin' that somebody's in for a surprise this mornin'. The gentleman said they weren't expected."

"Harley's nephew told me they had enough baggage for a good long stay," Abraham looked wistful, yearning for one more look at the swiftly vanishing pair.

"Yup, I stacked it on the back of the buggy and strapped it up good and tight." Otto turned back to the double doors that stood open beneath his brightly painted wooden sign. "Sure were good-lookin' animals," he said, with just the smallest trace of envy, as he surveyed his assortment of stock. "Never seen anything so fine in Forbes Junction before."

"We got visitors, boss."

Matt swept the hat from his head and wiped at the line of sweat that beaded his brow. His forehead furrowed as he glanced at Claude. "Anybody I wanna talk to?" he growled. If it was Clyde Hopkins or his daughter, they could just go hang, he decided sourly. They'd come close to being placed number one on his blacklist already. He wasn't sure he could tolerate being polite to them this morning.

Claude shook his head as he considered. "Nope. Never saw this pair before. Look kinda fancied up, they do. But they're sure bein' followed by four of the dandiest animals I've ever laid eyes on," Claude allowed, jutting his chin as he passed judgment.

"Animals? What're you talkin' about?" Matt frowned, his attention still centered on the yearling colt he was leading about the corral.

"You'd best come take a look." Claude headed away from the gate he'd been leaning against. "Miss Emmaline is standin' on the porch with her hand over her mouth, and if I ain't goin' blind in my old age, I think she's bawlin'. She sure is dabbin' at her eyes with her hankie, anyway."

Matt swung about, and his eyes narrowed, glittering darkly as he turned toward the house and led the colt from the corral. "Here, B.J.," he called shortly as one of his men emerged from the barn nearby. "Take this colt and rub him down good."

"Sure thing, boss." The young man reached for the lead rope. "Would you take a look at those horses!" he exclaimed, gaping at the retinue coming to a halt before the porch.

"Yeah, I'm about to," Matt answered, stripping his gloves and tucking them into his back pocket as he made his way with long-legged strides to where Emmaline stood. His eyes were focused on her and his attention was set on the slender woman who was busily blowing her nose with dainty brushes of the white hankie she kept in her pocket. Then, even as he watched, her mouth curved in a smile and she stepped down from the porch to greet the visitors.

Can't be too unhappy to see them, Matt decided, his pace slowing as he watched her approach the couple. He waited, several steps away, aware of the stiff posture she assumed, the stilted words of welcome she spoke.

"Grandmother, Grandfather...I'm so pleased to see you." Emmaline halted before them, and her eyes flicked from one to the other before she leaned to place a kiss against the lined cheek of her grandmother. It was accepted with a faint smile and nod. Then, as Emmaline turned to greet the tall, erect gentleman who flanked her, the woman eyed her with a gimlet gleam, noting each detail of her appearance.

"I can see it's a good thing we brought you something decent to wear, Emmaline," she said with haughty emphasis.

Emmaline flushed as she heard the words of censure. "I'm considered quite decent here, Grandmother," she answered quietly. "The heat seems to require lighter clothing."

"Good breeding requires a lady to always dress in an appropriate fashion, Emmaline. You look like a servant," she said crisply, as if that were a sin beyond redemption.

Emmaline swallowed a giggle and struggled to keep her features subdued. Indeed, her skirt and blouse were dead ringers for those that hung against the wall in Maria's room, having been cut from the same pattern, albeit from more costly fabric.

"I've been helping Maria in the kitchen," she answered with determined brightness. "She's teaching me how to make flour tortillas."

Her grandmother sniffed delicately. "Whatever that might be."

Emmaline cast a look in Matt's direction, and he answered the summons.

"Well, if we're real fortunate, we may just find them on the dinner table," he drawled, approaching Emmaline with one hand outstretched. She grasped it and drew him closer to her side.

"This is Matthew, Grandfather," she said with quiet pride. Dusty and rich with the scent of horses and hay, he stood beside her, and she watched as the stern gentleman from Kentucky took the measure of the man who had married his granddaughter.

The palm offered was gloved in fine kidskin. The hand that grasped it was callused and browned from years in the sun. Both gripped with strength, Matt's leashed in deference to the older man.

"Sir," Matt said, acknowledging Jonathan Rawlings with a nod.

"Mr. Gerrity." Keen eyes, deep-set and faded blue, met his, and Matt felt an unaccountable relief. The lined face was somber, the mouth unsmiling, but the man had a look about him, Matt decided, that was encouraging. Perhaps this unexpected visit might be good for Emmaline.

He turned his attention to the woman who watched him with gimlet eyes. "Ma'am," he said with a nod, one hand reaching to sweep the hat from his head. "We're more than pleased to welcome you."

"I'm sure we'll try not to discommode you any more than necessary," Clara Rawlings answered smartly. "We decided quite quickly to make the trip, rather than send Emmaline's things by rail. Can't depend on them not getting lost." She looked about her, barely repressing a shudder as she viewed the flat vista stretching away in all directions, with only the trace of low hills to be seen to the north. "I can't say that your surroundings hold much interest, Emmaline. I'm sure you're desolate without the beauty of your home about you."

Emmaline's mouth opened and then closed abruptly as she reformed the words that had almost blurted from her lips. "I've missed some of what I left behind," she said after a moment, "but there is much here to recommend our life."

Clara Rawlings's eyebrows raised as she looked down at the dust that coated her smart half boots, glanced once more at the sparse vegetation that stretched to the horizon, and shook her head in silence.

"It isn't what you're used to, Grandmother, but it has a beauty of its own," Emmaline said with quiet assurance. Then, not for the first time, she glanced at the string of horses, long-legged and gleaming in the sunshine, waiting patiently behind the buggy.

"We brought you a wedding gift, Emmaline," her grandfather said, his eyes intent on her. "Do you recognize your horse?"

"Yes, of course." Her breath caught in her throat as Emmaline looked her fill at the bay mare. The animal swished her dark tail and flicked her ears as she nickered softly. "Oh, yes," Emmaline repeated as she released Matt's hand and stepped eagerly around the buggy to where the four horses waited. She stood a moment, her face close to the rich sorrel-colored mare before she rested her cheek against the animal's muzzle. Her hand lay with familiar ease, brushing the soft forelock, even as her other arm reached to allow her fingers to tangle in the long, dark mane that lay against the mare's neck.

Matt felt a thickening in his throat as he watched, his hands thrust deep in the back pockets of his denim pants. She missed her horse, he thought with a touch of surprise. She hadn't really talked about her home that much, she'd just settled in pretty well and gone on with it.

His glance drifted back to the elderly couple who had turned to watch Emmaline's reunion with her Thoroughbred mare. A slight frown and a pursed mouth more than expressed her grandmother's opinion of Em's exuberance, he decided. The grandfather, on the other hand, wore a half smile that might be fainthearted approval, Matt thought.

Emmaline turned, her face flushed, her eyes gleaming with unshed tears, and spoke her thanks. "I can't tell you how much it means that you brought Fancy to me."

"Your grandfather suggested that since you've chosen to remain here for your sister's sake, you might be grateful for a decent horse to ride," Clara said with deliberate emphasis.

Precise and biting, the statement ground against Matt's ears, and his lips thinned as he held back the curse that surged within him. He drew in a breath, and his nostrils flared. The old biddy—how did she dare to suggest that Emmaline was stuck with no choice, either in family or in horses? Remain here for her sister's sake... without a decent horse to ride. He glared at Emmaline, as if she were the culprit, and caught her eye.

She stared at him, still digesting the snide remarks of her grandmother, and felt a twinge of apprehension as his eyes flared darkly, piercing her with the anger that rode him.

"I...I've been riding here, Grandmother..." She faltered, her mind searching for just cause for Matt's anger. "It's different... I've had to get used to a western saddle." She licked at her lips, suddenly gone dry, and her eyes pleaded with the man whose face had assumed a mask of indifference.

Gone was the angry glare, in its place a cold stare that confused her and set her heart to beating more rapidly.

If she'd married him just for Theresa, she'd been putting on a good show, Matt groused to himself, watching her search for words. She sure hadn't said any different to the old lady, either, he thought with scorn. What had given the woman such an idea? Surely not the wire he'd sent.

He remembered writing the lines and waiting till Harley Summers tapped it out on the wire. *Emmaline and I are married, making a home for Theresa. Send her belongings.* Seemed pretty simple, right to the point, he decided. Nowhere had he suggested it was a big sacrifice on Emmaline's part to spend her life in Arizona. Seemed like she ought to be glad she had a chance to live on her daddy's place again. Sure beat the hell out of spending the rest of her life with the dried-up old lady she called a grandmother, he reasoned.

"Well, I'm sure the stock here will improve if your husband has enough sense to make use of the stud we brought with us," Clara said firmly. "Rawlings Farm has always taken pride in their horses. Perhaps your sister would benefit from the opportunity to ride a Thoroughbred, also."

Enough was enough. "Sorry I can't offer you an even swap, ma'am," Matt drawled with cold purpose. "I haven't got much to offer. Emmaline's not up for grabs, and she's the most valuable commodity I've got." He shook his head in mock dismay. "I'm afraid my animals are used to hard work and hot weather. They'd purely go to waste back east with nothin' to do but eat grass and tote pancake-ridin' city folk about."

"I beg your pardon? Pancake-riding...what?" Her attention firmly grasped by the subtle insult wrapped in the meager apology he'd offered, Clara Rawlings lifted her chin and allowed her dignity to slip, just a bit. "We certainly didn't intend to trade horses, Mr. Gerrity. And certainly Emmaline is not to be spoken of in the same breath with animals that live in a barn. They are a gift to our granddaughter... one whose value I am sure you are not cognizant of."

Emmaline moved swiftly, frightened that the emotions flaring so openly were about to get out of control. Her grandfather reached to halt her, one gloved hand touching her forearm.

"It's all right, Emmaline. Your grandmother is feeling the effects of the long trip. I'm sure she didn't mean to be so outspoken," he said, his effort to defuse the situation apparent.

"Don't worry, Mr. Rawlings," Matt said. "I sure wouldn't want your wife to think I wasn't goin' to put the proper value on Em's gift. After all, four Thoroughbred racin' horses are just what we need out here in the desert."

"Matt!" Emmaline hurried to grasp his hand, her eyes pleading with him. "She didn't mean that the way it sounded."

"Well, since you married me for your sister's sake, and you didn't have a decent horse to ride, I'm sure glad your folks showed up to rescue you, sweetheart," he said emphatically.

Emmaline was torn between grinding her teeth at the cocky words he spouted and crying with frustration at the whole foolish argument that had sprung up between these two hardheaded people. His hand was hard and ungiving against hers, and she curled her fingers about the length of his determinedly, unwilling to let him hide behind the sarcasm of his words.

"Matt—" she began softly "—can't we go in the house and make my grandmother comfortable and continue this later?"

"Yes, do you have a place where I can rinse some of the dust from your countryside from my skin?" Clara asked condescendingly. "Perhaps a washroom of sorts?"

"We have a bathing room, Grandmother," Emmaline answered, "or you can wash in your bedroom. We'll bring a pitcher of water to you."

"You have spare rooms?" the woman asked, gathering her skirts to step onto the porch.

"Yes, ma'am, we've even been sleepin' on real beds for several years now," Matt said soberly as he finally returned the pressure of Emmaline's fingers. "Quit beddin' down in front of the fire a while back, in fact." Opening the screen door, he waited for Clara to enter.

Emmaline cast a look of entreaty at her grandfather, who nodded in tacit understanding and followed his wife into the cool interior of the living room.

"Humph...must have made some improvements since my daughter lived here." Clara looked about her, and then her gaze settled on the tall rancher who stood proudly by Emmaline's side.

"We do try to keep up with the times," Matt agreed, willing to cool the embers of the confrontation he'd kept aflame out of hurt pride.

The thick walls and the wide overhang were features that had been incorporated into the building of this home with one purpose in mind—that the cool night air be held through the daytime hours and the sun's rays be kept from the interior by the wide roof. As a result, except for the hottest summer days, the high-ceilinged living area of the house was a welcome respite from the heat.

"You have a lovely home, Emmaline," her grandfather said with warmth.

"Matt's mother had a lot to do with it, I think," Emmaline answered haltingly. "Grandmother's right. I don't think this was nearly as beautiful when I was a child."

"Can we find someone to help carry in our things, child?" Jonathan asked. "Perhaps I can help sort out the bags and boxes and get your grandmother's carpetbag for her."

Matt moved to the door. "I'll get a couple of the men to do it," he offered, appeased somewhat by Emmaline's words. She'd come to his defense, he realized. In her own way, she'd set herself on his side of the line. As he opened the door and stepped onto the porch, a look of satisfaction curled his lip.

Maria had outdone herself, Emmaline decided as the evening meal came to a close. Matt had been taciturn, offering little to the general conversation, his eyes heavy-lidded and veiled. Olivia was quiet, answering in single syllables the few questions tossed in her direction, her gaze measuring as she watched the visitors.

Emmaline was flushed and harried, though they had managed to eat without any major crises. But between ensuring that the conversation focused on the food and the trip from Lexington and helping Maria with the additional work of serving guests, she was at a fine pitch of exhaustion by the time dessert was served. She had helped with it, choosing to make this part of the meal as traditional as possible for her grandparents' benefit. Dried-apple pie was a safe bet, she'd decided, and although Maria groused about fussy eastern folk, she'd allowed Emmaline to cajole her into line.

With a grunt of farewell and a nod to the ladies, Matt took Jonathan to the barns, finally ready to supervise the settling-in of the four new horses and, in the bargain, listen to the older man talk at length of his own place in Kentucky.

Grudgingly he'd admitted that Emmaline's grandfather had more substance to him than a fancy suit of clothes and an overabundance of dignity. Beneath the stiff and starchy ways, lay a loving grandparent, Matt suspected. That he was not able to express his affection for Emmaline posed a conundrum. Maybe the old lady had him toeing the line, playing the part of the Kentucky gentleman to a fare-thee-well.

"You've a fine place here, Mr. Gerrity." The words interrupted his thoughts, and Matt looked up in surprise.

"I expect you could settle for Matt, if you've a mind to. 'Mr. Gerrity' sounds a mite dignified for a ranch hand."

The keen blue eyes moved over him in a slow appraisal. "I hardly think you qualify as a mere ranch hand," Jonathan Rawlings mused. "The man who talked my granddaughter into marriage on the basis of such brief acquaintance must be possessed of qualities that far surpass those of a simple rancher."

Matt's mouth twitched as a smile threatened to curl his lips. "Well, there's a little more to it than that. Maybe one of these days, I'll let you in on the whole shootin' match, but for now, we'll just call me mighty persuasive."

"Emmaline appears to be reasonably satisfied with her life here," the older man ventured.

Matt nodded his agreement. "Hope you're not plannin' on coaxin' her back east with you, 'cause I'd say she's not too unhappy with her situation."

"Got any close neighbors?" Jonathan asked as they headed out of the barn and toward the corral that flanked it.

"Yeah," Matt grunted. More's the pity, he thought.

"Someone, another woman, perhaps, for Emmaline to cultivate as a friend?"

Matt's snort of derision was spontaneous. "Not hardly. Deborah Hopkins and her daddy own the next spread, and they've been plottin' for years to put it together with this one." He leaned on the corral fence, his arms folded atop one rail as his boot lifted to hook over another. "There's been some hard feelings between us, what with Emmaline showin' up here and then us gettin' married so quick-like."

"The girl wanted you for herself?"

"Yeah, you could say that," Matt agreed, amused at Deborah's being described as a girl. The word was too innocent and youthful to suit Deb; she merited another, but at the moment he couldn't come up with one suitable.

"There's a townful of women who'll befriend Emmaline," he assured her grandfather. "They took to her real well, kinda took her under their wings, so to speak."

"She's been raised to be a lady," Jonathan said. "I expect it's been a real turnabout for her, living without the luxuries of home."

"Dunno," Matt muttered, his speech deliberately curt. "I probably wouldn't recognize a lady if I walked into one. Emmaline managed to get over her snooty ways in jig time. She fits in pretty good, now." His eyes were cool, the tightening of his jaw the only sign of anger he revealed.

The dry chuckle that split the dead silence came as a surprise, and Matt turned to face Jonathan Rawlings. His lined face was lit by merry eyes, and his mouth was bent with a wry grin. He offered an ungloved hand in a gesture of truce.

"Guess I sounded a bit pompous, didn't I? You have to understand that Emmaline is all we have, Matt."

"Well, she sure doesn't feel like a very valued possession, the way I see it." He reached reluctantly for the man's hand, shaking it briefly, unwilling to play at being friendly. "Emmaline is right where she belongs," Matt said finally. "We got married for our own reasons, one of them being our little sister. If she'd never heard from you and her grandmother again, she'd have lived through it. Since you've showed up and brought her those highfalutin horses, I guess you're welcome here. Just don't cut her down for choosin' to live on her daddy's place, and don't go makin' her feel any less a lady because she quit wearin' those harnesses under her dresses."

The white-haired man nodded his head slowly and straightened to his full height. "I think we understand each other, Matt. Perhaps we'd better go back to the house and serve as buffers for a while. I suspect Emmaline's grandmother is out to do some reforming, and I'm not sure my granddaughter is in a pliable mood."

"It's about time to close up for the night, anyway," Matt agreed. He glanced at the sun, which hovered just above the western horizon, its rays spreading in a glorious display of color against the wispy clouds. Not enough to forecast any rain, he noted stoically. A summer shower was too much to hope for, at least here on the flatlands. They'll probably get some up in the high country, he thought, his mind turning to the herd of horses that were summering to the north.

"Does he do his own evening chores?" Clara Rawlings asked with guarded horror. "Surely he has hired help to tend to such things."

Seated on the comfortable sofa in the living room, Emmaline struggled to be friendly. "Matt likes to oversee everything around here, Grandmother. I'm sure they'll be in directly."

The older woman looked about her with a critical eye. "I must say, the western influence takes away any chance of your home being conducive to formal entertainment, doesn't it?" she remarked. "It's too bad that at least this room couldn't have been a bit more... formal, perhaps." She looked about and shrugged delicately.

"Stiff and starchy, you mean?" Emmaline supplied helpfully. "I like this room—in fact, I like the whole house. It suits me," she stated with quiet finality.

"Well, you know where your home is, Emmaline. When all this..." She waved her hand expansively about the room. "When it's become too much for you to tolerate any longer, the train runs back to Lexington, the same way it made its way here."

"There's nothing for me in Kentucky," Emmaline said quietly. "My place is here, with Matt and Tessie."

"But we are your family, my dear," Clara said with emphasis. "Your bloodlines go back for generations. The name of Rawlings has meant something in this country for almost two centuries."

Emmaline shook her head. "Matt and Tessie are my family now. Tessie is all I have of my father."

"And that was no great loss." Clara sniffed in a dainty manner, touching her nose with a lacy handkerchief. "A roughneck from the beginning. How he ever persuaded your mother to come to this godforsaken place has always been a mystery to me."

"But she did come," Emmaline answered. "I wish now she'd never left."

Her grandmother raised her eyebrows in delicate dismay. "How can you utter such a hateful statement? She'd have died here in this miserable place."

"She died in Kentucky," Emmaline reminded her softly. "I don't think she was any too happy there, either."

"If it hadn't been for that hateful man, she'd still be alive, probably married to one of our own kind."

"She chose him. She must have loved him once," Emmaline said. "He was my father, and I loved him."

"He didn't have the time of day for you," Clara declared bluntly. "Spent his days riding around tending to horses and cows and left my poor child to wilt in this terrible climate."

"He had time to write letters to me after my mother took me away from him." Emmaline's gaze lifted to meet that of her grandmother.

"Did he?"

"You know he did," Emmaline told her. "He sent me letters for years. The only problem was, they were never given to me."

"There was no sense in keeping things stirred up, Emmaline. When you're older, you'll understand. Your mother wanted to protect you from his influence."

"I don't believe you." She spoke the words quietly, and with a total lack of emotion.

Clara Rawlings paled and rose to her feet. "I resent the implication, Emmaline. Your mother knew what was best for you. It was her decision."

"I don't think my mother ever made a single decision once she got back under your roof, Grandmother. She just became your little girl again, till the day she died."

"You think I kept these supposed letters from your father away from you?" Clara asked, her tone challenging. Her cheeks had flushed, and her eyes sought relief from Emmaline's steady gaze.

"I know you did. Matt told me."

"It's come down to that? You'll take a stranger's word over that of your own flesh and blood?" Clara had come close to losing her well-disciplined temper, embarrassed at being caught out in the lie she'd been weaving for years.

"Matt is my husband, Grandmother. He's far from a stranger. If he says so, I believe him."

"Well! In that case, I'm sure you won't be wanting us under your roof any longer than necessary. We had planned on visiting for a few days and then stopping along the way home to do some sight-seeing. But this certainly has changed our plans. I'll tell your grandfather he can rearrange our traveling schedule when he comes in the house."

Emmaline bowed her head in acquiescence, her heart aching for the love that had never been and would never be. She'd had a modicum of approval from the woman before her, but the love she craved had been withheld, and the breach made between them today might never be mended.

"Is she my grandma, too?" Tessie asked plaintively as Emmaline buttoned up a nightgown that fell only to mid-shin on the child.

"No, I'm afraid not." Emmaline turned Tessie before her to brush the long hair into a single handful. Separating it deftly, she braided the dark length, tying the tail with a short piece of yarn.

Tessie pouted, her lower lip protruding a bit as she pondered the situation. "She's not very smiley, anyway," she announced after a moment. "I think grandmothers are supposed to be nicer than that." Her chin lifted in a determined gesture. Clearly, if this was not her own kin, she was willing to face the truth of the situation.

"You're probably right, Tessie." Her fingers soothed the child's head as Emmaline tucked her against her own breast. The reluctance was in the past. A caress, a hug, even a moment of close contact like this—it was all becoming more and more common between them, and her heart rejoiced as Tessie's hand patted with sisterly affection against the arm that surrounded her.

"I don't need a grandma. I got you, Emmie," the child said stoically. She smothered a yawn and settled closer against the warmth of her sister's breast. "An' we both got Matthew," she whispered with satisfaction. "Don't we, Emmie?"

A memory of dark, unsmiling features and stiff, unbending posture, all bearing Matt's image, popped into Emmaline's mind, and doubtfully she quoted the words her little sister had pronounced with such assurance.

"Yes, we both have Matthew," she said quietly, hoping in her heart of hearts that it was true.

Chapter Fifteen

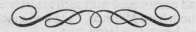

"Sorry you folks can't stay for a few days, Jonathan," Matt said cordially.

The change in plans had been announced before breakfast, and had been duly noted and accepted, as if nothing untoward had occurred.

"Clara finds the climate here to be enervating. She'll feel better when we get into higher country," the older man said, with a smile for Emmaline.

Matt looked quizzically at the Rawlingses, then cast a questioning look in Emmaline's direction. Something's escaping me this morning, he thought warily. The old lady's sure got a bee in her bonnet over something.

Clara picked at her food, a look of distaste drawing her mouth down at the corners. She sighed deeply, laid her fork aside and wiped her fingers with delicacy. Her eyes swept over her granddaughter. "I noticed that you've left off mourning, Emmaline." Mildness notwithstanding, the words were an accusation. Delivered as they were, in a casual tone, they caught Emmaline off guard, and she swallowed her mouthful with haste.

But before she could gather her thoughts or open her mouth to reply, Matt gently nudged her with his foot, and the glance she chanced in his direction was apprehensive. He was tight-lipped, and the movement of his head was almost imperceptible, effectively silencing her before she could formulate a reply.

"I asked Emmaline not to wear the black dresses she brought with her," Matt said briskly, his demeanor daring the older woman to start an argument.

Emmaline smothered a gasp of incredulous humor. Asked, indeed! He'd ordered her, was what he'd done. And there he sat, lying through his teeth.

"The climate here is too da—too doggone hot to wear the sort of stuff she hauled out here," Matt explained, faltering as he censored his blunt language. "Emmaline went to town and got some yard goods, and between them, she and Maria put together some comfortable things for her to wear. And then, when we got married, we thought you would be sending her things to sorta fill in the gaps in her wardrobe." His manner defied argument, and his hand moved across the table to cover Emmaline's small fist, which curled in a gesture of defiance by her plate.

I can speak for myself, she thought with a flare of temper. And then the warmth of that big hand cradling her own with such heated comfort penetrated her budding anger, and she looked up at the man who sat beside her. His brows were furrowed—it was a state that had seemed to be permanent for the past day—and his eyes were intense with a foreign emotion as he pierced her with his gaze.

Be careful, Emmaline. Don't be feisty this morning, he demanded silently. *Let me keep her off your back, at least in this, sweetheart.*

As if she read his mind, as if his thoughts penetrated the agile workings of her brain, she relaxed her fingers within his grip and unfurled it.

"Matt felt it was best to honor my father in other ways," she said quietly. Her chin lifted as she faced her grandmother, and she endowed the words she spoke with gentle defiance. "I like the clothing I'm wearing, and I appreciate Maria for being kind enough to show me how to put together skirts and blouses so quickly."

That Matt had been the instigator and had chosen the light fabrics she wore was a part of the truth she was loath to reveal. Indeed, his trip to town and the displaying of his purchases had been a battle of wills between them. Only his threat to burn her mourning clothes had allowed her to concede defeat with a measure of grace. That she reveled in the loose clothing and the freedom it afforded was a secret she hoarded, lest she give him a victory to tease her with.

"Well, I'm sure your father wouldn't have cared either way," Clara Rawlings said snippily. "He didn't have much regard for the niceties of life, as I understand it."

"You got that right, Mrs. Rawlings," Matt drawled. "Old Sam Carruthers didn't give two hoots for such fripperies. He wouldn't care what Emmaline wore, and my mother doesn't need a black armband worn in her behalf, either. She's alive in my mind, and that's all that counts."

Emmaline looked up in surprise at his words. That Matt should be so eloquent was a shock. Actually, now that she thought about it, those were the first words he'd spoken about his mother since the day they'd ridden north toward the high country, weeks ago. She smiled at him, eager to banish the chill from his demeanor, willing to take the first step in healing the strange breach in their fragile relationship, one that had formed with the coming of her grandparents.

He met her look, apparently in ignorance of the olive branch she offered, and ran his gaze over her with cool, dark-eyed intensity. She was doing all right, he decided. So long as she managed to keep the old lady at bay for just a while longer, Jonathan would have the woman hustled back to Forbes Junction and well on her way to Lexington. Then he'd get Emmie back to normal.

Except for the violet shadows beneath her eyes, she looked like she was managing...tired, but holding her own. He'd thought she was asleep when he crawled in beside her last night, but then it had occurred to him that she was playing possum. It had piqued him to think that her aloofness probably stemmed from the fact that her family was in the house. It would all be settled up in a day or so, he reckoned, rising and preparing to leave the table, casting one more glance at Emmaline. She met his eyes, and he was pierced by the unspoken plea that beckoned him. It was all he could do not to snatch her up from where she sat and haul her off to their bedroom to hold her and cherish her with tender touches. Later, he thought with resignation and more than a trace of anticipation.

Turning to the older man, he smiled, waiting patiently as he listened to Jonathan's compliments to Maria on the abundant breakfast she had served. "I declare, if we didn't already have two cooks in residence, I'd be offering you a fine position at our place in Kentucky, ma'am."

"Not on your life," Matt said with humor. "I'll remove the temptation, Maria, and take him with me," he told her as he rounded the table toward the door.

"Foiled again," Jonathan said playfully. "What are the plans, Mr. Gerrity?" he asked as he followed Matt toward the door.

"Thought we'd go for a ride, Mr. Rawlings. I'm headin' out to check with some of my men to the north of here."

"It's a beautiful ride," Emmaline put in eagerly. "Perhaps we could go along, Grandmother."

"I'm not sure you have an extra sidesaddle available, do you, Mr. Gerrity?" the older woman asked, wiping her mouth with the napkin from her lap and laying it precisely at the side of her plate.

"Hell's bells, I don't even have one of those goofy things," Matt said with honest scorn. "You'll have to ride with a real saddle out here, ma'am."

"I brought your riding costume, Emmaline," the woman said with a sniff, deigning to ignore Matt's burst of profanity.

"I wear a split leather skirt that belonged to Matt's mother," Emmaline said quietly. "I've been riding several times without my sidesaddle, and I've found it to be much more comfortable, Grandmother."

"I'm sure you managed to ride in sufficient comfort with a lady's saddle at home," the woman answered sharply.

Emmaline couldn't find it in her heart to lie. "I did ride astride, more than once, before I came here." she confessed, her voice subdued.

"Indeed?" The single word spoke volumes.

"Yes...the trainers let me when I rode the three-year-olds in the ring. It would have been confusing for them to have my weight unevenly distributed, when they were used to the men riding them astride.''

''I think there were several things going on that I was not privy to,'' Clara said coldly.

''Well, I think there were several things goin' on that Emmaline was not privy to, also,'' Matt said smoothly, turning back toward the dining room table.

''Matt!'' She turned to him, her eyes pleading. *Don't make a fuss,* she wanted to say. *Don't bring up the letters. I can't face another session with my grandmother,* she thought in despair. *Please Matt,* she begged silently. Her mouth quivered as she looked up at the tall man who stood before her. *Not now . . . not now . . .*

He understood. His head nodded, and he drew in a breath as he reined in the irritation that the gentlewoman from Kentucky managed to rile up so easily. Emmaline was riding the edge, he realized as he watched her blink back the tears that had risen to shine within the depths of her blue eyes. Her lips were trembling, and she was all in a fuss. The least he could do, he realized with a deeply drawn breath, was to keep his mouth shut and his thoughts to himself.

''You wanta come along, Em?'' he asked gently.

She hesitated for but a moment, and then better manners prevailed. ''No, I'll stay here with Grandmother. Will you be back for dinner?''

''I certainly need to be here by noontime, if that fits in with your morning, Matt,'' her grandfather interjected with an apologetic look. ''Emmaline's grandmother and I should be heading back to Forbes Junction this afternoon, in order to get the evening train.''

Matt nodded. ''We'll only be a couple hours. Tessie will be busy with her schoolwork this morning, won't she, Olivia?'' His attention turned to the young woman who still sat at the table with her charge.

''Do I hafta, Matt?'' Tessie piped up, wiggling in her chair as her dark eyes glittered with excitement. ''Can't I have a holiday today and be with Emmie?''

''I think it will be all right,'' Olivia said, her gaze veiled as it lifted to meet Matt's. ''I have some things to do in town. Perhaps I'll take the light buggy in, or ask one of the men to drive me.''

Matt nodded, satisfied for the moment that his household was in order. ''That'll be fine all around,'' he said, heading from the house, his boots noisy against the wooden floor of the hallway.

Behind him, Tessie slipped from her chair and rounded the table to clasp Emmaline's hand with her small fingers. ''We'll have fun, won't we, Emmie?'' she asked, with a look of hope lighting her fragile features.

A brisk nod was her answer, and with a giggle of delight, the child tugged at her sister, eager to enjoy her hours of freedom.

They were gone, and it was as if they had never been here. Emmaline's mind wove past each moment of her grandparent's visit, seeking one particle of comfort from the event. It was not to be. They'd left in the middle of the afternoon, leaving her numb with defeat. Finally, only the ceaseless chatter coming from Tessie's direction had been able to penetrate the dull lassitude that enveloped her. Only Tessie's pleading, jump rope in hand had brought a glimmer of interest to her blue eyes and caused her to put away her disappointment. She'd smiled her agreement, and taken up the lesson with her usual vigor.

The afternoon sun blistered the sandy ground, the heat rising in waves that forbade walking barefoot in the courtyard. Emmaline sat on a wooden bench tucked beneath the overhang, one tingling foot clutched in her hand, her fingers brushing quickly to remove the grains of sand that clung to her tender sole.

''I told you not to skip rope barefoot,'' Tessie reminded her airily. Parked beside her sister, she smothered an arrogant grin as she repeated her warning.

Emmaline cast her a glance that took in the amusement her small sister attempted to conceal. ''I sure wish you hadn't been right,'' she said mournfully, leaning closer to inspect the damage. The flesh was pink, but her sprightly movements had been quick enough to prevent actual burning, she was pleased to note.

"I never saw you move so fast, though," Tessie said, with twitching lips that struggled to hide her amusement. "You only jumped twice, but they sure were high jumps, Emmie."

From behind them, a chuckle announced a hidden watcher. "Yeah, that sure was some fancy steppin' you did, Miss Emmaline," said the man who lingered just inside the open terrace doorway.

Glancing over her shoulder, Emmaline dropped her foot to the ground, assuming a posture of indolence as she brushed at the sand on her skirt. "Spying, Gerrity?"

He was in shadow, but she sensed the difference in his mien, the subtle shading in his tone, the absence of the strain that had veiled his every word and phrase during the past day. A surge of emotion brought a quickening to her breath as Emmaline looked back at him once more. He's been protecting me, she thought, afraid they'd hurt me. The pleasure that welled up within her suffused her cheeks with a pink stain, blurring her eyes with unbidden tears as she considered the knowledge of her love for this man.

So quickly it had come, like a bolt of summer lightning, this overwhelming sureness that Matthew Gerrity owned her heart. She'd known, she'd really known, that it was all right before now, that she felt good about being his wife, she realized, aware that his gaze held her in thrall. But it was more than that, more than just "all right." She hadn't known this was how it felt, to love . . . to love.

She rose slowly, and Tessie reached for her skirt, small fingers tangling in the soft fabric.

"Where you goin', Emmie?"

Her smile was distracted as she looked down. "I thought I'd go indoors for a while, Tessie. It's pretty warm here." The words were breathless; indeed, she sensed a strange lethargy as she looked up once more at the man whose dark gaze seemed to pierce her to her depths. Lifting her hands to her mouth, she blinked at him from swimming eyes. Her lips compressed as her fingers moved upward against her face, until both palms were pressing against the flush that played across her cheekbones. Beneath her fingertips, she felt a trickle of moisture as a tear slid past the barrier of her lashes.

"Em?" His voice was low, but his movement was rapid as he straightened from the lazy stance he'd taken against the wall. "What's wrong, honey?" he asked quietly, his eyes intent on the glistening blue eyes that viewed him through a veil of tears. His hand touched her arm as she walked past him, but there was no hesitation in her step.

"I just need to wash my face, Matt," she muttered, intent on escaping to her bedroom.

"Emmie, are you cryin'?" Tessie asked in a wobbly little voice. She stood slump-shouldered, looking forlorn and abandoned as she watched her sister brush past. "You shouldn'ta teased her like that, Matthew! You made Emmie feel bad!"

Matt's attention swerved in her direction, pulled by the anguish that painted her words. "Emmie's fine," he assured the child, stepping to where she stood, then crouching before her to tilt her head back with one long forefinger beneath her chin. "She just got too hot out here in the sun," he told her, forcing a lightness to his voice he was far from feeling. "She didn't mind us teasin' her, sweetheart."

Behind him, he heard the closing of a door and knew it was the farthest bedroom down the hallway, the one he shared with Emmaline.

"Come on, Tessie. Let's go see what Maria has to offer us for a hot afternoon. I'll bet she made something cool to drink." Clasping her fingers in his, he led the child through the living room and into the kitchen at the back of the house.

"Maria, what've you got for Tessie to cool her off? She and Emmaline got all hot and bothered out in the courtyard."

"Maybe some nice buttermilk?" Maria offered with a teasing look at the child.

"Yuck!" Theresa answered inelegantly. "That's bad stuff, Maria. Don't we have any lemonade?"

"*Sí*, we can find you some, I'm sure," the housekeeper assured the child. "And you, Mr. Matt?"

"Nothing for me. Just let Tessie sit out here with you for a few minutes, all right?"

Without waiting for a reply, he backed from the room as Tessie followed Maria to the cupboard. Purposefully intent on muffling his footsteps, he approached the bedroom where Emmaline had retreated so abruptly.

The handle turned silently beneath his big hand, and he stepped through the doorway, his eyes seeking her slim figure within the room. The white curtains filtered the sunlight and its brightness was dimmed as it played across the floor. But caught in the midst of that shimmering, wavering brilliance was the slender form of his wife. She was a mound of clothing, topped by fiery curls that meshed with the sunlight. Her legs were drawn up, her arms encircling them tightly, so that her head, leaning upon her knees, gave her the appearance of a child, huddled against the cold. Or a small woman, curled within herself, he thought with a flash of intuition.

His approach was quiet, his boots silenced by the rug, and he squatted beside her, his hands dangling between his knees.

One large, callused palm lifted slowly and hovered over the back of her neck, where tangled curls were damp from the heat. She'd pulled them up, gathering them into her fist before she wrapped a piece of yarn about the upswept length and then left them to dangle in a mass of glorious confusion down her back. His fingers itched to bury themselves in that profusion of glory, and he clenched his fist against the urge.

She stirred, and her breath caught in a series of small sobs before she inhaled deeply, as if to stem the betraying sounds. Aware of the form hunkered beside her, she silently cursed the tears that stained her hot cheeks, not willing to allow her weakness to be so apparent to the man who waited silently next to her. That she should be so vulnerable to him was hard enough to cope with, without the knowledge he had captured her heart so quickly, so easily, and with such little effort.

All he'd had to do was be there, she recognized. All he'd had to do was be himself, that ever-vigilant, ever-protective, ever-aware husband she'd married and accepted into her secret self. For weeks, he'd woven his web about her, and she'd been too caught up in circumstances to recognize the strands of caring he'd secured her with.

If this is what it feels like to love a man, then I don't care for it, one little bit, she decided. Her head lifted, and she brushed at her eyes with the back of one hand, then swiped the dampness across the layers of fabric that made up her skirt.

"What do you want?" she asked in a muffled voice, not willing to face him with the evidence of her weakness still visible.

His palm possessed the fragile bones of her neck, where her nape was bent and the tender skin beckoned his touch. One knee dropped to the floor, and he leaned closer, allowing the other hand to curl about her face, turning it gently toward himself. His long, tanned fingers were cool against the hot flesh and the dampness that remained.

"What is it, Em? Did I make you angry when I teased you?" He waited as she stiffened, her eyes closing so that she didn't have to meet his gaze.

"No." The one word was abrupt, and her lips tightened, as if they held a multitude of syllables captive within their plush grip.

"Emmaline." It was a demand, as though he were tired of a guessing game he could not win, and his fingers tightened on the flesh of her cheek. "Will you look at me?" he asked, and again his voice made a command of the words.

Her eyes fluttered open, and the tears she had fought to contain within them beaded her lashes as she blinked once to clear the mist that clung. "I'm not a child, Matt. I don't get angry when you tease me. I might not appreciate it, but I don't take to pouting."

She focused on the perplexed look that furrowed his brow and pursed his lips as he watched her. Her eyes narrowed, for she was aware of the heartache in store for her if he recognized her foolishness. That Matt was more than willing to accept the responsibility of her as a wife was a certainty. That he was more than eager to seek the softness of her embrace during the long hours of the night was obvious. That he would welcome the words that her tender heart yearned to spill into his hearing was dubious, to be sure.

This marriage had been entered into for reasons that didn't include passionate promises and whispers of everlasting love. Matt seemed satisfied with the bargain he'd made. Emmaline had no intention of being any more open to hurt now than she'd been in the past.

For too long she'd waited, allowing those about her to deny her the love she craved. First her father had allowed her to be taken from him. He'd stood there and watched her leave and not lifted a hand to halt the process. The aching need for those big arms that had held her with such tender caring had never eased, she realized. She'd carried that same need all the way to the Kentucky horse farm where it had lain unquenched within the very depths of her heart for all of her growing-up years.

Only Delilah had given her the tender warmth of loving arms, and even that had become a memory since she'd become a grown girl, too big to be comforted by her nanny. Certainly the stern upbringing she received at the hands of her grandmother had not answered the cry of her heart. The memory of her sickly, often bedfast, mother was but a hazy recollection, she realized. The weak woman who had hated the Arizona sunshine had fared no better in the humid summers of Kentucky. Emmaline had often wondered if it had not been simpler for the woman who had birthed her to just lie abed and steadily allow her lingering reserves of strength to be depleted, day after day, than to make the effort of living.

Whatever her reasons, Theodora Carruthers had died in much the same way she lived, without a whimper of protest. In fact, the only time she'd asserted herself with any degree of firmness was the life-changing decision she'd made to leave the husband she'd grown to despise here in the everlasting sunshine.

"I wonder why my mother married my father," Emmaline said suddenly, blurting the words into the silence that had filled the room.

It was not what he'd expected to hear, and Matt gazed at her, dumbstruck. "What on earth brought that up?" he asked bluntly. His eyes scanned her rosy features and settled on the pouting fullness of her mouth. And then he grinned suddenly as she allowed those lips to tilt into a smile of her own.

A laugh that contained more than a remnant of a sob bubbled up from her depths. "I don't know," she admitted, a bit shyly, to be sure. Then she closed her eyes once more and shook her head. Her cheek brushed against the warmth of his big palm, and she inhaled sharply. "I tend to let my mind wander, Matt," she said ruefully, unwilling that he know all the various tacks she had taken in her meandering.

His sigh was verdant with the relief he felt. "Are you fixin' to be a woman for a few days, Em?" Relief enveloped him as he seized the thought.

Her reply cut short his sense of satisfaction and set him to puzzle-solving once more.

"Whatever do you mean, Gerrity?" Her eyes snapped open wide, and she frowned as she considered him. Then a flush coated her skin, washing up from her throat to pinken her cheeks once more. "If you're referring to my—" She broke off and bit at her lip. "If you mean what I think you mean . . . well . . . let me tell you, it's none of your business," she blurted out.

"Yeah, I guess I'm referrin' to what you think I am," he answered dryly, drawling out the words. "And it is my business, Mrs. Gerrity. Especially when it makes you all weepy and you start actin' like—" He broke off and rose, his broad hands clasping her about the middle as he got up, lifting her with him, until she hung within his grasp, her toes inches above the floor.

Her lower lip protruded, and she glared her frustration from sparkling eyes. "Will you put me down?" The words were muttered from between her teeth. "My personal business is not up for discussion, Gerrity!"

He brought her closer to himself, the muscles in his arms rigid and straining with the effort of holding her in midair. With their faces almost touching, he leaned forward, his lips brushing against hers. "I can find out myself," he whispered.

"How?" she blurted, and then her eyes opened wider once more. "Oh, no! Don't you dare even think it, Gerrity. You put me down. Don't you touch me!"

Her feet were swinging, attempting to do damage to his legs, and he laughed delightedly as he felt the bare toes against his shins. Her arms looped about his neck then, and she caught her fingers in the length of his dark hair, tugging and pulling at his head.

"Put me down, I said!"

"Can't. You're pullin' my hair out," he answered, wincing at the fierceness of her grip.

His own arms tightened, one sliding to clutch her around her middle, the other beneath her bottom, and he turned with her, carrying her to the big bed that centered the wall. Each step was accented by her words of protest, each word accompanied by another tug of her fingers in his shining hair.

Reaching his goal, Matt lifted one leg and slid it between hers. With that knee against the bed, he lowered them both to the mattress and allowed her to be cushioned in the feather tick as he let his weight fall against her slender frame.

"Oof!" She landed on her back and looked up to find his face against her own, his mouth twisted in a wolfish grin. "I'm really angry now," she sputtered as she released her grip on his hair and struggled to squeeze her hands in between their bodies.

"Well...if you're gonna get mad, I'll just hafta hold you here till you get glad, I reckon," he drawled, his mouth pecking eager kisses over every inch he could cover.

She squeezed her eyes shut against his attack, but it did little good, for her senses only became more attuned to his touch and she found herself lifting and twisting to capture the heat of his mouth with her own.

"I'm really mad, you know," she grumbled as his lips made the contact they'd sought.

"Ummm...are you now?" With leisurely pauses between each word, he made his way across her mouth, sucking at each lip in turn with small biting kisses.

"Matt!" she cried finally. "Will you listen to me?"

"Sure, honey, have at it." He inhaled deeply, lifting just enough to free her mouth to speak.

His eyes were warm and veiled with a look she recognized, and she sighed. "Somewhere out there in the house, Tessie is wondering what is going on in here," she said finally, flattening her fingers against his chest, urging him to give her space.

He did, lifting from her and resting his weight on his elbows—no easy feat, given the softness of the feather bed they lay on.

"Yeah..." His sigh was deep. "Is it too much to hope for that you'll be over bein' mad by tonight?" he asked, his brow wrinkled, his mouth downturned.

He looked like nothing more than a small boy begging for a treat, and she melted. "I'm not really mad now," she said, capitulating to his lure once more.

"No?" His fingers enclosed her face, and he narrowed his eyes as he watched her closely. "Tell me, Em," he asked quietly, his teasing mood held in abeyance. "What made you wonder about your mother a while ago? What were you thinking... or remembering?"

She looked at him and bit at her lower lip once more. "I think I need to know more about my father," she said finally. "I've never known him, not really. The memories of a small child are not very reliable, are they?"

He shook his head. "I don't know what you remember about old Sam, but I know something that may help you read his mind a little."

She was still, quiet as a doe in the twilight and just as pretty, he thought as she froze in place, her nostrils flaring just a bit and her mouth opening so that her tongue could touch the sudden dryness of her lips.

"Your letters—the ones Sam sent you—are here, honey," he said finally. "He put them away when they were sent back to him. He kept them for you."

Chapter Sixteen

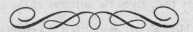

"Emmaline Gerrity, as I live and breathe," Ruth Guismann called from across the store, as if she were announcing the visit of a long-lost friend. "Haven't seen you since the party out at your place. Have you come shopping for supplies? Thought Matt sent someone in the other day."

Emmaline flushed as several heads turned her way, and then turned to close the door behind herself. She nodded to two women whose names she couldn't remember and headed for Ruth, thankful that good manners dictated she reply to the questions that had been fired in her direction.

"We just need a few things that Matt didn't think of. He remembered the coffee and bacon and such, but minor details like salt and vanilla slipped his mind. Maria was ready to stage a rebellion, so I told her to make a list for me." She rummaged through her reticule and brought forth a piece of paper with a dozen or so items scribbled on it.

"Let me see," Ruth said, reaching for the list. "I've been reading Maria's writing for years. Tell me all your news while I look this over and get things together."

But Emmaline's eye had been caught by a bolt of fabric left on the counter, and she ran her hand over it with open appreciation.

"Isn't that a pretty piece?" Ruth asked her as she breezed past. "It just came in on yesterday's train. Got a whole passel of dimity and batiste from St. Louis."

Emmaline lifted the bolt to unroll a yard or so of the fine material. Holding it up to the light, she admired the weave and the flowers that were scattered in a dainty array across

the cotton. "This would be lovely on Tessie for church,"
she said. "I think I'll have you cut me a piece, Mrs. Guismann."

"Ruth," the woman told her, depositing her armload of
supplies on the wooden counter. "I'm almost done, Emmaline. Just look around a little. There's a new shipment
of children's shoes in, too. I'll warrant Theresa has about
outgrown the ones her mama got her last fall."

The door opened behind Emmaline, and she glanced
over her shoulder. Deborah Hopkins was picking her way
across the store, plainly aware of all eyes fastened on her.
She made a beeline for Emmaline, a smile pasted on her
face.

"Well, if it isn't the bride!" she trilled. "I can't believe
you let Matt out of your sight. Or are you hiding him back
there?" She made a show of peering over the counter and
shook her head in a mocking gesture.

Emmaline gritted her teeth. "Hello to you, too, Deborah. My, it certainly is nice to see you getting around. I was
afraid all of the exercise you got on the dance floor might
have laid you up for a while." Before she could stop them,
the cutting words had passed Emmaline's lips, and for a
moment she regretted her lapse in manners.

But not for long, as Deborah shot a haughty look in her
direction. "Oh, I admit, I had to rest up after the party at
your place, what with dancing with every eligible man in the
territory until I was just about worn to a frazzle," Deborah said. "You know, I would have sent some of them in
your direction, but you were hanging on to Matt so tight,
it... well..." She leaned closer in a semblance of intimacy. "You know, you can't hold a man by being a clinging vine, Emmaline."

"If there's anything I've never been accused of being, it's
a clinging vine, Deborah," Emmaline said with a brittle
little laugh. "And, contrary to what you may think you
saw, the hands holding on so tight weren't mine. Matt just
can't stand to have me more than two steps away these days.
He's found lots about me to admire lately, I guess." Her
eyes lowered in a semblance of modesty, but her lips
twitched as she tried not to smile. This nastiness was con-

tagious, she realized. But then, manners had gotten her
nowhere with Deborah up to this point, and since they'd
been abandoned in favor of straight talking, she might as
well join the rest of these folk.

"Well, that ruckus you put on with that cowhand sure
was a shame to behold." The words cut in on Emmaline's
thoughts, and she blinked as she considered the charge
Deborah had made.

"Ruckus?" She frowned her bewilderment.

Deborah lowered her voice, speaking in a loud whisper.
"Matt sure was embarrassed by all the fuss, you know. It
made him look downright foolish, you taking off with that
man the way you did."

"Foolish? You think he felt foolish because I was almost kidnapped? Why, I heard he looked pretty heroic,
carrying me to the house and making such a fuss over me."
Emmaline took a deep breath, aghast at the accusation.
That Deborah would even suggest such a thing... that
anyone would believe Emmaline would run off...

Deborah's lashes fell, concealing her eyes and she
squared her shoulders. "Well, I'd never noticed Matt
Gerrity fussing over anyone in all the years I've known
him," she said snidely, as if doubting Emmaline's word.

She'd tried to control her temper, she really had. But this
woman really took the cake, Emmaline decided, speaking
her reply with wide-eyed sincerity. "Of course he fusses
over me all the time, being a new bridegroom and all. Why,
I could tell you..." She put her hand over her mouth and
giggled. "But then, being left on the shelf, so to speak, you
wouldn't understand such things." Her eyes narrowed, and
she hesitated a moment, then smiled in silky speculation.
"Or would you? No, of course not!" she said, denying the
subtle insult.

"I could have had him, you know," Deborah said with
a nonchalant gesture of her hand, waving it gaily before
Emmaline's face.

"Well, I'm sure he could have had you...if he'd wanted
you," Emmaline said agreeably. "But from what I heard,
he wasn't much interested. Maybe the samples you handed
out didn't tempt him."

Ruth Guismann approached, her face flushed, her eyes dancing with merriment as she interrupted the set-to she'd been eavesdropping on. "I've got everything together, Emmaline. How much of that dimity did you want cut for Theresa's dress?"

"Three yards should do it. Oh, and whatever else I'll need to make it up," she added. "Matt told me to pick up anything I wanted," she said, smiling sweetly. "He's so generous, you know."

Deborah leaned closer as Emmaline walked past her. One hand grasped Emmaline's arm with cruel intent, her fingernails digging into the tender underside.

Emmaline drew to a halt by her side, deciding to pacify the other woman somehow. Matt would not be pleased by the sharp words spoken before the women in the store who listened so intently.

Her resolution was shattered by Deborah's words of warning. "It's not over till you have a child, Emmaline. What if that day never comes?"

Emmaline stiffened, flushing darkly as the intimate details of her bargain with Matt were made known aloud.

"What do you know about that?"

"My aunt works for Mr. Hooper," Deborah said smugly.

"Then she should be ashamed of herself, telling things she has no business repeating," Emmaline said quietly. Snatching her arm out of Deborah's grasp, she sailed down the length of the counter to where Ruth waited.

"Sheriff Baines!" Matt's summons halted the lawman in his tracks. Turning from the middle of the road, he eyed the tall rancher with mild curiosity.

"Got a problem, Matt?" he asked, heading back toward his office with a deceptively lazy gait. Past his prime, he'd found an easy berth in Forbes Junction, but when matters called for it, he was known to live up to the reputation that had traveled with him.

Keen eyes viewed Matt Gerrity, and then, reassured that no immediate emergency prevailed, the sheriff waved a hand toward the hotel, just across the way. "How about a bite of breakfast?" he asked hopefully.

"Sure, I'll sit with you while you eat." Matt could afford to be agreeable. He lengthened his stride to catch up with the lawman. Tilting the brim of his hat a bit, he smiled. "Kinda late for breakfast, isn't it? Or are you keepin' town hours these days?"

They stepped up onto the broad wooden walkway that fronted the hotel and waited while a young boy held the door open for them to enter the lobby.

"Naw, I just can't bring myself to eat the stuff Hilda cooks for the prisoners. Sorta took my appetite this morning when I saw all that cold gravy and biscuits on Smokey's plate."

Matt led the way to the dining room archway and hung his hat on the rack provided. "What's old Smokey doin' in jail?"

"Drunk as usual." The lawman's words were succinct.

"Was he fightin' again?" Matt asked as the white-aproned waitress poured two cups of coffee into thick mugs. This time of day, the hotel abandoned its china cups, he was pleased to note.

Hailey Baines shrugged. "Naw, not enough to really hurt anybody. He just needed to cool off." The waitress approached once more, this time with a plate of eggs and pancakes in hand. With a small flourish, she placed it in front of the sheriff and turned her attention to Matt.

"You going to have breakfast, too, Mr. Gerrity?" she asked.

"How'd he get that served up so quick?" Matt asked, nodding at the plate of food that was occupying Hailey Baines's attention.

"We saw him coming," the waitress said, deep dimples showing her amusement. "As soon as he leaves his office about this time every day, the deskman lets us know and we put his eggs on to fry."

Matt grinned. "Better watch your step, Sheriff," he said in an undertone. "It doesn't pay to get too predictable."

"Well, I keep to a tight schedule," Hailey answered, pausing for a swallow of hot coffee. "They just try to accommodate me a bit."

"Coffee's enough for me this morning," Matt told the girl. "My schedule's kinda tight too," he added. "In fact, I don't want to be leaving Emmaline on her own for too long."

"You bring her with you this morning?" Hailey asked.

"For the most part, I'm not letting her get two feet from me these days. But I dropped her off at the dry goods with a list of stuff she's lookin' for, and I told her to stay there till I came back."

"Is this the same woman you had to track down in a saloon in order to get married?" His face was solemn, but his eyes gleamed with humor, and Hailey Baines was rewarded with a glare for his efforts.

"Emmaline's tamed down real well," Matt said. "She knows better than to trot around town by herself. She'll stay put."

"You got some problems out your way, Matt?" Having made short work of the plate of food, the sheriff raised his hand to the waitress, and she nodded at him.

"Yeah, you could say that. You were there the night of the party, when somebody tried to grab Emmaline right off the back porch," he reminded him quietly.

Hailey Baines nodded, his eyes intent as he listened. "Has there been anything else going on?" He glanced up as the waitress placed a plate before him, covered by a cinnamon roll that looked to be fresh from the oven. "Thanks, Molly."

"No, not since then. You knew about the shot that was fired the morning we got married."

The sheriff nodded. "Seemed like it was somebody looking for game, isn't that right?"

"That's what Emmaline wants to believe. I don't agree with her," Matt said. "Not after the incident with her saddle a couple of weeks after she got here."

"Too many coincidences, Matt?"

"Let's just say I'm not real comfortable without her tucked under my arm these days. And let me tell you, it's a mite difficult to run a ranch that way," he growled.

"Got any ideas? Why would somebody be after Emmaline? Nobody here has anything against the girl. And everybody thought well of old Sam Carruthers, far as I know," Hailey said.

Matt shook his head. "I thought at first it was just pranks, mean stuff, maybe someone wantin' her to go back to Kentucky. But when she was grabbed right off my porch, I decided it was more than that. Besides, anybody that knows me ought to know that I wouldn't be lettin' my wife run back east, no matter how scared she was."

"Is she?"

"Scared?" Matt grinned. "Emmaline? Not on your life. Mad's more like it." He shook his head, and the smile disappeared. "Fact is, Sheriff, I'd like it better if she was a little scared. She's certain she did enough damage to that bastard with her teeth to chase him off. I hated to tell her it was the screamin' she did that sent him flyin'."

"Either way, she was a lucky woman," Hailey said, pushing his chair back. "You done with that coffee yet?"

"Yeah, I guess so." Matt looked at his half-full cup and lifted it quickly, draining it with two swallows. "I just thought I'd let you know that I'm feelin' pretty uneasy about the whole thing. Almost like I'm waitin' for the other boot to hit the floor."

"Have you heard of any new hands being hired on hereabouts? How about your men?"

Matt shook his head. "I've had the same bunch for over a year. Haven't put on a new man since Kane hit town last summer. And he's worked out real well."

"How about Clyde Hopkins? He hire on anybody this spring?"

Matt glanced up and shrugged. "Not that I know of, but then, I don't spend a lot of time lookin' for new faces. Some of these hands come and go a lot, you know."

"Sounds like you've come up empty-handed, Matt," Hailey said as they sauntered toward the door. "See you tomorrow, Molly," the lawman said to the woman, who watched them leave.

"Don't you pay for breakfast?" Matt asked, fishing in his pocket for loose change.

"Naw, they give me a bill once a week. Keep your money, Gerrity. I'll foot the bill for your coffee. Seems like the least

I can do, after the meal I ate at your place the night of your party."

"Well, I'd better go round up Emmaline," Matt said with a sigh of frustration. "Guess I was snatchin' at straws this morning. Just thought you might have heard somethin' around town that I didn't pick up on."

"We'll just have to keep our eyes open, I reckon," the lawman said agreeably. "If I see or hear anything that rings a bell, you'll be the first to know. If anything goes wrong, you know where to find me."

"Well, right now I feel like I'm walkin' blindfolded," Matt told him, halting before the jail. "I don't know where to start lookin'. There just doesn't seem to be any reason for anybody to want to hurt Emmaline."

"Anybody mad 'cause she married you?"

Matt snorted. "Don't know who, 'cept for Deborah, and she's got no reason to squawk. Besides, she's not ornery enough to pull somethin' like this."

The sheriff tipped his hat at a jaunty angle. "Isn't there an old saying about a woman scorned?" he asked softly.

At Matt's quick, unbelieving look, Hailey shrugged. "Just thought I'd mention it. Might be worth thinking about."

"I told you to stay and talk to Ruth Guismann till I got back." Matt's hands rode his hipbones, and his eyes were dark with anger as they skimmed over her full-skirted blue dress, as if he were looking for some damage done to the woman within the yards of fabric.

"I told you, Matt. I got tired of waiting and just walked out to put my parcels in the buggy. I left the heavy stuff for you to carry out." Not for the world would she carry tales about Deborah. Besides, she was still feeling a bit shame-faced at her own part in the quarrel. Not only that, the store had become too small for both of them, and Emmaline had known she needed fresh air to cool her anger before she had to face Matt.

"Well, I don't want you roamin' around by yourself," Matt grumbled as he picked her up with both hands about her waist and swung her into the buggy seat.

"For heaven's sake! I know how to climb in here without you manhandling me," Emmaline sputtered, smoothing her skirt and looking about to see if they had been observed. "Don't make a fuss about nothing, Matt."

He untied the reins from the hitching rail in front of the dry goods store and stalked to the other side of the buggy, leaning in to speak to her. "Is this everything you bought?" he asked, nodding to the boxes he'd lashed to the rear.

"If you brought out two crates of groceries, you got it all," she snapped, her chin jutting angrily as she looked straight ahead.

"Then I got it all," he muttered, climbing up to sit beside her. He picked up the reins and slapped them easily on the broad back of the mare. Obediently she headed down the road, and at a second reminder broke into a trot.

"I saw Deborah inside the dry goods. Did you talk to her?" he asked.

"We spoke." Her words were muffled as she leaned to rearrange the packages she'd placed about her feet.

"What's in there?" he asked, his head nodding at the bundles.

"Some things for Theresa. She's grown a lot since anyone made her something to wear to bed. Her nightgowns are all too short. On top of that, she needs a new Sunday dress. I bought her a pair of patent-leather slippers to go with it," she said defensively.

"Well, we'll be stickin' pretty close to home, Emmaline, till things get settled down," he told her. "Tessie won't be needin' Sunday-mornin' clothes for a while."

"Surely you won't be keeping us from church, just because some idiot tried to . . ."

"That idiot could have hauled you away over his saddle without a whimper, if you hadn't sunk your teeth into him," he reminded her darkly.

"I refuse to let some outlaw make me a prisoner in my own home," she announced, her cheeks pink with anger.

"Aw, come on, Em." He smiled, attempting to coax her out of her temper. "We don't need to fight over this. I take it back. I won't keep you from goin' to church with Tessie. I'll just have to get you there myself from now on."

"You're going to church?" Arched eyebrows signaled her amazement.

"Yeah. I'm not a heathen, you know," he answered sharply.

"Well, if that isn't something of a miracle," she mused, her eyes glittering with amusement.

"You're not mad anymore?" He risked a glance in her direction.

"I wasn't mad to start with," she lied. "Just a little aggravated with you and your high-handed methods."

"Now what the hell does that mean?"

She pursed her mouth and attended his stony profile. "Just look at you! All up in the air and cursing up a storm. You seem to think that being my husband gives you the right to tell me what to do every day of the week."

She waited for the retort she was certain he couldn't resist tossing in her direction, but was greeted instead with silence.

His refusal to participate spurred her on. "Did it ever occur to you that you're getting upset over absolutely nothing? All I did was walk out of the store and put my packages in the buggy and wait there for you. You'd think I'd been looking for trouble, the way you act."

It was enough. He rolled his eyes in exasperation.

"Honestly, Emmaline, you sure do take the cake for pure ignorance this morning. There's a man out there somewhere who has every intention in the world of hurting you. Honey, he's already shot at you and tried to run off with you. Not to mention havin' you bucked off your horse. Just how much more does he need to do to get your attention?" He turned to glare at her, his worry forming frown lines that ridged his forehead beneath the brim of his hat.

"Well, I just don't think that ten o'clock in the morning, in the middle of town, is any time to be fretting about some outlaw giving me trouble. Besides, I was thinking that maybe the man who tried to grab me was just letting a prank get out of hand. Don't they do shivarees out here? You know, where the bride gets carried off for an hour or so?" She looked up at him, almost pleadingly, as if his reassurance would make everything right to her mind.

"Shivaree is one thing, Em. Kidnapping is a whole different mess of fish altogether. They don't even compare," he muttered beneath his breath. "You need to understand, honey—until we find out what's goin' on, you're gonna have to be careful."

"Well, I really can't see that there's any danger in broad daylight," she said with a sniff of defiance.

He glanced at her, and his eyes lingered on her mouth. Her lips firmly pressed together. His heart was touched by the woebegone look that painted her features, taking every trace of joy from her expression.

One long arm snaked about her waist, and with an easy movement he tugged her closer, lifting her until she was pressed against his side. "Take off your bonnet, Emmaline."

"Whatever for?" she wanted to know, amazed at his order.

"Do you have to argue over everything I tell you? Just do what I asked, will you?"

Her sigh was deep, but her fingers moved to untie the bow that had been fashioned beneath her chin. With a flourish, she swept the straw bonnet from her head and deposited it under her seat.

"There! Now are you happy?" she asked with another wave of her hand.

"Well, it sure makes it a lot easier to kiss you and nuzzle your ear, without all those flowers bobbin' in my face and that straw scratchin' my nose."

"You wanted to kiss me?" Her look was unbelieving as she turned to face him.

"Sure did," he said agreeably, and bent to do just that.

And then, as if it were for the first time, he tasted the freshness of her mouth, the soft, plush cushion of her lips and the fragile warmth just inside. His intent had been to take her mind from the cares of the day, to tighten the bonds between them, to revel for just a moment in the delight of her nearness. But so easily, her scent and the sweet savoring of her mouth beguiled him, and he was caught up in the kiss that had begun so innocently.

"Ah, Emmie, you taste so good," he muttered against her cheek. He drew in a breath and delivered a line of damp little pecks down the side of her throat, tilting her head with a nudge of his cheek, the better to find the pulse beat he sought. "Somethin' down here sure smells good," he whispered against her flesh.

"Ummm...probably the soap I washed with." She closed her eyes, relishing the feel of his mouth against her skin.

"Uh-uh. I don't think so, honey. It just seems like pure Emmaline to me. You smell just about like this all over, you know," he told her in a rough whisper.

"I do?" She laughed beneath her breath as he touched her throat with the tip of his tongue. "That tickles. You're making me have chill-bumps, Matt!"

His teeth drew in a bite of flesh, and he held it captive for a moment. Then, with a sigh, he relinquished his prize and puckered his mouth against the pinked spot with a loud, wet smack.

"Damn, you sure know how to hurt a guy, Em." He groaned, straightening in his seat and abandoning the project he'd undertaken with such enthusiasm. Sitting erect, he tilted his hat back with a nonchalant gesture, but his eyes were alert, casting a guarded look at their surroundings as he slapped the reins against the horse's hindquarters once more.

Emmaline watched his movements, attuned to his mood. Then, with a great to-do, she straightened her blouse, tugging at the gathered neckline and brushing at her hair distractedly. Casting another glance at him and worrying her bottom lip with her teeth, she considered his watchful stance.

"You're really worried, aren't you, Matt?"

He glanced at her. "Just give me a while to figure this out, okay Em? It'll all work out, I promise. We'll get to the bottom of it."

Slipping her hand inside the bend of his elbow, she squeezed the hard muscle of his arm. "Well, I'm not about to get into a dither over things. I know you'll take care of me. And I promise to be careful. I mean it. I'll do whatever you say."

"You know what? I've been thinkin', honey." Intent on changing the subject, he patted her hand and grinned in her direction. "You know what I told you the other night... about the letters your pa kept for you?"

Her eyes lit with delight as she rounded on him, twisting in the buggy seat to face him. "You know where he put them?" she asked eagerly.

His snort was answer enough. "Of course I do. I know where just about everything in that house is located. They're in a locked box in his desk."

"Well, why didn't you give them to me, then?" she wanted to know.

He shook his head. "I don't know. I guess I thought when the right time came, I'd know enough to get them out and let you have them."

Emmaline closed her eyes as a sense of satisfaction flooded her. I told you so, Grandmother, she whispered within herself. I knew Matt was right. I knew it! She settled herself tightly against his hip, facing the front of the buggy once more as she edged her hand atop his thigh, her fingers spread to tighten against the hard muscle. Her breast pressed against his arm as she nestled her shoulder against his side, and he took the hint, raising his arm to wrap it about her slender back. His big hand rested at her waist, cradling her ribs, with the softness of her breast teasing the backs of his fingers.

"When we get home, okay, Em?"

Her answer was a few seconds in coming. She drew in a breath, as if a momentous decision were in the making, and then nodded, the movement brushing wayward curls against his cheek as he bent closer to hear her reply.

"Yes, when we get home."

"So be it," he whispered. "When we get home."

The big chair cradled her body, holding her within its plush leather depths. In her lap, the letters were heavy, resting against her thighs with a strange warmth. Almost as if he were here, as if his own body were beneath hers in the chair, Emmaline felt her father's presence. Her fingers pressed against the topmost envelope and slid it from place, opening it with care. Her eyes filled with tears as she read the first words, and she blinked furiously, the better to see the strong script.

> My dear daughter,
> I pray your mama will read this to you. It is my hope that you will remember that your papa loves you and misses you every day. I send you hugs and kisses.
>
> Your loving papa

She folded the short note with trembling fingers and placed it in the yellowed envelope. For twenty long years it had lain atop the stack, tied with a leather thong, though probably the thong had been wrapped about the pile much later, she realized.

The second envelope was a little heavier, and she opened it carefully, as if to tear it might be a desecration to the man who had sealed it, posted it and then accepted its return with heart-rending regret.

> My dear daughter,
> The horses have gone to the high country for the heat of the summer. I sent along your pony, since no one here will ride it. She will be waiting for you when you return. Maria sends her love and prays every day in your behalf. I hope you are enjoying your visit with your grandparents.
>
> Your papa loves you.

He thought I was coming back! Why would he think that? she wondered. Did Mama lie to him when she left? Surely he must have known the leave-taking was final.

But apparently not.

Her eyes awash with tears, she fumbled with the envelope, carefully refolding the note to place it within. And then she discovered that a picture remained inside: a hand-drawn sketch of a pony, dappled with darker tones and adorned with darker mane and tail. Colored with wax crayons, it was surprisingly lifelike. And obviously a futile attempt to provide his child with a memento of her pony.

How he must have felt! she thought with a heavy heart. To know that he was forbidden to correspond with his daughter. That cruel and unknown hands kept his messages from the child he loved so well.

Her eyes wept copious tears as her fingers wrapped about the stack of letters, holding them closely against her breast . . . as if the love contained in those sheets of foolscap could somehow be transmitted to the child now grown.

"Oh, Papa," she whispered mournfully, her head bent as hot tears fell, to be soaked up by the voluminous skirt she wore.

"Emmaline." The soft whisper penetrated her despair, and she lifted her face to where Matt stood, just inside the door of his office.

"Ah, Emmie, your pa wouldn't want you to cry over those letters," he said tenderly. "He'd want you to read them and be happy."

Her head shook, slowly and mournfully. "It's so sad, Matt. Why didn't someone tell me he loved me?"

He strode across the room and knelt next to the leather chair that almost enveloped her in its depths. His broad palm tenderly cradled her cheek, and she allowed the weight of her head to rest against his greater strength. Her eyes were closed, and the tears had ceased to flow. Only a hiccuping sob escaped once, and then again, before she sniffed and stirred to search out her handkerchief.

He was there before her, loosening the red bandanna that was tied about his neck, easing it into her groping fingers and releasing his own hold as she blew her nose and wiped at the tears that trembled on her cheeks.

Her eyes opened, and she smiled at the sight of the red cloth she held. "I'll wash it out for you," she offered shyly, as if sharing his neckerchief was a very personal thing to be doing.

He shrugged and smiled his relief. "I've got lots where that one came from. Looked to me like you had enough tears and dribbles there to fill three of those little bits of hankies you carry around in your pocket." He shifted his weight to the other leg and leaned closer, tugging her head to rest against his shoulder.

"Maybe you better plan on keepin' a bunch of my bandannas right here on the desk while you finish readin' that pile of mail."

Her smile widened, and she nestled into the bend of his shoulder, her lips searching for the tender flesh beneath his jaw. Her whisper was warm against him, and he closed his eyes, to better savor the pleasure of her touch.

"I'll be all right now," she assured him softly. Fumbling with the stack of letters that had fallen into her lap, she drew forth the second one in the pile.

"Look, Matt. This was my pony.... I think her name was Ranger." She pulled out the crayon drawing and unfolded it with gentle hands, smoothing it carefully as she presented it for his inspection.

"Yeah, old Sam was some hand at drawing," Matt said. "That's a good likeness, you know. That pony only died about four years ago."

"Really? If I'd come back sooner, I might have seen him again?" The thought brought forth a trickle from the well of bitterness she'd carefully contained for many weeks. "How can I ever forgive them?" she asked, with little hope of an answer. "That's why they left early, you know. I had a big fuss with my grandmother, and she was terribly upset with me."

"I kinda figured that out, honey," he said soberly. "And as for forgivin' them for the past, that's somethin' you'll have to work out on your own, you know. If it makes you feel any better, I doubt if they realized how much harm they were doing."

"She must have known . . . My mother had to know how much I needed..." But her thoughts were too hard to form into words. "I'll come back to these later." She straightened the stack, moving the leather thong and tucking the second letter into place.

Matt pulled open the bottom drawer and picked up the metal box that had held its secrets for many years. His fingers lifted the lid, and she deposited her treasure within, one fingertip stroking the words on the front of the topmost envelope. *Miss Emmaline Joy Carruthers,* he'd written in bold, slashing letters. Her mouth formed a word, but it remained unspoken, and she allowed Matt to close the lid, locking the precious papers within.

Papa...

"The grandparents have left."

"I'll bet you were hopin' they'd take the city gal back home with 'em, weren't you?" His words were amused as he viewed the woman from beneath his heavy eyebrows. "It sure woulda saved me a whole lot of trouble."

"Don't be foolish," she answered briskly. "It'll take more than a visit from two old fogies to get her out of my way. She knows when she has a good thing, married to Matt Gerrity and owning half the ranch."

"Which do you want more? The ranch or Matt Gerrity?" The man approached her, his lips curved in a smile that bore no humor. "It's sorta up to me whether you get either one, isn't it, lady?" His voice was husky, his eyes dark with intent as they swept the length of the woman who leaned with indolent ease against the tree. One hand lifted, and grimy fingers brushed against her cheek. "I'm sure lookin' forward to tastin' this nice soft—"

She turned her face abruptly and his hand fell to his side. "Keep your hands to yourself," she told him, concealing her aversion beneath lowered eyelids. Her chin lifted in a haughty gesture. "You'll get your money after you keep your end of the bargain."

"Not only money," he reminded her, reaching to toy with the fastening on her cloak, grinning as he sensed her reluctance.

She looked at him impatiently and brushed at the fingers that sullied her garment. "Just do it." She moved away from his touch, then looked up at him.

"Just do it," she repeated, "and then..." Her smile was a promise.

"Don't think you'll get away from me tonight, lady."

Her senses reeled as she considered the threat he conveyed. "What do you expect?"

His hands drew her against him. His head was bent, his mouth inches from hers. "I could give you a good time right now, honey."

The scent of his whisky-tinged breath filled her nostrils and she shook her head, gasping for a breath of clean air. "Not here! Not now!" Her voice was not as firm as she'd like it to be and she stiffened in his grasp. "I have to go. I'll be missed."

With reluctance he released her. "When? I want to get this over and done with. You're gonna have to help out a little here. Gerrity's watchin' the woman like a big cat after a newborn calf."

She nodded. "Keep a sharp eye out. I'll do what I can."

Chapter Seventeen

"Can we go for a ride today?" Tessie's eyes were hopeful as she made the request. "I cleaned my plate," she added brightly, as if that might sway the verdict.

Matt's mouth curved in a smile. "Listen, punkin," he said, "you've got schoolwork to do."

She shook her head vigorously. "Not today. Miss Olivia said that I deserved a day off, 'cause I've been doing so good."

"Is that so?" Matt's eyes focused on the young woman, who was busily concentrating on her breakfast. "Olivia?"

She glanced up quickly and nodded her agreement. "If you don't mind," she added after a moment. "After all, if Theresa were in a regular school situation, she wouldn't even be into her books through the summer months."

Matt studied her for a moment. "Do you feel the need of a vacation yourself, Olivia? I hadn't thought of it before, but maybe you have family you'd like to visit, or friends, perhaps."

She shook her head. "No, Mr. Gerrity. I haven't anywhere in particular to go. My family is back east, you know, and we never have been especially close."

"Well, if you change your mind, let me know," he told her. "And as far as Tessie's studies go, I agree that she should not be puttin' in too many hours during the summer. She needs to be spending time with her sister, anyway. Emmaline's been wantin' to read some of her books to Tessie."

"What I'd really like to do is go for a good long ride with her," Emmaline put in. "I'm getting awfully tired of sitting around in this house, Matt."

He gave her a look of forbearance and attempted to soften his refusal. "Now, Em...you know we have to be careful."

"You mean *I* have to be careful, don't you?" she asked, aware that she was being more than rude, arguing with him in front of Olivia, but unable to resist seizing the moment in order to state her views.

"Emmaline..." he began, his tone urgent and stern.

"Matthew!" she said, mocking his intonation. "Just listen to you! All set to lecture, instead of suggesting a family outing with Tessie and me."

He stared at her blankly.

"A family outing?" As if the words were foreign, he repeated them and then shook his head.

"You're saying no without even considering the idea." It was a sharp accusation.

"This is a ranch, Emmaline, and I run it. If I don't keep my hand in and keep things moving and under control, we'll be in big trouble. I don't have time for 'family outings,' and I surer'n hell don't have time to argue with you this morning. Besides, you told me just a couple days ago you'd do whatever I asked."

"I knew you'd bring that up. And in case you didn't know it, I'm very aware of your duties around here. It's just too bad that one of them doesn't involve Tessie and me."

"Look, lady," he said wrathfully, aware of the audience they had managed to captivate with their dispute. "I'm involved up to my neck with you, in case your memory is a bit short. Tessie sure isn't doin' any complainin', and I've already devoted almost a whole day to you this week."

"When?" she demanded, and then waved a hand at him as she recognized what he was talking about. "You were planning on going into town that day, anyway. You said you wanted to see the sheriff, and I just went along for the ride."

Olivia's gaze swept from one to the other as Emmaline and Matt's voices rose in volume, her mouth pursed as she listened. Then, as they both drew breath at the same time, she cleared her throat and stood.

"I believe I'll go to my room, if you don't mind," she said quietly.

"Now see what you've done," Emmaline hissed as the young woman walked quickly through the doorway and down the hall. "You embarrassed Olivia!"

"I embarrassed her? Me?"

Theresa looked from one to the other, and her eyes filled with tears. "I didn't want to go riding, anyway," she said sadly. "Come on, Emmie. Let's just go read or something. Matthew has lots of work to do, I guess."

Tipping his head back, Matt took a deep breath and ran his fingers through the length of his dark hair, making runnels in the dampness left from his early-morning ablutions.

"Look, you two. Why don't we make a bargain, all right? I'll do what I have to this morning, and then, after we eat dinner at noon, we'll go for a ride together and head for the creek above the north pasture. Maybe Tessie can go wadin' and play under the trees." He looked hopefully at the females in his life, one of whom had eyes that had begun to glow with bright expectation.

"Oh, Matthew! I sure do love you a lot!" The cry was welcome music to his ears, and he crouched to catch the child who hurled herself at him. Her short arms wrapped about his neck, and she scattered kisses over his face.

"Well, that was answer enough, I guess," he allowed, rising as Tessie left his embrace to turn to her sister.

"Isn't that good, Emmie? I get to wade in the creek and everything," she said, waving her arms expansively.

"Well, Emmaline, are you gonna be as grateful as your little sister?" he asked quietly, more than willing to make peace. "I'd sure like a kiss from you, too."

With a look at the child who was bouncing up and down before her, Emmaline abandoned whatever hurt she'd sustained.

"It sounds wonderful to me, Matt," she said, her face alight with pleasure as she felt the tug of Tessie's fingers.

"Now you hafta kiss him," the child whispered loudly.

"Yeah, now you hafta kiss me," he repeated softly. His eyes gleamed with anticipation as he watched Emmaline's cheeks turn a delightful shade of pink.

She tilted her head and gave him a silent admonition. *Don't you dare, Matt Gerrity*, she thought. But he would not be denied.

In three long strides, he was before Emmaline. Long arms wrapped his wife in an embrace that drew her against the hard length of his body. And as his head dipped to allow their lips to meet, she heard the ecstatic giggle that Tessie could not contain.

"Matt!" The protest was muffled beneath his mouth.

"Ummm..." Whatever words she attempted to utter were swallowed up in the tenderness of his caress. His kiss spoke to her, as though it were an apology. Gently, he wooed her. Carefully, he touched her.

And, finally, he won her acquiescence, and she allowed the softness of her body to be absorbed into the broad structure of his own.

It was what he had waited for, this silent melting of her resistance, this warmth she gave so willingly.

"Ah, Emmaline...you sure do pack a mean punch. I reckon I'm just about the luckiest man hereabouts this morning. I've got the best armful of woman in the territory right here." Then, glancing down at Tessie, he grinned broadly.

"Not to mention the best little sister anybody ever had."

Emmaline pushed him away, aware of the flush that had taken possession of her. "Go on now," she said. "We'll see you at dinner, won't we, Tessie?"

"Yeah, we'll be waiting for you, Matthew," the little girl agreed eagerly, the morning stretching before her in a long series of minutes and hours.

"Boss, I hate to be carryin' tales, but I think you're gonna hafta do somethin' about that last hand you hired." Claude's lined face was concerned as he stood at the corral fence with Matt, both of them leaning with elbows propped on the top rail. Beneath the cloudless sky, the new arrivals from Kentucky, Thoroughbred mares, were circling the pole fence, tossing their heads, their tails high and flying, their glossy coats shimmering in the sunlight.

Frown lines furrowed Matt's forehead, evident when he tilted his hat back with one long finger. "Are we talkin' about Kane?"

Claude nodded glumly. "Yup, shore are. I'm thinkin' he's slackin' off on the job."

"He's up with the herd," Matt told him shortly. "How would you know what he's doin'?"

"That's the whole thing. Tucker saw him in town the other day. Kane tried to bluff his way out of trouble, but old Tuck said he acted mighty sneaky about the whole thing." Claude switched feet on the bottom rung of the fence and scratched at the back of his head beneath the brim of his hat. "He even tried to make Tucker swear not to tell you he'd seen him."

"Well, if that don't take the cake," Matt said, his eyes narrowed thoughtfully. "What you s'pose he was up to, Claude? And who on God's green earth was doin' his job while he was lollygaggin' around in town?"

Claude shrugged and shook his head, but his eyes sparkled as he glanced up at his boss. "Think mebbe he went to town to visit with one of the ladies at . . ." He glanced behind him, lest any female ears should be within eavesdropping distance. "Well, you know what I mean," he said with a dry chuckle.

"If he's that hard up, he needs to ask for a replacement," Matt growled. "I won't stand for a hand takin' off like that, leavin' a hole where a body's supposed to be standin' watch."

"Well, the problem is, I guess it's not the first time he's been seen round and about," said Claude evasively.

Matt's face darkened and he glared at the man next to him. "You been holdin' out on me?"

Claude shook his head. "Not really, boss. I just sorta took care of it the other time, thought maybe he had snuck down to see a fancy lady, but seems to me like he shouldn't be all randy again so soon. That's when I thought it best to fill you in."

"Well, damned if that ain't just what I need," Matt blurted. "There's not a multitude of extra ranch hands layin' around on the ground this time of year. Fact is, they're about as scarce as water in a dry well these days."

"Yup, that's about right," Claude put in sympathetically. "You gonna go up there and talk to him, boss?"

Matt shook his head. "Haven't got the time to spare, not today, any which way. I promised to take Emmaline and Tessie out for a ride this afternoon after dinner, and standin' here chewin' the fat with you isn't gettin' my work done, either. I'm runnin' behind, and that's a fact."

"Goin' swimmin' up at the creek? I'll bet Miss Emmaline will get a boot outa that."

"I don't know if I can get Emmaline to go wadin', let alone getting in the creek for an all-over wet-down," Matt admitted. "But Tessie is tickled for the chance to go riding and kick off her boots. They're both sufferin' from a good case of cabin fever."

"Sounds like you got your day all laid out for ya, don't it? You need me to give you a hand with those two-year-olds this morning?" Claude asked, holding out his hand with a piece of sugar in it for one of the mares to take.

"Wouldn't hurt any." Matt grinned as he watched the long-legged animal approach. Prancing, her dark mane flying as she tossed her head, she presented a pretty picture, he thought. The delicate nostrils flared as she scented the treat held out so alluringly, and she approached with reined eagerness, as if she would not embarrass herself by being too anxious.

"Sure are good-lookin' animals," Claude said in an undertone.

"Kinda skittish?" Matt wondered.

"No, just a mite fussy about who gets on 'em. I been leadin' them around with a saddle and blanket, gettin' them used to the idea. I put Earl up on one yesterday. He's just a skinny little runt, and that mare took to him real good. She turned her head and give him the once-over, and then tucked her neck and set off to pickin' up those feet like a real lady."

"What do you think about breeding them with my stallion? Maybe see what they throw?" Matt asked thoughtfully.

Claude peered at him knowingly. "I'd bet last month's pay that that there thought's been chasin' around in your mind ever since they arrived."

Matt shrugged. "Be interestin' to see what we get, wouldn't it?"

"Yeah, a long-legged cow pony could make short work of a lot of miles, get from here to there a whole lot faster. Those little ladies can sure stretch out and cover ground when they get movin'," Claude said with approval.

"Yeah, well, let's get some bridles on these two-year-olds and start puttin' them through their paces," Matt told him as they headed for the tack room. "By the way, I've got a rancher from down toward Phoenix comin' here next week to give us a once-over. I'll need to take a trip up and bring back a couple of the horses for him to look at. I think he's interested in these colts I've been workin' with."

"Guess we'd better get with it, then," Claude said agreeably, hitching up his denims as he stepped a bit faster. "We sure don't want to keep your ladies waitin' at noontime, do we?"

The creek was running high, the water flowing over the pebbled bottom in a flowing current. Tessie stood in midstream, the water almost to her knees, her denim pant legs rolled up as high as she could get them.

"My papa bought me boy's britches in town," she'd explained to Emmaline, the first time they rode together. She'd displayed them proudly, as if they were highly prized.

"I'm so glad you remember so much about your father," Emmaline had answered, a trifle wistfully.

"He was your papa, too, Emmie," Theresa had reminded her solemnly. "Don't you remember things about him?"

Emmaline had shook her head. "Not much, Tessie. Just a little."

The little girl had sighed sadly. "I feel sorry for you, Emmie. Sometimes I miss him a lot, and my mama, too, but I remember lots of good stuff, like how he used to carry me around and tease me and everything.''

Emmaline smiled to herself as she remembered the arms Tessie had wrapped about her sister's neck and the soft kisses she'd bestowed upon her cheek that day. I've finally done it, she thought with a sense of triumph. I've managed to gain her trust and maybe a good share of her love.

She looked over at Matt, who was sprawled on the grass beneath the trees at the water's edge. He'd refused to take off his boots, only removing his hat and rolling up his shirtsleeves in the heat of the day. Now he catnapped, watching Tessie from beneath heavy lids, aware of each splash and ripple she made as she chased minnows in the streambed.

This is what I needed, Emmaline thought, drawing up her knees and circling them with her arms, lowering her chin to rest there as she kept an eye on the man before her. The breeze played through the branches overhead and across the sparsely grown meadow that lay to the north. The sun had about dried up all the green, Emmaline thought sadly, realizing how important it was to take the herd up north in the summer.

Matt stirred, and she watched as he stretched, hard muscles rigid beneath the shirtsleeves, chest expanding as he took a deep breath and then crossed his hands beneath his head, closing his eyes once more.

I never get tired of watching him, she marveled to herself. *All the days and weeks I've been here and all the time we've been married—it seems like I should know him by heart, I've looked him over so often.* She laughed softly, smothering the sound against her knees.

"Somethin' funny, Em?" he asked lazily. Attuned as he was to her every movement, he'd known the moment she turned her concentration on him, felt the warmth of her gaze with a second sense that surprised him with its accuracy. He knew the moment she entered a room, or when she walked up behind him, his body registering her approach. Whether by the faint scent that accompanied her or the whisper of her skirts, or by the inner ear that told him she was near, it mattered not. *Fact is, I'm gettin' a bit wrapped up in this woman. More than a bit,* he realized ruefully. *More like head over heels.*

She smiled and shook her head. "No, nothing funny, really. I was just enjoying the afternoon." Not for a minute would she admit her abiding interest in his long, lean body. In the dark hair that rode his collar and the hard line of his jaw, and the broad, callused hands that handled a small child and a half-trained horse with equal care.

He was all the man any woman could wish for, she thought, not for the first time. She didn't blame Deborah for wanting him so badly. For a moment, she felt almost benevolent toward the woman who had lost her chance at Matt Gerrity. She wondered how many other women wanted him. Maria'd suggested more than once that the man who ran the Carruthers Ranch was much in demand among the unmarried females of the territory. She'd bet he'd broken his share of hearts all over the place.

His chest rose and fell in a slow, easy rhythm as he dozed, and her hand yearned to brush at a lock of hair that fell across his forehead. Clenching her fingers, she denied the impulse, lest she wake him. He needed his rest, she thought with a secret smile, seeing as how he hadn't slept a whole lot last night. Her smile widened at the thought, and she covered her mouth with one hand, holding back a betraying chuckle.

"Now what are you grinnin' about, Emmaline?" Matt asked in a husky growl. One eye opened, and then he glared at her from between half-closed lashes. "You look like the cat that swallowed the last of the beefsteak."

"Not me!" she vowed, waving her hand at him teasingly. "I was just thinking that you really needed a good nap today, an old man like you."

She unwound her arms from about her knees and scooted across the grass to where he lay. Easing herself close to his sprawled body, she lifted his head and edged herself beneath, her lap providing a pillow for him.

"Somebody kept me awake for a good long time last night." He looked up at her with just the trace of a grin curling the corner of his mouth. "Some woman kept pesterin' the daylights out of me till past midnight, and me such an old fella," he repeated mockingly.

She allowed her fingers to brush at the recalcitrant lock of hair that lay across his forehead, relishing the warmth of his skin. But her grin taunted him, as if she must deny the tenderness she gave. "Listen to you, Gerrity," she hooted. "There I was, trying to sleep and you kept... well, you just..."

His smile widened and both eyes opened, one hand reaching up to capture her chin. "I just what, Em? All I did was..."

"What are you talking about?" piped up the small voice of the child who had paused in midstream to join in their conversation. "Are you fussing again, Matt?"

"Naw," he drawled. "I'm just raggin' at your sister, Tessie. I'm thinkin' she needs to get her feet wet and let some of her orneriness out the bottom of her soles."

"Can she come wading with me?" Tessie asked, her eyes dancing with anticipation.

"Sure she can," he answered. "I'll even help her take her boots off." And, so saying, he rolled over and tugged at the leather boots Emmaline had curled beneath her. He stretched her legs out before her, and within seconds had pulled the boots from her feet, the stockings following in short order.

"These are my stockings!" he said in an aggrieved yelp of accusation.

"I only borrowed them." Emmaline scrambled about, snatching her bare feet from his grasp. "All I had were long ones, and they're too hot."

"Well, seems to me you raided my small-clothes drawer without my knowin' it." He reached for her with a threatening growl. "What else you got on that belongs to me?" he wanted to know as he pulled her across the grass by one foot.

Tessie giggled, hands on her knees, as she watched from the creek. "Don't let him get you, Emmie."

"You just let go of me, Gerrity," Emmaline sputtered, her legs jerking wildly as she attempted to escape his grip. "I don't have on anything else that belongs to you. Nothing else would fit me!" She giggled, bending to pry his fingers from her ankle.

He watched her, amusement rife upon his features, his fingers circling the fragile bones, immune to her pulling and tugging.

"Think you're tough, don't you?" she cried, panting as she bent first one finger back, then another, unaware that only his good humor allowed her to move even one fingertip from its place.

"Yeah, I'm sure tougher than a little bit of a citified girl in men's stockings, anyway," he told her teasingly.

"I stopped being citified a long time ago, and you know it, you big ugly ranch hand," she told him, panting between each word as she vigorously struggled against the fingers circling her ankle.

"Get him, Emmie!" cried Tessie, wading closer to the bank as she enjoyed the tussle beneath the trees.

Switching her methods, Emmaline got to her knees, closer to the man who held her with a lazy grip and laughed idly at her struggles. Her hands fell against his chest, and her fingers became stiff weapons, poking at the rib cage that lay beneath the gray cotton shirt he wore.

"Oof . . . that's not fair!" he yelled, a wide grin splitting his face, even as he began to laugh aloud and twist away from her marauding fingers.

"He's ticklish, Emmie!" Tessie cried. "You've got him now!"

"I give, I give!" Matt's hands waved in the air, freeing her from his grip. "You don't fight fair, Emmaline Gerrity," he accused her, rolling out of reach of her hands.

"Ha! Who says?" She scrambled to her feet when she saw his eyes narrow, and felt excitement twist through her belly when his mouth curled in a feral grin.

He crouched and was then on his feet, but she'd been warned, and with two running steps she was in the water, splashing with uncaring abandon, holding her leather skirt high as she escaped the long reach of his arms. Looking down at his own boots, Matt grinned.

"Think you got the best of me, don't you?" His eyes crinkled as he watched the woman he had married turn to face him. Upstream by several yards, she was a sight to behold. Her hair escaping the braid she'd twisted it into early in the day, her hands tugging at the leather of her split skirt to keep it from the water, she stood in dappled shade and sunlight.

"Only for the moment, I'm afraid," she admitted with a laugh. "But at least I'm cool." She stirred the lazy current with her toes, kicking up a riffle of water with one foot. Her legs were slender and long; her skirt was well above her knees, and the soft curve of her calves was half beneath the flowing stream.

"You sure are a sight to behold, Emmaline Gerrity," he said softly, his humor vanishing with the emotion that clutched at him. His heart had begun a steady thudding within his chest, and his hands were clenched at his sides. He gazed his fill, as though he would imprint the sight of the woman before him on his memory for all time.

"Matt?" Her whisper carried the several yards between them and brushed against his hearing. "Why are you looking at me that way?"

He shook his head. His eyes were alight with a gleaming, glittering heat, which penetrated her through the heavy atmosphere that hung between them. She waded slowly in his direction, holding her skirt higher, so that the leather would not be dampened by the water that splashed about her legs.

"Matt?" She asked once more, frown lines settling between her eyes.

He moved abruptly. "Come on, Em. I'll give you a hand up the bank," he offered, his gaze intent on her face.

"I'll help her, Matthew," Tessie offered, reaching out her small palm to her sister as she neared her side. "I can walk without holding up my pants. I'll hold her arm and help her so she doesn't fall down. It's kinda muddy on the edge."

"Thank you, Tessie," Emmaline said, her concentration broken, a gentle smile forming on her lips as she looked down on the small sister who had rallied to the cause. "You just give me a push when I get one foot up on the bank, all right?"

"All right!" Tessie fell into place, switching to walk behind and ready to give her able assistance.

Matt watched, his palm outstretched, then bent to grasp Emmaline's left hand as she relaxed her hold on the folds of her skirt. With a deft movement, he hauled her toward him, her feet brushing over the grass as he wound both arms about her waist, lifting her easily from the stream. He looked at Tessie, who had one small foot on the creek bank, the other at the water's edge.

"Can you make it, short stuff?" he asked, ready to help if she spoke her need.

She nodded her head and clambered up easily, standing beside them. "I think we should get Emmie some pants to wear, Matt. Then she wouldn't have to hold on to her skirt all the time." She looked disapprovingly at the leather that hung to boot-top length. "Why don't we?"

"Ladies don't wear pants, according to your sister's grandmother, Tessie," Matt said with a grin.

"Heck, Emmie isn't no lady," the child said scornfully. "She's just Emmie!"

"Hear that?" he asked the woman he held with a possessive grip. "You aren't a lady. Your sister just said so."

She made a face at him, wrinkling her nose and pushing her lips into a pout. "Is that so? Well, what would you call me, Gerrity?"

His eyes raked her features and wandered to where her collar lay open at her throat. With three buttons undone, the fabric was tugged against her flesh, exposing the soft, rounded slope of her breasts. His lids were heavy as he surveyed the pale flesh, and he breathed deeply as she hung quietly in his grasp.

"Well, Miss Emmaline," he said in appreciative tones, "I'd guess I'd have to say that you're all woman."

"I can't keep sneakin' around to meet you," the darkly clad man said angrily. "I don't need you checkin' up on me all the time."

"Things are at a standstill," the woman said. "When are you going to handle this? Do I need to get someone else to do it?"

"No!" The single word was harsh and loud. "I just need to know that things are going to work out all right for me," he said, more softly. "When this is all over with, I want to be sure I get what's coming to me."

"How about a sample?" she whispered alluringly, sauntering closer to where he stood beneath the sheltering tree. Her hands rested against his shoulders, and her eyes lit with a teasing glance. She rose on tiptoe to place a warm kiss against the seam of his lips, a whispering touch that brought him to instant attention.

His arms surrounded her harshly, and he bent her backward, his mouth opening to capture the fullness of her own. A guttural sound was born between them, and she shrank from his touch, pushing at the width of his chest with gloved fingers.

"Hold still, woman," he grunted harshly. "You owe me this much, anyway. You've been teasin' me and tauntin' me for weeks. I'm only takin' a kiss or two, and damned if I haven't got more than that coming, not to mention the money you promised me. You're lucky I'm not askin' you for full payment yet."

She held herself stiffly in his arms, holding her breath as her nose rejected the sweaty odor of his unwashed body. "One kiss," she agreed tightly, aware of her precarious situation. "We're too much in the open here, you fool," she muttered. "Be done with it!"

He laughed—it was a sound of dark promise—and once more forced her head back with the harshness of his openmouthed caress. He helped himself to the forbidden fruit he'd craved over the past days and nights.

"I'd give a lot for a dark night right now," he murmured against her lips.

She pushed from him, and he released her reluctantly. "It's broad daylight, you fool. Get on back where you belong. I don't want to hear from you until you make a move on her. I'm tired of waiting."

"Yeah," he said, his hands adjusting the fit of his trousers. "That goes for both of us, lady."

Chapter Eighteen

"Till we meet . . . till we meet . . . God be with you till we meet again." The voices rose in harmony, echoing from the high sloped ceiling and resounding from the bare wooden walls. The unadorned pews were nearly full, ladies waving woven fans, gentlemen openly using their white handkerchiefs to mop the perspiration that slid in abundance down into their collars. Their relief at the end of the closing hymn was palpable, and the final notes rang out with vigor as the congregation readied themselves to leave the church.

Seated next to a window, Matt had savored each stirring of air that penetrated the open sash, his eyes trained with staunch discipline on the earnest demeanor of Josiah Tanner. Attending Sunday-morning church was way down on his list of chores, but it hadn't been as bad as he feared. Matter of fact, the Reverend Tanner had made some pretty good sense. It had been years since he'd darkened a church door. He'd watched Emmaline go alone, with only Maria for company, several times, but today was different. Emmaline had asked, and for Emmaline . . .

He followed her down the aisle, his eyes on the flowers that bobbed atop her bonnet, his own hat in hand. Ahead lay the churchyard, where the congregation had gathered in small knots, most of them probably talking about Matt Gerrity taking up space on a church pew, he thought ruefully.

"Good to see you this morning, Mrs. Gerrity," the preacher said cordially. "Glad to see that Mr. Gerrity could make it."

Matt eyed him suspiciously, but could detect no malice in the remark. "Good talk you gave, Preacher," he commented as he settled his hat in place.

Emmaline's head turned in his direction. "Sermon, Gerrity," she whispered.

He glared at her. "He knew what I meant, Em."

"It doesn't matter what it's called, so long as the congregation heeds the message," Josiah Tanner told them with good humor.

Emmaline nodded stiffly, and Matt grasped her elbow, hustling her down the steps toward the open wagon they'd traveled in. Tessie had made her way out of the small church ahead of them and was at the gate, another young girl at her side.

"Looks like Tessie's located a friend," Emmaline said softly, unbending as she caught sight of the child in earnest conversation.

"That's the preacher's girl. She hasn't had much chance to see her since my mother died. I suspect you've managed to figure out that I've never been a big hand at church-goin'," Matt said, his eyes tender as he watched his young sister. Caught in the noontime sunshine, the little girls presented a picture that tugged at his emotions. Emotions that were more in evidence these days, he admitted to himself. Since Emmaline had entered his life.

"Maybe we can ask to take her home with us and spend the day." Emmaline's words were low, not meant for Tessie's hearing, and her eyes were intent as they savored the happiness that brightened the little girl's features.

Cold reality nudged Matt as she spoke, and he shook his head at her. "Can't do that Em. It's bad enough I risked trouble bringin' you and Tessie to church. I sure can't take a chance on totin' somebody else's young'n along till we get things settled."

She sighed deeply and nodded. "I suppose you're right. I just wish Tessie had friends closer at hand."

The little girl whirled to greet them as they approached. "Matt, this is Rose," she announced. "I used to see her at church when Mama..." Her voice trailed off as she spoke of her mother, and Emmaline stepped forward quickly to place a caring arm across the small shoulders.

"I'm so glad you had a chance to talk to Rose, honey," she said warmly. "Maybe another Sunday she can come home with us after church and spend the day. Wouldn't that be fun?"

Tessie nodded and blinked at the tears that had gathered. "I'd like that, Emmie." Subdued, she turned back to Rose, and the two little girls whispered together as they wandered toward the buggies and wagons.

"Why, if it isn't the newlyweds!" Ruth Guismann broke away from a small group of women and approached, smiling broadly. "We've been meaning to come out for a visit, Emmaline," she said. "You know the ladies made you a quilt, don't you?"

Matt stepped back, willing to leave his bride to the tender mercies of the womenfolk, aware there would be no leaving for a few minutes, now that the clutch of females had begun to descend on Emmaline.

Hilda Schmidt hurried to Ruth's side. "Maybe we can drive out tomorrow morning," she suggested with a sidelong glance toward her husband. "I'll just get Otto to harness us up a wagon first thing after breakfast."

Ruth looked uncertain as she mulled over that idea. "I had in mind an afternoon visit," she began. And then, with a determined lift of her chin, she amended her thoughts. "I'll just tell Mr. Guismann that he's going to be in charge of the store for a few hours. We can be on our way early, and back by noontime."

Emmaline's gaze went back and forth between the ladies, amazed at their management of her schedule. In her experience, folks waited for an invitation before visiting. Obviously, these women were unused to the more genteel method of handling things. Either way, it certainly looked like she was having company in the morning.

"I'm sure I'd love to have you visit," she said graciously.

"Well, there'll be a couple more coming along," Ruth told her. Reverend Tanner's wife will probably want to call on you, and maybe Julia Hooper, too."

Emmaline's mind was racing. She'd have to get Maria to make some cakes, or pastries, perhaps.

As if she'd read her mind, Hilda Schmidt reassured her. "Now don't you worry about a thing," she said airily. "We just want to visit for a bit and bring out the quilt the ladies made for you."

Emmaline's smile was distracted, but she rallied valiantly. "I believe Matt is looking to leave now," she ventured, waving a hand in his direction.

Indeed, he had untied the wagon and horses and waited near the gate. Relieved at the excuse, she backed away, making her goodbyes in short order.

Hustling Tessie into the back, Matt tugged her dress down about her legs and made her comfortable on the quilt Maria had provided. "All set, short stuff?" he asked with a grin.

Her nod was solemn and her eyes were a bit teary, but she waved and smiled at Rose, who had retreated to stand by her mother's side.

"Maybe Rose's mother will bring her along tomorrow," Emmaline said. "She could play with Tessie."

"Tomorrow?" Matt asked. "What's goin' on tomorrow?"

Emmaline waved her own farewells to the ladies gathered by the gate, then turned back to Matt and smiled uncertainly. "Some of the ladies are coming to call. Hilda and Ruth said probably the preacher's wife would want to come along."

He was quiet for a moment. Maybe he could get something done without looking out for trouble for a change. "Suppose they'll stay the day?" he asked idly.

She looked at him in alarm. "Surely not!"

He shrugged as he urged his horse into a ground-eating lope. "Thought they might be comin' out to visit a spell," he went on. "Sure would be nice for you to have a little company, wouldn't it?" *And keep you out of trouble for a while,* he thought with furtive hope.

"Well, they'll be there for an hour or so, anyway," she said. Her eyes sought his face, resting on the strong profile. His hair was getting long. Maybe she should cut it a bit, even it out just above his collar. She traced the hard edge of his jaw with her gaze to where the dark line of his eyebrow ended. His lashes were heavy and stubbed, half lowered against the noon sun, and the faint shadow of his beard was dark against his skin.

He's mine, she thought with a surprising surge of possessiveness. He might not know it yet, but one of these days, she'd tell him. The love that had been stored within her for so long spilled with abundance from her heart as she gazed her fill. The narrow line of his lip intrigued her, and the cleft in his cheek, containing a hidden dimple within amused her. Only when he was relaxed did it appear, and then not often. He'd probably laugh if he knew she admired his dimple, she decided. She leaned closer to him, one hand finding its way within the bend of his elbow to rest with a touch of intimacy against his arm.

"You all right, Em?" he asked, bending to scan her face.

"I'm fine," she assured him brightly.

"If you say so." His mood was distracted for a moment, as he peered into her eyes. Then, patting her hand, he concentrated on his driving, viewing the horizon once more. His eyes narrowed as he watched for movement, a flash of color, anything that would foretell danger.

It wouldn't do to concentrate on Emmaline when there were other things to think about. But then, there wasn't anything to stop him from enjoying the touch of her hand against his arm, the intermittent clenching of those slender fingers against his skin, even though the cotton of his shirt muffled their effect.

"Roll up my sleeve, Em," he said gruffly, lifting his hand from hers. He kept his eyes averted, watching the road ahead as she opened his cuff and carefully and evenly turned back the sleeve to just above his elbow.

"Kinda warm today," he allowed, flexing the muscle of his forearm as he enjoyed the coolness of the breeze.

"Let me reach the other one," she suggested, leaning across him to complete the task.

The press of her breast against his arm as she maneuvered in the seat brought him to attention, and he grunted a muffled word beneath his breath.

"There . . . isn't that better?" she asked, settling herself once more at his side.

He looked down at her and waited, but she was remarkably unaccommodating, to his mind. With another barely audible grunt, he lifted her hand from her lap and wound it through his arm, till her fingers rested once more against his bare flesh. With a final pat against the back of her hand, he left it there and returned his attention to the horse and the road before him.

Rose had been tucked into the back of the two-seated wagon, between her mother and Mrs. Hooper, her feet swinging as she anticipated a morning with Theresa. It had more than met her hopes, what with playing in the courtyard and taking turns with the shiny new jumping rope Theresa's sister had brought with her. They'd sprawled in most unladylike postures in the shade offered by the house overhang and played with the colored jackstraws for almost an hour. And only when the sun rose almost overhead and vanquished their shady spot had they run with carefree abandon to the barn.

There Claude had been persuaded to saddle Tessie's horse and had allowed them to take turns riding in the empty corral, keeping a watchful eye as he replaced part of the fence. Until the twice repeated "Yoo-hoo" from the house announced her imminent departure, and a crestfallen Rose had been scooped from the back of the patient horse and sent on her way.

Claude headed for the house himself, his duties as watchdog over, minding the call of Maria's bell on the back porch. Dinnertime, his stomach told him, and not any too soon.

The disconsolate face of Theresa at the table put a damper on the meal. "I don't see why Rose couldn't stay for a while," she said pitifully. "Maybe even a few days," she added hopefully.

Emmaline's eyes met Matt's dark gaze and, receiving the message there, she smiled ruefully. "Not this week, Tessie."

"Too much goin' on," Matt put in firmly. "Give it a rest, Tessie. We'll have Rose come out again."

The child subsided with little grace, and pushed the food about her plate with disgruntled movements of her fork.

"Tessie, if you can't sit up and eat your dinner, maybe you'd better just go to your room," Matt said finally.

Without a word, the child slid from her chair and left the dining room, her lips firmly pursed in a pout that gave silent testimony to her state of mind.

"Matt!" Emmaline's word of appeal was waved away with one motion of his big hand.

"She has to learn, Emmaline," he said firmly, "she can't have her way all the time."

"Well, you could have been a little nicer about it," she grumbled beneath her breath.

"You both need to learn how to follow orders." He glared at her from beneath lowered brows, then finished the meal before him, intent on heading back to his chores.

"I only promised to obey, not follow orders like a ranch hand," she reminded him with spirit.

His sigh was patience personified. "Don't start now, Em. I've got my afternoon all planned out, and it doesn't include lookin' out for you and Tessie. Just stay in the house, will you?"

She bit her lip. It wasn't really fair, she supposed. Matt had to work in the hot sun, out in the western part of the ranch, rounding up several of the beef yearlings to be sent to town this afternoon. Abraham Guismann held them in a lot on the edge of Forbes Junction and then had them butchered when he needed fresh meat to sell from his store.

Any way you looked at it, it was bound to be a long afternoon for Matt and the two men who would work with him. She, on the other hand, could look forward to a quiet few hours, perhaps reading with Tessie or cutting out a new nightgown for the child, with Maria's help.

Her mouth tilted in an apologetic smile as she watched the tall man across the table. He'd stood and leaned against the back of the chair, one hand spread against the white tablecloth as he surveyed his wife.

"I'll stay inside and keep an eye on Tessie," she promised, willing to ignore his spouting orders this once.

Relief rode his expression, and he nodded and straightened. "Come give me a kiss, Em," he told her, his eyes narrowing as he made his way to the end of the table, waiting till she met him there. His gaze warmed her, sliding like thick syrup down the length of her, admiring the slim lines and rounded curves of her figure beneath the blue muslin dress she wore.

She's a beauty, he thought as he reached for her, uncaring of Maria's eyes as she made her way from the kitchen to clear away the remains of the noon meal.

He embraced her roughly and bent his head to capture the pink fullness of her mouth. Scooping her against him, he closed his eyes, every sense attuned to the movement of her body against his.

She leaned into his strength, her arms slipping about his neck with familiar warmth, her mouth forming itself to the heat of his caress. Inhaling his dark, masculine scent, she nestled against his hard chest, concentrating on the warm possession of his mouth.

His chuckle was muffled against her as he nipped lightly at her bottom lip, and his hands moved leisurely across her back, then settled at her waist.

"Hell, Emmaline, I'll never get anything done today if I'm not careful. You sure taste good, lady," he muttered, against her flesh.

"You only asked for a kiss," she reminded him. "No, I take that back, you commanded me to kiss you." Her mouth smiled against his, and she whispered softly, her lips brushing against his with every syllable, "You'll notice, I obeyed, just like a good wife."

"Damn," he growled, setting her aside with purpose and scowling at the teasing light in her eyes. "You are a handful, girl." He snapped his leather gloves from his back pocket and thrust his hands into them, his frown well in place.

"You'll be the death of me yet, Emmaline Gerrity," he grumbled, heading for the hallway. "Just stay put, you hear?"

* * *

The sadness inherent in the story never ceased to move her, and today was no exception, Emmaline thought as she wiped tears that flowed, blurring the words on the page before her. *A Tale of Two Cities,* leather-bound and dog-eared, lay in her lap as she mourned the heroes of that day, sniffing her sadness and enjoying the coolness of her bedroom.

There'd not been a word from Tessie in hours, she realized. Probably taking a nap or playing with her doll, she thought with a damp smile. She urged herself to her feet, realizing the length of time she'd spent indulging herself.

The book replaced on a shelf near the bed and her face splashed with water from the pitcher on her dressing table, she set off to look for her small sister. With only a perfunctory rap on Tessie's bedroom door, she opened it and peeked inside. The room was empty, the window open to the courtyard, the curtains hanging to either side in the stillness of the afternoon.

"Tessie?" she called quietly, inquiringly, even as she recognized the silence of the empty room.

Stepping back, she frowned and headed for the kitchen. "She's probably pestering Maria," she whispered to herself, her face brightening at the thought.

But she wasn't. The kitchen was empty, Maria having retired to the wide veranda at the front of the house, away from the sun, where she sat dozing, a pan of beans in her lap.

"Tessie's not here?" Emmaline scanned the yard, looking for the small figure. But to no avail. Tessie was not on the low porch with Maria, and with only the sparse bushes and low ground cover for concealment, she was obviously nowhere in sight.

Maria's head lifted and turned, her eyes blinking away the residue of her nap. "Isn't she with you? Or in her room?" she asked, frowning her confusion.

Emmaline shook her head. "I was reading. When I went to look for her, she was gone." She shaded her eyes with one hand and looked out from the house, as if she might spy a small form on the horizon.

"She wouldn't have gone out there," Maria said. "There's nothing there but what you see, and even less of it farther south."

"Where's Olivia?" Emmaline asked urgently. "Maybe she took Tessie for a walk or something."

"Huh!" Maria's grunt was disparaging. "I haven't seen her all afternoon. That woman is never around lately. I think maybe she has finally taken her eyes from Mr. Matt and settled on one of the cowhands."

Emmaline's look of disbelief was obvious. "I can't imagine that would be her style," she said bluntly. "But if she isn't with Tessie, maybe I'd better look in the barn." Her steps were hurried as she walked to the end of the veranda. Stepping off, she headed around the side of the house. She moved quickly, breathing deeply, aware of her rapidly beating heart and the sudden, dreadful anticipation that gripped her.

The path to the barn had never seemed so long. The air had never been so still, and the sky never so blue.

"No, ma'am, I sure ain't seen her," Claude said, removing his hat and smoothing down his sparse gray hair. "Come to think of it, her horse was in the corral before dinnertime. Maybe... Naw, one of the hands probably put it away."

"Her horse?" Emmaline's heart pumped faster. "Is the mare still here?"

"Aw, I'm sure it is, ma'am. Let's just take a look down here in her stall." He moved as he spoke, his gait quick, his arms pumping.

The stall was empty, and Emmaline's throat was suddenly filled with a lump that threatened to choke her.

"Well, mebbe she's out yonder in the corral. Might have missed her before," Claude mumbled beneath his breath as he swung wide the half door that led outside.

"Well, I'll be switched," he growled, casting a worried look about the pole-fenced area. "You don't suppose that young'n set off for a ride by herself, do you?"

"I don't know. She was mad at Matt at the dinner table, and he sent her to her room, you know."

"Yeah, I heard, but she oughta know better than to ride out of here alone. I'll take a walk around and see what I can see, anyway."

"Saddle my mare." Emmaline's tone left no room for argument, and Claude recognized that.

"I don't know that you should do that, Miss Emmaline," he said, his face reflecting his doubt. "I just know Mr. Matt won't like it."

"'Mr. Matt' isn't here, and I am," Emmaline answered.

The three young steers were determined to be a handful, but the cow pony took it in his stride, and Matt made his way to Guismann's store in short order. It was a dusty job, and he had his mouth set for a schooner of beer at the Golden Garter when he'd completed his business with Abraham.

"I hear the sheriff was going to head out your way this afternoon," Abraham told him. "Said it was important."

Matt's eyebrows rose. "Is that so?"

"He might still be around. He was in here 'bout half an hour ago or so." He calculated the credit to Matt's account, writing the amount in his large black book, then watched as Matt's tall figure left his store.

The sheriff's office was empty, and Matt stood on the boardwalk, hands on his hips, as he considered his next move.

"Sheriff's over at the hotel, lookin' for the deputy," a small boy volunteered as Matt looked back at the empty jailhouse.

"Thanks, son," he answered, his stride hurried as he made his way across the street.

The lawman and his young aide were just stepping from the hotel door as he approached. Hailey Baines looked worried.

"Got something to show you, Matt," the older man said soberly. "A poster came in this afternoon I want you to see. We were just about to head out your way to show it to you."

"Where is it?" His frown had deepened, apprehension roughening his voice.

Hailey pulled it from his inside vest pocket and unfolded the heavy paper. "Can't tell for sure. The drawing's kinda blurred, but it sure as hell looks like one of your hands. It says here he's wanted for killin' a man in a barroom fight in Texas."

"Let me see." Almost snatching the paper from the sheriff, Matt scanned it quickly. "Aw, hell!" He closed his eyes and shook his head.

"What do you think, Matt?"

"You know what I think, Hailey. If this isn't Kane, my apologies to the man. But I'd lay odds that I've been payin' a gunfighter good money out at my ranch."

"Let's take a ride, boy," the sheriff told his deputy, and the young man hurried off to retrieve the horses tied in front of the jailhouse.

"My horse is over at the livery stable," Matt said, hustling down the street as he spoke. "I'll meet you there in a minute."

"Matt!" The call was strident, and he turned to answer it.

Hailey Baines stood in the middle of the street, his face was pulled into a worried frown. "Where's Emmaline?"

"Emmaline?" As he spoke her name, he felt a wave of apprehension wash through him. "She promised me she wouldn't leave the house this afternoon. I sure as hell hope she keeps her word."

"There might not be any connection, Matt," Hailey assured him. But the frown remained well in place.

Chapter Nineteen

The water in the creek was just as cool, rippling over the stones and washing about her feet, as it had been the last time she stood here. But today was different, and Tessie looked about with disconsolate eyes as she waded half-heartedly along the bank.

Miss Olivia had said that it would be a secret, that they didn't have to tell Matt about riding out here, but Tessie had begun to worry even before the ranch house was out of sight. Now the deed was done, and her small countenance darkened as she thought about it once more.

"But then," she whispered, her face brightening a bit, "it will be all right. Miss Olivia knows where I am, and she said she'd send Emmie out to get me in a while." It was all the excuse she needed. Her smile was relieved, with the situation once more to her liking. Between her dismay and anger, and the urging of her teacher, she had justified the ride to the north with childish reasoning.

"Matt will be sorry he was so mean to me, when he can't find me anywhere," she said to herself. The water splashed about her ankles, but the joy she'd found here last time was missing today, she realized.

Her horse stood just a few feet away, absorbed in the grass that grew near the creek, his reins tossed over the limbs of a bush. She'd slid from his back slowly, worried that her brother would be angry. Taking her horse from the corral without permission was enough to get her the whipping Matt had promised, but never given, for major misbehavior.

Tessie's eyes were filled with tears of self-pity. "I'm really mad at you, Matthew," she said stiffly. "You were mean to me." Her mouth was drawn into a sad little moue and her hands were stuffed into the puffy pockets Maria had sewn with such care onto her pinafore.

"I wonder if he'll be worried about me...." Kicking at the water, she watched it splash on the hem of her dress, even though she held it in both hands, high above the stream. Turning about, she headed back the way she had come and finally climbed up on the bank, where she sat dejectedly, a picture of woe.

It was quiet, only the rippling water and the sound of the horse snuffling in the grass, and an occasional sniffle from the child who sat hunched over by the creek bank, disturbing the silence. The heat of the afternoon lay heavy upon her, and Tessie yawned into her hand, looking about her sleepily.

Finally, with a little sigh of discontent, she lay down on the grass, curling her legs up beneath the dampness of her skirt and resting her head on one arm.

"I'll just rest a little bit, before I go back," she promised herself in a whisper. "I wonder why Emmie didn't come to get me yet? An' I just bet Matt's gonna be awful mad at me," she said mournfully, as several more tears slid from beneath her heavy eyelids. And then she slept.

The ride to where they had picnicked hadn't seemed nearly so long last time she came this way, Emmaline thought impatiently. That afternoon had been joyous, a few hours she had tucked into her memory and had taken out to examine several times already. Matt had never been so relaxed, so teasing, so filled with laughter.

And she was certain Tessie had headed this way. "If she's not out here, I won't know where to look," she admitted to herself as Fancy followed her lead, heading north toward the stream.

Filled with the disappointment of losing Rose's company after such a short visit, Tessie'd been fit to be tied, she knew.

"I should have spent the whole afternoon with her." Emmaline grumbled aloud, chastising herself. "Maybe Olivia went with her." The thought was hopeful, but then, as quickly as it had come, she realized the futility of it.

Fancy's gait had slowed with Emmaline's ponderings, and now she urged her forward at a lope, heading for the picnic spot, catching sight finally of the line of trees that bordered the creek. Within her heart, she was hoping against hope that Tessie would be there.

The sight of a riderless horse in the distance, grazing beneath the trees, caused her knees to tighten against the sides of her mare, and Fancy broke into a gallop that mirrored the urgency of her rider. So intent was she on the small mare she recognized as Tessie's, she failed to notice the horse and rider approaching at an angle from the west, less than half a mile away.

Reaching to rub her hand against the neck of her mount, she leaned forward in a silent plea for speed, and the mare responded, her hooves pounding the earth with a muffled cadence. Suddenly, from her left, Emmaline heard the sound of rifle fire, and she turned to look, her hands tightening on the reins. Her eyes focused disbelievingly on the rider who approached, his gun pointing skyward, his horse angling in toward her.

"Who on earth—" She risked a second glance at him, at his face, covered by the bandanna he wore, and her heart skipped a beat. A certainty that Tessie was in danger flooded her mind, and she hesitated, drawing up tighter on her reins. Fancy obeyed, skidding to a halt in a dusty cloud that surrounded them.

He held his rifle at the ready, and Emmaline watched his approach with frustration filling her, her fear for Tessie holding her there. "If he knows Tessie's out here..." Her whisper was almost a prayer. And again she breathed words beneath her breath. "Oh, God! Keep her safe! Don't let anything happen to my sister."

"You're a smart lady," the rider said mockingly, riding his horse near her. "I thought a little rifle fire would get your attention."

"Who are you? What do you want?" she blurted out, her eyes intent on him, hoping against hope that he would not look toward the small horse that was cropping grass just a few hundred yards to the north.

"Well, I reckon you'll find out all that, lady," he said with a mirthless chuckle. "You just ride over some closer to me, and I'll wrap a little rope around your hands, and we'll take a ride. I'll lead you along as sweet as you please."

She glared at him, barely able to endure the look gleaming from his gaze. Just the thought of his hands on her filled Emmaline with disgust, and she shuddered visibly. "Are you the same one who grabbed me off the porch?"

Even with the bandanna covering his nose and mouth, she could tell he was smiling, his eyes narrowing as they roamed over her. "Recognized me, huh?" He motioned to her to come closer, a rope held in his hand. "If you're thinkin' I don't know your little sister is over yonder, yer dead wrong," he told her with raw menace in every word.

Her heart thumped mercilessly in her chest as she digested his threat. Getting him away from Tessie was her prime concern, and there was no guarantee that allowing herself to be trussed up would turn him away from the child. Turning in her saddle, she glared at him again, and then, feigning surprise, looked over his shoulder.

"Who's that coming?" she cried.

"Where?" He stretched his neck, then turned a bit as he searched the horizon to the south.

It was exactly what she had hoped he'd do, and she dug her heels into the sides of her mare with desperation. Loosing the reins and leaning forward against Fancy's neck, she sent the Thoroughbred galloping. The animal stretched out above the ground at a pace that left her pursuer behind.

Heading northwest, away from the stream, away from the man who shouted and spurred his own mount into action, Emmaline rode her mare with desperation. The knowledge that she was heading away from the ranch was a deterrent, but staying clear of Tessie was more important.

Ahead, the ground rose, and she urged Fancy on, sensing that over the ridge she would be out of sight of her pursuer for a few moments. Maybe...

Her eyes widened with surprise as another horse and rider appeared before her, coming into view as if he had been awaiting her arrival. But it wasn't a man, Emmaline realized with amazement. Seated atop a cow pony, holding a gun aimed in her direction, was a woman, riding astride and watching her with a smile.

"Olivia." Emmaline breathed the single word and slowed the pace of her horse, tugging at the reins. Fancy side-stepped, dancing impatiently as she tossed her head.

"Stay right there," the teacher said, aiming a revolver in Emmaline's direction.

"Olivia!" Again she breathed the word, but this time with dawning comprehension.

"Stay where you are," the man said, riding up behind her.

With startling clarity, she looked about, realizing she didn't have any options to speak of. There didn't appear to be any way she could escape. Certainly there would be none if she was tied and led by the reins.

I haven't anything to lose, she thought despairingly. If they want me, they'll have to catch me. There was no other direction to head in. She was boxed in on the south and northwest. Ahead lay mountains and the high country. Her chances were as good there as anywhere else.

Fancy responded, almost as if she read the mind of her rider, and even before Emmaline gave her the signal, she had burst into a ground-eating run that surprised both of her enemies. Just long enough for her to be yards away, they sat in stunned silence.

"That bitch!" the man spit out with evil intent.

"Calling names won't do any good. Shoot her!" Olivia told him. "Take aim and kill her now."

"I'll catch her," he said, even as his horse set off at a gallop.

"Damn fool. I'll do it myself, then." She gritted the words out between her teeth, drawing her rifle to her shoulder. The barrel wavered as she took aim, closing one eye as she tried to sight in on Emmaline's back. The Thoroughbred was blurred in the gunsight, racing with the speed of her sire and dam multiplied by the urging of her rider.

Olivia grunted and squeezed the trigger, then opened both eyes to watch as the horse crumpled to the ground. Fancy lifted her head and made a terrible noise, almost as if she were screaming in distress, and then shuddered as she lay flat against the hard ground.

"Fool woman!" the man shouted, jumping from his horse and running the few feet to where Emmaline was sprawled. "Probably killed the horse. It's bleedin' like a stuck pig!"

He bent to turn Emmaline's silent figure over, noting the lump that was already appearing on her forehead. Then, turning his attention to the horse that lay just a few feet away, he watched as the animal struggled to rise to her feet. Blood streamed from her left hindquarter, and he moved closer, shaking his head angrily as Fancy sank once more to the ground.

"Never mind the horse. Just pick Emmaline up and let's get going," Olivia said from behind him.

He pulled the kerchief from his face and turned to snarl at her with impotent rage. "I was hopin' to take that horse with me when I go. I coulda sold her and made a few bucks in the bargain."

Olivia rolled her eyes in disgust. "You're already making a few bucks from me," she reminded him darkly. "Now see if the bride is still breathing, will you?"

He shrugged dismissively. "She's alive. I already checked." Bending, he picked up her limp form and stepped to his horse. Holding her beneath his left arm, he lifted her, laying her inert body across the saddle. He stepped into the stirrup to settle himself there, picking her up to lay her across his thighs.

"Let's go," he said roughly, heading north with his burden.

"It would be easier to just leave her here. All you'd have to do is put a bullet in her head, and you could leave, just get out of the territory," Olivia snapped.

"I don't shoot women," he said angrily. "If she dies all by herself up there in that line shack, that's one thing. Shootin' her isn't my way of doin' things."

"I don't want to be away from the house much longer," Olivia told him.

"Then go on back. Just remember to have my money out behind the barn after midnight," he said. Tilting his hat forward over his eyes, he looked his fill, his eyes measuring and chill. "Don't forget what else you owe me," he reminded her, each syllable precise and filled with promise. Then, turning his back, he urged his horse forward.

She glared, frustration rife upon her features. The sun was well on its way toward the horizon. It wouldn't do for her to be missing at supper time.

"Where's Emmaline?" Matt's words were sharp and urgent.

"She went after Theresa," Maria said, her hands buried in the folds of her white apron as she stood on the porch. She'd been pacing the areas around the house for over an hour, and only the sight of Matt with two other riders had relieved her anguish.

"Where'd Tessie go?" Matt asked angrily. "They were both supposed to stay in the house."

"I know! I know!" Maria cried. "But the little one left while I cleaned the beans for supper and Miss Emmaline was in her room. When we knew she was gone, Miss Emmaline went after her. She thought Tessie probably went to the stream where you took them the other day."

"Did Tessie ride? Who saddled her horse for her?" His voice lowered to an alarming softness as he spoke, promising retribution to the culprit.

"It was already saddled, boss," said Claude, coming from the barn at a run. "She and her little friend were ridin' in the corral before dinner, and she snuck back out here and took the mare before anyone knew it."

"Awww..." Matt spun his horse about and muttered words beneath his breath that made Maria's eyes widen.

"Will they be all right?" she asked pitifully, lifting her apron to cover her face, knowing that she would receive no answer.

Matt wheeled away, his horse ready to lunge into a gallop, but then the sight of a lone rider approaching from beyond the corral brought him to a halt. Drawing rein abruptly, he bent to reassure his horse, quieting the animal's prancing with soothing words.

The sight of Olivia astride a horse was a surprise to Matt. He hadn't even known she rode; in fact, he'd never separated her from the vision of a teacher. Now he watched her ride toward him, his eyes narrowed, his every sense alert to an unknown danger.

"Where've you been?" The question was quiet, but the penetrating gaze sweeping horse and rider was chilling. She halted her mount near him, lifting her hand in a gesture of supplication.

"I went looking for Theresa," she explained, her cheeks flushed, her clothing dusty from her ride. "She said she was going to play at the stream, even after I told her not to."

He frowned at her impatiently. "Why didn't you make sure she stayed home?"

Olivia shook her head helplessly. "I did everything I could, Matt. She promised me she wouldn't go out of her room, and I believed her. I thought she'd be all right."

He grunted, accepting her explanation, and relented, waving a hand in apology. "Go on to the house, Olivia. I take it you didn't find Tessie?"

"No..." She hesitated and bowed her head. "I wasn't sure where the creek was, and I was afraid I'd get lost, so I came on back."

Matt grunted and shook his head. Fool woman. About as worthless as they came. His thoughts turned from the limp figure before him and focused on the source of his problem.

Emmaline.

"Let's go, Hailey," he said, heading due north and leaving the lone woman behind him to watch.

It wasn't a long ride, but he was impatient, leading the way with Hailey Baines and Tad close on his heels. Only a few miles past the home pasture, easily reached by a small child on a sturdy mare, he saw the line of trees. In the light of the setting sun, he spotted the mare, and his breath escaped in a deep sigh of relief.

"There's the horse." He pointed her out to the men who rode with him. Hailey nodded and flashed him a look of understanding.

"See her yet?" he asked, squinting as he slowed his horse to a trot.

"Yeah, over there by the creek," Matt answered, his heart thudding when he spied the small, silent figure.

"She's stirring, Matt," Hailey said quickly. "I saw her hand move.... Look, she's stretching."

A grin of relief spread over Matt's face, curving his mouth even as his eyes closed for a moment. The hot rush of emotion threatened to unman him as he saw the form of his sister rise to stand as she watched the approaching men.

"Matthew!" she cried plaintively, reaching her arms to him. "I had a bad dream, an' I heard a gun shootin' and everything." She swallowed her sobs and wiped at her eyes. "I didn't know it was gonna start gettin' dark. I slept a long time, I think."

He was off his horse and beside her, scooping her up from the ground and holding her closely. "I swear, short stuff, one of these days I'm gonna give you the whippin' of your young life!" he said gruffly, even as he hugged her and buried his face against her hair.

"You always say that, Matthew." She giggled. "You won't whip me!"

"Well, I might," he said, holding her away from him to look over her rumpled clothes and bare feet. She seemed to be in one piece, he noted, lowering her to the ground and looking about.

"Where's your sister?" he asked, frowning once more as he saw no sight of her. "Where's Emmaline?"

Tessie shook her head. "I don't know. She was supposed to follow me here, but she never came, and I fell asleep."

He scanned the horizon as she spoke, and his brows lifted at the story she told. "Who said she was going to follow you? Did Emmaline tell you that?"

"No," the child said, shaking her head. "Miss Olivia said I should come here, and she was gonna tell Emmie to come, too."

"Different story than we heard," Hailey murmured beneath his breath. He turned his horse and trotted the animal back to where he'd spotted tracks earlier. Matt watched him go, and his stomach tightened with apprehension.

"Tad..." Matt motioned the deputy closer. "Take Theresa home, will you? Put her up on her horse and get her in the house without seeing Miss Olivia, if you can manage it. I don't want Olivia near her. Make sure Maria or Claude stays with her till I get back. This whole thing is gettin' more involved all the time. I'm beginnin' to have some gut feelings that Olivia's... Well, it just isn't makin' sense." He looked at Tessie quickly, not wanting to frighten her. "Enough said, I guess."

Waiting only long enough to see the nod the younger man gave him, he set off after the sheriff, who had begun heading north, his head bent, watching the ground before him as he rode.

"What do you see, Hailey?" he asked as he rode up beside him. "Is that two horses or three?"

"Looks like three along here. Then, over there—" he pointed to the west a ways "—there's another set going back to the ranch."

"Do you 'spect these are Emmaline's tracks?" Matt asked, bending to one side to inspect the fresh hoofprints, which were barely discernible in the dusk.

"It's not a shoe from the blacksmith shop in town, or from anywhere around here. See that depression there at the toe? I'd say these mighta been made by one of them new horses Miss Emmaline's folks brought her." He sent his mount into a trot with a light touch of his toe, and kept his eyes lowered. "These other tracks look like half a dozen others I've seen lately. Probably from this area, maybe even one of your horses."

Matt looked grim. "That's what I'm afraid of," he admitted. "It's almost too dark to track much farther, isn't it, Sheriff?"

Hailey Baines cast a look at the sky, the horizon and the encroaching darkness. "For a while, maybe. We're due for a clear sky tonight, and the moon is pret' near full, so we should be able to keep movin'. Can't see far ahead, but up close we'll make out all right."

"How long since they came this way?"

Hailey shook his head. "I ain't no damn Indian, Matt. You're lucky I can track as well as most white men hereabouts. Maybe better than most," he added with a modest grin.

"I always said you were a patch of still water," Matt told him, riding just to one side and behind the lawman. "I'd give a little bit to know where you came from and what you did there."

Hailey grunted and shook his head. "That's an old story. One I don't tell."

"Well, I can't think of anyone else I'd rather have along on this trip," Matt told him bluntly, then looked ahead to where the mountains rose in the distance.

Emmaline was cold, chilled to the bone, and her first instinct was to reach down for the quilt that lay at the foot of the bed. She shivered and huddled into a ball, aware in that instant that her hands were asleep, folded together at her waist. She attempted to wiggle her fingers and failed, sensing a tension about her wrists that confused her. She tried to brush the cobwebs from her mind.

Her eyes flickered open and she shielded them from the glow of the fireplace, her lashes drooping a bit to absorb the glare. Fireplace? There was no fireplace in the bedroom. In fact, it didn't even feel like her comfortable bed.

She turned her head and groaned, suddenly aware of the pain that radiated from her forehead and encompassed the rest of her crown and the back of her neck. *I feel like I've been here before.* The memory raced through her mind, confusion blurring her thoughts. *No, that was when I was* bucked off Brownie, she remembered suddenly, stirring against the rough blanket beneath her.

"Awake, are you?" The man emerged from the corner of the room, clad in darkness, his clothing fading into the background, as though he had appeared from the depths of the night.

She straightened her arms to fend him off, lest he touch her again, and her eyes fastened on the rope knotted about her wrists and cutting into the flesh. Her gaze swept the room, the rough log walls, the small table and stools drawn up beside it. The fireplace was stone, built against the far wall, and as small as the room was, she felt the warmth of it against her outstretched hands.

Yet she was chilled, and again she shivered, her brow beaded with cold sweat. She lifted her head and was overwhelmed by waves of nausea, and frightened as her vision blurred once more. She squinted, and the man became two vague shadows before her.

"What do you want with me?" she asked, her voice slurring and pathetically weak.

"What I want and what's gonna happen is probably two different things," he answered enigmatically.

She peered at him. "Do I know you?"

He shrugged. "Maybe, maybe not. I've been around, but mostly up here."

"Here?" She looked about her again. "Where are we?"

"About ten minutes away from a dandy fire. Soon as I get my gear together, you'll be on your own. Except for the trusting fool over there in the corner."

She narrowed her eyes, her gaze seeking the far side of the room. As though a pile of blankets had been cast aside, a motionless heap lay just beyond the firelight. "Who—" she began.

"Had to get him out of the way," the man told her bluntly. "Didn't plan this quite the way it turned out, but I reckon it'll all be the same in the end."

A muffled groan from the corner, accompanied by a thump against the wall, alerted her to the fact that the third person in this room was very much awake and aware.

"Sorry, Jackson. Haven't got a thing against you. I jest can't afford to leave anybody to carry tales," the man said darkly as he stepped into the light. A blanket was rolled across his back and he carried a bundle wrapped with a rope. Approaching the cot where she lay, he bent lower and touched her face with the back of his fingers.

"Too bad I don't have time to spend with you, lady. I think I coulda enjoyed an hour or so of your company, but I'm afraid the boss man will be hot on my trail before long, and I'm gonna have to make tracks."

She shuddered at his touch and turned her face away, her mind more confused than ever. "Why are you doing this?" she asked weakly.

"You shouldn'ta married the man, honey. If you'd been half as smart as you thought you were, you'da gone back east and left things as they were here." His chuckle was dry and rusty, and his face was too close for her to focus on.

"What did it matter to you?" she managed to say, her voice wispy and querulous.

"Not me, honey. The lady that hired me. She wants your man, and she don't care what she has to do to get him."

"Where... What did you do with Tessie?" she asked, panic alive within her as she remembered the small child by the creek bank.

"Nothin'. Didn't do a thing. She wasn't part of the bargain. Jest you, lady. Fact is, without the kid, Gerrity wouldn't even need—" He glared at her suddenly. "You don't need to know any more," he said bluntly. "Won't make any difference to you in a little while, anyways."

The muffled sounds from the corner erupted once more, and her assailant turned away to glare at the man who lay there in the darkness. "No sense in gettin' yourself all in an uproar, Jackson. If you'd gone back to the ranch when I told you to, you'd be well out of it now."

"Kane..." The single word was a guttural sound in the room.

"Got your gag off, did ya? Won't do any good, ya know. Those knots are tighter'n a hangman's noose."

The man called Kane stepped to the door, and Emmaline watched as he opened it wide, allowing the night air to enter, the scent of pine reaching her nostrils as the breeze filled the room.

"'Fraid this is it, folks," he said. "Sorry I can't stay to watch the fire, but I'm headin' out to collect my pay. If I got it figured right, it'll be dawn before the boss man gets here. He'll never track me in the middle of the night. An' by then, you'll be a pile of ashes, and he'll be—"

"Don't count on it." Emmaline cut in, her voice growing stronger as she felt the anger surge within her. "He's not stupid, you know. He'll have this all figured out."

"Well, in that case, I'd better move on out and stay a step or two ahead of him, hadn't I?" He reached through the doorway, to where a length of pine lay waiting on the ground. Bringing it into the room, he laid the green needles and the topmost part of the long branch in the fireplace, where it burst into flame, pitch spitting as it crackled with a radiant glow.

Carrying it to where the small table sat, he put it on the floor beneath. Within seconds he had piled firewood loosely over the branch, and Emmaline watched in horror as the dry kindling caught the flame and blazed into an eager inferno that reached toward the underside of the table. Kicking the stools closer, until they, too, toppled into the growing fire, he stepped back and squinted at Emmaline, then grinned with satisfaction at the man in the other corner.

"Sorry I can't stick around, but I'm runnin' behind like the cow's tail as it is," he drawled, backing to the porch as he spoke. The door slammed shut, and immediately the room was filled with heat, the flames reaching toward the fireplace as though drawn there by their counterparts.

"Jackson?" Emmaline's voice was edged with fear.

"Sorry, ma'am," the man answered. "I'm tied tighter than a pig in a poke."

Emmaline lifted her hands to her mouth, her teeth fastening on the rope that bound her, even as she saw the first smoky haze surround the cot where she lay. She bit hard at the heavy rope and shook her head. A pain slashed through it from forehead to nape, and she groaned aloud and closed her eyes, but all the while her teeth tightened and tugged against the knot.

"This sure is takin' a hell of a lot longer than I'd like," Matt growled as he followed the sheriff up the steep grade. In the fading light, he searched the ground before him, looking for whatever the lawman followed so carefully.

"We're losin' the moonlight," Hailey said, urging his horse forward at a faster clip. "But I have a notion we're not far behind them."

The wind blew steadily down the slope they followed and brought with it a tangy blending of pine and the humid scent of the night. Matt scanned the crest of the rise, then began the downward trek into the fertile valley below.

"Damn. I've got two men down there," he said angrily. "Sure hope they had their eyes open. Maybe they saw somethin' goin' on." He turned to Hailey. "Why in hell would he come here? Doesn't make a whole lot of sense to me."

Hailey shook his head. "I'd lay money that's where he took her, Matt."

"Let's go," was Matt's guttural reply as he scanned the valley. He straightened suddenly, his hands clutching the reins in a reflexive grip. Before him, at the edge of a stand of trees, where the rough cabin stood, he saw a flare of light. Then a slender flame lit the sky, penetrating the eerie darkness that settled about the small shack. His head tilted back as the faint scent of woodsmoke reached him, and his heart began to pound with an increasing beat.

"Hailey!" he called in a strident shout. "Look there!" He stretched forth the hand that held his rifle at the ready, pointing at the flames that licked the crest of the roof.

"Yeah, I see it," the lawman answered, already urging his mount into a gallop, skirting the rocks and shrubs that dotted the terrain. Within seconds, he was no longer in the lead, as Matt Gerrity overtook him. Bending low over the neck of his stallion, Matt rode with breakneck speed, his lips moving in a silent plea, his only thought the woman who was in peril.

* * *

Emmaline watched as the flames crackled and grew, enveloping the table and crawling up the legs, filling the small cabin with smoke. Fire shot upward, spreading to lick at the low ceiling, and then making its way down the walls. *It's too late,* she thought in despair. *The roof is on fire.*

Her eyes closed, and she felt helpless tears slide from her eyes. "Listen, ma'am!" came a shout from the corner, and she inhaled sharply, choking on the smoke that filled the small room. From somewhere on the outer edge of her awareness, she tried to focus on Jackson's words, but then she heard another shout, and then another. She stilled, listening.

As from a distance, a gunshot resounded, followed by more shouts. Once more a shot split the air, and she heard a commotion that seemed to come from nearby.

"Damned if that don't sound like the boss!" A grim laugh from the corner broke her concentration, and she inhaled another lungful of smoke, coughing harshly.

"Hang on, missus," Jackson told her. "I'd swear that's Matt Gerrity thumpin' around out there."

Emmaline's head was throbbing with pain. Every cough vibrated within her until she sensed that the darkness was closing in once more. "Matt," she whispered, raising her hands to cover her mouth as much as she could, ducking her head against her chest to escape the smoke that had crept down the wall behind her and was surrounding her body.

"Emmaline!" The door burst open, and two men rushed in, Matt in the forefront, scanning the room. Spotting her body on the cot, he reached her quickly. Then, in two long strides, he was halfway to the door.

"Help me, Gerrity!" called the man from the corner.

"That you, Jackson?"

"I got him, Matt," Hailey Baines told him, dragging the trussed cowhand outside, just as the flames reached the low ceiling of the cabin.

Matt ran heedlessly, aware only of the need to carry his precious burden away from the scorching heat and soaring flames. His arms tightened about her as he fell to his knees and bent over to peer into her face.

"Em!" he called urgently. "Emmaline, answer me, damn it!" He leaned forward and placed her on the ground, his hands pushing haphazardly at her hair, holding it back from her face. Quickly he ran his fingers over her shoulders and down her arms, finally reaching her hands. Working at the rope that bound her, he rid her of it in seconds, his hands gentle as he touched her swollen flesh.

She coughed again, gagging and choking as the night air flooded her lungs. A groan escaped from between her open lips, and she gasped once more, turning her head to one side as she drew in another breath.

"Emmaline." The single word was choked within his throat, and he felt the misting of his eyes as he scanned her pinched features. She looked so fragile, he thought, one hand lifting to brush at the smudge that marred her left cheek. Her breast rose and fell as she sucked fresh air into her lungs.

"Em . . . I almost lost you," he whispered, damning the blurring of his vision as his eyes filled and overflowed. "Oh, God, Emmaline . . ." he groaned, leaning over her and lifting her against himself. She was warm and alive, and his heart cried out a silent prayer of thanksgiving to the God he had all but forsaken. Emmaline's God . . . who had heard the cry of his soul and given him back the woman he held.

She murmured against his face, her mouth soft as she brushed his cheek. "Matt? It was you? You're really here?" The words were broken and breathless, but he rejoiced in them.

"I'm here, Em," he assured her, his mouth pressed against her throat. "I'm here, sweetheart."

"I like it when you call me that," she breathed. And then a shiver trembled throughout her body as she curled into his chest.

"Let me put my shirt around you," he said quickly. "You're cold, Em." He placed her on the ground and undid the buttons, stripping it from himself, then wrapped her in the warm cotton, unaware of the cool night air that touched his bare arms. His body was clad in the light undershirt he wore, and her eyes sought him, running with concern over his chest and arms.

"The gunshots— You didn't—?" she asked, seeking reassurance about his well-being.

"I'm fine," he told her, rising to his feet. "I've got to take care of things. You just lie there and wait. I'll be back in a few minutes.

The night air was cool, clean, and smelled like every good thing Emmaline had ever imagined. She lay on the hard ground, curled on her side, Matt's shirt wrapped around her shoulders and back, and closed her eyes. Breathing deeply, she coughed once, and then again. Her wrists hurt where she'd tugged at the knots, chafing her skin, before Matt untied the ropes.

"Hang on, Em, I'll be right there." Matt's voice came from across the clearing, at the edge of a stand of trees. She watched as his form emerged from the shadows. Behind him, a horse with a burden draped across its saddle followed, led by the reins he carried.

"He's set to go, Sheriff," Matt called out.

"So is old Jackson here," Hailey answered, mounted on his horse and trailed by the man who had shared the cabin with Emmaline.

"You all right, Jackson?" Matt asked, leading the horse toward the two riders.

"Yeah, just kinda embarrassed to be caught with my pants down, so to speak. He caught me off guard, boss. I swear I didn't have a suspicion till he laid me out cold. He told me to go back to the ranch on a cockamamy excuse, and I thought maybe he had a lady friend comin' out to visit, what with all the quick trips to town he'd been makin' lately. But I told him no anyways. Next thing I knew, he bushwhacked me."

"Well, he won't be causin' any more trouble for anybody," the sheriff said soberly. He tugged at the reins, and the horse fell in behind his own. "Can Emmaline make it back all right? Is she doin' okay?"

"She'll be fine," Matt told him gruffly. "Don't wait on us. We'll be right behind you."

Emmaline heard the hoofbeats of the three horses fading as they ran away at a steady pace. Above her, a dark shadow formed, limned by the fire that was still blazing across the clearing.

He was big against the shadows. His fists were clenched at his sides, his feet were spread, and his pants were tight against the muscled length of his legs. Her eyes were nourished by the sight of him. He squatted next to her and reached one hand out to brush the hair from her face, his gentle touch a sharp contrast to the rugged silhouette he presented.

"I'll take you home, Emmaline," he said roughly. Reaching for her, he lifted her, rising easily and holding her against his wide chest as he turned to where his horse was tethered.

She closed her eyes and took a deep breath. Then, through the veil of tears that would not be denied, despite the rapid blinking of her eyelids, she peered up at him. His face was drawn in harsh lines. He was stern and forbidding in his anger, but she smiled anyway.

He was hers and she loved him, and that was all that mattered.

Chapter Twenty

The ride back took longer than he'd planned. He rode easily, not willing to submit Emmaline to any more jostling than necessary. Then there was the matter of his horse carrying a double load, what with Emmaline riding before him. Her head leaned against his shoulder, and her eyes closed—for now. He feared that any moment her eyes would open to search for a trace of her Thoroughbred mare.

Matt gritted his teeth, remembering the moment he'd put his rifle against the proud head of Fancy and pulled the trigger. When he found her, she'd been lying there, blood still pulsing from the wound, soaking into the dry ground. She'd been barely alive as she lay in the crimson pool, with her left hindquarter shattered by the blow of a bullet. The sight had come close to breaking his control, so angry was he at the futile loss of the animal. Not to mention the personal loss to Emmaline.

He hesitated at the crown of the southernmost ridge of the mountains and made a deliberate choice. Although it would take an extra hour of riding, he swung to the east to detour around the area where Emmaline had been thrown from her stricken horse.

She hadn't even noticed, so weary and headsore was she. Her occasional murmur told him she was awake and aware of his arms about her, but the limpness of her form against him sent a message of its own. Once more she had been hurt, again she had barely escaped grievous injury. The

memory of the flames that had come within scant feet of
her bound body brought a shudder that racked his spine.

Involuntarily he held her closer, bending his head to bury
his face against her curls. She responded, resting her fingers against the back of the leather glove that held the reins.
In the faint light of dawn, he looked down at her hand,
noting the dark bruises, the scratched fingers, the dried
blood on her forearm.

Was it her own? Maybe it had come from the scrape on
her cheek, or the abrasion on her forehead where the
swelling had begun to subside.

"I should never have gone to town yesterday," he whispered, almost silently, condemning himself without pity.
"Should have stayed close by, kept a better eye on things."

She stirred against him and squeezed his hand.
"No...don't say that, Matt. It was my fault for not
watching Tessie."

He pulled back on the reins, bringing his horse to a halt,
wrapping the leather around the saddle horn. His callused
hands lifted her from the saddle before him and turned her
until she was lying across his lap, her head cradled by his
left arm, her legs across his thighs. Stripping his gloves
from his hands, he pocketed them. Gently his fingers
brushed at her face, wiping away a trace of ashes, leaving
a smudge against her cheek.

His heels touched his horse lightly, and the animal tossed
his head and broke into an easy trot.

"You and Tessie are my responsibility, Em. I wasn't there
when you needed me." It was a statement of failure, and he
felt the dark tentacles of self-censure envelope him.

"No, Matt," she said, more firmly, her blue eyes focused on his face. "I was in charge of Tessie. Don't blame
yourself."

He smoothed back her hair and bent to kiss her forehead, careful lest he press too firmly against the injury
there. "I reckon there are three of us totin' around a pile of
guilt this mornin'. Tessie felt pretty bad when we found her,
and by now she knows that you were in a peck of trouble,
too. I'll warrant she's parked on the porch, waitin' for us
to hit the horizon along about now."

"How much farther?" Emmaline asked him, her lashes drooping once more as she nestled against his chest.

"An hour or so," he answered, reining his mount to swing past the eastern side of the creek, having crossed it farther north, where it barely made a stain on the dry ground. Coming from a deep spring, it flowed year-round, but during the summer it soaked up a lot quicker than in the cooler months.

"Want to stop and rest awhile, Emmaline?" he asked, his eyes intent on the rise and fall of her breasts, the even measure of her breathing. She had coughed and choked at first; but once he had her in the air outside the cabin, she'd settled down, only occasionally inhaling deeply, as if she needed a cleansing breath to fill her lungs.

Jackson had done enough gasping and gagging for both of them, he decided. He'd been closer to the source of the fire, surrounded by the heavy smoke before Hailey was able to get to him. It had been a close call, and once more his anger at the man who was responsible rose within him. Futile anger, with no target to vent its fury upon.

Except for the woman who waited at the ranch house. The quiet, ladylike female who had come close to costing him the woman he— His thoughts focused on the word, one that been almost foreign to his vocabulary.

Hell, she's under my skin, that's all there is to it, he decided with a scowl that would have frightened anyone who knew him well. *She came flittin' around, smart and sassy and ready to argue about everything and anything. What's more, she sure as hell hasn't acted like she's head over heels about me,* he thought, glaring down at her darkly.

Anyway, I wouldn't know what love felt like if it was starin' me square in the face. In fact, if I told her I loved her, she'd probably just… Damn it all, it's hard to say what she'd do.

Love. How the hell do I know what love is supposed to feel like? Just because I like havin' her in my bed, that doesn't mean anything. But it did, and his mouth twisted in an unwilling smile as he admitted the fact to himself.

He tightened his hold on her, caught up in the flood of tender emotion that enveloped him. Well, one thing was for sure, he vowed—she was his and he'd be switched if he let her get out of his sight again.

He watched her for a moment, savoring the feel of her, the softness of her bottom beneath his hand as he lifted her higher against his chest. *Damn, she never looks at me the way she does Tessie,* he thought glumly. *She's about as prickly as a cactus with me. And damned if she don't like to fuss at me.*

Except in the dark hours of the night. His grin was cocky as he thought for a moment of laying Emmaline down beneath the trees by the stream.

And, as if she sensed his thoughts, she stirred against him, grumbling beneath her breath.

"Matt...you're squeezing me!" she said plaintively, her eyes flickering open, accusing him even as he laughed aloud at the petulant look she wore.

"Sorry, honey." He was thankful she could not read the randy thoughts that had prompted him to hold her so tightly. "We're almost there, Em," he promised her. "You'll be in your own bed in just a little while."

"I want to see Tessie," she murmured, her eyes closing once more.

"Soon, Em. Soon."

The confrontation with Olivia had been brief, her stunned surprise at seeing Emmaline proof enough to condemn her in Matt's eyes. She'd been conniving for weeks, perhaps longer, he realized. Her placid demeanor had vanished when Hailey Baines took her firmly by the arm and told her she was under arrest. Complicity was the accusation he'd leveled in her direction, and she'd hotly denied it.

"I've done nothing wrong!" she'd snarled, and then condemned herself with her arrogance. "You have no proof, anyway," she'd said with haughty smugness, her eyes on the body of Kane Burton as he lay across the saddle of his cow pony.

"Proof? Not in writing, maybe," Hailey had drawled. "But the word of this little girl will go a long way in court. You lied to her and sent her out on a horse alone, telling her that her sister would come to fetch her."

"A child's word against mine?" Olivia sputtered.

"She shot my mare out from under me," Emmaline said softly from her seat on the porch, where Matt had deposited her at her own insistence. She'd looked at Olivia with sad eyes, aware that no one had mentioned Fancy in her hearing, and only too conscious of the significance of that lack.

"I was aiming at that ranch hand," Olivia had blurted.

"You told him to kill me," Emmaline had reminded her. "And then you said you'd do it yourself."

"You're an upstart." Olivia had flung the words at her. "Matt would've married me sooner or later, if you'd gone back where you came from. I know that's what his mother intended to happen when she brought me here, and he was becoming interested in me. You never belonged here, anyway," she'd snarled.

Olivia had cursed her then, using vile words that drove the color from Emmaline's face and caused Matt to pick her up and carry her into the house. Behind them, the small group had dispersed. The sheriff, his deputy and their prisoner had headed for town, Olivia on the seat of the buckboard, Kane's body secured on the wagon bed. Claude had volunteered to drive her, his eyes alight with satisfaction as he glared his finest in her direction.

Now the quiet of the house surrounded them. Tessie had been tended to, had viewed Emmie's bruises with tender eyes and kissed them with damp smacks guaranteed to make them better in jig time, she'd said.

The room was dim, the windows draped to keep out the bright light of day, and Emmaline was a small bundle beneath the sheet he'd thrown over her. He'd been careful taking off her clothes, pulling off the leather skirt that had probably saved her from more scrapes, if its condition was anything to go by.

He'd felt his frustration rise to a peak when he washed her. The rope burns on her wrists were proof of her struggle to rid herself of her shackles as the fire burned inside the cabin. Her poor hands had borne the brunt of her fall, showing numerous deep scratches. He washed her face, hearing her sigh of pleasure when the cool cloth bathed her throat and her breasts, removing the scent of the fire and the dust of the trail.

She had rolled to her side, unaware that her only covering was the muslin sheet, too weary to dispute his instructions.

"Were you really getting interested in Olivia, Matt? Before I got here, I mean?"

The snort of denial was spontaneous, and Emmaline smiled as Matt sputtered a reply. "She's got a mighty big imagination, is all I can figure out."

"I knew she had eyes for you," Emmaline whispered.

Matt shook his head. "I want you to sleep, Em. Just close your eyes and try to rest, you hear?"

A sigh of satisfaction escaped her lips as he lay beside her and enclosed her in his embrace. His fingers tangled in a cluster of curls, crushing the vibrant locks within his palm. His other hand had followed the curves of her slender form, roaming at will down her side, as if he sought reassurance that she was whole, safe and secure—here in his bed, where she belonged.

The weight of his arm was heavy across her ribs, his hand, cradling her breast, was warm and familiar, and Emmaline's first thought was one of thanksgiving. Not for a moment had she doubted that Matt would rescue her. Even when the fire sent smoke billowing and flames were creeping across the ceiling, she had not doubted his ability to free her from the cabin.

She sighed, relishing the warmth of his body behind her, his chest against her back, and his arms containing her, sheltering her. Suddenly she needed to see him, needed to face him. She turned within his embrace, shifting until she was tucked beneath his shoulder. Then she tilted her head, the better to look into his face.

His eyes were open, scanning her features, as if he wanted to reassure himself about her well-being.

"Hi, Em," he whispered, his voice raspy with the remnants of sleep.

"Hi." She stretched and yawned, one hand rising to cover her mouth. Then she relaxed once more against his shoulder, aware suddenly that there was only a thin layer of muslin between her flesh and his gray cotton shirt.

"I don't have anything on," she said accusingly.

He grinned. "I know. I'm the one who put you to bed, remember?"

He backed away from her, allowing her head to fall to the pillow, and heard with amusement the small cry of protest she uttered. Standing, he stripped off the denims he wore, sliding his smallclothes with them, then deliberately removed his shirt. Switching the sheet to one side, he crawled in next to her and lifted himself on one elbow to consider the injuries she'd sustained.

"I'm fine," she protested as she watched the frown gather on his brow, knowing what he sought as his eyes traveled over her face.

He raised the sheet, stifling her protest with one long finger across her lips, and looked his fill, aware of the pinking of her cheeks as she tolerated his perusal. There were bruises on her breasts, along one hip and down the length of her thigh. Probably where she'd fallen from Fancy, he decided. He'd wiped her hands clean, and the scratches were already beginning to heal, scabbing over and looking not nearly so vicious now.

He lifted each hand separately, his mouth paying homage to her fingers and the palms in turn, his kisses warm and damp against her flesh.

"I love your hands, Emmaline," he said as he trained his eyes on the slender fingers. That had slipped out pretty well, he thought.

"You do?" She sounded amazed, and he grinned at her reaction. "Why ever would you love my hands?"

"They're part of you, for one thing," he drawled. "I love your hair, too," he told her, releasing her hands to run his fingers into the wealth of copper-toned curls that spread out upon her pillow.

"Matt? The last time you said anything about my hair, you only liked it." His fingers tugged a bit at her teasing, and she squeaked a protest and tried to sit up. But he would have none of it. His weight shifted to hold her where he wanted her. Subsiding with barely a murmur, she pressed her lips together and waited.

"I love all the parts of you, Emmaline Gerrity," he said finally, his eyes having finally come to rest on her face, wary and hesitant as he gauged her reaction.

She swallowed, and her tongue made a journey from one side of her mouth to the other, tracing its way across her top lip and then back along the plush line of the bottom one.

"All the parts?" she asked breathlessly.

He nodded solemnly. "All of them." His eyes slid down her body, pausing as they tenderly bathed her breasts with approval, and then continuing until he noted the curling of her toes and the tensing of the muscles of her belly.

"You love me, Gerrity?" she asked, with a delicate emphasis on each word.

He nodded and waited for her reaction.

It was beautiful beyond belief. Her expression was almost like that which she had bestowed on Tessie at times, and yet it was different. She was blossoming before him like the cactus on the desert to the south. Damned if she wasn't the prettiest thing he'd ever laid eyes on, with that soft mouth and those blue eyes filled with wonderment.

"Oh, Matt!" She looked at him helplessly, blinking until a single tear overflowed from each eye, to vanish into the hair at her temples.

"Oh, Matt!" she repeated in a soft whisper, as if they were the only words she could speak.

"Emmaline?" He was prompting her, willing her to give him the words her eyes were speaking silently.

She reached for him and buried her face in his throat, her mouth open against his skin. In a whisper that brought a shiver of delight to his soul, she answered his plea.

"I've loved you for such a long while." It was a breath of surrender, a giving of herself, and he cherished the moment, holding her close, relishing the softness of her curving length against his hard body.

"Since when, Em?" he asked against her ear, his breath warm, his mouth damp, his lips moving against the convoluted curl of her flesh.

"I don't want to tell you," she said primly. "You'll gloat."

"No..." he told her with a chuckle. "Just tell me."

"Since before the night in the hotel...since that afternoon."

"That afternoon?" He was puzzled. "Before we got married?"

She nodded her head. "Well, after the first time...but before the second time. When you sent for a bath for me and had someone bring in my wedding clothes."

"That made you love me?" he asked incredulously.

She peeked a look at him, her cheeks rosy, her mouth pursed, her eyes gleaming with joy. "You knew what I needed, Matt. You were willing to stand before the preacher and do the whole thing up right, and I knew then that I was glad we were getting married."

"Coulda fooled me," he growled, intent on touching her tender flesh, his hand brushing against her arm and across her shoulder.

"I was afraid, you know," she confided softly.

"Of me? I wouldn't hurt you, Em," he told her quietly.

"No...just of everything. You know, the loving...the part when you..." She groaned and turned her face from him. "You know what I mean!"

"Doesn't hurt anymore, does it?" he asked in a silky whisper.

"No."

"Got a headache, Em?" His whisper had deepened into a husky growl.

She shook her head. It was a small, infinitesimal movement.

"How bad do you hurt, honey?" The words were barely audible as he buried his face against her throat.

"Only down my side, a little," she allowed.

"Hmm...not here?" he asked, his hand cupping the soft weight of her breast.

"A little, near my ribs, I think."

"Hmm..." He scooted down till his mouth settled with feathered kisses on the bruise that marred her flesh. "I know you didn't have Tessie kiss this one," he told her.

"Matt!" She cuffed at his ear with a restrained touch, her voice reproving.

His eyes narrowed as he lifted to look more closely at the bruise, and his mouth tightened as he thought of what she had suffered at the hands of Kane Burton and Olivia Champion.

"Are you sure I won't hurt you, Em?" he asked soberly as he struggled against the urge that drove him to possess her.

"I need you, Matt," she whispered. "I need you to touch all the places that hurt, and drive away all the bad memories."

He framed her face with his palms, holding himself back from crushing her into the bedding. The words came more easily this time, and he spoke them with tenderness. "I love you, Emmie. I'll always love you," he promised. "I'll take care of you and Tessie for the rest of my life."

She sucked in her breath with a sob, and he stiffened. "Don't you cry now, Emmaline. You hear me? Or I'll never tell you that again," he vowed.

"I cry sometimes when I'm happy," she admitted, blinking back the tears that threatened to slip from her eyes.

"Are you happy?"

She nodded. "I love you, Matt." She slipped her arms about his neck and drew his face to hers, nibbling at his lips and stretching against his hard body.

It was an invitation he couldn't resist, and he responded as she'd known he would. With the power of his passion restrained, lest he crush her beneath him and take her before she was ready to accept him, he moved against her. With his strength harnessed into gentleness, he caressed her, moving with careful precision, caging the desire that would have had him surging against her tender body, his hands and mouth worshiping the fragile flesh he had bared to his inspection.

She twisted, her body reaching for him, her hands grasping to tug him closer; but he quieted her, whispering and coaxing until she could no longer contain the plea of her heart.

"Matt...please. I need you to..." Her movements were agile as she readied herself beneath him, her fingers searching between their bodies to lay hold upon the hard, thrusting length of him. And then she sighed, sobbing her relief as she brought him to herself, surging upward as she captured him within her flesh.

"Emmie," he murmured, "I love you," and realized anew that it was true.

Tessie was full of questions, and her eyes were big as she looked from Matt to Emmaline at the dinner table. "Won't Miss Olivia be coming back anymore?" she asked. "Did you send her away 'cause she lied to me, Matt?"

He shook his head, choosing his words carefully. "Sometimes people do bad things, short stuff," he told her soberly. "Miss Olivia lied to everyone. She caused a lot of bad things to happen, and she has to be punished for it."

"I'd sure never do bad stuff, Matt," the child assured him as she tucked into the meal on her plate.

"I know you wouldn't, honey," he told her, flashing a smile at Emmaline.

"Who's gonna teach me now?" Tessie asked. "Maybe I'm old enough to go to real school, don't you think?"

"Not yet," Matt said firmly. "In another year or two, maybe."

Emmaline laid her fork down and rested her arm on the table in front of her. "Maybe I could be Tessie's teacher for a while," she suggested quietly. "I think I could keep up with her, at least for a couple of years."

Matt grinned his approval, and she relished the warmth of his smile. "I can use the same books, and add a few of my own," she suggested. "I think she was pushing Tessie a little, anyway. Maybe we can lay off the lessons for the rest of the summer, and take them up again in September."

"How does that sound to you, short stuff?" Matt asked the child.

"But I can go to real school next year?" she wanted to know.

"We'll see," Emmaline said, making no promises.

"We've got another project to work on, you know, Em," Matt reminded her with a wolfish gleam in his eye. "You may be up to your neck in—"

"Matt!" she admonished him, her cheeks flaming.

"Suppose we might have already taken care of it?" he asked innocently.

She gave an exasperated groan. "Will you behave yourself?" Her eyes flew to where Tessie sat, her fork halfway to her mouth, her eyes flashing with interest in the guarded conversation.

"Well," he conceded, "I guess we could talk about it later. I'm feelin' pretty perky this evening, anyway, what with sleepin' half the day away." His eyes sparkled as he set to with vigor, eating the dinner Maria had prepared as a celebration for them.

Emmaline poked at her food, aware of places on her body that would be tender for days to come, conscious of the weariness that still held her in its sway. And more aware than ever of the man who sat at the end of the table, his knee almost touching her own beneath the concealing folds of the white tablecloth.

He loves me, she thought with a sense of wonder. He said so, she remembered with a flush of pleasure as she recalled his impassioned words.

"Emmaline?" His voice nudged her into awareness, and she looked up to find him leaning toward her, his gaze intent on her face.

"Yes?"

"Are you all right?" he asked. "You looked like you were..." He shook his head, descriptive words escaping him.

"I'm fine, Matt. I've never been better, in fact. A little tired, a little sore, and a whole lot happy."

"Me too," Tessie chimed in. "I'm a whole lot happy, Emmie. We're really a family, aren't we?" she chirped, already far removed from the near tragedy that had threatened their lives.

"Yes, we're a family," she agreed. "At least we're the beginning of a family," she amended with a smile. "Just the beginning, Tessie."

Epilogue

"Should we tell Oswald Hooper?" The question was spoken into the darkness, and Matt frowned.

"I thought you were sleepin' already," he said accusingly. "You need your rest. Besides, unless old Oswald is blinder'n a bat, he probably knows already."

"If you don't quit picking at me, I'm going to change my mind about this," she threatened. "I've been resting every afternoon and eating everything Maria pokes at me. I'll sleep when I please, thank you!"

"Damn, you're a spitfire these days, Emmaline Gerrity!" He turned to her and scooped her against him, his hands tender as he arranged her to his satisfaction. She wiggled against him, and he groaned.

"Now, cut that out, Em," he told her. "I'm doin' my best to take care of you here, and you just won't let me."

"I have a real need to be taken care of tonight," she told him soberly, snuggling closer.

His hand swept up beneath her gown and rested with a possessive gesture against the roundness of her belly. "Are you sure it won't hurt him?" he asked. "'Course, I can be real careful. In fact, I can probably think of something new that will—"

"Matt! I'm fine. The doctor said that this baby is about as safe as he's ever going to be in his life, right now. He told me that it would be a good two months before he's born, and—"

"He? He? Emmaline?" he asked hopefully.

"I thought you wanted a boy," she reminded him.

"Yeah, I guess," he agreed. His hand moved against her swollen flesh, and he grinned in the darkness as a small limb poked into his palm. "Feels like a boy's foot to me," he said solemnly.

She giggled and nestled against him suggestively.

"Tell you what," he said, lifting her gown higher and easing her from its confines. "I'll look things over, and little Sam and me'll take a vote."

"A vote?"

"Yeah, we'll decide just how to go about this tonight. And just you wait till I tell you a new idea I thought of today while I was gettin' your stud into the breeding pen."

"Gerrity, will you behave?"

His mouth was seeking, his hands were urging, and his voice was husky with the need he carried with him like a second skin. "I'm tryin', Em. I guess there's just no hope for me, is there?" he said sighing against the tender flesh of her breast.

"Umm...not much, Gerrity," she agreed. "But I'll keep you, anyway."

*   *   *   *   *